Hustlin' Divas

Also by De'nesha Diamond

The Diva Series

Hustlin' Divas

Street Divas

Gangsta Divas

Boss Divas

Anthologies

Heartbreaker (with Erick S. Gray and Nichelle Walker)

Heist (with Kiki Swinson)

A Gangster and a Gentleman (with Kiki Swinson)

Fistful of Benjamins (with Kiki Swinson)

Published by Kensington Publishing Corp.

Hustlin' Divas

De'nesha
Diamond

Kensington Publishing Corp.
http://www.kensingtonbooks.com

DAFINA BOOKS are published by

Kensington Publishing Corp.
119 West 40th Street
New York, NY 10018

All Kensington Titles, Imprints, and Distributed Lines are available at special quantity discounts for bulk purchases for sales promotion, premiums, fund-raising, educational, or institutional use. Special book excerpts or customized printings can also be created to fit specific needs. For details, write or phone the office of the Kensington Special Sales Manager: Kensington Publishing Corp., 119 West 40th Street, New York, NY 10018. Attn. Special Sales Department. Phone: 1-800-221-2647.

Dafina and the Dafina logo Reg. U.S. Pat. & TM Off.

ISBN-13: 978-1-61773-818-0
ISBN-10: 1-61773-818-2
First Kensington Trade Edition: November 2010
First Kensington Mass Market Edition: July 2012

eISBN-13: 978-0-7582-7861-6
eISBN-10: 0-7582-7861-6
Kensington Electronic Edition: July 2012

10 9 8 7 6 5

Printed in the United States of America

This is dedicated to my native hometown: Memphis.

Welcome to Memphis, where when the sun goes down, shit starts popping off. The three major female gangs ruling the gritty Mid-South are the Queen Gs, who keep it hood for the Black Gangster Disciples; the Flowers, who rule with the Vice Lords; and the Cripettes, who are mistresses of the Crips.

If you want to survive, drop your head and mind your own business. In a city that leads the United States in violent crime, the women here are as hard and ruthless as the men they hold down. Your biggest and last mistake is to try to play them, fight them, or even love them.

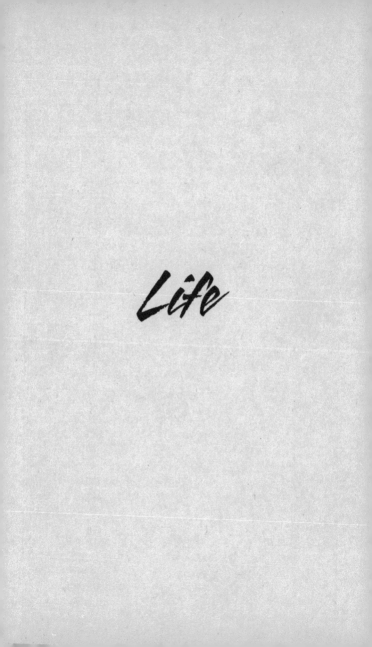

Life

1

Ta'Shara

September . . .

At 8:15 a.m. the halls of Morris High School are already crammed with a bunch of lil niggas who didn't want to be here—me included. It doesn't matter that I'm in the top 5 percent of my class and that I already know the colleges I want to apply to next year. I hate this shitty school and look forward to the day I can roll up out of the here for good. Real talk, I have plans—big muthafuckin' plans that don't have shit to do with holding down none of these wannabe grown niggas repping bullshit gangs and bragging about how hood rich they are while they blast they way to the jail or the graveyard.

It isn't that I don't understand the struggle. Hell, I didn't come up with shit either. No money. No home. No parents. The only thing I did have was a crazy-ass sister who loved the streets despite the fact that they don't love her.

"Ta'Shara!" Essence's unmistakable babylike voice squeaks above all the other miscellaneous conversations floating down the hall.

"What up, E?" I say, jerking open my locker.

Essence reaches my side, out of breath. "Have you finally lost your goddamn mind?"

I know exactly what my girl is yapping about, but I'm not in the mood to try and explain myself. "Don't start." I grab my precalculus book and check my lip gloss in the small mirror on my locker's door. "It was a mistake and it won't happen again." I slam the door closed and try to go on my merry little way.

"A mistake? Girl, do you—"

"Your ass ain't cute," Qiana sneers, poking out her hip and mean mugging me while her neck twirls on overtime.

I roll my eyes and smack my perfectly round booty at Qiana. "That ain't what your man said last night."

"Oooh!" The other niggas littering the hallway instantly jump into the mix.

Qiana, a compact shawty dressed in black jeans, black T, and sporting a lopsided Louis Vuitton cap, steps forward, popping her bubble gum. "Hands off Profit, bitch. I catch you rubbing your stank-ass titties on him again and I'm going to personally slice your ass up."

"You mean these titties right here?" I cup my shit, knowing they put Qiana's minus-A cups to sleep. "Don't hate on Profit just 'cause you eyeballing my shit. If he was a homo thug, then I guess his ass would try to get with you and those dried-up Flowers you run with."

"Dayum!" some inconsequential nigga in the crowd hollers.

Qiana's already-burned toast complexion darkens as fire leaps into her eyes.

I'm not the least bit surprised that Qiana and her dyke

friends with the Vice Lords' Flowers feel bold enough to
step to me like this. I sort of expected the shit when I let
my guard down and got caught hugging up on Profit
after homeroom—a serious violation since Profit's family run with the Vice Lords, and guilt by blood means
that he's VL property as well.

Despite the ring of Flowers behind Qiana, Essence
and I hold our ground, ready for the jump-off. The Flowers are infamous for jumping chicks and forcing them
into their shitty-ass gang. The school is littered with
bitches repping for the three dominate gangs in shady
M-Town: the Black Gangster Disciples, the Vice Lords,
and the Crips.

I'm in a unique position. Like Profit, I have a little guilt
by blood situation myself. My older sister, LeShelle, is the
head Queen G, riding with the Black Gangster Disciples. In the grand scheme of things, Qiana is just a lowly
chicken head and she knows fucking with me means
death.

Qiana grinds her back teeth and stares me down. She
knows her options are limited. "Let's just see what Fat
Ace got to say about Profit dipping his dick in trash."

I flinch. If anybody has the power to shut us down, it's
Profit's menacing brother. "Get your snitchin' ass out
my face."

"What's going on over here? What is going on?" Principal Davis shuffles his tall, lanky frame through the crowd.
His old ass always gets nervous whenever too many niggas are clustered together.

I turn my back, considering the situation squashed for
the moment. Beside me, Essence exhales a long breath.

"Girl, you're playing with fire," she whispers as we
make our way down the hall. "That bitch can't keep
water, and you and Profit's scandalous situation is going
to reach Fat Ace—and LeShelle."

My mind races a mile a minute. *What are we going to do?*

"What the hell were you thinking about, kissing him like that in public? Y'all were supposed to keep y'all shit on the DL."

"I know. I know. But Profit kept fuckin' around and pinchin' me on my titties."

"Well, I hope it was worth it. 'Cause now y'all shit is wide open, and the blowback ain't going to be nothing nice. You feel me?"

Now my head hurts. Profit and I didn't ask for none of this gang bullshit, and neither of us feels like we should be beholden to a bunch of laws and bylaws that we never agreed to. We've been feeling each other for the past six months, ever since I caught him peeping me out in German Town. I'd just tagged along with Essence to visit her uncle out there in a nursing home. . . .

German Town was the latest spot white folks had flocked to, trying to get away from niggas. I remembered being stunned at the pristine sidewalks, mowed lawns, and fancy cars flying down the roadway. It felt like another universe to South Memphis, where bullets fly and drug fiends reigned supreme. Essence and I turned the day into an adventure and hung out at Wolfchase Galleria, snickering and cheesing at all the uppity white folks.

In my heart, there was a little jealousy about how the different classes carried themselves. They acted and were treated like the whole world was theirs. Their clothes were nicer. Their cars were hotter. Hell, if I didn't know better, I would've sworn the damn air was fresher.

"Hey, Ta'Shara," Essence whispered. "Ain't that nigga checkin' you out?"

"Hmm?"
zel and gla
food court
place. It did
ing glance,
with a bas
against him
until that

"Oooh,
Essence t
that?"

"Nah.
my pretzel,

I took my time glancing
did, I wasn't prepared fo
twinkling from beneath
heart started playing
was cut low; but
Rican grade tha
help of greasy
"You ain
smiled,
teeth.

gaze caress every inch of my body. It
had not to peek back at him. I then decided to give the
brother an opening by telling my girl I was going back
up to the Auntie Anne's Pretzels counter for something to
drink.

"You want anything?" I asked.

"Nah, girl. I'm straight."

I stood up and switched my hips all extra because I
wanted the yellow cutie to see what I was working with.
Up until the previous year, I had been a late bloomer.
My older sister, LeShelle, had got her tits and ass in junior high while I had to wait until I was a sophomore in
high school. Now that I got them, I sure as hell knew
how to flaunt them. And it didn't matter how much junk
food I ate; being the star on the track team kept my waist
small and my long legs firm and shapely.

"I'd like a Coke," I told the woman behind the
counter, and then wiggled a hand down the front pocket
of my jeans for some change.

"I got you," a deep baritone said from behind me. A
second later, a Lincoln was slapped on the counter.
"Keep the change."

...ver my shoulder, and when I ... the big, caramel-brown eyes ... a fan of long, curly lashes. My ... hopscotch in my chest. His hair ... could tell he had that good Puerto ... had a nice wave and shine without the ... products.

...'t got to stare that hard, baby. I'm real." He *...itting me with perfect rows of pearly white*

...cut my gaze away and grabbed my drink.

"What, you just going to take a nigga's drink and roll?"

I strutted off.

"Oh, your momma must not have raised you right."

I stopped. "Don't be talking about my momma. You don't know shit about me."

My anger only made his smile wider. "I know you're rude as hell. Does that count?"

"What, I'm supposed to bend over because you dropped five dollars? I ain't impressed."

My potential boo licked his fat, luscious lips as his gaze dropped to my ass. "I ain't said shit about bending over, but if you put that fat onion in my face, I'm going to give you something to remember me by."

A delicious thrill slivered straight down to my panties, despite me holding on to my mad face. "Is that how your momma taught you to talk to a lady?"

"Oh, so it's a'ight for you to talk about my momma, huh?"

"Answer the question."

He held up his hands. "My bad, shawty. I didn't know that you were going to try getting all brand-new on a brotha." He adjusted his collar as if it were an invisible tie. "Excuse me, miss. May I ask you your name?"

I crossed one arm beneath my breasts and sipped on my Coke as I weighed my decision.

He stood, waiting and doing his damn best to mesmerize me with his deep-pitted dimples.

"Ta'Shara," I finally said, offering my hand.

"Ta'Shara," he repeated.

My name sounded sexy tripping from his lips, and I felt that same thrill hit my clit and dampen my panties some more. "And what's your name?"

"Profit." He straightened his shoulders and licked his lips. "But you can call me your boo."

I cocked my head. "What makes you think I ain't already got a man?"

" 'Cause you standing here flirting with me."

My lips twitched upward. "I'm just talking to you because you were crying about your five bucks."

"Tsk, aww, Momma. Don't play me. That ain't no money. Come with me and let me show you how I roll." He cocked his head.

"Nigga, I don't know you."

"What, you scared now?"

"I'm just stating the facts." I went back to sucking on my straw. "You could be a mad rapist or a murderer or something."

"Yeah, right." Profit hooked his fingers through the front loops of my jeans and pulled me so close my titties pressed into his chest. When I didn't resist, his smile turned cocky as hell. "Now do I look like a killer to you?"

I wanted to answer, but being all up on him like that made it hard to think about anything other than wondering what his fine ass looked like naked.

He laughed at me, his breath all spearmint fresh. "Do you put all niggas through this much drama when you know they feeling you?"

"There you go crying again. Your momma must not have breast-fed you when you were a kid."

"There you go talking about my momma again." His beautiful brown gaze lowered to my round titties. *"But if you're offering to breast-feed a nigga, I might let that shit slide."*

There was a hot moment of temptation. No little nigga had ever gotten me this hot. Plus, there was just something about his cocky ass that felt like the ying to my yang.

"C'mon, lil momma. I'll take you and your little friend shopping."

Essence, who was just inches away at a wrought-iron table, perked up at that shit.

"A'ight. Cool." I hit him with the full power of my white smile.

"Yeah!" Essence sprang up like a Pop-Tart.

Wanting to see what Profit was working with, we hit every store in the mall, waiting to see when he would cry uncle and start cussing our asses out. It never happened. Profit peeled Benjamins off a fat knot of bills and made it rain at each cash register with a smile.

"I think this nigga is serious," Essence whispered when her feet started hurting, and she was ready to go home.

I was thinking the same thing.

"So, can a nigga get the digits, or are you just going to play me?" he asked once he helped load our shopping bags into Essence's old Ford Escort.

I folded my arms and stared. *"Where you from?"*

"Here."

"German Town? What, your people got money?"

"My people do a'ight, but I ain't from German Town. I meant Memphis. South Memphis, to be exact."

I frowned. "I'm from South Memphis. How come I ain't seen you before?"

"Been down in the ATL for a couple of years with my moms, but the stress of being a single mom tryna raise a black son was too much, so she sent me to live with my father and big brother, Fat Ace."

My heart dropped. "Fat Ace . . . is your brother?"

"Ah, shit," Essence swore, crossing her arms behind her. "Give this nigga his shit back and tell him to get ghost."

Profit's face twisted. "Damn, shawty. Slow your roll. What, you kicked it with my brother or something?"

I stepped back and shook my head. "I can't be fuckin' around with the Vice Lords. My sister would fuckin' kill me."

"Whoa. Whoa." Profit tossed his hand up. "I ain't in that gangsta bullshit. I make my own moves. You feel me?"

"I hear you talking, but . . ."

"But what? You don't believe me?"

"I'm saying it don't matter. I ain't in the game, either, but it don't mean that I ain't caught up in the politics of the situation. My sister is Python's main chick. Do you know who he is?"

"I heard the name around. I've only been back in Memphis a couple of weeks."

"Well, he's the head nigga of the Black Gangster Disciples. That means he's your brother's number-one enemy. Those niggas been beefing since my ass was in grade school."

Profit paused, and then in the next second shrugged it off. "That shit ain't got nothin' to do with us."

"You can't be that naïve," I said with my heart twisting in my chest. I was really feeling this nigga, too.

Despite Profit's reassurances, there were flickers of concern about the situation in his face. But being a true stand-up nigga, he didn't like being told that he couldn't have something . . . or someone. That was the day we hatched the idea of us seeing each other on the serious down low. The only other person who knew the deal was Essence, and she had my back like a muthafucka.

Now, because of one slipup, our shit is wide open. When LeShelle finds out, the blowback is going to be nothing nice.

2

LeShelle

Datwon Jackson is standing in the center of Momma Peaches's cramped house, sweating like a runaway slave. Fear is a scent every Gangster Disciple killer thrives on, and we are all eyeballing Datwon's trembling ass while he takes his sweet time stacking money in front of our leader—and my man—Python.

I smirk at the weak-ass nigga. I know what the fuck is about to go down, and I can't wait for my man to deal with the weakest link in our organization. Had it been me, I would've toe-tagged his ass a long time ago. But he's Python's blood—who knows how he's going to handle this situation.

"Somebody shoot this dumb mutherfucka," Python hisses after taking one glance at the money stacked on the table and knowing that the shit is short.

An arsenal of handguns is lifted and aimed at Datwon.

I smile as I stand behind Python, ready for the shit to go the fuck off—which always happens when you get a bunch of niggas together.

"Whoa, whoa, whoa, mutherfuckas. Whoa." Datwon's eyes bug out as he jacks up his hands. "Python, how you going to kill me? We're cousins, man!"

"Nigga, you're like my fifth cousin twice removed and shit. Ain't nobody going to be crying foul over that bullshit," Python sneers. His big, bulky, chocolate frame is littered with tats of pythons, teardrops, names of fallen street soldiers, and, more importantly, a big six-pointed star representing the Black Gangster Disciples. Python isn't just a member of the violent gang; in Memphis he is the head nigga in charge. Everybody in South Memphis knows my nigga don't fuck around when it comes to his money, drugs, territory, and women—in that order.

The seriousness of the situation hits Datwon like a ton of bricks. The young nigga's face twists like he smells something nasty while his eyes manage to squeeze out a few tears.

That shit only angers Python even more. "Nigga, is you about to start crying and shit?"

The surrounding brothers snicker and cheese. It takes everything I have not to start instigating shit by yelling, *Put a cap in his ass*. This was a family situation. Everybody needs to fall back and let Python handle his.

Python snatches off his shades and rakes his black gaze up and down his cousin. Despite his hard-earned muscles, Python has a face only a mother can love. But the brother has presence, power, and mad respect. "If you going to be big, bad, and bold and steal from a nigga, then man up." He hammers a fist hard against his own chest. "Pump that shit out and meet Lucifer like a fuckin' soldier."

"I'm trying," Datwon cries. "But, Python, I didn't—"

Before Datwon can finish the sentence, Python snatches his burner from the hip of his jeans and straight shoots his cousin in the foot.

"Aaagh!" Datwon hits the warped and dusty hardwood floor with a quickness.

Everyone jumps back and watches the family drama unfold like it was some shit on cable.

I smack a hand over my mouth to prevent myself from laughing out loud.

Python scratches at his scruffy face with the side of his gun as he walks over to his cousin and squats down.

Datwon grabs his bleeding foot and carries on with the theatrics. "C'mon, Python. You know I got a lil man and shit I gotta take care of. I'm planning on marrying his momma next week at the courthouse. Please don't kill me. I don't know why the shit is short. I'll get whatever is missing back to you. I promise. I promise. Just don't kill me."

"Nigga, quit all that hollering. You're embarrassing yourself—and me."

To Datwon's credit, he does attempt to quiet down, but then he starts snotting up.

"Lookie here, *cuz*. I'm going to be brutally honest with your ass. I don't think this is the business for you. You sloppy with your shit. Word is you bumping your gums to anybody who'll stand still long enough, and now you got Momma Peaches on my ass twenty-four/seven. A nigga like me don't need the extra stress. You feel me?"

Datwon whimpers.

"Now, I'm going to cut your ass a break, and in return

I want you to keep your punk ass out of my face. If not . . . the next bullet"—he places the gun against Datwon's chest—"is going to hit where it counts. We clear?"

Datwon meets his cousin's black stare to see what most niggas usually saw: death.

"We clear?" Python presses.

"Clear." Datwon swallows the knot clogging his throat and damn near chokes to death.

Python nods and stands. "One of y'all niggas take this punk muthafucka to get fixed up. And the rest of y'all get this shit cleaned up. Momma Peaches is going to be here any minute, and she's going to be pissed if she sees blood and shit."

Niggas get busy as Python dumps his cash into a Hefty bag and then sweeps the shit over his shoulder.

I have to admit I'm turned on, watching my man do his thing. Nobody comes harder or keeps it more real than my thuggish boo. Every nigga up in this joint knows that shit—just as they know that it takes the baddest chick in the 901 to handle his ass. And there's no doubt about it; I'm that chick with the tightest pussy, the meanest head game, and the quickest trigger finger.

From the moment I'd laid eyes on Python, I wanted to be the Bonnie to his Clyde. Real talk there's something dangerous and sexy as hell about his ugliness. I ain't the only one who feels that way. My nigga has five different seeds running around by five different bitches; all of them just as ugly as they daddy.

But none of that shit fazes me. Those little niggas were all on the scene before I claimed the throne as head bitch of the Queen Gs—the female gang that keeps the Disciples, or what most around here called *6 poppin'*: Sexed up and stress free.

I have only one true responsibility in life: looking out for my sixteen-year-old sister, Ta'Shara. We came up in

the foster system. Nobody seems to know shit about
what happened to our parents. Guess we're supposed to
believe that we just sprouted out from under a rock or
some shit. So for most of our lives, we moved from one
home to another, watching people collect checks for taking us in. Shit changed when my booty rounded and my
titties sat up. Suddenly I had to endure a few foster daddies and uncles who liked to play with my pussy and
stuff my mouth with a different kind of lollipop in the
middle of the night.

None of those muthafuckas paid attention to my tears
or gave a shit that I'd gone to bed with my asshole bleeding. In fact, no one gave a shit until I saw one of them
seriously eyeballing my little sister. I finally took action
by slicing up one of those child-molesting muthafuckas
while his ass was sleeping. Then suddenly *I* was the
crazy one and had to be locked up in a group home.

For two years, I was separated from my sister. The
hardest part was always wondering how Ta'Shara was or
what she was doing. Would some doped-up muthafucka
put her through the same hell I went through? Those
couple of years was when I realized that I had seriously
fucked up and had failed my sister.

How could I do my job looking after her from a damn
group home?

However, that was where I had gotten my education in
street politics. Drugs and boosted loot floated in and out
of that group home like it was a fucking flea market. Despite all the heavy shit I could get my hands on, my drug
of choice was weed—purple haze, to be exact. That shit
made everything better: food, sex—just fucking life.

I first heard about the Queen Gs while lying in bed at
that place. This dyke bitch, Sameka, just straight raped
this chick Lovey with some metal dildo because she
thought the girl jacked one of her chains. Nobody helped

the girl because no one liked her big-boned ass. The next day, Sameka found her chain and realized the shit wasn't missing after all. When someone suggested she apologize to Lovey, Sameka smirked and claimed the bitch enjoyed the shit.

And she must've, because to this day, Lovey is still Sameka's main bitch. But back then, seeing the power that Sameka wielded was mind-blowing to me. Bitches jumped when Sameka said jump, and they jacked who she said needed to be jacked.

The only thing was, I didn't know how to go about asking to join the Queen Gs. At first, I worried that I would have to let that mean bitch rape or beat my ass. Turned out, I had great reason to worry because that was exactly what happened. Four chicks held me down and took turns beating my ass. Shit. I had to stay in bed for damn near two weeks after that shit, but it was a small price to pay for the kind of world that opened up to me after that.

Next thing I knew, I was flying high, boosting shit from Hickory Ridge Mall for Momma Peaches's network and jacking cars headed out to the Tunica casinos. It wasn't great money, but it was enough to make sure I kept decent clothes on my back and something other than chicken in my belly.

When I finally left the group home and was placed with my sister at the Douglases in midtown, I felt like I'd been sent to another planet. The biggest change was in Ta'Shara. She thought she was good and grown and didn't have to listen to me anymore.

Where I had been hard and jaded, Ta'Shara believed her shit didn't stink, with her straight As and being a star on the track team. What really hurt was Ta'Shara thinking that I was crazy whenever I tried teaching her slow ass about how to navigate through the politics of the streets.

Ta'Shara just acted like she was above it all, not recognizing that it was my status that kept her safe—not only from the other Queen Gs but also from the Flowers and the Crippettes. But that was cool with me, seeing how my sister might actually have a chance of escaping Memphis's rat hole and actually making something of herself. If that happened, then maybe—just maybe—it would make some of the bullshit I've gone through worth it.

When I was rising up the ranks, I was a good foot soldier, but I wanted more and set my sights higher. In order to do that, I needed to do something that would catch the HNIC's attention. That meant locking down Python, a nigga who got his name for all the damn snakes he has slithering around his house. Python's kryptonite is pussy—the tighter the better. He especially likes girls who have a different look. Ever since I can remember, people have told me I look like Chilli from TLC. Who knows, maybe I really had Indian in my family.

At sixteen, I got a fake ID so I could strip at Python's club, the Pink Monkey. From the moment I stepped out on the floor, I made sure I put niggas in a trance: winding my hips and popping my oil-slick booty like my damn life depended on it. But the Benjamins didn't start raining until I showed that I could swallow a big, long banana whole. That night, Python gave the order to bring me to his office. . . .

I was so excited. At the time, this was nothing more than a power move, if all went right. Of course, there was no guarantee that Python wouldn't just fuck me and then put me back out in the stable, so somehow I had to make that first meeting memorable.

When I stepped into his office, it was smoky as hell.

My weedology degree told me that Python was puffing on some blueberry AK-47. I was high before I even got to the center of the room. Up until that moment, I'd seen Python around the way, but never close enough to actually get a good look at him. But standing there in that room, staring into that face, I knew my life would never be the same.

I must've stood there forever while he inspected me in my string thong and white flower pasties. While he looked at me, I kept an eye on the red and silver corn snakes that swirled around his meaty arms and hands.

I knew then what I had to do. None of the girls liked Python's snakes, and to be honest, I wasn't too keen about them either. But on that day, I pushed all that bullshit to the back of my head and walked over to his chair unbidden.

"Can I play with your snake?" I asked in a schoolgirl voice that caused the side of his lip to curl. I'd never seen a smile that made someone even uglier, but for some reason the shit turned me on so hard that my pussy started swelling right before his eyes.

Python stretched out one hand and allowed one of his friends to slither up the center of my belly and then up between my breasts.

I smiled and locked gazes with Python, letting him know that I wasn't scared of a damn thing.

His lips spread wide as if recognizing that he'd finally found his ride-or-die chick. When he licked his fat lips, I saw that the nigga had had his tongue surgically forked to look like that of a snake. I couldn't wait to feel that shit smacking my clit. No doubt, he knew how to work it.

The corn snake slid up over one shoulder and then looped around my neck. Still I didn't flinch. Python stood up, yanked down his baggy jeans, and showed me a cock that was long, veiny, and black as coal—all ex-

cept the head. The head was more milk chocolate and looked like an overbaked muffin top. As he stared at me, precum started to drip from the tip.

"You got a pretty pussy," he said flatly. "But I want some ass."

That shit threw a monkey wrench in my plans. I was already wondering how I was going to stuff that fat head into my pussy, but my ass? Suddenly I remembered all those nights when I'd gone to bed crying, bleeding in my panties. I seriously didn't think I could do it.

But this was a chance of a lifetime. Becoming Python's girl meant no more menial carjacking and drug-muling shit.

"Whatever you want, Daddy," I said, wiggling my ass as if I couldn't wait for him to split me wide open. And that was just what the fuck he did—rammed into me raw and fucked me with no remorse.

If I'm proud of anything, it was of my ability to not shed a single tear. Instead, I should have won an Oscar for all the panting and moaning I did. Lucky for me, he had a quick nut that night and blasted off all over my back.

"You a good little soldier, Ma," he praised. But seconds later, I was shown the door.

For six months, I thought I'd ripped my asshole for nothing and went back to playing my position on the poles and doing a little drug-muling on the side until word started circulating that Python had put his latest baby momma, Shariffa, in the hospital because he caught her ass cheating. Nigga she was cheating with was found on the side of the road in a car that had so many bullet holes it looked like black Swiss cheese.

To this day, the Memphis police still had the case open with no leads.

Of course, everybody knew who sent that nigga to the

*devil's door. Just like every bitch in the Queen Gs was
hyphy for the number-one position even before the ambulance showed up to take Shariffa to the hospital.*

*I'd hoped and prayed to catch Python's attention
again, but I was never in a position where I could see
him, much less be alone with him. But one night after my
set at the club, there he was, wanting another go with my
ass. Without missing a beat, I turned it up to him and
then braced myself for a rough ride.*

*Python didn't disappoint. He turned my asshole into
a crime scene and then hosed it down with a thick, heavy
load. Determined not to have him just roll up on out of
there, I washed him down and then gave him a sample of
my mean head game and let him know how tight my
pussy could grip his meat. I candy-coated that black
cock from its head to its balls. The shit was crazy explo-
sive.*

*I loved it. It was like fucking a dangerous beast that
was trying to pound the lining out of my pussy. I fell in
love with that muthafucka that night, and I promised
myself that I would do anything and everything to become the Head Bitch in Charge—and I succeeded.*

That was three years ago.

"C'mon, baby," Python says, pulling me out of my
memories. He hands me the Hefty bag of money and
then smacks me on the ass. "Get the molasses outcha
ass. Momma Peaches is going to be here any minute."

"Okay, Daddy. Whatever you say."

3

Momma Peaches

"**Y**ou leaving today, Momma Peaches?" Bonita shouts from three cells down.

I cock a half smile. "Hell, yeah. I'm tired of looking at all these damn gray-haired pussies up in this bitch. I'm getting out of here and finding my ass a young buck to breast-feed." I lick my fingertips and then smooth down the edges of my hair while I waited for the guards. "These slow muthafuckas need to hurry the fuck on. My nephew is going to do it up and throw his auntie a surprise welcome-home party."

Bonita's cackle bounces off the cement walls. "It ain't a surprise if you know about the shit."

"Maybe not, but a party is a party. And nobody throws a party like my baby Python."

"I know that's right," Bonita agrees. "I got hold of some shit at one of his parties some years back, and I swear to God my ass was high for six damn months. His ass be slanging the good shit for real."

I snicker. "You going to do something, then you might as well be the best. That's what I always say." I tap my foot, impatient. Ten months on lockdown was more than enough for me, and way too much time for the amount of shit the police found in my car. Hell, I didn't even know the shit was in the car. If I had, I would have invited my bingo girls over and had myself a party.

The only reason my innocent-grandma act didn't work was because I had a rap sheet a mile long, and everyone in the department knew my nephew. I'm getting too old to be dipping in and out of jail for bullshit. I can't remember how many times I'd told my knuckle-headed nieces and nephews not to be stashing shit at my place. One of these days, there's going to be a fuckup and I'll have to serve some real-ass time, and then I will really be pissed.

I am what most of the young kids nowadays call an old-school lady gangsta. I'd been in the game since back in the '50s when my nana Maybelle vowed not to return to the cotton fields in Mississippi. Niggas were free, but in their neck of the woods, cotton picking was still the only thing most of them knew how to do. But on Beale Street, the economic situation was a different story entirely. From the music, gambling, and drugs, black folks was coming up and pissing off a lot of white trash.

When I first started out, I helped run numbers up and down Beale Street. Nana Maybelle was a trip. She went toe-to-toe with a lot of niggas trying to hustle her out of her operation. She didn't play that shit and was known for busting a hollow point in people's ass in a hot minute.

At ten, I wasn't allowed to pack heat, but Nana May-belle taught me how to wield a straight razor. By sixteen, I must've sliced more than a hundred niggas trying to jack my shit. They all found out the hard way that Nana Maybelle and I were cut from the same cloth.

Sixteen was also when I fell in love for the first time; he was this fine redbone named Manny. It was also the first time I had ever seen a black man with green eyes. Manny had charm and style and could play a mean saxophone. People came from miles to hear his ass play. Men wanted to shake his hand. Women came hoping to land themselves a husband.

I wasn't really any different, especially after I ignored Nana's rule about keeping my legs closed at all times. But there was just something about that green-eyed devil that made me want to do things I didn't even understand. The fact that he was twice my age only made the situation better in my eyes. I wasn't fucking around with no boy. I had a grown man teaching me how to work the greatest prize God gave women—a pussy.

It's been more than fifty years, and I remember that first nut like it was an hour ago. . . .

Manny wasn't no big nigga. He was an even six feet tall, lean and smelled like Lifebuoy soap. But what was so memorable about Manny was the way he played my body like it was his beloved saxophone. That nigga was never in a rush. Making love in his crammed apartment with just one slow, rotating fan was hot, sticky, and nasty—in a good way.

I didn't get shit past Nana Maybelle. She knew the morning after that some nigga had busted my cherry just by the way I was walking. Instead of scolding me, Nana Maybelle just shook her head and told me, "A hard head makes a soft ass."

For months I had stars in my eyes. It was just a mat-

ter of time before Manny slipped a ring on my finger. 'Course, Manny didn't get the Western Union wire on that shit. Manny quickly educated me to the ways of a playa. He had more bitches than the Southland Park's dog tracks. I denied the truth for a while until I caught him in a back alley with his head buried beneath some chick's skirt.

Enraged, I sliced up the girl and landed in the back of a paddy wagon. Back then, the police didn't give a fuck about black-on-black crime. I stayed about a night behind bars, and the next day I was right back in Manny's arms, listening to his sweet lies about how that bitch meant nothing to him. I was the one he loved. Yet, when I pressed for a ring, he silenced me by drumming his thick tongue against my fat clit until I was practically climbing the walls.

"Damn, baby. You taste like peaches," he moaned.

This was about the time a lot of brothers were getting angry about this white boy who had stolen the Negro sound off Beale Street and was now making mad money. Once one white boy starts stealing, then they all of them start stealing. It went over hard for a lot of musicians like Manny, who wasn't making anything more than chump change. Manny's depression and frustration led him to heroin. It was the drug of choice back in those days.

In the beginning, it really opened Manny's mind and he was creating some wonderful music. Before long, people were tossing around the words *music genius* and Manny's ego became a beast. He hooked up with a few promising bands, and he kept believing that his big break was just around the corner.

Nana Maybelle saw how much cash was being moved around with this drug craze and got into the game bigtime. With the money rolling in, she bought herself a big *house and a fancy car and was straight confusing white folks to just who this Negro woman thought she was. But then, just like now, money talks and bullshit walks. She slung a couple of dollars around and cops left her the fuck alone.*

I benefited as well. My cheap clothes were replaced by silk dresses, fancy hats, and seamless stockings. When Manny and I stepped out, people said we gave Dorothy Dandridge and Harry Belafonte a run for their money.

But all good things must come to an end.

Manny never did get his big break. He never put a ring on my finger. And he never kicked his heroin habit.

Despite those things, I held on—until one of Manny's baby mommas called me and told me that Manny had died of an overdose while she was sucking his dick. I never knew if the latter part was true, but it didn't help that the woman who called was the same bitch I'd sliced up years ago.

Nana Maybelle did spare me the I-told-you-so speech, but I was crushed all the same. The only thing Manny left me was memories and a small heroin habit of my own.

"Maybelline Carver!" a female guard shouts.

I spring to my feet. "Here I go!"

"Got your walking papers, girl."

"It's about damn time." I stroll over to the bars just as the guard shouts for them to be opened.

Women line their cells to yell their well-wishes, and some of the haters shout that it was just a matter of time before my old ass would be back. Lord, I hope not. On the condition of my parole, I'm strapped with an electronic tag around my ankle along with a curfew. However, as the officer is fitting the device around my left ankle, it takes everything I have not to bust out laughing.

I catch a few questionable looks, but I straighten my face and thank the officer when he's done. When I stroll out of Memphis's Federal Correctional Institution, I spot a black Escalade with a driver who resembled my best friend Josie's grandbaby, Arzell. It has been a minute since I've seen him, but baby boy has developed into a fine specimen.

"Boy, look at you," I say, approaching. "C'mon over here and give Momma Peaches a kiss."

Arzell clearly doesn't want to engage in any PDA, but everyone knows that I'm the momma Queen G in the nest, and he does what he's told.

I hug him tight and then playfully squeeze his ass.

"There you go." Arzell chuckles. "I've been warned about you."

"What?" I ask innocently.

"Just get in the car." He laughs, opening my door. When I turn, he pays me back by smacking me on the ass.

"Whoo!" I glance over my shoulder and receive a wink from the young buck. "Yeah. I'm going to fuck you. Watch." I climb into the large vehicle before one of the cops gets the idea to run his face through their database and come out here and arrest his ass for any host of reasons. "A'ight. I'm ready for my party!"

Arzell frowns. "What party, Momma Peaches?"

"Boy, don't play with me," I sass, mushing the side of his head. "Python better be throwing me a party or I'll turn that big nigga over my lap."

"Now *that's* some shit I'd like to see."

I grinned as I look over at him. *Damn, he's a fine young buck.* "How old are you now?"

The side of Arzell's face cocks up. "Twenty-three."

"That's old enough." My gaze skitters down to his lap, but with his baggy jeans, there's no way for me to know what he's packing.

"Old enough for what?"

"You'll find out," I tease.

Despite being a "senior citizen," I never bought the notion that at a certain age a woman is supposed to put her pussy out to pasture. If anything, good and regular sex does wonders for migraines and keeps up one's flexibility. It also helped that, over the years, I've made sure to keep my cute figure in check. In my case, black sure in the hell doesn't crack, and my skin is just as smooth as it was in my early forties. My hair is just as healthy and bouncy as ever. I keep just a small silver patch in the front and dye the rest of it back to my natural color of off black. The bottom line, I never have and never will have a problem getting a man—of any age.

As we roll through town, I'm once again struck by how my beloved Memphis is one part clean and picturesque and two parts dirty and run-down. The drug and gang wars have the city by the fucking throat, and there's no sign of it ever letting go.

I feel no guilt over my part in the drug game. All my life, I, like Nana Maybelle, have been making a way out of no way. I wear the title of Momma Queen G or Momma Peaches proudly. The men and women with the Black Gangster Disciple are my family. That's the way it is and the way it'll always be.

The minute I spot my brick house, a big ole smile stretches across half my face. I smack my lips, ready for both a drink and a fat blunt to make me feel oh so lovely. Before the Escalade even comes to a full stop, I'm already opening my car door and preparing to hop out.

"Hold up, Momma Peaches. I got you." Arzell cuts the engine and rushes to help me out.

"Baby, don't get it twisted and start treating me like I'm some lil old lady. I got this."

"A'ight." Arzell tosses up his hands. "It's all you, Momma."

"And don't you forget it." I lift my head and stroll up to my front door, knowing full well that Arzell's big, young chocolate eyes are following each sway of my hips. As I suspect, the front door is unlocked and when I step into my house, the place is pitch black.

"Humph," I say, playing along. "I wonder why it's so dark in here." I flip the switch by the door. Niggas jump out of the woodwork like cockroaches.

"Surprise!"

I light up while tears burn the back of my eyes. "Now this is what I'm talking about. Somebody pass me a blunt and let's get this muthafuckin' party started!"

4

Yolanda

The music from Momma Peaches's welcome-home party is bumping so hard all the walls up and down Shotgun Row are jumping and trembling. But nobody says shit because everybody loves Peaches—me included. As far as I'm concerned, Peaches is like a second momma, only better. She has always tried to look out for me, despite the fact that I'm a little hardheaded. Still, I have nothing but love for the feisty old lady.

Back in the day, she saved me from my drunk, no good daddy (though I found out years later that he really wasn't my daddy) when he came at me with a broken beer bottle. Peaches had stepped in, bold as you please, asking him what the hell he thought he was going to do with that bottle. Daddy charged toward Peaches. However, Peaches had something for his ass. Instead of slicing her up, *he* got sliced. Hell, she was so fast, nobody even saw when she'd reached for her blade. It was just swish-swish-swish—like some old Zorro shit, and the nigga went down, grabbing his face and hollering like a bitch.

My momma, Betty, was pissed about that shit, and to this day blames Peaches for chasing her man off.

"Shit. Betty should be grateful—I did her ass a favor," Peaches would always say whenever Betty's venom dripped into her ears.

I agree.

I don't even remember how old I was when the shit went down. My *daddy* had already banged me up pretty bad because he claimed I'd back talked him. Maybe I did, maybe I didn't—I don't remember. However, I *do* remember laughing my ass off when Peaches lopped the nigga's ear off.

Peaches looked at me like I was crazy. But the shit was just funny. After that, people up and down Shotgun Row started saying that my elevator didn't quite reach the top. Teachers told Betty on the regular that I was slow and needed to be on Ritalin. Keeping it real, the shit was just a legal high and turned me into a zombie.

Teachers and the neighborhood kids still called me slow no matter how hard I tried to be like them. There was nothing I wouldn't do to be popular. I used to let people borrow what few good clothes and toys my momma scraped up only for them not to return them or fuck them up before giving them back. In junior high, a few of the kids were curious about my Ritalin, so I let them try it. I got into some major shit for that. Soon after, a boy I liked, Jimmy Gaines, gave me a box of Lemonheads to let him put his dick in my mouth. I did it—and then the next day another boy asked, and then another.

I finally became popular—at least with the boys. They even gave me the nickname Lemonhead.

I didn't care. Boys loved me, especially when my body started to resemble a Coke bottle, and I proved that I was a certified freak when it came to sexing the 6 poppin' crew. School turned out not to be my thing; books always hurt my head. So I dropped out in the ninth grade and started hustling. When my momma couldn't afford my medication, I turned to the street shit and found it all made me feel about the same.

But now I'm tired of just being a mule, hauling shit everywhere and spreading my legs for every foot soldier in Python's crew and getting next to nothing for my troubles. I might not be book smart, but I know that shit ain't fair. Other bitches started moving up the ranks faster than me, and they didn't do half the shit I did.

My gaze cut across Momma Peaches's living room to where LeShelle is doing her old stripper pole routine all up and down Python's leg. I can't stand that bitch, always flossing shit Python laces her with, thinking that all the Queen Gs are here just to lick her ass. The bitch thinks she's the shit just because she looks half Indian. So? Most of us niggas up in here are mixed with some other shit. Hell, I know my ass is rounder and can clap harder than hers. Ain't that all a bitch needs to lock down a nigga—that and to know they way around the kitchen?

Sure, Python is a little hard on the eyes, and he does freak me out with all those damn snakes, but being with his ugly ass means money, power, and respect. There isn't a bitch up in here who isn't feeling that.

He also has a slew of rug rats running around Memphis, and all his baby mommas are laced up nice, rocking Chanel this and Gucci that even if they are still

living in different projects. Everybody keeps waiting for
her ass to drop another seed, but it's been three years and
LeShelle's belly remains empty. Word on the street is
that she might be wifey, but she will never be wife with
a rotten-ass belly. That's why I'm looking to get in
where I fit in.

"Damn, girl. You keep staring at LeShelle, she's
going to come over here and smack the taste out your
mouth."

I glance over my shoulder to see KyJuan, one of
Python's old road dawgs, flashing his platinum grillz.

"You got a big-ass sign that says 'HATER' flashing
on your forehead. Better turn that shit off before you
embarrass yourself," he jokes above Jay-Z's latest joint
while puffing on a blunt so fat it looks like a Cuban
cigar.

I calmly reach over and remove the blunt from his
mouth and toke on it for a few puffs. "I just don't see
what she got that I ain't got. That's all."

"She keeps the nigga happy. That's all that matters,
ain't it?" KyJuan looks down my white, mesh, see-
through top, drooling over my large ebony-tipped nipples. "Damn, you believe in advertising your shit, huh?"

"When you got it, you flaunt it, right?"

His gaze roams as he smacks his lips. "Sheeit, girl.
How did you get all that ass into those booty shorts?"

"One cheek at a time." I puff out a ring of smoke and
smile into his chocolate eyes. I can tell by how low his
eyelids are that he's already fucked up, but I also know
that he's higher up the food chain than the wildin' out
foot soldiers I usually deal with.

"Is that blood in my carpet?" Momma Peaches harps,
squinting down at the floor.

KyJuan props one hand on the wall above my head

and continues talking to my titties. "Looky here, are you
rolling with anybody here?"

I brush my braided blond extensions back from my
face. "No. Why?"

" 'Cause I'm thinking about raping your fine ass," he
says, smiling. "Damn titties got my dick hard." He takes
a swig from his beer bottle. "For real, those muthafuckas are staring me straight in my eyes. Hypnotizing a
muthafucka."

I smile. I'm used to getting this kind of reaction from
niggas. "You ain't got to do all that, Daddy," I say in my
best seductive schoolgirl voice, which I've perfected.
"I'm feeling you, too."

"For real?" He smacks his lips some more and then
glances around. Every inch of the place is crawling with
muthafuckas. A few card tables have been propped up,
and serious dominoes and poker games are under way.
In between those, soldiers are grabbing Queen Gs left
and right and are rocking the same two-step no matter
what's spitting out the speakers. "Let me holler at you
out back." Without waiting for a response, KyJuan takes
my hand and leads me toward the back screen door.

"Damn, Python," Peaches complains. "I told you to
convince Datwon to get out of the game—not shoot his
ass."

Niggas laugh.

"Peaches, how about a dance?" Rufus asks, squeezing in between her and Arzell. Everybody knows he's
been sweating Peaches for decades.

"If you don't get your old ass up out of my face!"

The crowd roars again.

There are even more niggas crawling outside, most of
them hanging by the grill and food table, loading up on
grub like they ain't ate in weeks. The rest are either

dancing or leaning against the back fence and swigging down Buds.

"Shit." KyJuan cups his meat like his hard-on is getting to be too much to handle.

I smile at his frustration. In my head, I'm calculating. If I can lock down a lieutenant like KyJuan, maybe my hustlin' days are over. I can be one of the Queen Gs who spends her time shopping and rocking the latest fashions. This nigga isn't Python, but surely he's the next best thing.

"Ain't no thang, Daddy. I live just a couple of doors down." I puff out another smoke ring and feel my eyelids go heavy. I look at the blunt and wonder about all the sudden tingling sensations spreading throughout my body. Hell, it was stronger than the shit my best friend, Baby Thug, be rolling. "What's in this shit?"

"Ayo, man. That's a KyJuan specialty blend. My shit going to have you feeling *loverly*." He rubs on my arm, but then does a sneak wraparound and squeezes my booty. "Damn, girl, you thick as hell."

I giggle and lick my lips. "C'mon, Daddy. Let me hook you up." I take him by the hand and then proceed to start stumbling out the yard.

KyJuan laughs. "Aw. You're feeling the shit now, huh?"

I laugh. Saying that I feel good is a serious understatement. At some point while I try moving through the crowd, I'm convinced that I'm not walking but floating through the scene with Lil Wayne's old hot track "Lock and Load" blasting through the street. Suddenly, the air is charged with a different kind of energy—a dangerous energy. The hairs on the back of my neck stand up as I glance to my left and then to my right.

My gaze locks onto a dusty brown Chevy Impala cruising down the crowded street. Behind the wheel, a short muthafucka with thick cornrows and cheap mirror sunglasses catches my attention and blows my high. *Who's that muthafucka?* But my brain is working slower than usual.

"FORKS UP!" KyJuan yells, shoving a hand against my back, tripping me out of my pumps and sending me careening toward the sidewalk.

I scream just as my exposed skin hits concrete and I scrape a good foot along pebbles, broken glass, and God only knows what else.

POP! POP! POP! POP!
RA-DA-TAT-TAT-TAT!

Bullets fly everywhere.

Startled and hysterical screams fill my ears while I'm still a little dazed and confused. An army of Gangster Disciples pours out the houses on Shotgun Row, guns blazing. There's a loud screech from the Impala's tires, and the evening air is blanketed with the scent of burning rubber.

POP! POP! POP! POP!
RA-DA-TAT-TAT-TAT!

The Impala attempts to make a sharp turn off the street but instead crashes into a parked black Escalade. Disciples proceed to turn the Impala and the three niggas inside it into Swiss cheese. When I sit up, I watch as the dead bodies jump and wiggle around as a barrage of bullets hits them.

"YEAH! YEAH!" KyJuan starts jumping around, throwing his fist in the air. "FUCK THEM NIGGAS UP!" He runs over to the car just as most of 6 poppin' crew are pulling the doors open and jerking bodies out. KyJuan is one of the first to start stomping the niggas into the ground.

I pull myself off the sidewalk and then inspect my

legs and arms to see what the damage is. Relieved to find only a few cuts and bruises, I start laughing about the near-death experience.

WHOOSH!

I glance up to see the old Impala now ablaze. I can't feel sorry for those niggas, even if I wanted to. What the hell were they thinking rolling through our hood and attempting to do a massive drive-by? Everybody in Memphis knows that Shotgun Row is the muthafuckin' heart of the Gangster Disciples' territory. Clearly these niggas were trying to impress somebody and got caught up.

KyJuan races back over to me, shooting his gun straight into the air. "YEAH! YEAH! You see that shit?" He stumbles. "Whoa."

I smile. "For sure. You handled yours, Daddy."

"Damn straight." His greedy eyes roam my figure. "I done smoked me some la, capped me some Vice; all I need is some pussy to call it a day."

I frown as my gaze falls to the blood soaking his T-shirt. "Did you get hit, Daddy?"

KyJuan follows my line of vision and then looks surprised. "Oh shit." He lowers his gun and pulls up his T-shirt.

All I can make out is blood and pulverized flesh before he slumps to his knees. "Those muthafuckas!" He swears under his breath, drops his gun, and then passes out.

I stare at my golden ticket to rising up in the Queen Gs and can't believe my eyes. I walk over to him on bruised knees and check for a pulse. When I can't find one, my tears swell. "Now what the fuck am I going to do?"

5

LeShelle

I'm high as hell, grinding my hips and clapping my ass in Python's face when these pussy, punk muthafuckas start blasting down Shotgun Row. Next thing I know, my arm is on fire and Python is shoving me to the floor and reaching for his chrome. There isn't even time for me to question what the fuck is happening before he charges the front door with the rest of the set.

But it's hard to keep a good gangsta bitch down. I roll up off the floor and reached for the 9 mm I keep strapped to my right calf. Even Momma Peaches goes for her cast-iron umbrella stand and rises up with an HK SL8 assault weapon, ready to rock-a-bye any nigga who gets in her way.

In the short time it takes for me to hustle my way to the front yard, the brown Impala has crashed and niggas are pulling bodies out of the car and stomping their asses like cockroaches. I start to run over to add my high-heeled pumps into the mix when someone sets that shit on blaze. Niggas whoop and holler, acting like they just got their freedom papers.

"Is y'all sure that's all of them?" Momma Peaches asks, clutching her weapon and peeking around the corner of the front door like some real commando.

I laugh. "Yeah, those trick ass—" From the corner of my eye, I see KyJuan drop like a stone.

"FUCK!" Rage twists Python's face before he plows through a crowd of niggas and hoofs it up the cracked sidewalk.

I race after him. My heart pounds in the center of my throat. Everyone knows that Python and KyJuan have known each other since they were baby seeds. They grew up and blew up together. They were the kings of Shotgun Row, and the thought of some miscellaneous niggas rolling through our block and blasting one of them off their throne is just too much to wrap my brain around.

Python drops to his knees and snatches KyJuan away from the chicken head crouching over him, but it's clear by the way KyJuan flops over and the amount of blood painting the concrete that the Grim Reaper has collected one king and is marching him toward heaven's ghetto.

"Fuck these muthafuckas!" Python jumps up and throws punches in the air. "I want to know who the fuck sanctioned this shit, and then we ride the fuck out."

"Vice, man," a foot soldier says. "I know I've seen that one dude dumping and running with those dirty niggas. You feel me?"

"McGriff," Python hollers as he heads back toward the burning Impala. "Verify this shit. Are those niggas tagged?"

An army of Disciples launch an immediate search of

the two dead bodies that had been pulled from the wreckage. There are no flags, and none of the tats identify a gang affiliation.

"These muthafuckas are clean."

"What the fuck?" Python reaches their side and performs his own search. "You ain't going to tell me that these niggas just decided to pop off down here by they damn selves."

"Could've been just an initiation stunt," McGriff offers, shaking his head, his hand still clutching his chrome.

Python lifts his foot back and delivers a hard, swift kick to one of the dead man's head. It's clear he's hot. Heat rolls off of him in waves. "These muthafuckas had names. I want them, plus where they lived, who they people is—you feel me? And if we get *any* muthafuckin' confirmation that Fat Ace's ass had anything to with this shit here, we're blazing this city up. Six poppin' five droppin' tonight, baby. You feel me?"

"I feel you, man." The men fist pound.

With flames and black soot coiling up toward the darkening sky, Python turns his attention to the hundred deep surrounding him. His six-foot-five frame suddenly looks ten feet tall as he starts looking niggas one by one in the eye. "This shit here won't stand. Niggas got us confused if they think they can roll down our shit, disrespecting Shotgun Row or any other block we got on lock." His black eyes cast back up a ways, where his road dawg still lay in the street. "Somebody get something to cover my nigga up. Show some muthafuckin' respect!"

A few Queen Gs scramble to carry out the order.

Python sniffs one time, but no tears drop from his eyes. "Niggas want to blast, we blast. We going to let the muthafuckas who are behind this shit know that they started a war! You feel me?"

"HELL YEAH!"

"We will not rest until we earth every one of those grimy muthafuckas!"

"HELL YEAH!"

The crowd of blue and black cheer their agreement, and some even shoot off a few bullets into the air.

I smile, loving how my man commanded everyone's attention and respect. As I start to pump my fist into the air, that fiery pain surges back into my arm. How in the hell did I forget about that? I glance down and suck in a sharp breath as I notice my thin, bubble-gum-pink top darken with blood.

"Shit!" With my right hand still holding my nine, I use the tip of my pinky finger to pull up my short sleeve and reveal my gushing wound. "Shit! Shit! Shit!"

Despite the amped-up crowd, I catch Python's attention. In a flash, he's standing next to me, examining the wound. After a sec, one corner of his thick lips quirks up. "I can take care of this for you, Ma."

I try to smile back, but my arm feels like straight fire now, and as sure as my ass is black, I know every member of the Queen Gs is watching me, so the option of crying like a bitch is completely taken off the table. To clamp down on the pain, I grind my teeth together as Python leads me back through the crowd to Momma Peaches's spot.

"Get the fuck out of the way!" Python shouts, storming through the front door.

Niggas part like his ass is Moses.

We make a beeline to the kitchen.

"Let me get my shit," Momma Peaches says, returning my weapon back to its hiding spot before rushing for the first-aid kit.

"I need some ice," Python says calmly.

Baby Thug, a short, thuggish shawty just barely kiss-

ing five feet with little mosquito bites for titties, quickly
jerks open a couple of cabinets, grabs a large Glad bag,
and then fills it with ice. Shortly after, the bag is pressed
to my bullet wound.

I hiss but still manage to fight back tears.

Python's chest swells with pride. "That's right,
Shelle. You can handle this shit." He takes my gun from
my clenched hand and sets it on the counter.

Momma Peaches whirls onto the scene like a hurricane. "How we doing in here?" She pops open the white
box and starts pulling out bandages and medical tape.

"We're numbing the shit up," Python says, moving to
the stove and turning on an eye.

"Good. Good." She turns toward the crowd at the
kitchen door. "One of you niggas get me some alcohol.
Either scotch or some whiskey."

"Get me something for her to bite down on—a stick
or something," Python adds as he sets a large knife on
the glowing stove eye.

Fear knots in my chest. My heart races. My head
spins.

"Don't worry, baby. I'm about to fix you on up." He
moves back to my side and removes the ice bag. "That's
long enough with that." Python produces a second knife
and runs it under some cold water from the sink. "Now
this shit might hurt for a minute, but you man up, baby.
A'ight?"

I nod.

"Here you go, man." Lethal, another lieutenant, steps
up with a nasty little stick. He doesn't even bother to
wipe off the dirt and bugs.

Momma Peaches notices my scrunched-up face and
snatches the stick from Lethal's hand and runs it under
the sink. "Better?" she asks.

I nod, though all I want to do is scream for them to

get the fuck away from me. The stick is shoved into my mouth with Momma Peaches's simple instruction to "Bite down."

Python smiles and wraps one of his large hands around my wounded arm and lifts it so that he can have a better look. Then I watch as the cold, wet knife descends to my arm like a hawk. In the next second, my entire world is nothing but pain as Python's knife digs around in my arm.

I growl and hiss, and then my teeth clamp down so hard that the stick snaps in half—but not a muthafuckin' tear drops.

"That's right, Shelle. Hang in there. I almost got it."

When the bullet eases out of my bloody arm, I expect some relief, but it doesn't happen. Blood continues to gush and the pain is relentless.

"C'mon over here by the sink," Python says.

Momma Peaches removes the knife from the stove's eye.

I spit the sticks out of my mouth and try to walk on legs that feel like they are filled with Jell-O. By sheer will alone, I make it over to the sink with my audience doubling in size.

"Goddamn." One bitch winces. "Shouldn't we be getting her ass to a doctor or something?"

Python leans my arm over the sink and reaches for the bottle of scotch. "Take a deep breath."

Again, I follow orders, but damn near faint when the first drops of liquor splash against my arm. Suddenly Momma Peaches is right there to help hold me up. Still, I don't scream or cry.

But the comments from the peanut gallery continue.

"Aw, hell naw."

"Sheeit!"

"Yeah, that's my gangsta bitch right here. Niggas,

y'all checking this shit out? Is my girl a soldier or what?"

There's a rumble of agreement and even a few cheers for me to hang in there.

"Some of y'all could learn a thing or two," he boasts as he splashes scotch all over my arm. "I ain't going to call out no names, but I know a few of y'all would be hollering my damn ear off right about now."

"Not me!"

"Nuh-uh!"

Python rolls his eyes and then sets the bottle aside.

My ego doesn't even trip. It takes all I have just to hang on. *You can do this. You can do this.* I repeat the words until I start to believe it. But then Python reaches for the heated knife his aunt has taken off the stove. Tears finally rise up and sting my eyes, but I blink those muthafuckas back as I watch Python bring the knife closer.

He licks his lips with his snakelike tongue. Python loves inflicting pain. It doesn't matter on whom. "Now I'm going to seal this shit up. A'ight?"

I draw in a sharp breath and summon courage from parts of my body that I didn't know existed before I finally give Python the nod to go ahead. *You can do this. You can do this.* Yet, doubt starts creeping up my spine. *You can do this. You can do this.*

"Look at me, baby," Python commands.

My jittering gaze makes its way up to my man's black eyes, and a strange calm settles over me as I stare into his soulless depths.

"Ready?" he asks.

I swallow as sweat blankets my face. "Ready."

Python presses the scorching knife against my skin.

My head explodes with pain while the sound of my skin sizzling fills my head. A scream rips from my throat before I have a chance to stop it. But it isn't a bitch scream. It is more guttural and Herculean—like a nigga trying to bench-press twice his body weight.

More importantly, no tears fall.

Pride polishes Python's black eyes as he finishes sealing my wound and then wrapping my arm up with a tight gauzy bandage. When it is all over, he stands and inspects his work as police sirens fill the air. "You're a bad bitch, baby." His face twists into a menacing smile as he tilts up my chin. "Don't ever let anyone tell you different." He leans down and slithers his forked tongue into my mouth for a kiss.

I smile against his thick lips. *Damn straight, I am—and don't you ever forget it.*

6

Melanie

"**W**e have a code purple reporting off Utah Avenue. Car thirty-four, are you still in the area?"

I groan and ground my teeth. Utah Avenue—better known as Shotgun Row. I've been on the force for four years, and I'm so sick of all the gang activity in this shitty-ass place I don't know what to do. It's dusk, there's a blood-orange glow settling over the city I call Hell's Paradise, and I'm more than ready to take my ass home, jump into a warm bath, and blaze up a fat blunt to relax my nerves.

"Car thirty-four, you roger?"

My partner and pain in my left ass cheek, Detective Keegan O'Malley, chuckles and reaches over for the hand radio. "Thirty-four, copy. We're on our way."

"Roger that, thirty-four. We have reports that there is

eleven-forty-four on the scene. Car forty-three and fifty-four will assist."

"Shit," I spat. "We're probably rolling up on a war."

"If we're lucky."

I side eye O'Malley. No doubt my adrenaline-junkie partner is just looking for an excuse to shoot at niggas. The muthafucka is always acting like this gang shit is some kind of fucking video game and he's the big exterminator who is going to rid Memphis of gangbangers. I suspect most of that blustering comes from all the steroids his ass be pumping. Oh, he would deny the shit, but I know nobody's neck is supposed to be as thick as a tree trunk.

Sure, O'Malley works out all the time, but the shit still doesn't seem natural. When he isn't in the gym, his ass is at a gun range. He's a perpetual soldier who'd traded in shooting at sand niggas for the real thing. In Memphis, the badge is a license to shoot first and ask questions later—and nobody dares challenge that shit. The city at large knows what kind of battle we're in with these street gangs, and they don't ask too many questions as long as it appears that we're doing our jobs.

Appearances aren't everything.

The truth is much more sinister.

O'Malley laughs, his bald head rocking back and forth. "Don't look at me like that. The sooner we get over there, the sooner we get off the clock and you can go back home to play with your *cat*."

"Don't start that ignorant shit with me," I hiss, pressing the accelerator down to the floorboard as I whip around cars, trucks, and a little old lady taking her sweet-ass time trying to cross the road.

"What?" He laughs, cracking himself up. "When was the last fuckin' time you even went out on a date, Detective Johnson?"

"That ain't none of your goddamn business, O'Malley."

He tosses up his hands, still smirking. "Fine. But if you ever need someone to scratch that itch—"

"Don't even fuckin' finish that goddamn sentence."

"—I'll be willing to take one for the team."

As O'Malley's laughter explodes from his chest, I imagine ramming his Mr. Clean head into the dashboard until I bust his face wide open. I can't stand his racist ass, and I find it exasperating that he thinks shit is cool between us.

Far from it.

In the meantime, I bide my time. I don't want to complain to my lieutenant—mainly because he'll take my complaint to the captain, who just happens to be my father. It isn't easy being the police captain's daughter. Everyone is always eyeballing me to make sure I'm not receiving any special treatment. What they find instead is that I have it harder than anyone else. From the police academy to now, Captain Melvin Johnson made sure my superiors pushed me harder than everyone else. He wants to break what he calls my iron will so that I'll quit and take my ass to college and law school like he always wanted.

But Daddy Dearest found out that his only daughter is just as tough and hardheaded as he is. Instead of receiving my colleagues' envy, most times I garner their sympathies, which is worse.

For the most part, I have a reputation for being a bitch. I don't put up with or take any shit from anyone. I'm strong. Five-eight, curvy, and no one can pinch more than an inch on my toned body.

During my short time on the force, I have been shot at more times than I care to count. One Latina *puta loca* managed to get a blade into my left side.

I fucked that bitch up over that shit.

Of course, the very thing that makes me so good at my job usually scares niggas off. I'm loud, domineering, and maybe a little quick to throw the first punch. But this is what happens when a woman works with and hangs out with a lot of men. I start talking and acting like them. Once that happens, it's just a matter of time before people hurl names like *dyke* and *carpet-muncher*, thinking the shit is funny.

It isn't.

My personal life isn't anybody's muthafuckin' business. Never has been. To this day, I have never told anyone Christopher's father's name—or that we still get it on from time to time. Sure, some know, but they never got the information from me. So I put up with the jokes, the bullets, and the occasional broken bone because . . . Hell, I don't know why. It isn't like the job pays well, and respect in the black community is nonexistent. Maybe I'm addicted to the drama and the danger.

Shit. That means me and O'Malley do have something in common.

With lights flashing and the police siren blaring, we fishtail onto Shotgun Row with tires screeching. We're instantly jolted back to the serious situation at hand when we spot a burning car at the opposite end of the road.

I slam on the brakes and jump out. In a flash, my weapon is out of its holster and gripped tightly in my hands. Everyone on the block hustles out of the way, a lot of them laughing and pointing fingers.

"Niggas got what the fuck they deserved," a small voice shouts.

I whip my head around. "Who got what they deserved?"

A boy, who can't be more than ten, glares back at me

with dark eyes that seem to belong to an old soul. "The muthafuckin' Vice Lords. Who the fuck you think, bitch?"

"Watch your mouth," O'Malley snarls.

The young boy just rolls his eyes.

That's when it hits me. The odd smell I'm picking up is the scent of burning flesh. One hand comes off my weapon as I press a finger against my nose in a weak effort to block the stench. "What happened here?" I bark at the kid.

His face immediately twists in disgust. "What? I ain't no snitch, bitch."

A few of his friends, all young with old faces, snicker in support. "Yeah, bitch. We ain't snitches!"

"What the fuck did I tell you?" O'Malley leaps forward, acting like he's ready to knock one of the boys off their bikes.

"Easy, O'Malley." I roll my eyes. This Rambo wannabe muthafucka is going to get our asses blazed up on this damn street. I know every one of these niggas is packing more heat than the U.S. Army out here. I glance around the street. Just then, two backup patrol cars blaze onto the scene.

Our backup exits their cars, weapons drawn.

The hair on the back of my neck stands at attention as my eyes shift to one of the houses that has a yard full of people with music blaring. At the fence, an army of brothers stand with their arms crossed and their gazes daring me to walk my ass over to them. The whole scene makes me nervous, but they have it twisted if they think that Detective Melanie Johnson is some weak-ass bitch who can't do her fucking job. I've earned my badge, and I'm not afraid of no muthafucka.

To prove my point, I holster my shit and stroll over to the fence with my chin up. About a hundred sets of eyes follow me to the fence. "Anybody want to tell me what the hell happened here?"

No one moves. Not even so much as an eye twitches.

"Somebody saw something," I press.

Silence.

"Maybe we should call in a few wagons and haul everyone down to the station and ask our questions there?" My gaze shifts to each face on the front line. "You all look like fine, upstanding citizens. I'm sure none of you have any outstanding warrants or anything like that."

Finally, a few gazes shift around.

"Ain't nobody seen nothing," a deep, gravelly voice says from behind the front line.

People shift and then part like the Red Sea.

Python steps up with a stony expression. "You're wasting your time here."

I draw a deep breath and cock my head. "Why don't you let me be the judge of that?" A long glaring contest ensues. The only reason I'm the first to break the eye contest is because the dueling blares from the approaching fire truck and ambulance catch my attention.

"Anything?" O'Malley asks, walking up beside me.

"Of course not," I answer. "As usual, everyone hears no evil and sees no evil."

A corner of Python's lips curl as his eyes rape my curvy frame. "Don't forget 'speak no evil.'"

I stop my lips from kicking upward. "Smart-ass." I turn away from him and mumble under my breath, "I'm sick of this gang bullshit. Go ahead and destroy this city. Why the fuck should I care?"

7
Ta'Shara

The Douglases are cool people. After a lifetime of bouncing around from one shitty foster home to another, the man upstairs finally did the Murphy sisters a solid and brought Reggie and Tracee Douglas into our lives. The middle-class couple lives in a two-level, beige and gray stone craftsman bungalow on the edge of picturesque midtown. The lawn is green, the house is clean, and the neighbors are freakishly friendly.

The first biggest thrill when I first moved in was that I had my own room—mainly because LeShelle had been still walled up in a girls' home. Those first two years were like a dream as the childless couple rained money on everything from clothes to the latest computer gadgets. In the beginning, I resisted letting the Douglases buy my love. I kept waiting to peek out their hustle. I wasn't stupid. LeShelle taught me early that *everyone* had a hustle.

At night, I kept counting the minutes and hours before my new stepfather started creeping to my door. Since LeShelle wasn't there to shelter me, it would be my turn to cry into my pillow while some grown-ass man ripped my young pussy to pieces. But night after night, Reggie Douglas never darkened my bedroom door.

Soon the days rolled into weeks and then months, and all the Douglases pushed was me getting an education, talking all this shit about how I can do or be anything as long as I put my mind to it. That shit was funny as hell the first hundred times I heard it. However, after a while, I realized that the Douglases were serious. They were a walking, talking public service announcement. If you had an education, you can do this, or if you had an education, you can do that.

Reggie is a history professor at the University of Memphis, and Tracee works part-time for the public library. They are complete squares. Books litter their house from one end to another. Most times if they weren't reading a book, they were talking about one.

The first time they took me to the public library, they made it a big production, like it was a trip to Disney World or something. They gushed over just getting ready, and they were overly giddy during the short drive to the cement and glass building.

I didn't see what the big deal was. That place had just as many books as the Douglases had at home. Then they made the big announcement: I was allowed to check out my very own book. *Whoopie!* It took everything I had not to roll my eyes. Were these people serious? But with their wide eyes on me, I felt tremendous pressure to pick out a really good book, something that would impress them, something worthy to talk about at the breakfast table. I must've roamed those shelves for hours before finally settling on Edward Bloor's *Tangerine*. I knew it was a good choice by the way Tracee lit up like a Christmas tree.

After the first year, I concluded that Tracee and Reggie didn't have a hustle. What you see is what you get. For a young girl of thirteen, it was a refreshing and welcome change of pace.

I began to trust them.

Then I began to love them.

It was odd at first. My feelings for the Douglases sort of felt like a betrayal to LeShelle. It was supposed to be just the two of us against the world, but life wasn't working out that way. LeShelle was in a group home, and I was on my own.

I wasn't stupid or naïve. I understood my sister got sent away because she was trying to protect me. But the Douglases offered something that was almost impossible for me to turn down: hope.

Inspired by my foster parents, I thought long and hard about what Reggie and Tracee were saying; then I started dreaming about my future instead of how to just survive the present. What if there was another life out there for me—something better than what the streets were promising? LeShelle wasn't the only one I knew going in and out of juvenile hall. Hell, it was damn near everybody around me, including my best girl, Essence. She got popped on her thirteenth birthday after going on a home burglary spree out in Cordova with a group of Queen Gs.

That wasn't the life I wanted for myself. Not if there was the possibility for something more. So I started to pay attention in school and found that I was a natural at math and science. Tracee mentioned that I would probably make a good doctor one day—and the idea stuck. *Dr. Ta'Shara Leigh Murphy.*

It had a nice ring to it.

Then a year later, LeShelle showed up. I was thrilled at first, but then I saw how much my older sister had changed. She was harder, louder, bitter, and rabid for the illusion of power, money, and respect that the street life promised. At the Douglases, everything went to hell in a handbasket—fast. At every chance LeShelle got, she'd curse out the Douglases, refuse to go to school, and rarely returned home. The times she did, she reeked of marijuana, sex, and alcohol.

I hated to admit it, but I was actually embarrassed by my sister's behavior. She was like a bull in a china shop, determined to break every dish that stood in her way. There were many days I wished she would just go back to the group home so the Douglases and I could go back to being happy, living our quiet suburban life. It was a horrible thing to wish for, but night after night I watched the Douglases pace and fret over LeShelle's whereabouts. Soon my wish became a prayer. Then one night, God answered my prayer. . . .

It was late. LeShelle was dead set on proving that Reggie Douglas was no different than any other nigga and that he was just lying in bed with his perfect little wife but was dreaming that he was fucking one of us. LeShelle claimed that she caught him watching her switching her ass around the house. I didn't believe it, so my sister set out to seduce him—to prove me wrong.

I tried to talk her out of it—tried to convince her that Reggie wasn't like our other foster fathers and uncles, but LeShelle wanted to prove that the Douglases weren't worthy of my love and blind devotion. She preached that I needed to get my head out of the clouds and get back into the real world, where street smarts were all that a bitch needed to get by.

LeShelle took a hot shower, oiled her body down, and then split her inky black hair into two ponytails. "Men love the idea of fucking lil girls. That's why they always asking, 'Who's your daddy?'"

I frowned. I wasn't aware of that tidbit.

"Watch and learn," LeShelle said with a smug smile, and then headed downstairs wearing nothing but a pink towel wrapped around her incredibly grown-up curves.

Reggie had fallen asleep watching ESPN in his favorite chair in the living room. I was scared—that my sister was right—and that I was wrong. If Reggie failed the test, would this set off a pattern of him creeping to our bedrooms? If he passed, would he be so angry that he would kick us both out? At first, I just paced around in my room, but then my curiosity started getting the best of me, and I crept toward the stairs so that I could at least hear what was going on. I didn't need to bother, because when Reggie Douglas woke up, what I heard— what the entire neighborhood heard—was an explosion.

"WHAT THE FUCK DO YOU THINK YOU'RE DOING? GET THE FUCK AWAY FROM ME. PUT SOME FUCKIN' CLOTHES ON! TRACEE!!"

I had just barely made it back to my room when Tracee fumbled out of the master bedroom and raced toward the stairs. "REGGIE? WHAT'S WRONG, REGGIE?"

My heart pounded everywhere: my head, my throat, my chest, my stomach. This was it. LeShelle had fucked it up for the both of us. Hot tears burned the backs of my eyes as hatred started boiling in my veins.

"THAT'S IT! SHE HAS TO GET THE HELL OUT OF HERE! DON'T TELL ME TO CALM DOWN!"

LeShelle raced back into our bedroom; her entire face was purple with anger and embarrassment. "Get your shit. We're getting the fuck out of here!" She pulled out the torn duffel bag she had from the girls' group home and started shoving clothes in it.

I didn't move.

LeShelle crammed on a pair of panties and tight jeans. "Didn't you hear me? I said get your shit!"

"I'm not going," I hissed through my gritted teeth.

LeShelle froze as her homicidal gaze leveled on me. "What the fuck did you just say?"

"I said I'm not going anywhere," I repeated, my hands balled into fists at my sides. "I told you not to go down there."

"Don't you fuckin' start with me," LeShelle said, determined to assert control. "I ain't got time for your bullshit. Get your shit!"

"I'm not going."

"YES THE FUCK YOU ARE."

I swallowed and shook my head. "I like it here, LeShelle. Besides, where are we going to go?"

"Anywhere is better than these Huxtable wannabe muthafuckas." She shoved on a Detroit Tigers jersey and matching cap, its gray and blue colors easily identifying her with Gangster Disciples. "Now stop standing there like a scared chicken and c'mon."

"No."

LeShelle moved so fast that I barely registered what was about to happen, and by the time my sister's hand whipped across my face, it was too late. I reeled back and hit the wall. For a few seconds, I felt like one of those cartoon characters with stars rotating around my head and a few tweeting birds. When I touched my burning face, it was soaked with tears.

"When I tell you to do something, you fuckin' do it, bitch! Now get your shit!"

"SHE'S NOT GOING ANYWHERE." Tracee burst into the room and thrust herself in between us. She was a tall woman, at least six feet, but flat chested and rail thin. On most days it looked like a good, stiff wind could snap her in two, but tonight she looked strong enough to take on Superman himself and stood a damn good chance of winning.

LeShelle's head whipped around toward the usually timid Tracee. *"She's my sister. She goes where the fuck I tell her to go."*

"No. That's not how it works here." Tracee lifted her chin. *"I'm the head bitch in this house, and you will leave my man and my daughter alone."*

LeShelle glared, but Tracee seemed unfazed.

"I'm not afraid of you, little girl." She straightened even taller. *"I've already called Family Children Services, and they're coming right now to march your fast ass up out of here tonight."*

"Don't bother." LeShelle's head swiveled back toward me as she said, *"I'm leaving."*

I watched my sister as she stomped back over to her duffel bag and collected her things. There was no mistaking the anger, betrayal, and humiliation etched into her face as she tried to cram everything she owned into the tattered bag. I wanted to explain my decision better, but Tracee stood guard, watching my sister like a hawk. But what could I really say to make my sister understand?

LeShelle stormed out of the bedroom and then out of the house and never returned. Eventually, word got back to me that my sister was dancing over at the Pink Monkey. Some time after that, she had launched to the head *of the food chain as Python's latest wifey. Our paths crossed every now and again, but things were never the same between us and I doubted they ever would be. . . .*

I shove an old picture of me and my sister back into the top drawer of my vanity and try to wipe the memories of that old fight out of my head, but I have a sinking feeling that that blowup will be nothing compared to what will happen when news of me and Profit reach Shotgun Row.

I reach for my hairbrush the same time my cell phone starts buzzing against the vanity's glass top. On the ID screen, the words My Boo causes my lips to curl upward and my heart to start skipping around in my chest.

"You know our shit is all on Front Street now, right?" I spit angrily.

"Damn, baby. Hello to you, too." Profit chuckles into the phone.

I roll my eyes and struggle to remain mad. "That shit you pulled wasn't cool, boo."

"Hey, it ain't my fault that your ass is so fine I can't keep my hands off of you."

I cluck my tongue but can't keep the grin off my face. "See. You can't even be serious."

"Sure I can. In fact, the main reason I'm calling is so I can apologize."

For a brief moment, I pull the phone away from my ear so I can make sure that I am talking to who I think I am. When I put the phone back to my ear, Profit is laughing.

"That's right, baby. I said it. A brother can admit when he's wrong."

"I guess there's a first time for everything." I stand up from the vanity table and start walking around the room.

"So, are you going to accept my apology or just leave a nigga hanging?"

"Of course I accept it." I huff out a breath. "But it doesn't stop the fact that the damage is already done."

"Then maybe we should hook up and put our heads together on how we going to handle this."

I draw in another breath and shake my head. "I don't know."

"You don't know?"

"Look, baby, I just don't think it's a hot idea to risk being seen together again."

He chuckles. "C'mon. Now, I ain't said nothing about us going all public. Besides, we've been able to keep our shit tight for six months, haven't we?"

"Yeah, until you fucked up," I snap, a little harder than I intended.

A strained silence stretches over the phone.

I suspect that my secret boo is struggling not to curse me the fuck out. I know him well enough to know that he doesn't like it when people mouth off at him, and there have been more than a few times when he had to tell me to check my slick mouth when talking to him. He never wilds out or anything; he just has this cool way about handling me without me feeling handled.

"Are you finished now?" he asks. His deep baritone is like warm honey in my ear. "Have you got all of that shit out of your system?"

Contrite, I shrug my shoulders with my bottom lip poked out.

"Good. Now come over here to the window and let me in."

I whip my head around and am stunned shitless at seeing Profit's beautiful dimpled smile beaming back at me. "What the fuck are you doing out there?" I gasp into the phone.

"What does it look like?" He laughs. "I'm out here risking my neck tryna see your ass." He taps my window. "Now get over here before your pops catches me out here and starts blasting at a nigga."

I blink out of my stupor, toss my phone down on the bed, and then race over to the window. "I don't fuckin' believe you." I turn the silver lock and open the window. "Damn, Profit. What the fuck were you thinking?" I ask as he climbs inside. Once he's in, I glance back out. "How the fuck did you get up here?"

Still laughing, Profit wraps his strong arms around my waist and then nuzzles a kiss along the column of my neck. "Now what difference does that make? I'm here now." His soft lips move to just behind my ear, causing every inch of my womanhood to tingle and throb. "All you need to know is that I miss your fine ass." His large, basketball player–like hands dip down in between my legs, where he massages my swollen clit through the seam of my jeans. "Did you miss me, too, baby?"

Since I'm moaning, there's no point in saying anything other than the truth. "You know I did." I still have sense enough to reach up and jerk my bedroom curtains closed before we give everyone on my street a good peep show.

"If you missed me so much, how come you ain't actin' like it?" His teeth lightly skimmed my lower earlobe. "How come you ain't ripping out these clothes, Ma?" His hands move back up but make a beeline toward the top button of my jeans.

I draw in a shaky breath and then slap the top of his hand as I pull away.

"Damn, lil ma. What's up?"

"Nigga, you know what's up." I smack him on the chest. "This shit is serious. What are we going to do?"

Profit rolls his eyes. "We ain't gotta do shit . . . just mind our p's and q's. The shit will blow over."

"Please say that you're fucking joking." I blink at him.

"What?" He tries to pull me back into his arms.

"Nigga, this ain't Atlanta where we play paper gangstas. This is the real shit here in Memphis. Niggas pop out they momma's pussies wearing colors. Don't tell me I'm telling you shit you don't already know."

"Shara," Profit insists, tugging on my white cotton T and smiling directly at my creamy milk-chocolate breasts. "Niggas talk. That's what the fuck they do. We can't control that shit." His hand roams up my flat belly and then cups my shit as if that's all it takes to calm me down.

"Puh-lease." I push him and his octopus arms away from me. "Niggas also shoot—or did you forget that shit?"

"Tsk." Profit rolls his pretty-ass eyes and hits me with his large dimples. "You're taking this shit too serious, Shara. Ain't nobody sweating what the fuck we're doing. Neither one of us are in the game. We can do what the fuck we want." He eases back on me and sucks on my bottom lip. "I done told my brother that shit and you have told your sister. If anybody steps to us sideways, then we'll handle that shit. End of story." His hands return to my jeans and snap them open before I can stop him again. "Your problem is that you worry too much."

"You don't worry enough," I say, mushing him in the head.

He tugs on my lip again and then dips his tongue inside my warm mouth until I start moaning again and pressing my marble-sized nipples against his chest. His dick quickens and my titties tingle.

What the fuck? I can't even stay mad at this nigga. I turn my face until my lip pops away from his gentle sucking. "C'mon. You know that shit ain't true. It's just a matter of time before LeShelle starts blowing my phone up. Hell, if it wasn't for some big fuckin' party they're throwing tonight, she would be doing the shit right now."

"Fuck! Will you stop worrying about your whack-ass sister and start concentrating on your man?"

My eyes bug, but before I can jump on my high horse, Profit tosses up his hands. "All right, all right. I was out of line," he says, forcing a smile back onto his face. "I'm sorry." He kisses me tenderly. "Forgive me?" Another kiss.

However, I'm hip to his game. "You ain't foolin' no-body. You just want some pussy."

Profit's lips broaden. "Nah, nah." He tugs me toward the bed. "I don't just want *some* pussy. I want the best pussy." With just two fingers, he gives me a little push and watches as I fall backward onto the bed. "You know you got the best, right baby?"

I laugh as he jumps down on top of me and removes my cotton T-shirt in one swift move.

"Oooh. There my babies are." He grins and drops his face and tries to smother himself in between my breasts.

I start laughing at his foolishness.

"Ta'Shara?" Tracee's voice floats from the hallway.

I clamp my mouth shut just as Profit's head pops up from between my titties.

We watch in horror as the doorknob twists and rattles in vain.

I expel a relieved breath. At least I'd locked the door. *Thank God.*

"Ta'Shara, are you in there?" *Knock. Knock.*

Scrambling off the bed, Profit loses his balance and falls over the side, hitting the floor with a loud "Ooof!"

"Ta'Shara, honey? Are you okay?"

"Umm, yes, ma'am."

"What was that noise?" The doorknob rattles again.

"Uh . . . uh, I just tripped." I reach down and pull up the bottom of my comforter before whispering, "Hide."

Profit frowns as he peeps under the bed. "Yo, I don't know what you got under there."

"Why is the door locked?" Tracee asks, rattling the door again.

"Will you stop playing and get under there?" I whap him on the back of the head and then help cram him under the bed with my dust bunnies.

"Ta'Shara?"

"I'm coming." I jump up and grab my T-shirt from the other side of the bed. Clutching it against my chest, I jerk open the door. "Hey!"

Tracee jumps back and then runs her gaze over me. "What are you doing?" she asks suspiciously.

"N-nothing. I was just getting ready for bed."

"What was that noise?" Tracee glances over my head and peeks into the room. "I thought I heard you laughing with someone."

"I, um, was on my cell phone talking to Essence," I say, thinking quickly. "We were just laughing about something that happened today at school."

"Oh." Tracee's gaze returns to my open and honest-looking face. "Well, try to keep it down in here. Reggie has a migraine."

"Yes, ma'am. 'Nite."

Pop! Pop! Pop!

Tracee and I jump, but then share an awkward

smile. The sporadic gunfire usually starts around nine o'clock and is like a soundtrack to the gang violence that's creeping toward midtown.

"Well, you better get to bed," Tracee says after taking a breath. "Good night." Tracee smiles but casts a final look back into the room before I shut the door in her face—and lock it.

Pop! Pop! Pop!

"Yo, Ma. Your moms be bugging," Profit says, crawling out from under the bed with a goofy grin.

"Keep it down," I say, tossing my T-shirt and hitting him on the head with it. "Trust me, you don't want Reggie to find you in here."

Profit jumps to his feet and quickly draws me back into his arms. "I'll be quiet if you'll be quiet." He unhooks my bra and peels the straps from my shoulders.

Once upon a time, I vowed that I would wait until I was married before I had sex, but that shit flew out the window when I met Profit. Hell, I didn't even make his ass wait. On our first date, he flashed those diamond-sized dimples one too many times, and the next thing I knew, I was screaming for Jesus and my pink Wednesday panties were hanging from his car rearview mirror. I don't have anyone to compare him to, but as far as I'm concerned, our bodies were made for each other.

We click. We flow. We are soul mates. I know this as well as I know that I need air to breathe. Profit completes me—and this small life I've managed to carve out with the Douglases. Now I just need to figure out some way to hold it all together, at least until I can roll the hell up out of Memphis.

Pop! Pop! Pop!

Profit enters me with one smooth stroke and stares lovingly into my eyes while I try to control the volume on my moans. He doesn't make it easy for me either. He hooks my legs over his shoulders and tears up my G-spot, my T-Spot, and my Z-spot.

"Oh . . . Profit . . ."

Pop! Pop! Pop!

"Shhh. Shara . . . baby," he hisses, trying to handle how hard I'm throwing my pussy back at him. We go at it until our bodies are slick with sweat and words of love are whispered back and forth.

Pop! Pop! Pop!

I roam my hands around my man's waist and then lower to grip his tight ass. The feel of his muscles flexing and relaxing and the intensity of his caramel-colored eyes keep me wetter than a waterfall. Outside my door, I swear I can hear my foster parents climbing the stairs and heading to their bedroom for the night.

Pop! Pop! Pop!

"Oh . . . Oh . . ."

"Good night, Ta'Shara," Reggie and Tracee call from outside my bedroom.

"Oh!" Pop! "Oh!" Pop! "Oh!" Pop!

In order to keep me quiet, Profit smothers my mouth with kisses and at the right moment swallows my orgasmic cry while my foster parents close the door to their bedroom.

I drift down from my cloud and start giggling.

"You think that shit is funny?" Profit asks, laughing. "Earlier, you were all scared they might come in here and put a cap in my ass. Now that you got your nut, it's fuck me, is that it?"

I laugh. That's something I love doing with Profit as much as having sex. He's funny and goofy and then can flip the script and can be serious and no-nonsense.

"Ah, I see how you do a nigga with your selfish ass." He tickles my sides, but when I start wiggling around, his dick gets harder.

I smile at the feel of his dick thickening and throbbing. "Oooh. What's that?" I ask, rolling my hips and watching my man's face twist with pleasure. "You like that, baby?"

His mouth sags open. "Damn, baby. Hold up." He struggles to catch his breath.

"Nah, nigga." I pick up the speed. "You were talking all that shit. The truth is you can't handle this sweet pussy, can you?"

He tries to laugh it off, but then I hit a particular sweet spot and instead he starts sounding like a man who just caught the Holy Ghost.

"Uh-huh. I didn't think so." I roll him over and take the top position. "You like how I work this dick, baby?" My hips whine, bounce and then roll some more.

"I fuckin' love it." Profit pulls my body close so he can pop an erect nipple into his warm mouth. "I fuckin' love you, baby," he rasps.

I stop. "What?"

"I don't stutter and your ears don't flap." Profit smiles and rolls me back over. "I said I love you and I mean that shit." His hips start moving again. This time his strokes are so deep I think his dick is banging against my heart.

"I love you, too," I confess. My heart pounds in double time.

Our eyes lock.

"Then that's all the fuck that matters." Profit cups my face in his hands while he continues his deep stroking. "Promise me that you'll always remember that, baby."

"I . . . I promise."

Pop! Pop! Pop!

8

Momma Peaches

Every time I open my eyes in the morning, I thank the good Lord for blessing me to see another day. As far as I'm concerned, there are a lot of muthafuckas who don't make it this far in life. For whatever reason, the man upstairs sees it fit for my old ass to still be roaming around in these streets just like he sees it fit to deliver the fine buck snoring next to me to really give me the proper homecoming I needed.

Now that the cobwebs have been knocked off my pussy and the sun is shining on my new chocolate boy toy, I'm in the mood for some flapjacks. I smile and peel back the white cotton sheets on my big ole cherry poster bed and swing my legs over the side—well, my one good leg and my one half a leg. I reach down and rub the bottom nub of my left leg and then have to remind myself that the ache I feel isn't real and that I'm still suffer-

ing from what the doctors called phantom limb—the
sensation that a missing limb is still attached—but it
never really works.

   *I had lost the leg in '73, fucking around with Leroy, a
small-time hustler who thought his ass was Priest from*
Super Fly. *Hell, everybody blew his head up about that
shit, just because he was light-skinned and could rock
out a hot-comb press better than most. I don't know why
I was attracted to bad boys. I just was. Their swagger,
their danger, their fuck-the-world attitude would get me
and keep me wet better than any nigga working a nine-
to-five with full benefits.*
   *It was the same summer my baby sister, Alice, was
sent up to Nana Maybelle's place since our momma kept
spitting out babies every nine months like clockwork.
When Alice showed up, the whole Manny affair was six
years in my rearview mirror, and I was trying to trick
niggas before they could trick me. What love had to do
with shit was my anthem long before Tina Turner got
some sense knocked into her screaming ass.*
   *Momma Maybelle was still in the game but was start-
ing to show less heart about staying in it. Niggas were
starting to get too wild, weren't respecting long-held
codes of honor on the street, and snitching became a
new pastime down at the precinct. Still, Nana played the
game smart and kept those Irish muthafuckas off her
doorstep by contributing to the right people's retirement
funds.*
   *In '73, I slipped up one more 'gin by catching feel-
ings with Leroy's pretty ass. And it had a lot to do with
his ass rocking double digits in the dick department and
introducing me to white people's favorite drug of choice:
cocaine.*
   For a while, I just let him have that. After years of

fighting that heroin habit Manny had left me with, the last thing I wanted was to get hooked on some new shit. But I had to admit, Leroy's ass was a lot of fun whenever he was on that shit. He played more, laughed harder, and just downright tore my pussy up in the bedroom like his tight ass had batteries in it. Back in those days, drugs had a certain hierarchy. Any ole nigga could get their hands on some weed and heroin, but cocaine meant your ass had some dough.

It first started at a red light in the basement party over at my best friend Josie's crib. Everybody and anybody was bumping and grooving in that muthafucka that night. The women were rocking big-ass afros and equally big hoop earrings and ridiculous high-platform shoes while every man in there wore their baddest pimp gear, Leroy included.

"I don't understand why it got to go up in my nose?" I had naïvely said after watching people do lines or just scoop the shit up with their own private stock with tiny gold spoons that they wore around their necks.

"Why ask why?" Leroy snickered as he chopped up his shit with a razor and made two distinct lines. "All that matters is that the shit works." He then rolled a twenty-dollar bill and snorted a good six-inch line into each nostril. When his head sprung up, his golden eyes looked as if they were suddenly made of glass. The smile that came over his face was both sexy and contagious.

"Hey, girl." Josie slapped me on the back and cheesed in my face. "Glad to see you made it out." Josie was decked the fuck out in a bright red Jersey dress with a halter top that gave every nigga in there a good view of her full D cups. "At least there are two hot-looking bitches up in this piece." She laughed.

"You ain't lyin'," Leroy said, his lustful gaze raking Josie up and down.

I popped him on the back of his head. "No, you ain't, nigga."

"What?" He cheesed. "I was just fuckin' with you. I wanted to see what your ass was going to do." He squeezed my leg playfully and gave me the I-want-to-fuck look.

"Uh-huh." I couldn't hate on my girl because she looked just like Diahann Carroll from that TV show Julia. She had her pick of niggas despite her ass being married to one who had a real j-o-b down at the post office.

"Hey, Leroy. How about giving me a whiff of that shit? I can hook you up later," Josie said.

Leroy laughed in her face. "Bitch, please. This ain't Give Me, Tennessee."

"Humph!" She rolled her eyes and twitched her legs. "Peaches, can you talk to your man? This is supposed to be a party and shit, and his ass is being stingy."

"Go on, girl. I ain't in that shit. That's between y'all."

"All right, then. You want me to break him off some pussy payments?" She raised her pencil-thin brows as if to say that she was serious.

"Get cut if you want to, bitch," I sassed.

"All right. All right." Josie reached in underneath her left breast and pulled out the small roll of bills she had taped under there. "Take the last of my allowance money, muthafucka."

Leroy smiled and handed over a few packets of white powder. "Nice doing business with you."

"Whatever, muthafucka." Josie rolled her eyes. "I'll catch you later, Peaches."

"All right, girl." My gaze skimmed back around the dancing crowd. No doubt that every one of those mutha-fuckas was either drunk or high as hell, but so far there wasn't any shit poppin' off.

Leroy's nose vacuumed up another line.

"That shit that good?"

"Fuck yeah." He smirked. "You wanna try it?"

Maybe it was the Colt 45 or maybe it was just that good-ass weed that was floating around that had my curiosity finally get the best of me. "O-okay," I said, pinching my nose as if to get ready. "I'll try it this one time."

Leroy lit up. "Trust me, baby. Once you get a taste of this shit, you'll be thanking me for the rest of your muthafuckin' life. I guarantee it'll have your ass flying to the moon." He laughed, rocking his hips to Curtis Mayfield's fly-ass tracks and bumping into a few annoyed party guests.

"Nigga, watch where you're going," an O. J. Simpson look-alike muthafucka snapped.

Leroy tossed up his hands. "Peace, love, and soul, my nigga." He chuckled. "Now, baby girl, you want to hit this shit or not?"

"Stop tryna sell me, Leroy. I said I'll try it." I laughed, mushing him in the head. "Now show me what I need to do."

"Sho'nuff, girl. Sho'nuff." He smacked his hands together and ordered people to move out of his way before copping a squat back down next to the coffee table. "Now, we're just going to give you enough to get you started." He sprinkled the white powder onto the glass surface and quickly produced two beautiful white lines of coke.

My heart raced. In the back of my mind, I could hear my nana's stern warning, but that shit was drowned out with the crowd and Leroy's singing.

"I'm your momma. I'm your daddy. I'm that nigga in the alley." He handed over the dirty twenty-dollar bill while bobbing his head. "I'm your pusher man."

I took the bill, leaned down, and then tried snorting

*the first line just like I'd seen him do, but the first whiff
had my nose on fire.*

"Keep going, keep going," Leroy coached.

*Like a fool, I listened to him and completed snorting
up both lines. When I lifted my head, I couldn't help but
wave my hand in front of my nose. But then a second
later . . . shit, things just started melting away. Stress.
Pain. Heartbreak. Just about every fucking thing. All
that was left were these wonderful sensations swirling
inside my brain and in my body.*

*"Got to get mellow now. Gotta be mellow, y'all,"
Leroy crooned, smiling in my face. "You feeling that
shit, baby?"*

I could only manage a goofy grin.

*"Aww, shit. What did I tell you?" He stood and pulled
me to my feet just as* "Little Child Runnin' Wild" *started
grooving from the Tannoy fifteen-inch gold speakers.*

*Chest to chest and pelvis to pelvis, Leroy and I
grooved and grinded against each other like we were the
only two people in the room. "You know what I like after
having some really good nose candy?" Leroy asked me,
spreading his large hands over my thick booty.*

*"I think I might have an idea," I said, knowing that
my panties were already wet as hell.*

*Five minutes later, we were fucking on top of a giant
pile of fake fur and leather in the coat room. No. It was
better than fucking. That coke had awakened sensations
in my pussy that I had never felt before, to the point that
each stroke was like having a mini orgasm.*

*An hour later, we took our private party back to my
bedroom at Nana's house. As luck would have it, Nana
was out her damn self doing her own thing, leaving
twelve-year-old Alice asleep up in her room. I did a couple more lines, and sometime during the night, I heard*

my bedroom door creak open. Fearing that it was Nana returning home, I swiveled my head to investigate.

"Alice, what the fuck are you doing in here?" I barked.

My twelve-year-old sister's eyes bugged—most likely from seeing Leroy's yellow, sweaty ass still drilling its way to China between my legs.

"Get the fuck out of here," I snapped. "Go back to bed." I dropped my head back down and moaned out my pleasure while my liquid candy-coated Leroy's dick.

Alice didn't move.

Through the mesh of my lowered eyelashes, I caught her still standing at the door. "I said get the fuck out of here!"

Leroy chuckled. "Let the girl be. Maybe she's learning a thing or two." He wrapped a muscled arm around me and quickly flipped me onto my back. "You see how much your sister like this good dick I'm throwing at her?" he asked Alice.

"Leroy, stop playing. . . . Oh . . . shit. That's my spot, baby."

"Hell, yeah. Big Daddy knows how you like it." He opened up my ass cheeks and showed all my business to my little sister. "Shit is good, ain't it, baby?"

Again, I caught sight of my sister. "A-Alice . . . oh . . . shit. Damn it. Don't make me tell you again. NOW GO!"

Alice finally slammed the door.

Leroy laughed. "Ah, baby. She's got to get her education somehow. Might as well be at home."

I meant to tell him that shit wasn't funny, but then his hips picked up speed and he pounded my pussy something lovely. I lost count of how many orgasms I had and how many lines of coke I did in just one night. Later, I opened my eyes to find my bed empty. Fuck, I didn't really mind, given how delicious my body felt. The only reason I got up was because I had to piss like a muthafucka.

I stumbled out of bed naked and crept out of my room to the bathroom down the hall. It wasn't until I was on the toilet with my face cradled in my hands that a sound caught my ear and caused the hairs on the back of my neck to stand at attention. I stopped my piss in mid-stream and strained my ears, trying to hear it again.

I did.

"Alice," I whispered, popping up off the toilet and racing as best I could to my little sister's room. When I burst through the door, it was my turn for my eyes to bug out and my stomach to twist into painful knots.

Alice turned her tear-soaked face toward me, but she couldn't say anything because Leroy's big gorilla hand was clamped over her mouth.

"Peaches, you come in here to join us?" Leroy asked, still stroking between my sister's legs.

"Muthafucka, get the fuck off my sister!" I made a running leap toward the bed, landed on his back, and pounded away at his head. "You sick muthafucka. She's just a kid!"

"Wh-what the fuck! Get off me." With one powerful swing back, Leroy sent me careening toward the wall. I hit headfirst and then barely registered the rest of my body smashing a close second and then dropping down on top of the wooden nightstand below. Amazingly, I didn't stay down for long. I bounced up, grabbed an American eagle brass lamp that had fallen to the floor, and swung at Leroy's head as if I were Reggie Jackson.

When the brass connected with his skull, there was a loud, sickening crack! Leroy was lifted off a whimpering Alice, who jumped off the bed with bloodstained thighs.

"I'm going to fuckin' kill you!" I leaped back onto the bed, my fists flying.

Leroy was feeling no pain. The muthafucka turned on me so hard and vicious that I could hardly comprehend what was happening other than he'd grabbed me by the throat and was whaling on me like I owed his ass money.

"Have you lost your muthafuckin' mind, bitch?" His fist crashed against my jaw like I was a grown-ass man. "Do I look like some punk muthafucka to you? Huh?" He switched up and hit me with a right hook.

I reached up and dragged my nails down Leroy's mug shot. I could feel his skin and blood scraping off.

He howled out in pain but retaliated with a one-two punch.

I tried to scream, but my mouth was quickly filling up with blood. Time and space became a blur. I even forgot that I was supposed to be trying to fight back. My mind was just spiraling into a black abyss.

"You just wanted all this good dick to yourself, didn't you, baby?" Leroy changed up, squeezing my titties like he hadn't just beaten the shit out of me. "You ain't got to worry about a damn thing. There's plenty of this good dick to go around." He snatched my legs open and rubbed the head of his bloody dick over my clit.

Pop! Pop!

"What the fuck?" Leroy roared.

Pop! Pop!

I felt Leroy jerk.

Pop! Pop!

My eyes flew open when it felt like my left leg had been slammed by two hot pokers.

Leroy slumped over on the bed. His big golden eyes were still glossy but lifeless. I struggled to pull myself up.

At the doorway, Alice stood with tears streaming down her face, blood pooling on the floor between her legs, and Nana Maybelle's gun smoking in her hand.

I blink out of the old memory, sigh, and glance down at my prosthetic leg on the floor—complete with the electric tag that the po-po strapped on yesterday. If I had a nickel for every dumb muthafucka I've come across, I would be one rich bitch, that's for damn sure. I strap on my leg and climb out of bed.

Arzell stretches out a muscled arm, pats the empty space beside him, and then lifts his head from the pillows. "Where you goin', Ma?"

A big smile blooms across my face. "I'm fixing to knock the funk off this body, and then I'm going to hook my boo up with some good ole homemade flapjacks. Would you like that?"

"Fuck yeah." Arzell rolls over onto his back with a big Joker smile. "That's what I like about you older women. You know how to take care of your man." He stretches his hand down and wraps it around his early morning hard-on. After a couple of pumps, a few drops of precum ooze from the tip.

"Looks like Momma needs to fix you up first," I say, edging back over to the bed.

"You know it." He spreads his legs wide.

I just love these young boys. Their dicks are always just a little harder than they heads. "In that case, come to Momma."

9

Yolanda

A week after KyJuan had been shot down in the heart of Gangster Disciple territory, an unofficial war was declared against the Vice Lords. Hell, it isn't safe for any nigga to be out on the streets: young, old, male, or fucking female. It really doesn't matter because the wildin' out members who aren't waiting for no verification on who sent them niggas blazing down Shotgun Row are just straight blasting everything in sight. Python has the power to reel these niggas in, but he doesn't seem to be all that interested in doing so. He is content to hold the whole city hostage until somebody starts talking—mainly Fat Ace.

For the time being, Fat Ace is MIA. No matter how many ears and foot soldiers Python has patrolling the streets, no one has seen this muthafucka nowhere. How the fuck they can't find a three-hundred-plus-pound muthafucka is beyond everyone's comprehension.

True to his word, the minute the *Commercial Appeal* printed the names of the shooters in the paper, Python sent a team of GD assassins to roll up on those niggas' families and wipe out what was left of their family trees. The rash of gang violence dominated the nightly news, and Memphis PD washed the streets with blue lights each and every night.

I keep my head down and my mind on my fucking job. For the time being, that's still muling shit into Memphis's fine prison system. At this point, the job is a breeze. The top dogs know just who can be bought with pussy and who needs to be cut in on the profits. The money flowing out of the joint is the best money to be made, since our people on the inside make three times what the shit is worth on the street.

My cut is decent, but even decent money isn't cutting it no more when I keep dating niggas who are in my pockets more than I am. Every time I turn around, it's "Can I borrow twenty dollars for this?" or "Can you run to the store and get me that?" That's the problem with just dealing with lowly foot soldiers; ten times out of ten they spend their money faster than they make it.

I know that I need to get my act together so I can get my kids back. Family Children Services took all three of them because my mother kept reporting that I wasn't taking good care of them, which is bullshit. I fed my damn kids. They just looked poor because that's how they damn looked. Probably took after they damn daddies, even though I'm not sure who they all are.

The Queen Gs are like a substitute family within the family, and just like most families, it tends to be dysfunctional as a muthafucka. Sometimes there's just as much fighting going on inside the set as there is fighting such bitches as the Flowers or the Crippettes. Brothers of the struggle tend to cast their nets in their own pool or bring in new bitches who don't know shit about gang life. Either way, there's a lot of man stealing or sharing, and I'm just as guilty as anyone.

If I'm going to change my situation, I need a higher-ranking nigga within the Gangster Disciples. Someone who slings big money. Since my dreams and hopes were derailed when KyJuan died, I need to cast my net again.

"I'm thinking about gettin' a job down at the Pink Monkey," I blurt out to Baby Thug as we cop a few cases of beer at the J & W Liquor Store.

Baby, pretty much my only true friend in the set, busts out laughing at my ass before turning away and strutting up to the counter.

"What's so goddamn funny?"

"You," she says, setting her shit down. "You may have the body, but you sure as hell don't have the rhythm."

I move up behind her and set two more cases down. "What the fuck you know? I can dance."

Baby jams her hand into her pocket and pulls out a fat roll of money. "Girl, I ain't talking about just rocking your hips in time to the music. Your ass got to be able to work it down at the Pink Monkey. Those girls don't be playing when they hustlin' for that paper—bending and twisting their bodies like pretzels." She shakes her head. "You are going to have to really up your game."

The old black man behind the counter squints his brown and jaundiced eyes at us.

"So?" I say. "I can do that shit, too."

"Bitch, please. Half the time you be tripping over air." Baby glances up at the old dude behind the register. "What the fuck? Your arthritis acting up, nigga? How much?"

The man lifts a trembling, withered finger and shakes

it at Baby. "Ain't you the girl who came in here and robbed me last week?"

Here we go. I roll my eyes.

"Ain't nobody robbed you, old man," Baby snaps, her face twisting like she's offended. "Now how much the fuck do I owe you?"

"Yeah. You were the one," he says, bobbing his head.

Quick as lightning, Baby's gat is in her hand, and a red light glows in the center of the man's forehead. "For the last time, old man, I *said* nobody fuckin' robbed your ass."

Grandpa's hands shoot up in the air as his nervous gaze shifts toward me. "Don't look at me. I didn't rob you either."

"All right. All right. My mistake." He licks his lips.

There is a small tinkling sound and then a foul odor drifts toward us.

Baby sniffs. "Muthafucka, did you just piss on yourself?"

"And shit," I add.

The old man swallowed so hard we can see his Adam's apple bobbing up and down.

Baby lowers the gun. "Damn. You're a nasty muthafucka." She tosses a few bills on the counter and then grabs the cases of beer by their cardboard punch-out handles and marches out the door. Once outside, Baby glances over at me. "Damn, Yo. Why in the fuck didn't you remind me we robbed this muthafucka last week?"

"Shit, girl. I can't keep up with that fuckin' shit."

We quickly hop into Baby's tricked-out royal blue '68 Impala and burn rubber back toward Shotgun Row. Nobody dares tell Baby that she looks like a thirteen-year-old teenager behind the wheel, including my ass. I know my girl is sensitive about her size and wouldn't hesitate putting a cap in someone's ass if they mentioned it.

"Are you still going to braid my hair?" Baby asks when we pull up to the curb of my momma's house.

"Shit, I guess so. I can go fill out an application down at the Pink Monkey afterward."

Baby shuts off her engine and climbs out from behind the wheel. In the distance, a series of gunshots catches our attention, but no one on the street trips. It's probably just business as usual. "You're really gone take your no-rhythm ass down there?"

"Fuck you, Baby."

"You going to keep saying that shit to me and I'm going to take you up on it."

I may be a little slow from time to time, but I'm more than aware that Baby is interested in more than just friendship with me. It's just too bad I don't feel the same way about her, because Baby is really cool peoples. I know for a fact that she treats the girls she dates like fucking queens, spending time and her hard-earned paper on them. But it never really lasts long, because Baby says women are just as scandalous as the niggas I deal with—maybe more so. I think it's debatable.

"Hey, y'all. Whatcha up to?"

Baby and I turn around to see Pit Bull, a large Queen G who is as husky as the two pit bulls she's always walking up and down Shotgun Row.

"Nothing. Just hanging for a little while," I answer.

Baby elbows me and hisses, "Why the fuck you always talking to that bitch?"

"What? I'm just being nice," I whisper back.

Pit Bull jams a hand on her hip and rolls her eyes. Her dogs, Barksdale and Hoover, growl at us. "You two muthafuckas know I can hear y'all, right?"

"And?" Baby snaps.

"Whatever. You two homo bitches deserve each other." Pit Bull tugs on her dogs' leashes and continues her flat-footed stroll down toward her own crib.

"You just mad that nobody wants your funky ass," Baby yells.

Pit Bull flips us the bird.

Baby turns toward me. "Why the fuck you always talking to that heifer? You know I can't stand that bitch. She don't do nothing but talk shit behind everybody's back."

I know that, but I still struggle with that childhood need to win people over no matter how many times my ass gets burned. "C'mon, girl. Get in here so I can do your head." I turn and swish my ass up my momma's porch steps.

The moment we enter the front door, our eyes land on Betty sitting in her La-Z-Boy and eyeballing *Wheel of Fortune*. As usual, the house smells like a combo of Vicks VapoRub and Bengay.

"Hey, Ms. Turner," Baby greets with a lazy wave.

Betty exhales a long breath and just ignores her.

We keep it moving and unload the beer in the refrigerator before we take out two cold ones that were already chilling in there.

"We going to be in my room, Ma," I say, not expecting or receiving an answer.

"I hate to talk about your momma and everything, but that shit ain't normal." Baby pops open her beer.

"Normal?" I laugh, grabbing my Blue Magic hair grease and fat-toothed comb. "What the fuck is normal on Shotgun Row? This dirty, cracked-out muthafucka ain't exactly what they put on postcards, now, is it?"

"Yeah. You right. You right," Baby concedes. "But that woman ain't said shit to me in the seven years I've known her. Nothing. Nada. I think if I waltzed in here on fire, she couldn't be bothered to piss on me to put the shit out."

"Don't worry. You ain't the only one."

Baby shakes her head, chugs down half her can of beer in one gulp, and then burps so loud that the neighbors probably heard her.

"Gross."

"You know that shit turns you on." Baby winks.

"Stop playing and get your ass over here," I say, sitting down on the edge of the bed and spreading my legs.

Baby rushes over and drops down on the floor in front of me. "Can you hook it up in that crisscrossed style Allen Iverson had in that picture I showed you last week? Remember that?"

"Yeah, girl. Hold your head still." I start in on one end of Baby's cornrows. I actually like braiding people's hair. It is a surprising talent that came naturally to me. All I have to do is see a style one time and I can duplicate it, no problem. A lot of the girls in the set who don't really care for me often cheese in my face, get me to do all kinds of complicated styles, and then pay me little or nothing for it. Everybody except Baby. She always breaks me off what some of those girls who work in the salons be charging—and most times a little more.

"Now this is what the fuck you need to be doing to pull you some extra money," Baby says. "You know you got mad skills."

"Sheeiit!"

"What?" Baby asks, trying to glance over her shoulder.

I jerk her head back around. "Keep your damn head still."

Baby snickers. "Whatever. You know I'm right. You don't need to be sliding your ass up and down no damn pole like the rest of those trifling hoes, tryna catch a dollar. You need to see if Ms. Anna will rent you a chair at her salon."

"Please. I hear those bitches at the Pink Monkey be dragging in six to eight hundred a night."

Baby's head jerks back again. "In Memphis? At the Pink Monkey? And you believe that shit?"

I frown.

"See, that's the problem with you, Yo-Yo. You're too trusting. You believe every muthafuckin' thing these trifling bitches be spitting. Six to eight hundred a night. Shit, this ain't Vegas. Those same hoes be running up and down the Row tryna sell they food stamps for damn near thirty cents on the dollar."

I suppose Baby has a point.

"Niggas around here always tryna act like people in those stupid-ass hip-hop videos when in reality they got they rims on some rent-to-own bullshit, and they gold chains are steady turning they necks green while slinging on the street corners."

"Don't hold back—tell me how you really feel." I turn Baby's head again.

"I'm just keepin' this shit real. You know how I do," Baby says, rocking her neck. "I hate this shit. I hate I ever joined up in this muthafuckin' gangbang bullshit."

"Girl, don't let none of these niggas hear you mouthing off like that."

Baby clucks her tongue. "Fuck them niggas. They can suck my dick."

I mush her in the back of her head. "If you hate the shit so much, why did you get in? Or better yet, why don't you get out?" I ask, since I can't imagine anyone forcing Baby to do a damn thing she doesn't want to, her size be damned.

"Shit. Everybody is cliqued the fuck up in this city.

Disciples, muthafuckin' Vice Lords, Crips, Bloods, and let's not forget those grimy LMGs still floating around this sonabitch. A nigga always need somebody to have they back while they tryna make this paper. NahwhatImean?" Baby shakes her head. "Shit here in Memphis ain't organized like it is up north or out west. Niggas be banging just 'cause they ain't got shit else to do."

I shake my head. "You looking at all this shit wrong. The Gangster Disciples is family. It ain't perfect, but it's better than the shit I grew up with in this muthafuckin' house. I just need to lock down a chief, an enforcer, a governor—some damn nigga with some damn money, power, and respect so I can move the hell up out of here and I can get my damn kids back. And I'm going to make that shit happen. One way or another. Watch."

10

Melanie

"**W**e have an eleven-ninety-nine off the three thousand block of Sharpe Avenue. Car thirty-four, are you still in the area?"

I reach toward the center of the patrol car console and snatch up the hand radio. "Car thirty-four, roger. We're on our way." I quickly stand up between the open car door and yell to O'Malley. "We gotta roll!"

O'Malley's head snaps away from the suspected drunk driver, who's having a devil of a time getting through the first six letters of the alphabet.

"We have an eleven-ninety-nine," I answer the unspoken question, and then jump in behind the wheel.

"You're one lucky motherfucker," O'Malley tells the red-faced driver as he shoves his driver's license back at him. "Go home and get your drunk ass off the street!" He jogs back to the car.

"Yes, sir, officer, sir." The good ole boy's glassy blue eyes light up as he gives a two-finger salute and stumbles back to his black F-450 pickup truck. "Y'all have a good night."

O'Malley barely gets his ass into the passenger seat when I slam on the accelerator and rip a sharp right to head out to the Orange Mound district to answer the call of an officer in need of assistance. Given the general address, there's no doubt that we're racing toward danger. Orange Mound is well-known Vice Lord territory.

I handle my cruiser like an Indy 500 driver and make the ten-minute drive in under three. The second we're out of the car, a series of shots are either fired at us or around us. It's hard to tell. Weapons out, I hear O'Malley speak into his shoulder radio and report shots fired with possible gang activity.

I'm more puzzled as to why the fucking street is so goddamn dark—that is, until I hear glass crunch beneath the soles of my shoes. I glance down and then up at the light pole. "Fuck!"

Instantly alarmed, O'Malley barks, "What is it?"

"These muthafuckas shot out the damn streetlights," I hiss.

RAT-A-TAT-TAT-TAT!

I duck down and sweep my gun out in front of me.

RAT-A-TAT-TAT-TAT!

The blue track light on top of our patrol car shatters, and Sharpe Avenue is once again bathed in darkness.

"What the fuck? Guess they don't want our asses seeing shit," O'Malley states the obvious.

"Shhh!" I strain my ears to try and pick up any little sound. I'm not about to get my ass shot up because he wants to crack jokes. Tugging in slow, steady, deep breaths, I master keeping my heartbeat under control, but the adrenaline rushing through my body is the best kind of high I've ever known. I'm scared but my body feeds off danger. To my right, I hear the shuffling of feet. "POLICE. STOP OR I'LL SHOOT!"

RAT-A-TAT-TAT-TAT!

I have never moved so fast in my life, but I can hear the bullets as they slam into the concrete where I was standing just seconds ago. Together, my partner and I return fire in the direction of our shooter.

"Aww, shit," someone shouts before a thud meets my ears.

O'Malley and I rush to approach the sound; our guns sweep in circles. We reach the perpetrator moaning and groaning on the sidewalk but remain mindful that there could be others.

"Shit, man. Y'all muthafuckas shot me," the dude moans.

"That's what the fuck you get when you shoot at cops, you dumb motherfucker." O'Malley delivers a vicious kick to the man's side and then moves his foot around his moaning body. "Where the fuck is it?"

"Where's what, muthafucka?" the perpetrator challenges through gritted teeth. "I ain't got shit. You need to be getting my ass to the doctor."

"Humph! Yeah, we'll get right on it, asshole." O'Malley kicks him again. "As far as I'm concerned, your life can bleed out right here on this dirty-ass sidewalk. That's what most you niggers do out here, anyway, ain't it?"

I grind my molars and cut a sharp gaze toward O'Malley's dark silhouette while he whales on the guy. His slick mouth is exactly the reason I want to put a cap in his ass my damn self. It's like he doesn't see or care that my ass is black too. "O'Malley, ease the fuck up, man."

"Yeah, *O'Malley*," the perpetrator groans. "Fuckin' ease up, man."

"Shut up. Now where the fuck is the gun?!"

"I don't have a goddamn gun, you stupid, racist fuck. I wasn't the one shooting at your ass. I was tryna get out the goddamn way of you two nonaiming muthafuckas. Shit. Where in the hell do they teach you pigs how to shoot?"

At the very real possibility of him not being the shooter, my hackles jump back up and my grip tightens on my Glock. My partner grows quiet as well but removes his handcuffs from his hip. With one hand, he keeps his weapon and locks down the suspect with the other. Something shatters behind me, and I spin around shooting. I just barely make out a dark figure racing toward an old church.

"POLICE! STOP OR I'LL SHOOT!"

Our second perpetrator runs at top speed, and I take off after him.

"Johnson!" O'Malley shouts after me.

I don't answer as I go full throttle, making good use of those many years of being a track star in high school and police academy. I close in and am just inches from reaching out and bringing him down, when suddenly both of us hit something that knocks our legs out from under us. Hitting the ground hard, I still manage to keep hold of my weapon, but the runner is able to scramble and bounce back up faster than me and is a ghost before I know it.

"Shit." I look back down to see what I'd stumbled over, and I'm just mildly surprised to find that it's a dead body.

To my great relief, more sirens fill the air, and seconds later a small army of lights wash the street in blue. Thirty minutes later, two ambulances arrive—one for our weaponless and wounded suspect and one for a fallen officer, Detective George Holmes, the cop we'd raced there to try and assist.

Detective Holmes's body is pumped full of holes. I question what the fuck a plainclothes cop is doing in this section of town by himself. Judging by the expressions on some of my colleagues' faces that very question is dancing inside their heads as well. I look around, trying to come up with a plausible scenario, but everything that races across my mind is shady as hell.

Detective Holmes had been hailed as the next super-cop in the *Commercial Appeal,* someone the city hadn't seen the likes of since my father's heyday. But clearly his ass wasn't bulletproof.

"Everybody just wants to fuck the police in this motherfucker, right?" O'Malley roars, pained by losing one of our own. "Just fuck the police!" He starts marching toward the gurney on which our wounded suspect lies, waiting to be lifted into the back of the remaining ambulance.

I quickly jump into action and try to pull him back. "O'Malley, don't do it. Walk the shit off," I urge. This is the part I hate, always trying to rein in a partner who acts an ass before he thinks shit through. His specialty is blurring the lines of questioning a suspect and beating the holy shit out of them.

"Nah. Fuck that," O'Malley roars. "I'm sick of these ignorant niggers terrorizing these damn streets. This damn city is like a fuckin' war zone with these damn ghetto hamsters running around, thinking life is a damn video game." He wrenches out of my grasp and keeps marching toward the gurney, which is surrounded by paramedics.

"All right, who is your friend out there?" he barks at our suspect.

I reach my partner's side, hoping some more shit isn't

about to pop off, especially now that curious residents are starting to mill outside their houses, people who can be possible witnesses to what will undoubtedly be described as police brutality before the eleven o'clock news.

"Hey, hey. Get away from me, man. I already told you that I wasn't the one shooting at y'all."

"If it wasn't you, then it was one of your fuckin' *homeys,* right? Your partnas, your family?"

"Man, you don't know what the fuck you're talking about."

"Oh? Is that right?" O'Malley challenges.

"Yeah. That's right, asshole."

My hackles start to rise again. O'Malley is definitely about to do something stupid.

"So you're just a fine upstanding citizen out for a stroll in one of the most dangerous Vice Lord territories? You think I'm stupid enough to believe that, you dumb fuck?"

The tall brother shifts his incredibly big, brown eyes toward me. "Is he for real?"

As expected, O'Malley's temper snaps and he delivers a hard right hook to the boy's wounded shoulder.

"Aaaargh!"

The paramedics jump in shock, the group of nosy and curious residents gasp and point, and the boys in blue quickly form a protective ring around the back of the ambulance.

"What the fuck?!" our suspect yells. "Y'all just going to stand by and let this muthafucka treat me like Rodney King and shit?" He cradles his bleeding shoulder.

"That's right, because you and your Vice Lord pussies just killed a *cop!*"

"Man, I done told you that I ain't have shit to do with all that."

O'Malley socks him another blow.

"Aaaargh! Shit! Shit! Shit!"

"Did you see that shit?" a curbside witness asks loudly.

People start shaking their heads, and the paramedics start looking jumpy.

"S-sir, I need to ask you to back away from the patient." A paramedic attempts to push O'Malley back.

"Get the fuck away from me." He smacks the man's hand away. "I'm interrogating a suspect, and you're interrupting official police business," he yells. "Gangsta Homey is a fuckin' cop killer."

"I told you I ain't killed no cop!" the suspect yells, his eyes blazing.

"O'Malley, you're causing a scene," I hiss. "We can do this another time," I insist.

"If it wasn't you, then it was one of your friends, and you both can go down as far as I'm concerned."

Despite the pain, the boy manages to laugh in O'Malley's face. "Whatever, man. You ain't got shit on me and you fuckin' know it. And don't be false flagging me as some gangbanger 'cause I don't rep no set, and you ain't going to find nobody that's going to say I do."

I shake my head. The shit didn't sound right. "You're not Vice but you feel comfortable strolling through VL territory unstrapped?"

"That's right. Ain't nobody going to fuck with me down here—other than you two shooting-challenged muthafuckas."

O'Malley cocks his fist back again. Our suspect flinches and the paramedics and I all move to shove O'Malley away from the boy.

"All right. All right. I'm cool," O'Malley says, opening his fist as a sign of surrender.

Everyone eases back.

I look back at our suspect, who surprises me by flashing two large dimples. "You're not Vice Lord but clearly you enjoy the luxury of their security. So who are you?"

The kid's lips spread wider as his gaze shoots back over to O'Malley. "Just another nigga, I suppose."

"Give me a name," I say, annoyed. "Your government name."

"Raymond Lewis," he says. "But my friends call me Profit."

I almost shit a brick.

11
Ta'Shara

"**W**ake your ass up, bitch! Profit's been shot!" Essence shouts into the cell phone. "Girl, all these people blazing up my phone saying that the po-po capped his ass over in Orange Mound."

"Wh-what?" My eyes spring open as my heart leaps into the center of my throat. "Say that shit again." I rip the sheets off my body and tumble out of bed.

Click. Click.

"Hold on, girl. That's my other line."

"Wait! No! Essence?" There's no use; she has already clicked over to the other line. "Shit." I turn on my night-light and then rush over to my chest of drawers with my cell phone still pressed against my ear. With one hand, I start pulling shit out and not really giving a fuck if it matches or not. "C'mon, E. Hurry the fuck up," I hiss, impatient for my girl to come back on the line.

"T, you there?"

"Yeah, girl." I stop with just one leg jammed into a fresh pair of jeans. "What the fuck is going on? Is Profit okay?"

Essence clucks her tongue. "Giiiirrrl, they saying that some serious shit was going down over off Sharpe. There's a dead cop and everything."

My legs nearly drop me on the spot. "But is *he* all right?"

"Everybody saying he's still breathing, if that's what you mean."

Relieved, I close my eyes and whisper a prayer of thanks before I return my mind to some of the other shit my girl is saying. "They ain't saying Profit killed a cop, are they? I know he wouldn't do no shit like that."

"Fuck, girl. Everybody saying different shit. One chick said that he went fuckin' Tony Montana on their asses, and I had someone else tell me that he just got caught being at the wrong place at the wrong time."

I'm stressed again. "Where is he now?"

"The hospital, I guess. They said the ambulance came and got him."

"Which one?"

"Shit. I don't know."

"Find out and then call me back. I'm going to finish getting dressed."

Essence laughs. "And just how in the fuck are you going to get there? We ain't got a car, and the buses have already stopped running for the night."

I stop for a moment. "Don't worry about it. I'll take care of it. You just find out where he's been taken and call me back."

"All right, girl." Essence clucks her tongue. "I'll call you back in a few."

I disconnect the call and rush to finish getting dressed. Seconds later, I shut off the lights again and then creep out of my bedroom. The hallway seems endless as I try to make my way down as quiet as possible. There's no time to feel guilty about what I'm doing. My man needs me.

Once I reach the stairs, each board in the floor is squeaking loud enough to wake the dead. I hold my breath until I reach the bottom of the stairs. When it seems like the coast is still clear, I race over to the black bombé chest in the foyer and retrieve Reggie's car keys. Less than a minute later, I'm rolling in his new Lincoln MKS out the driveway with the headlights off. It isn't until I get down the road to the first stop sign that I feel safe enough to turn the muthafuckas on.

Impatient for word from Essence, I dig my cell phone out of my jeans pocket and hit her back.

"Yo, girl. I was just about to call you back," Essence says after one ring.

"What did you find out?"

"The Med off Jefferson."

"Shit." I glance up to see what street I'm on. "Do you know how to get there?"

"Yeah."

"I'm on my way to pick you up," I say.

"Pick me . . . in what, bitch?"

"I'm driving Reggie's car."

"What?" Essence erupts in stunned laughter. "You jacked your foster parents' ride? Have you lost your damn mind?"

"Nah. Nah. It's cool. I just need to make sure that I'm back before Tracee wakes up at five." A white car appears out of nowhere. I drop the phone and slam on my brakes. "Shit. Shit." The back end of the car fishtails, and before I know it, I'm going sideways toward a curbside fire hydrant. My hands clench the steering wheel just before the back end of the car hits.

"No. No. No." I quickly jump out of the car and rush around to inspect the damage. My heart sinks at the sight of the busted taillight, but I'll have to think of a lie at another time. I have to get going. Once back in the car, I rummage around until I find my cell phone on the floorboard. "E? Give me ten minutes and be outside." I end the call and drive the car off the curb and back onto the street. From then on, I keep my eyes wide and my foot a little lighter on the accelerator.

True to my word, I make it to E's grandmother's place, just a block from Shotgun Row, in ten minutes. I sigh in relief when I see Essence standing outside, because the last thing I want to do is stop or get out of the luxury sedan on this side of town and at this time of night.

Essence jumps into the car, laughing. "Damn, girl. What the hell happened to the taillight?"

"You don't wanna fuckin' know."

"Shit. Are you sure you can drive this big mutha-fucka? I ain't survived this damn neighborhood just so your no-licensed ass can kill me in a fuckin' car wreck."

"Don't you start that backseat driving. Just tell me how to get to the damn hospital."

"Whatever. Just go up to the light and hang a right."

I take off down the street with my heart still racing and my palms sweating. "Did you hear any more news? What else are people saying?"

"Ah, girl. A bunch of bullshit now," Essence says, opening the glove compartment and checking shit out. "Niggas are now making shit sound like Profit went at the po-po with artillery of shit. Took out one cop and went at it with this one big, racist muthafucka who was still pounding on his ass even when the paramedics were tryna resuscitate him and load him in the ambulance."

"What?" I rake a hand through my hair. "They saying he almost died?"

Essence clams up as if she's suddenly afraid to tell me more.

"Well? Spit it out!" I pull my gaze from the road to look at my girl. The suspense is killing me. God help me. I don't know what I'm going to do if anything happens to Profit. He means everything to me.

Essence stops nosing around in the glove compartment and turns in her seat to face me. "Look, I hate that I gotta be the one telling you all this, but the bottom line is I just don't know what really happened and neither does any of them gossiping niggas. So just take a deep breath and calm down." To get me started, she starts sucking in air and rolling her hands to encourage me to do the same thing.

I roll my eyes only to get punched in the shoulder. "Oww."

"Take a deep breath," Essence insists.

Scared of getting punched again, I do as I'm told. Then from the corner of my eye, I see a patrol car. "Turn around and put on your seat belt."

Having her own inner cop scanner, Essence is already ahead of me and is locking the belt across her waist. "Be cool. Be cool. Be cool," Essence recites under her breath as the car rolls to a stop right next to a Memphis patrol car at a light.

I lick my lips while my sweaty hands clench the steering wheel. I just hope the cops don't look our way, because I don't fit the description of someone who could possibly own this luxury sedan, and my learner's permit requires that I drive with an adult. While the light is taking forever to change, I chance a look to my right. My heart stops short when my eyes crash with a female officer's.

I'm going to jail. I'm going to jail. I'm going to jail.

I swallow the lump in my throat and resolve that if the blue track lights come on, I'm jamming my foot down on the accelerator and making a run for it. I'm not going anywhere until I see for myself that Profit is okay.

The traffic light turns green. The police car moves forward and hangs a left.

"Whooo, giiirl," Essence sighs. "That shit was close. I just knew our asses were about to be like those white bitches Thelma and something."

"Thelma and Louise," I say, finally easing off the brake.

"Yeah, them," Essence cosigns. "I even got my gat ready."

I glance over in shock. "What the fuck? You got a gun? Since when did you start toting that shit?"

"Since the last time Qiana and those Flower bitches tried to roll up on me in the girl's bathroom at school. Bitch got me confused if she thinks she's going to catch my ass slippin'."

Shaking my head, I clamp my mouth shut.

"What? You wanna lecture me now?"

"Just tell me which way to the hospital."

"Take a right up here on Adams." Essence glances back over at me. "I don't think it's right for you to judge me. Not everybody got it as good as you do. These muthafuckin' streets out here ain't no joke. A bitch gotta do what she fuckin' gotta do."

"I ain't said nothing."

"But you want to. I can tell."

I spot the hospital up ahead and breathe a sigh of relief.

Essence shakes her head, but she squashes the argument since I'm not going to indulge her. We quickly park the car and race toward the emergency room entrance. The muthafucka is packed. Old, young, crying babies—everybody. What's worse, it looks like they've been here for a long time.

"Aww, shit. I hope our asses ain't going to be here all night," Essence complains, looking around.

"Shut up and come on." I weave my way up to the reception desk. "I'm looking for Raymond Lewis. I believe he was brought here. I'm his girlfriend."

The woman behind the counter definitely has molasses up her ass and is clearly in no rush to get off the phone or address my concerns.

Essence hip bumps me out the way and starts banging her hand on the counter. "HELLO!" *Bam! Bam! Bam!* "Get the fuck off the phone and help my girl out. Damn."

The receptionist levels a dirty look at Essence. "Keisha, let me call you back. I got a couple of hood rats in my face."

"WHAT?" Essence is heated and reaches toward her pocket.

I panic and grab my girl's wrist and give her a look to be cool. "Please forgive my friend. I'm just looking for Raymond Lewis. I was told that he was shot tonight."

"Aren't they all?" The woman turns toward her computer and finally searches for the information we need.

A few minutes later, we're racing toward Profit's room in the intensive care unit. But seeing a large group of niggas flagging Vice Lord colors outside his door, Essence slows down. "T, I don't know about this," she hisses.

I'm not listening. My brain refuses to process that we're actually running toward danger.

"T!" Essence tries again, but at seeing me continuing on, she follows through to have my back. "I swear to God, if we live through this, I'm going to fuckin' kill you myself," she whispers when she catches back up with me.

"Just chill out."

There are at least twenty people outside the door, and every one of them is now looking at us.

"Who the fuck are you two?" one burned-toast-looking muthafucka asks, twisting his face and mean mugging us.

"I-I'm Ta'Shara. I came to see Profit."

The young Vice Lord rakes his gaze over us. "Profit isn't exactly up for visitors at this time."

"Okay. Sorry to bother y'all." Essence grabs my arm and attempts to pull me away.

I snatch my arm back and refuse to budge. "He'll want to see me. I'm his girlfriend."

The small group starts chuckling.

"I ain't heard nothing about Profit having no girlfriend. If you ask me, you two look like a couple of chickens he's probably just fuckin' around with."

"How would you know? You look like the last time you seen pussy was when you were coming out of one," I snap back.

"Oh shit," E moans.

"Now get out of my way so I can see my man." I hold my ground and stare the asshole down.

"Aww. That young nigga got himself a feisty bitch," another nigga with thick dreads and a mouthful of gold laughs and cheeses.

"Who the fuck you calling a bitch?" Essence and I snap in unison.

"All right. All right. Simmer down." A woman I hadn't noticed until now steps forward. She's dressed like the other niggas, but she doesn't look like a dyke or nothing. She is actually very pretty, yet still looks like a bitch you don't want to fuck with.

"You say you're Profit's woman. Fine. We mean no

disrespect. Go on in," she says, stepping out of the way to let us through.

Essence looks like she can't believe what we'd just done.

I'm already over it. I'm focused on only one thing, or rather one person. The moment I push through the door, Profit's head snaps up from his cell phone and a look of surprise lights up his face. "Shara. I was just about to call you."

Relieved, I fly into the room as my tears flow. I even ignore the man sitting in a chair on the other side of the bed. "I was soooo worried about you." I try to wrap my arms around him. "Don't ever scare me like that again."

"Easy on the shoulder, baby." He chuckles.

"Oh." I glance down and gently touch his bandages. "Boo, what happened?"

"Just another day in the hood, Ma. You know how it is." Profit smiles tenderly while tears continue to skip down my face. "You really love a nigga, don't you?"

"What kind of question is that? Of course I do." I sit down on the edge of the bed and cup his face in my hands. "I love you more than life itself, baby. Now and forever." I lean in close and pour my heart and soul into a kiss that sends my mind reeling.

When at long last our deep kiss is reduced to small, nibbling pecks, Profit smiles again. "You know sometimes a nigga just needs to hear the words."

Gently, I lean closer and whisper in his ear, "I love you. I love you. I love you."

He laughs. "I love you, too, boo."

From the other side of the bed, a man clears his throat.

I pull back, but then suck in a stunned breath when my gaze crashes into Fat Ace.

12
LeShelle

Python's forked tongue drums against the head of my pink pearl like it's playing the congas. Indescribable pleasure unfurls from the center of my clit and radiates outward until I tremble and shake like I'm experiencing an internal earthquake. Nobody gives head like this nigga. Hands down that fucking tongue is a monster, dipping and sliding in my pussy until I'm fucking spelling his name backward. "N-O-H-T-Y-P."

Python groans and then reaches down and spreads my ass cheeks wide. The man is a fiend when it came to ass, and he knows as long as he hooks me up right on eating my pussy, I'll take him busting my little asshole open like a muthafuckin' soldier.

"Sssss," he hisses, sounding like Beauty and Beast, the two pet black ball Pythons slithering around the bed with us. In fact, just as Python is gliding his thick, sausage-sized finger in through my back door, Beast coils around my right thigh and then stretches across the downy V of my open pussy. Beauty is doing her own thing, gliding in perfect figure eights up and around my full C cups. The scaly feel of the snakes' skin against mine is erotic as hell. Pressure building, my hands clench the red satin sheets while my mind spins like a pinwheel.

Whenever Python puts it on me like this, I feel like nothing and no one can ever come between us. I would lie for this nigga, kill for this nigga, and even die for this nigga. There isn't a day that rolls by that I don't let him know that shit either. All I have to do is keep playing my position, and soon I'll go from wifey to wife.

"Awww . . . .shit!" That wicked tongue slaps my clit just right, and I scream in total abandonment. Python stays put, gulping down my thick, creamy candy until it coats every inch of his throat.

"That's some good shit, Ma," he praises, lifting his ugly head and smiling, his face twisted and scarred. Fucking him is like fucking the devil himself: dangerous, wicked, and powerful.

I rock my hips, anxious for his fat dick to split my ass in half. "That's not all that's good, Daddy," I flirt, moving Beauty from my breasts and sitting up. "Let me get you ready." I reach for his pound of meat and stroke it to life.

"Ssssss," Python hisses, and then flicks his tongue at me. "You hungry, baby?"

"Always." I roll my tongue across his thick lips.

"Then c'mon. Let me feed you." He eases onto his back and folds his hands behind his head as he waits for me to sink my hot mouth over his straining cock. "Ssssss. That's it, baby. Show me how much you love me."

I have no problem doing just that. I slurp, spit, and vacuum his gooey nut up from his balls and then pop my cherry-red lips off the fat head of his cock in time to watch my dessert gush and splatter everywhere.

"Sssss. Damn, baby. Clean that shit up and give me a little taste." He grabs his dick and smacks my face with it.

I bend my head and use my tongue like a baby wipe, licking him clean and polishing him up before easing toward his twisted lips and sharing his salty tang with a deep kiss. He loves that nasty shit, plunging and swishing his tongue inside my mouth for any remaining residue of himself.

"Sssss." He grabs my fat ass. "You know what time it is, baby?"

"Mmmm. You want some of this hot ass, Daddy?" I press a kiss against his scarred cheekbone and then nibble on his ear. "I betcha got some more sweet candy in that fat dick for me, don't you?"

"You know it."

He cruelly pinches my nipples and I moan. Hell, this shit is nothing compared to the bullshit I grew up with. Plus, there's a small part of me that's beginning to like the pain, if not love it. My growing pleasure from pain surprises me. It's becoming like an addictive drug. The adrenaline rush is insane.

"Wait. Wait." He sits up and reaches over to the black lacquered nightstand and pulls out a plastic bag.

My heart skips a beat.

"All right, baby. Climb up on Daddy."

I smile, knowing better than to protest or complain. "You got it, baby."

Straddling his hips in the backward cowgirl position, I open my cheeks wide so he can watch the show and cram every inch of his fat dick into my tight ass. My inner muscle clenches around him like an iron fist.

"Sssss. Twerk that shit, Ma."

"You got it, Daddy." I go straight to work, bouncing,

grinding, and then bouncing some more. Python hisses and curls his toes as a tactic to delay busting his nut too soon. I don't know what it is about ass that sends this nigga straight to the moon, but as long as he wants it, I'm going to toss it up and make sure that he gets plenty of it.

Beauty and Beast slither up and coil around my waist as if they can't stand to be left out of the action. Ten minutes later, I'm still at it, my body slick with sweat and one snake now around my neck and the other one sliding its way toward its daddy. Everybody is hissing in this muthafucka.

Without warning, Python flips me over so I'm on all fours. Pain sparks from my wounded shoulder and causes my arms to collapse, but before I can utter a sound, he jams a plastic bag over my head, cutting off my oxygen. He twists the bag around his fist so tight, my eyes bulge in shock.

Wait. I wasn't ready! Panic settles in before I can get my mind right. I try to suck in air but only manage to draw in a mouthful of plastic. My fingers claw at my neck.

"Sssss, baby. This shit is locking up tight," Python praises as he rams his fat, ten-inch cock into my ass like a jackhammer. "Ssssss."

Hold your breath. Try not to breathe. The small voice in my head grows harder to hear. My world is collapsing while a rainbow of colors splash before my eyes. But . . . my body tingles—deliciously so. Every pore is having mini orgasms. I hear blood rush through my head, and I begin to rise outside my own body.

"Take this dick! Take it!"

I'm losing consciousness. The vibrant colors slowly fade, but there's still a bright light shining in the distance.

Python roars and releases the bag as his hot nut blasts onto my ass and then all over the python tattoo on the center of my back. "Sssss. Goddamn, baby."

The sudden rush of oxygen is a shock to my system. I cough and wheeze as he pulls the bag from my head. Tears sting the back of my eyes, but I fight the mutha-fuckas back with everything I have, which is harder than when he dug the bullet out of my arm. Weak but still tingling, a smile softens the corners of my lips.

"Sssss. You liked that, didn't you, baby?"

"You know it, baby," I croak, and force a smile on my face.

Python smears and swishes his seed around my back with his still-rock-hard erection. When my back is good and glazed, he orders me to clean him up again. By the time it's all over, we're sated and passing a fat cigar-sized blunt between us.

I snuggle close and absently trace the numerous bullet hole scars on his chest. He'd been shot seventeen times since he'd been inducted into the gang life, and none of them came close to killing his ass, but seventeen niggas got dropped for the attempt. "You feel good, Daddy?"

"Fuck. You know you got the sweetest ass in Memphis." He winks and flicks his wicked tongue out at me.

"All for you." I smile and accept the blunt for my toke.

"It better be." He reaches behind me and squeezes his prized possession. "If I *ever* catch another nigga digging in my spot, I'll fuckin' squash that ass, Momma." He pulls the blunt from my lips and takes another hit. "Believe me greasy on that shit."

I love it when he gets all possessive. It's the only way I can tell he really cares. But I also believe I'm not the only bitch in the Queen Gs he's throwing dick to—but at least he isn't stupid enough to throw shade over my game in front of my face, and neither are any of his gangsta hoes. Long as we keep that shit going, everything is everything. The number-one problem between us is trust. Python doesn't trust no fucking body, except for Momma Peaches, and sometimes he be looking at her sideways, too.

"What?" Python asks.

"Hmm?" I glance up from his tattooed and scarred chest.

"What the fuck you thinking so goddamn hard about? I can damn near see smoke coming out of your ears." He chuckles and passes the blunt back. "Tell your man what the fuck is on your mind."

"Mmmm. My man," I croon. "I love the sound of that."

"You better like that shit. You're the Bonnie to my Clyde, ain't you, girl?" He kisses me again.

"You know it, Daddy."

His thick lips stretch into another grotesque smile. "That's why I fuck with you. Your ass is down for any and everything." His fingers drift lightly over my sore neck. "You know how to really get a nigga off. You play your cards right and nigga just might have to wife you."

I light up. "Really?"

"You keep passing these tests, baby girl. Word is bond." He takes the blunt from my hand, stubs it out with his fingers, and puts it aside. "Now get on up here and sit on my face. Daddy still hungry."

My body is still tingling and wet, but I quickly climb up into a sixty-nine and melt like butter when he parts my cheeks and tries to suck the nut he'd just planted there a few minutes ago out my ass. Before I can blast my own cum all over his face, Dr. Dre's classic "The Chronic" blasts from his cell phone. With his "business before pleasure" motto, he reaches over to the night-stand.

"Talk to me," he says, answering his phone with my ass still hovering above his face. Then the energy in the room saps out when his baritone voice drops to a dangerous level. "Say that shit again." He slaps me on the ass, and I scramble off him. "Gather some top-notch niggas. We're rolling through." He jumps out of bed as he disconnects the call.

"Daddy, what's goin' on?" I ask, leaping out of the bed after him.

"We finally found that nigga." He laughs, snatching his clothes off the floor.

"Found who?"

"Who the fuck you think? Fat Ace. Nigga is up at the Med visiting some muthafucka." He grabs his gat. "We're going to handle this shit tonight."

I turn toward my own clothes. "Hold up. I'm coming with you to earth this muthafucka!"

13
Ta'Shara

The stench of evil rolls off of Fat Ace in waves and threatens to choke me. For years I've heard of the man. As with most stories about niggas on the street, I don't know what's true and what's urban legend.

To say that Fat Ace is a big man would be an understatement. To say that he is fat would be a downright lie. Truth of the matter is, Fat Ace, even folded into a metal chair, is a giant. His chest alone is as massive as the side of a mountain, and as far as I can see, his arm muscles even had muscles. His head is the size of a sixteen-pound bowling ball and just as black and shiny on top. His eyes are hidden behind a pair of black shades, his nose is large but not broad, and his lips, framed in a thin goatee, are big and thick.

Fat Ace and Profit look absolutely nothing alike.

"Appears that you've been holding out on me, lil

bro." Fat Ace's voice is low and rough, like his throat has filled with shards of broken glass. "This your girl?"

A corner of Profit's lips kick up as he reaches out and grabs my hand. "That's right. This is my shawty, Ta'Shara. Baby girl, this is my brother, Fat Ace." He winks at me. "I bet you can't guess why they call him that."

When Fat Ace laughs, his chest rumbles and the entire room vibrates.

Essence inches closer to me and Profit. I don't know what to make of this muthafucka either.

"My lil nigga always got jokes." Fat Ace smirks, shifting a toothpick from one side of his mouth to the other.

Even though I can't see his eyes, I can feel them roaming over my body.

"I don't think I've ever seen you around before," Fat Ace says suddenly. "Where do you stay?"

It's a loaded question and everyone in the room knows it.

My fingers clamp around Profit's while Essence practically becomes closer than my damn shadow.

"Nigga, will you squash that bullshit? How you going to sit there and interrogate my woman? You see her ass cares for a nigga." Profit lifts my hand and brushes a kiss against my knuckles.

Fat Ace cocks his head at his younger brother. "How the fuck you gone tell *me* what to do, lil man? In case you forgot, we're in the midst of a muthafuckin' war with those grimy ass Gangster Disciples. Muthafuckas dropping our family like a fuckin' bad habit. They started this shit and we going to finish it."

I sense Essence reaching toward her pocket, but I'm too afraid to say anything or try to warn her. All I can do is pray that my girl don't do anything stupid—like get us killed.

"Trust when I say these muthafuckas got people

everywhere. To be straight up, I don't know these two bitches from Adam."

It's on the tip of my tongue to check his ass for calling me outside my Christian name, a habit most niggas learn early, but this time fear chokes off my vocal cords and I can do little more than just stand here and take the verbal abuse.

"Bro, again, this is my woman. We've been kicking it for a long while now. I ain't going to abide you calling her all kinds of bitches."

In that moment, I witness something that I've either never seen or ignored in my man. No, he isn't as large and domineering as his brother, but there's a quiet strength about him that hints at a darkness that lies just below the surface. I feel it and I have a sneaking suspicion that Fat Ace feels it as well.

"I know you're tryna impress your girl and everything, but I suggest you get that bass up out your voice," Fat Ace says, reclaiming authority.

"I . . . we stay over off Cowden in midtown," I squeak.

"There, are you satisfied?" Profit challenges, annoyed. "My girl ain't into all that gangbanging bullshit. I told you before that you can have that."

Fat Ace continues to smirk. "What you call gangbanging, I call street politics." He stands up from his chair and towers over all of us. "And you're looking at the muthafuckin' president of these here United Streets." He reaches up and finally removes his sunglasses.

My heart drops to the soles of my feet when I look into one brown eye and one milky white eye. The sight of it curls my stomach. I want to look away—I try to look away, but I just . . . can't. I'm riveted by what I'm seeing.

"Look, I didn't risk coming up here to watch you face fuck your girlfriend or argue with you over bullshit. I just wanted to see for myself how you were holding it down." He slaps hands with his brother, and they add a small fist bump for unity. "I heard how you handled your shit like a true soldier with that racist pig O'Malley."

"You know that white nigga?"

"Sheeeiiit. Everybody knows that slick muthafucka. Always rolling through the sets like he owns the whole fuckin' city. If you ask me, the wigga just wish he was out here making this real paper. The muthafucka always jack niggas shit without an arrest. NahwhatImean?"

Profit bobs his head. "I can see that shit. Muthafucka has a real chip on his shoulder. His ass is pissed that he had nothing to charge me with. Maybe it was a good thing I wasn't strapped."

"Nah. You could have easily blasted your way through those fools."

I'm dying to ask again what happened, but I figure I'll get a clearer answer once Fat Ace leaves.

"But I tell you what, your boy is a crazy muthafucka out there. He damn near got my ass killed." Clearly Profit left out a name on purpose. "I don't know what the fuck he was doing with that cop, but you might want to check to see if he's on that shit."

Fat Ace bobs his head. "Yo, leave that shit to me, man. I'll handle it. You just chill the fuck out and take care of yourself." Another slap and a dab. "You rolling up out of here tomorrow?"

"Yeah. First thing, man. I don't like all this hospital bullshit."

"A'ight, then. I'll make sure someone picks you up. One, nigga." He slides his shades back over his eyes and tilts his head toward me and Essence, who'd become a mute during this whole time. "Maybe I'll see you around again, shawty."

I just stare at him.

Fat Ace laughs and then strolls toward the door. "Let's roll out," he tells his people before the door swings closed behind him.

I finally expel the air I had trapped in my lungs and then immediately glance back over my shoulder at Essence.

"Don't say shit to me," E snaps through gritted teeth. "I'm so fuckin' mad at your ass right now I can hardly see straight." She jerks her gaze away and folds her arms.

Profit lifts and kisses my hand. "You do realize that we just came out of the closet?" His eyes sparkle. "Sort of speak."

"It didn't seem as if we really had a choice."

Profit laughs. "Damn, Ma. You should feel special. I ain't never introduced a girl to my family before like that. And I damn sure haven't been willing to take no beatdown over them either. 'Cause trust my brother's right hook ain't for the faint of heart." He pinches my cheek. "Ain't that at least worth a smile or something?"

"Profit, what happened?" I ask, needing some answers.

Smiling, he reaches up and brushes his hand against my cheek. "C'mon, baby. I don't want you to be all worried about that shit. Everything is fine now. That's all that matters."

"You're lying up here in the hospital with a bullet hole in your shoulder."

"It's no big thang, baby girl. Really. It's just a little sore."

"What. Happened?" I insist.

He looks as if he is going to hold out, but seeing how visibly upset I am, he caves. "Ah, baby. I'm not all that sure my damn self. I was just out chillin', hangin' with some friends. One of the niggas said that he had to roll and stack some paper and asked if I wanted to come with. Shit. He said it wasn't goin' to take too long, and I've known him for a hot minute. I didn't think shit of it, you know?"

"Okay."

"Well, the nigga has been known to smoke a few too many las from time to time, and before we rolled out, I wondered if the muthafucka was too blazed up, but you know, sometimes it's hard to tell. Anyway, we get over on Sharpe, then suddenly I can't go into this church where he's supposed to be meeting up with someone. He just wanted me to hang outside for a few and then we were going to keep it moving." Profit shook his head. "But a few minutes after he entered that building, all hell broke loose. I was just tryna get out the muthafuckin' way.

"I guess my boy was carrying some serious firepower in that dufflel bag he was carrying, 'cause this nigga was shooting up the joint: cars, streetlights—you name it. Yo, really. It was all a fuckin' blur. I got caught up 'cause my ass wasn't strapped."

"Wait," Essence jumps in. "You were over in Orange Mound strolling without your gat like it was a muthafuckin' park?" She twists up her face. "What? Are you stupid or something?"

"E!" I elbow my girl.

"What? Even a third-grader knows better than that shit."

Profit laughs. "Ease up off of her, Shara. She's right. Around here, if your ass ain't dodging bullets from other niggas, you're dodging them from the po-po. Trust. I've learned my muthafuckin' lesson."

RAT-A-TAT-TAT-TAT!
POP! POP! POP!

"What the fuck?"

I jump. "That can't be . . ."

POP! POP! POP! POP! POP!

RAT-A-TAT-TAT-TAT!

"Niggas are up in the muthafuckin' hospital shooting?" Essence says, looking as stunned as I felt.

"Ace," Profit whispers, and then jumps out of the bed to rush toward the door.

I quickly leap forward and grab his good arm and whip him back around. "You can't go out there. What do you think you're going to do?"

POP! POP! POP! POP! POP!

RAT-A-TAT-TAT-TAT!

"I gotta go help my brother!"

He turns, but I hold firm. "How? By throwing yourself in front of a bullet? You don't have a weapon!"

POP! POP! POP! POP! POP!

RAT-A-TAT-TAT-TAT!

"I gotta do something," he shouts, and wrenches his arm free.

"Wait!" I turn toward Essence. "Give me your gun."

Essence digs into her baggy pocket and pulls out her 9 mm.

Profit's eyes light up as he runs over and takes the gun. "Got an extra clip?"

Essence bends over to her ankle and produces a second clip, then looks at me. "What?"

"Y'all stay right here," Profit says. "I'll be right back." He races toward the door, his naked butt cheeks flashing through the split up the back of his hospital gown.

POP! POP! POP! POP! POP!

RAT-A-TAT-TAT-TAT!

For a full three seconds, I try to stay put, but I can't. "E, I'll be right back!"

"TA'SHARA, NO!"

14

LeShelle

Python and I roll out of Shotgun Row with a dirty dozen Gangster Disciples and with enough artillery to go hard with the muthafuckin' Taliban. Everybody is amped the fuck up, and I'm feeding off the danger and testosterone in Python's ink-black '77 Monte Carlo like a dope fiend. Behind us is the second group in a honey-colored '71 Cutlass with McGriff at the wheel. The murder train is rolling through Memphis, and niggas are going to die tonight.

"Six poppin', five droppin'," Lethal barks.

"FUCK YEAH!"

Everyone wraps their blue scarves around the lower half of their faces and then checks or slaps in their clips, me included. I hope I'm the one to put a bullet in the center of Fat Ace's large skull. A kill like that would clinch the deal on Python giving me his last name. No question about it.

The moment we hit Adams Street, we see the hospital looming large in the distance. It's been only a few minutes, but it feels like it's taking forever. Fantasies of how this shit can go down start to fill my head. I bounce in my seat and feel my nipples get harder than a muthafucka while my clit throbs to the same beat of my racing heart.

"There that muthafucka go right there," Python hisses, grabbing his TEC-9 and jamming hard on the trigger.

RAT-A-TAT-TAT-TAT!

Those bitch-ass Vice Lords duck and scatter like the muthafuckin' gutter rats they are. Half of them race back through the glass doors of the hospital, and the others dive behind parked cars or vans, but they quickly come up with their heat and start firing back.

POP! POP! POP! POP! POP!

RAT-A-TAT-TAT-TAT!

Two cars of GD assassins unload and start blasting at anything and everything that moves. It straight up sounds like we're in the middle of a war zone. We dump so much heat at the thick glass doors that the muthafuckas explode, and glass falls like rain. Inside, people scream and try to get the hell out of the way. A few aren't successful. Collateral damage.

I feel a few bullets whiz by my head, singeing wisps of my hair, but I never once blink or stop shooting. One big, greasy muthafucka pokes his head around the bumper of a Toyota and lifts his gat, but I pick him off, slamming two bullets into his forehead.

With four Vice Lords spilling their blood on the concrete, Python leads his crew in toward the entrance. He isn't going to pass on this fucking opportunity to put Fat Ace's ass in the earth for nothing in the world. None of us are—even with the sound of police sirens suddenly filling the night air. No surprise, those grimy mutha-fuckas hightailed it out of the main lobby. Judging by the droplets of blood on the floor, the muthafuckas sepa-rated.

"Split up," Python barks. He and a few of the crew take off in the direction of the emergency room.

I end up running behind Lethal, G-Blast, and Lil Chuckee toward Radiology. I'm so high off the adrena-line that is pumping through my veins it feels like I'm floating. One good shot, I pray. That is all I need and this shit is a wrap.

POP! POP! POP! POP! POP!
RAT-A-TAT-TAT-TAT!

I jump and turn around. The gunfire starts coming from the opposite direction. "Fuck!" I take off running. G-Blast and Lethal run past me, but my long legs don't keep me far behind them. But suddenly shots start ring-ing out in yet more directions. Are we surrounded?

Before I can react, the side of Lethal's head ex-plodes, and he's literally propelled sideways and smashes up against the wall.

I try to slow up, but I'm running so fast that when Lethal goes sideways, his long legs clip me and cause me to fall face-first. At the last second, I try to break my fall by thrusting my hands out, but the minute they hit the floor, my gun goes flying and pain ricochets up to my wounded shoulder. My arm bends like paper and my face smacks the ground so hard that I'm sure every bone is broken.

Lil Chuckee pivots and once again starts shooting at the muthafucka coming from the elevator bay. "What, muthafucka, you want some of this?"

POP! POP! POP!

G-Blast turns back and also starts unloading bullets.

POP! POP! POP!

Despite the pain, I open my eyes and see a tall muthafucka in a hospital gown blasting at us. With reserved strength and determination, I lift my head and glance around for my 9 mm. It's about a foot away from me. I stretch out my hand even though I know I won't be able to reach it.

Hurry up and crawl, bitch!

POP! POP! POP!

Not wanting to draw too much attention to myself by popping up on my knees, I belly-crawl inch by painful inch until I'm able to grab hold of the gun with just the tips of my fingers.

"Arrrgh! FUCK!" G-Blast curses, his blood squirting and splashing across my outstretched hand a second before he drops dead next to me.

Lil Chuckee hangs in there, keeping our mysterious gunman distracted while I finally manage to get a firm hold on my weapon.

The nigga's bullets pound across Lil Chuckee's chest: His body jerks around before he finally drops to his knees beside me, dead. My blue rag falls from my face as I take aim.

Then my eyes start playing tricks on me when I see Ta'Shara run up behind the mysterious shooter. From across the hospital, our gazes meet, and, shocked, I lower my weapon, but the movement catches the dude's attention and he now takes aim at me.

"NO!" Ta'Shara screams, attacking the dude from the side just as he fires off a shot. The bullet goes wild as they crash to the floor. "LeShelle, don't shoot. Run!"

But I can't. I'm too shocked to process until my sister screams again, "RUN!"

Police sirens blare like surround sound, and I finally push up off the floor, gun in hand, and run to catch up with my set. The emergency room is wrecked, with glass, blood, and bullet holes everywhere. When I run through with my gun up in the air, everyone screams again and tries to duck and dodge out of the way. Right outside, there's more exchange of gunfire and now the sound of tires squealing. I hustle out to get back into the action and just barely make it to Adams Street in time for Python to spot me and allow me to dive in through the open window. For a few heart-pounding seconds, just my upper body makes it inside while my feet kick in the air.

"McGriff took a plug out that muthafucka!" Python shouts as I crawl over other niggas to get all the way into the car.

When I'm in, I glance out the front and see that we're giving chase to a chromed-out black Escalade. "Is he dead?" I ask, wiggling into a spot between Killa Kyle and Tyga.

"If not, he will be soon," Python declares as we close the distance between the Escalade. "FORKS UP!"

Our crew leans out of the car and starts blasting. The back window of the SUV shatters, and the Vice Lords return fire. But our gun chase is a short one, as an army of blue lights appears in Python's rearview mirror.

"FUCK!" Python jerks the wheel and damn near rolls on its side as we turn onto the next street. Ten minutes later, we've ditched the cops and our cars at Goodson's Autoshop.

While everyone is still amped up and giving each other dabs and shoulder bumps, my thoughts are still tangled up with my baby sister. What the fuck was she doing there? What is her association to that muthafucka who took out three Gangster Disciples? And what will it mean for me when Python finds out?

15

Melanie

"**W**e're rolling out," O'Malley says, slamming the phone down on his desk and hopping out of his chair. "The niggers are busy tonight."

"What?" I frown and look up from our detailed account of tonight's shooting. Any time a police officer discharges their weapon, let alone when they actually hit someone, there are piles of paperwork that serve one purpose only: covering their asses.

"Crazy muthafuckas are shooting up the damn hospital," he says, rushing toward the door.

"You're shitting me." I have no choice but to jump up and follow, as do a few more officers when they receive the call.

"Sometimes I think that every major city just took their gang members and flushed them down the toilet, and they all popped out here in Memphis." He holds up his hands. "Keys!"

I unsnap them from my belt hook and toss them to my partner without breaking stride. "Which hospital?"

"The Med," he growls angrily. "The same place we just left about an hour ago." O'Malley shakes his head. "How much you want to bet this shit has something to do with that punk muthafucka we shot tonight?"

I don't answer.

"I knew we should've pressed charges on that arrogant asshole."

"We didn't have anything on him. Everything pointed to him being an innocent bystander."

"Fuck that. He was guilty. They all are."

"What the fuck is that supposed to mean?" I snap. "Not every black person is in a gang."

"Sheeeiit." He sneers. "You can't prove that shit to me. Haven't you been paying attention to what the fuck is going on out here? Kids killing kids over bullshit, and if a few bullets hit someone else, oh well, fuck it." O'Malley shakes his head. "Congratulations. You people survived nearly two hundred and fifty years of slavery, only to win the freedom to kill your damn selves. Way to go!"

He makes a sharp right, and my head nearly hits the side window. "Don't you start in on that racist bullshit," I huff. "I'm not in the mood. Gang crimes aren't a race issue; they're a fuckin' economic issue, and you damn well know it!"

"Bullshit." He takes a sharp left. "These muthafuckas just don't want to learn nothing but how to shoot, steal, and deal. They don't give a fuck about anything or anybody else. They're nothing but domestic terrorists. I wish I could just gather them all up, put them in one building with a ton of guns, and let them go at it. We wouldn't have to kill them—they'd kill themselves. It could be their Alamo."

"Do me a favor and shut the hell up." I grind my teeth together. There's no point in arguing with an idiot. It'll only bring me down to his level, but *goddamn* I'm tired of listening to his mouth. We swerve onto Adams Street and speed toward the hospital. As we draw near, the sound of gunfire penetrates through the wail of our sirens. We approach without our blue tracking light, which was shot out in the previous gunfight..

"There those muthafuckas go!" O'Malley jams his foot down on the accelerator. "I swear to God I want to kill every one of these bastards."

I reach for the radio and report our position to dispatch. Suddenly, a swarm of gangsters spill out of the hospital, shooting their way toward their cars. "They're going to get away."

"Not if I have anything to fucking do about it," O'Malley says.

I watch as one group struggles with a large man to a black and chrome SUV, and my heart jumps in recognition. A larger group, flagging blue and gray, race toward two cars and peel after the SUV, slowing only briefly as one last member dives through an open window.

O'Malley stays hot on their tail as the three cars tear away from the Med and then continue their gunfight. "Can you believe these bold, coony muthafuckas?"

I cut a sharp look to my left. "O'Malley." I grit my teeth. "You let one more muthafuckin' racist slur come out your mouth, and me and you are going to have a serious misunderstanding up in this bitch."

He smirks, knowing damn well that he's getting under my skin. We close in and then suddenly the black Monte Carlo peels sharply to the left, and the yellow Cutless goes right, leaving the SUV going straight. O'Malley makes a choice and at the last second hangs a left to chase after the black Monte Carlo. The other patrol cars split up as well.

I grab our radio and report our new pursuit position. However, O'Malley's driving skills aren't as sharp as mine. The Monte Carlo is able to shake him as they near the Bethel Grove area.

"What the fuck?!" He whips his head around, trying to judge or guess which street the damn car had ducked down. "Did you see which way they went?"

"Maybe you passed them?" I suggest.

O'Malley makes an illegal U-turn and starts searching the streets again. After what feels like forever, I say, "We lost them. Let's head back to the hospital, see what the damage is."

O'Malley dismisses my suggestion. "Fuck that shit. I know those gangsta niggers are around here somewhere. I'm not leaving until I find their asses."

I simmer.

"What's that?" O'Malley asks, slamming on the brakes. Suddenly he's excited again.

"What's what?" I ask, annoyed. I'm just ready for this long-ass night to end.

O'Malley shifts the car in reverse and backs up. "That," he says, pointing.

I try to follow his gaze. "I don't know. It looks like an auto shop."

He smiles. "Bingo. How much you want to bet they're in there?"

"How do you know?"

"If I had to ditch a couple of cars, that's exactly how I would do it." He smirks, turning toward the shop. "I bet they're in there thinking they pulled a fast one on me."

I roll my eyes; everything's always personal with this asshole. "Even if that was true, do you know how many fuckin' auto shops are on this road alone?" I reason. "What makes you think they're in that one?"

"I can just feel it." He glances over at me. "I can just smell these banging porch monkeys."

My eyes narrow as I jab a finger toward him. "When we get back to the station, I'm fuckin' you up."

"How about you just fuck me and we call it a night?" He winks, laughing.

"Not even if you were the *last* thing that resembled a man."

He chuckles and stops the car. "It's a damn shame. A woman as fine as you going without."

"Trust me. I'm getting more dick than I can handle," I sass back as we make our final creep toward the Goodson's Autoshop. I grab the radio and report our position and then request backup.

O'Malley reaches for the door and opens it.

"Don't you think we should wait?" I ask.

"I'm just going to take a peek." He gets out and shuts the door.

I roll my eyes. This hardheaded muthafucka is going to fuck around and get me killed one of these days. I climb out of the car behind him with my hand on my weapon, but I just barely clear the right side of the car when bullets start flying.

POP! POP! POP! POP! POP!

RAT-A-TAT-TAT-TAT!

The windows on the patrol car shatter and bullets slam into the car. A few blaze a little too close to my head as I dive for cover.

Then I can hear shoes shuffling everywhere.

"GO! GO! GO!" someone says.

"POLICE. STOP OR I'LL SHOOT!" O'Malley shouts.

POP! POP! POP! POP! POP!

RAT-A-TAT-TAT-TAT!

When bullets stop slamming into the car, I start to pull myself up, but before I can get to my feet, someone jumps into the patrol car. I half expect to see O'Malley, but instead it's some kid who looks more like a girl than a boy. I aim my weapon, but before I can demand that the kid get out of the car, the punk fires at me. I dive back out of the way again.

My attacker shifts the car in reverse and speeds backward. "What the fuck?" I can't believe the muthafucka just stole our police car. "These some bold muthafuckas."

I turn around to see O'Malley racing down the alley at full speed behind two large men. "Shit." I take off after him. Once again my long legs eat the distance up in no time.

POP! POP! POP!

I turn the corner to see one man down and one man cornered at a dead end with his hands in the air, O'Malley's weapon trained on him.

"Well, looky what we got here," O'Malley taunts. "My main man Python." He chuckles. "I'd know that ugly face anywhere. How you doing, Python? Or should I say Terrell?"

I lock eyes with the overseer of the Black Gangster Disciples and then glance over at my partner. I know damn well that O'Malley has no intention of making an arrest—at least not before having his own sort of fun with him. I look over at the other body just a few feet behind my partner.

"So what do you got to say now, big man on the block?" O'Malley asks. "Any last words?"

Python's demonic laughs fill the back alley.

"What? You find this funny, muthafucka?" O'Malley challenges. "You don't look so fuckin' big and bad to me."

I roll my eyes and walk around my partner to check

the other body. He's definitely dead, his hand still clutching his 45 mm.

"On your knees," O'Malley barks.

I glance up to the drama that's unfolding between Python and O'Malley. My gaze once again locks with the smirking gangsta. He is clearly enjoying egging my partner on.

O'Malley growls, "I *said* on your knees."

I move away from the dead body to stand behind my partner. The sound of police sirens alerts us that our backup is on the way.

"Oh, you're a stubborn muthafucka, huh?" O'Malley says. "It seems to me that I have myself a hell of an opportunity here. Don't you think?"

Python doesn't answer.

"I can just take you out right here. Huh? Then again, you niggers multiply like cockroaches. You kill one, there's another one to take its place. But you know . . ." The corner of O'Malley's lips kicks up. "In your case, I just might be willing to take my chances, *nigger!*"

I've had enough of his bullshit. I smile and quietly lift the dead man's 45 toward the back of my partner's head and pull the trigger.

The back of O'Malley's bald head explodes like a melon as his body pitches forward and then collapses in a heap on the concrete.

"I done told you about that nigger shit," I say.

"Took you long enough," Python says, moving away from the wall and looking down at O'Malley's dead body. "I didn't think he would shut up."

I laugh. "I don't think that's going to be a problem anymore."

Python smiles as he strolls over to me and lifts my chin. "Either way, I appreciate you coming through for your man." He leans down and kisses me.

16

Momma Peaches

The moment Python peels out of Shotgun Row, word leaks about Fat Ace's whereabouts. Soon after, members of the set spill out of their houses and turn the whole street into a spontaneous block party. Niggas started blasting music and shooting their guns in the air as an early celebration. There's no doubt in anyone's mind that the dirty dozen McGriff selected would handle this situation with Fat Ace once and for all.

Of course, I never seen a party I didn't like, so me and my boo climb out of bed and go mingle. Given that it's past midnight and I'm not allowed to be out of my house, I simply remove the electronic tag on my prosthetic leg.

"What's going on out here?" I ask, strolling out my front door.

My next door neighbor, Chantal, scratches at her unkempt hair and repositions her two-year-old son, who's wearing the Gangster Disciples colors and smells like he has a full shit load in his diaper, on her hip. "They've found Fat Ace. Python has gone to handle this business himself."

POP! POP! POP!

"ALL IS ONE!" some corner boys shout.

"UNTIL THE WORLD BLOWS UP!" the rest of the crowd shouts.

Everyone cheers as more guns are waved into the air.

POP! POP! POP!

The corners of my lips kick up. "I knew we'd find that fat fucka sooner or later." I spot a couple of Queen Gs and snap my fingers. "Hey, you two, let me have a hit of that shit." I continue to snap my fingers as Baby and Yolanda turn and jog up my porch steps.

"Be careful. That shit got a powerful kick," Baby warns.

I roll my eyes. "Chile, please. My ass has been smoking these muthafuckas since before you were an itch in your granddaddy's sac." I pop the blunt into my mouth and then fill my lungs with a deep toke only to find out that the lil girl wasn't playing. My eyes droop, my lips go numb, and my mind just fucking takes flight.

"Told you." Baby Thug grabs the blunt back and hands it to Yo-Yo.

"Goddamn that's some good shit," I say, already wavering on my feet. "What the fuck is in that?"

A wide smile stretches across Baby's face. "It's my own special blend. I only smoke it on special occasions. And cutting the head off those fake-ass slobs is a hell of a good reason to get blitz, nahwhatImean?"

Yo-Yo takes a deep drag. "My girl knows how to hook shit up, don't she?"

"That she does, chile. Puff, puff, pass," I joke, reaching for the blunt again and rocking my hips to the booming bass from one of the car's stereo systems. "Chantal, you want a hit of this?"

"Nah, Momma. I'm straight."

"Everybody going to have to watch they back for a while. You know the streets are going to be on fire after this," Baby says.

"Fuck. They started this shit as far as I'm concerned. If you can't stand the heat, get out of the muthafuckin' kitchen." I take a second hit and know that shit is going to have to be the last tug. "Go on, girl. You can have the rest. That shit gone have me fuckin' embarrassing myself after a while."

"Hey, Peaches," Rufus calls from the fence. "Sho look good this evening." His eyes rake me up and down.

"Nigga, don't start begging me for no pussy. I ain't got time for that shit tonight."

Rufus just shrugs his shoulders. "One day. Watch and see."

Arzell returns to the porch, carrying two beers. "Gotcha something to drink, Momma." He hands a chilled bottle over to me and then gives my ass a good smack and squeeze in front of the whole neighborhood.

"Whoooaa!" A few niggas snicker and point at us.

Arzell gives everyone the middle finger. "Fuck all y'all, muthafuckas!"

"Don't worry about them, baby. They ain't nothing but a bunch of haters 'cause they can't get at this. Muthafuckas don't know pussy is like fine wine—it only gets better with time."

The brothers howl.

Arzell smirks and then jogs off the porch to go talk shit.

"So what's goin' on with you, Yo-Yo?" I ask. "What you been up to? I haven't been able to catch up with you since I've been back home."

Yolanda shrugs her shoulders. "You know how it is. Doing a little bit of this and a little bit of that so I can stack some paper."

"Get your kids back yet?"

Yo-Yo takes another powerful pull on the rapidly disappearing woolie. "Nah. Not yet." She shrugs. "But I'm working on it. Got me a job over at the Pink Monkey today."

"Humph." I lean back and check her out. "Well, ain't nothing wrong with working what the good Lord gave you. You just make sure you stay one step ahead of the game. Don't let those niggas gas you up on some bullshit or you'll be poppin' out more crumb snatchers you can't afford to take care of."

She drops her head.

Even though I'm pretty fucked up, I realize that I hurt the girl's feelings, and knowing what the girl has been through, I ease up. "Chile, don't pay me no mind. You do what you gotta do to get your babies back, girl." I shake my head as another old memory starts to emerge through my drugged haze. When it's all said and done, it's up to the woman to provide for her babies. And sometimes we gotta stack money any way we can. . . .

April 1985. I had my arms full with trying to take care of Nana Maybelle. She had suffered a stroke a few weeks prior, and she was having trouble regaining the use of her left side. Medical bills ate through Maybelle's nest egg in just a matter of months. The good times were officially over for the Carver women.

Alice, six months pregnant, had moved back into the

house after much back-and-forth with her latest boyfriend, Jerome. Neither one of them was any use to me. The muthafuckas partied all night and slept all day. For years, Nana and I tiptoed around Alice, mainly because we felt guilty for what Leroy had done to her twelve years ago. Maybelle felt bad because she wasn't home that night, and I felt bad for obvious reasons.

Given the rape and her age, the courts ruled Leroy's murder as a justified homicide. However, Alice was never the same again. She got into trouble, flunked out of school, and just overall didn't give a fuck about anything. Then there were the men. Where I liked bad boys, Alice loved dangerous boys.

It was unclear where Jerome came from. His story changed damn near every day. And if you asked him too many questions, he'd become agitated and start cussing muthafuckas out. Around town, he'd been known to jack cars in broad daylight and shoot niggas over dice games. He even shot one nigga because he'd snuck a chicken leg out of Jerome's Kentucky Fried Chicken bucket. He straight up just didn't give a fuck.

I had to check his ass almost on the daily and came close to slicing his throat when I caught his ass stealing money out of my purse. Still, Alice defended him and refused to put him out of the house.

She also defended him whenever he hauled off and beat her ass for any and everything. I didn't understand. Alice had blossomed into a beautiful woman. Pretty face, big titties, small waist, and a thick ass. Everywhere she went, niggas damn near got whiplash trying to holler at her. She could've had any nigga she wanted, but for some damn reason, she wanted this illiterate, nasty, Jheri curl–wearing, gold-toothed, stank-breath muthafucka who dressed like Tubbs on Miami Vice.

The few times that I tried to push the issue, Alice had

*cussed me the fuck out. And the one time I'd jumped in
the middle of one of their fights, trying to defend Alice,
the bitch turned on me and tried to beat my ass. So I decided to let her do whatever the fuck she wanted to do. A
hard head made a soft ass.*

It wasn't easy staying on the sidelines. Jerome would
beat Alice so bad sometimes that I just knew she was
going to miscarry one day or even be killed herself. If
that day ever came, I didn't know what I was going to do.

Money became such an issue at the Carver house that
I tried to take over the family business, establish some
connections, but Jerome fucked all that shit up, too.

"He's gotta go!" I shouted after discovering I was
missing a couple of bricks I had kept stashed in a loose
board beneath my bed. "I can't take this shit no more!
Niggas die for shit like this."

"Calm down," Alice said, rolling her eyes. "You don't
know whether Jerome took your shit. Maybe you have
another nigga roaming around the house while you're
high as fuck and passed out." She cocked a half smile at
me. "It's happened before."

Our gazes clashed.

"So what? I'm supposed to let this muthafucka run
all over me for some mistake twelve years ago? Fuck
that. Enough is enough. The past is the past. It's time to
fucking move on from that shit. He's stealing money out
of our pockets, food out of our mouths. We got bills in
this bitch. You think the muthafuckin' lights stay on because people at Memphis Light and Gas just love our
black asses? Nah. He's gotta go."

Alice rolled her eyes again and smacked her heavily
glossed lips. "The last time I checked, this wasn't your
house. Nana Maybelle said that we could stay here as
long as we wanted."

"I tell you what. When Nana can wipe her ass again,

then she can have a vote. But as long as my ass is hustlin' in this muthafucka to keep the lights on, then what I
fuckin' say goes."

Alice teared up. "So, what, you're putting me out?"

"I didn't say that you had to go anywhere. Jerome
needs to take his dusty behind somewhere else—back to
Atlanta, Birmingham, or wherever the fuck he says he's
from this week."

"If he goes, then I go," Alice said, playing her best
card.

"Then I'm going to miss you," I said.

Alice's face fell. "You'd do that?"

"Nobody pimps me out. Not you and certainly not
some drip, drip Jheri curl muthafucka who's ruining all
our good sheets."

"Fine. Fuck you, bitch. If it wasn't for me, your ass
wouldn't even be here now."

I shook my head. "It's not going to work this time. I
appreciate and am grateful that you saved my life that
night, but I can't keep living like this. I'm sorry for what
Leroy did to you—for my part in what happened—but
I've got to draw a line, Alice. Jerome has to go."

"Your part? The whole fuckin' thing was your fault.
You brought that nigga in here . . . to my bed. Now you
wanna stand there and judge me on how me and my man
get down? Well, fuck you. You got a lot of fuckin' nerve."

I shook my head. "I'm not changing my mind about
this, Alice. I don't owe—"

"Bitch, you owe me your life." Alice winced and
clutched at her belly.

"What's wrong?"

"N-nothing." She doubled over. I rushed to her side,
but she stubbornly pulled away. "Get away from me. I
don't need your help."

"Don't be stupid. Do you need to go to the hospital?"

Alice didn't answer. She stayed doubled over, drawing in several short breaths until the pain subsided.

"I'm calling nine-one-one," I decided.

"No." *Alice stood, seeming to have recovered.* "I'm fine, so stop pretending you give a fuck."

"Alice . . ."

My sister didn't stand around to hear whatever I had to say. She simply turned and marched out of the room. An hour later, she had packed her and Jerome's shit and stormed out. Nana Maybelle was hurt but understood that I had to do what I had to do.

Alice and Jerome spent the next two weeks sleeping in his black van. For the first week, Jerome sold some of the brick he'd lifted from my stash. They partied hard with the rest. Alice kept telling herself that she wasn't doing that much coke and that her baby was going to be fine. Then she tried crack for the first time and had long spells when she forgot that she was pregnant altogether.

Two weeks later, Jerome sold the van out from under them, leaving them to roam from one shitty motel to another. Then he sold his gold teeth. None of the money lasted long. Then Jerome had the bright idea to pimp Alice out, even though she was now seven months pregnant. She refused at first, but after being slapped around for a little bit, she changed her mind. Niggas didn't give a fuck that her ass was pregnant. She was still pretty with a fat ass.

But the money wasn't coming fast enough for Jerome, so he concocted a plan to hit two check-cashing joints off Lamar. "It's just a smash-and-grab, baby. Ain't shit going to go wrong," he said. "We roll up in there, get that money, and we'll be set for a while—at least until Junior comes," he said, reaching over and rubbing her big belly.

"I don't know."

"What the fuck don't you know?" Jerome yelled. "We need the money, don't we?"

Alice sighed. "Yes, baby." She was getting tired of this same argument from him.

"Then what's the problem? It's tax refund time. You know these muthafuckas have mad loot in there. We hit this one and then the one over off Winchester, and I'm telling you we'll be set."

Alice remained unconvinced.

"Looky here." He sniffed and then sat next to her on the rumpled motel bed. "If it makes you feel better, after the job, we can get a couple of rocks and have ourselves a little party." He leaned over and nibbled on her bottom lip. "You'd like that, wouldn't you?"

Just the idea of getting high had Alice smacking her lips in anticipation. Fuck. They did need the money, and the little chump change she made with these broke niggas around Memphis was barely enough for a couple of rocks, let alone for some food and shit. In the back of her mind, she knew the shit she was doing was fucked up, but, damn, she couldn't help herself at this point. Life was too fucking hard to deal with when she wasn't high. Of course, she could always go home, but that would require her tucking in her tail and kissing her sister's ass. She couldn't do that.

Not yet anyway.

"Goddamn, Alice. What the fuck is there to think about?" he exploded, jumping to his feet. "If you ain't going to help me make this paper, then I need to cut your ass loose and find me a bitch who knows how to be down for her man."

Alice panicked and pushed herself to her feet. "Baby, baby, calm down." She tried to pull him into her arms.

"Nah, nah. Your ass ain't doing nothing but slowing a nigga down. You know how much pussy I've turned down, *fuckin' around with you? And I'm talking about some good pussy, too."*

She drew in a sharp breath as his words punched her in the gut.

"Do you appreciate shit? Nah. You just fuckin' whine and complain."

"I'm sorry, baby. I'm sorry." Again, Alice tried to pull him back into her arms. *"I'll do it, baby. I'll do it. Chill."* She rained kisses across his face, hoping to erase all thoughts of him leaving her.

Jerome's lips twitched up. *"You mean it? You'll do it?"*

She smiled and led him back over to the bed. *"Of course, baby. You know I'll do anything for you."* Alice unzipped his jeans and pulled out his fat dick. Jerome may not have been much to look at, but nigga had the best dick she'd ever had. It was long and veiny, with a thick muffin-top head. Jerome's toes would curl every time she squeezed that shit to the back of her throat and slobbered on it.

"Oooh. That's my girl," he sighed, keeping his calloused hands against the back of her head and occasionally forcing her to choke on his shit a little longer than she wanted to. *"You love me, baby?"* he asked, looking down at her and admiring her work.

Alice bobbed her head but kept working that dick.

"And you'd do anything for me?"

She bobbed again.

"Good girl."

The next day, Alice didn't ask where Jerome got the guns, but they hopped a bus to the mall and hot-wired a nice green Buick for their getaway car. Alice hadn't held a gun in years, and when Jerome tried to hand her a .38, she couldn't get herself to take it.

Irritated, Jerome thrust the gun toward her. *"Will you stop fuckin' around?"* He scratched his dry and lint-filled Jheri curl. *"I ain't got time for your bullshit today."* He licked his lips and glanced around the parking lot. *"Now, you're going to go in first, and I'll come in behind you and cover the door."* He reached in his jacket and pulled out a Hefty bag. *"All you got to do is point the gun and tell them to fill up the bag."*

"I gotta ask for the money?"

"Shit. I gotta watch the door, make sure nobody comes in there. You got the easiest part of the job." He shook his head like he was dealing with a fucking idiot. *"Now put this shit on."*

Alice took the black wool cap that would double as a mask.

"We go in. You point the gun, demand the money. Two minutes later, we ride out. Got it?"

Alice nodded but then felt a sharp pain in her stomach. *"Oooh."*

"What the fuck is wrong with you now?" Jerome snapped.

"N-nothing. I'm fine," she lied, and then reached for the door handle.

"All right. Let's do this shit!" Jerome jumped out of the car and did a sort of half walk, half run across the parking lot.

Alice struggled to keep up. Each step she took caused another spasm of pain to shoot up her body.

"C'mon, c'mon," Jerome demanded, rolling his arm as if that was going to light a fire under her ass or something.

But as Alice stepped up on the sidewalk of the L-shaped strip mall, she suddenly felt a rush down between her legs. She looked down and saw that she had wet herself. *"J-Jerome. I . . . I think—"*

"What the fuck are you pissing on yourself for?" His face twisted in disgust. *"Goddamn it. I knew that you*

were going to fuck this shit up." He started pacing and looking around. "I need to get this fuckin' money."

"It's all right, baby," she said, trying to smile again. "I'm all right now. I'm cool."

He eyed her warily. "You sure?"

"Yeah. Yeah. We're just going to be in and out, right?" More pain shot through her; this time it seemed as if it was coming from everywhere. She struggled not to double over and wail like a muthafuckin' banshee, but there was nothing she could do about the sweat pouring like a waterfall from her hairline.

"All right, all right. Cool," Jerome said, his eyes shining.

Alice knew that look. His ass was fiening bad. She rushed to the glass door of E-Z Check Cashing, but she wobbled more than she walked.

"Your mask," he hissed.

She nodded and pulled the wool cap down over her eyes and then ran into the building, pointing her .38 at the woman behind the counter. "This is a stickup, bitch! Give me all your money."

An older woman wearing a crooked black wig threw her hands up in the air. "Don't shoot me!"

"I—Ow!" Alice clutched her side. "I ain't going to shoot you as long as you do what—Ow!" She tried to squat.

The older woman eyeballed her for a few minutes. "Are you okay?"

"I-I'm fine!" Alice tried to steady her weapon. "Just put the money in the bag." She thrust out the Hefty bag, but then once again couldn't stop herself from trying to squat in the middle of the room. "Oh, fuck!"

"Ma'am, are you about to have a baby?"

She ground her teeth together as a way to bite down on the pain, but it wasn't working. "I just . . . I just need to sit down for a minute." Alice glanced over her shoulder to see where the hell Jerome was. He hadn't come inside with her as planned. He was pacing back and forth outside, waiting for her to come back out. "Shit."

"Do you need for me to call the doctor or something?" the woman asked, making her move to push a button behind the counter.

"N-no," she panted. "Just fill the bag . . . argh!" She squatted all the way down to the floor. There was no doubt about it—the baby was coming. NOW.

The woman rushed around the counter to help, but the minute Jerome spotted her doing that shit, he came charging into the building, blasting. She screamed as six bullets slammed into her chest and propelled her backward.

Alice screamed, too, but more because it felt like she was being torn in half.

"What the hell are you doin' on the floor?!" Jerome yelled, looking around. "Where the fuck is the money?"

"B-baby!"

"What?"

"The baby is coming!"

Jerome blinked. "What? Right now? You can't have that shit right now."

Alice tried to breathe in short puffs but then ended up growling when her body forced her to push. The sharp pain she was experiencing earlier had now become all consuming.

"Fuck this shit!" Jerome snatched up the bag, raced around the corner, and quickly started pouring open drawers into the bag, but it wasn't much. "What the fuck is this?" He clutched just a handful of twenty-dollar bills. "This can't be all of it!"

"J-Jerome." Alice gulped and tugged at her pants. She needed to get them off. "Hel-help!"

He ignored her. He was too busy sweeping shit off the counter and turning over filing cabinets until he finally stumbled across a bank safe.

The bell jingled over the door, and a guy wearing a mechanic's jumpsuit walked in. "What in the hell?"

Still panting and sweating, Alice grimaced as she glanced up. But before the guy could say anything else, Jerome started shooting again. The brother ducked and dodged and raced back out of the building like he was related to Olympic star Carl Lewis.

"Fuck!" Jerome kicked a desk for having missed the guy. He turned back at the safe. He pulled on the lever, banged on it, and then even attempted to pick it up, but it wasn't budging. In the distance, police sirens wailed. "Fuck! Fuck! Fuck!"

"Aaaaargh!" Alice felt the baby crown. "Jer—Aarargh!"

Finally giving up, Jerome jetted back around the counter. "Get the fuck up. We gotta go!"

"I . . . whew, whew . . . I can't. Aaaargh!"

The sirens grew louder.

Jerome grabbed her by the arm and attempted to tug her toward the door, but Alice just screamed louder. "Fuck this shit. You're on your own." He grabbed her .38 from off the floor and stuffed it in his pocket.

"Wh-what?"

He bolted toward the door.

"Wait! Jerome! Don't leave me! Jer—Aargggh!" She clutched her stomach and pushed down again.

The bell jingled as Jerome flew out the door, leaving her to deliver her baby right next to the dead woman on the floor.

Love

17
Ta'Shara

I sit mute in the police interrogation room. It's been damn near six hours, and I still haven't had my one phone call. Not that I'm in any hurry. My mind is running rampant with wild scenarios of Tracee and Reggie doing everything from beating, yelling, grounding, or even turning me back over to foster care. Still, I have no intention of talking. I'm not dumb. There's nothing more dangerous on the streets than being labeled a snitch.

I have no doubt whatsoever that Profit is sticking to the script as well. No way will he give up his peoples or even Essence, for that matter, for the illegal gun. Our story is simply that we were at the wrong place at the wrong time. Essence's burner is the only thing that can potentially trip us up. Where did it come from, and how did Profit get it?

Profit lied, saying he grabbed it off one of the dead

victims, but there was one old dude huddled behind a potted plant that no one saw who reported to the police that Profit had raced into the lobby blasting at the thugs coming in from the streets. Then I stun everybody and said that gun was mine.

After that, I shut the hell up.

Now, an annoyed Officer Tanner stretches his long, lanky frame back into the metal chair across from me and expels a tired breath. In his eyes, it is clear that he would like nothing more than to wrap his hands around my throat in order to finally get some answers.

"C'mon, Ta'Shara. You look like a good girl," the officer says with a belittling smile. "You just got yourself caught up in a bad situation. Maybe you thought being in a gang was cool or something. Maybe your boyfriend, Profit, talked you into joining or something. I get it. Girls like bad boys."

I laugh.

"What? You think this shit is funny?" he challenges. "I got fifteen dead bodies on my hands. Eight of them innocent civilians who didn't have shit to do with this damn gang war bullshit. They went to the hospital seeking medical assistance and ended up with bullets in their heads for their trouble. And you find that funny?"

I shut down at his combative tone.

He stares me down. "Now where would a good girl like you get a nine millimeter with the serial number filed off?"

Silence.

"You want to know what I think?" he asks.

I fold my arms under my breasts and just glare at the man across from me.

"*I* think that the gun belonged to your boy. *I* think it's the same weapon that was used to kill a cop last night over in Orange Mound. I'm willing to bet my life on it."

I roll my eyes and shake my head. This asshole was waaay the fuck off base.

"That shit is going to be confirmed when we run ballistics on the weapon. Are you sure you still want to claim that the weapon is yours? That could place you at the scene of another crime."

"You do what you gotta do," I say evenly, and stop myself from flashing the annoying cop my middle finger.

"All right, smart-ass." The cop jumps up from his seat, the metal chair flipping backward and banging against the floor. "I'm sick and tired of this bullshit. I'm sick and tired of seeing you young *gangstas* holding this damn city hostage. I grew up in this city." He paces in front of the table. "It used to be a good place to raise a family. Home of the blues and Elvis Presley. Tourists flocked to this city for good music and good barbeque. Now we bag bodies like it's a goddamn third world country!"

My expression doesn't change. This pig ain't getting shit.

"Fuck it!" He turns, kicks the chair, and finally storms out of the room.

I exhale and my shoulders deflate before I swipe the tear away before it rolls down my face. I didn't have shit to do with happened tonight, and I ain't about to let some racist muthafucka pin the woes of the world on my shoulders. I have bigger problems—the main one being LeShelle.

I still can't believe my older sister was just seconds away from putting a bullet into Profit—and then him turning to polish her off. Shit. Everything happened so fast. It was amazing that I had even recognized LeShelle when I came running into the waiting room. What would've happened had I not chased after Profit? I shift around in my chair, ready for these muthafuckas to either charge me with something or let me go.

Two hours later, they finally release me to my foster parents.

A relieved Tracee sweeps me into her arms and squeezes me so tight I come close to suffocating. I don't complain, mainly because I can feel Tracee's thin frame trembling as she plants kisses over the top of my head. "Thank God," she sobs. "I was so worried."

My gaze shifts over Tracee's shoulder to Reggie. A mass of thin worry lines monopolize his forehead and his dark eyes.

"Are you all right?" he asks gruffly.

I nod as tears sting the backs of my eyes. I remain silent after hours of interrogation and here, after just a few seconds with foster parents, I want to confess everything. The last thing I want them to believe is Officer Tanner's outlandish lies about me being involved with a gang. They have done so much for me, and I don't want them to regret it.

"Good." Reggie coughs and clears his throat before turning away, but not in time to hide the flicker of disappointment on his face. "Let's get out of here."

Tracee finally pulls back enough for me to breathe and then loops my arm through hers before leading me out of the precinct and to a rented Nissan. Once I'm in the backseat, I hand Reggie his car keys and tell him where his car is parked at the hospital, but I don't tell him about the busted taillight. For that, I wait until he sees it for himself.

"I'm sorry," I mumble weakly.

Reggie remains silent, which only makes me feel worse. *They're going to send me back.* My mind scrambles for something I can say or do to make things up to them, but I can't think of a damn thing. Tracee scoots behind the wheel of the Nissan and tells me to come sit next to her in the passenger seat since Reggie will take his car straight to work.

I climb out of the backseat and walk over to the passenger side. Briefly, I catch Reggie's eyes, but he quickly turns. I sniff but am unable to keep my tears from splashing down my face. Opening the passenger door, I glance up at the hospital. There are still teams of police cars and media vans littering the front—a reminder that last night's shooting wasn't just some nightmare. I sit down and buckle my seat belt and then cast a final glance at the hospital, trying to guess which window belonged to Profit or whether he was still even there dealing with his shoulder.

"What were you thinking?" Tracee asks the moment she shifts the car into drive. "A gang?"

"I'm not in a gang," I mumble.

"The police said—"

"The police don't know what the fuck they're talking about."

She whips her head toward me. "Watch your mouth, young lady!"

I drop my head. "Sorry."

"I don't know what the hell has gotten in to you," Tracee starts again. "After all Reggie and I have done for you."

The tears return. "I know." I sniff and try to mop them up with the back of my hand. "But I swear to you, I'm not in a gang."

Tracee shakes her head as if she can't bring herself to believe me. Now that she has reassured herself that I'm all right, she shifts gears and is showing her disappointment. "Does any of this have anything to do with your sister?"

I stiffen. "Why would you ask that?"

"I don't know. Maybe because sneaking out of the house, stealing Reggie's car, and being involved in some gang shoot-out sounds more like something LeShelle would do." She pulls up into our driveway and parks.

I look away.

"Well?" Tracee presses. "Does any of this have anything to do with LeShelle?"

More tears burn the backs of my eyes. No matter what has happened between me and LeShelle in the past, there's no way I can or will sell her out—despite what it might cost me. I turned my back on my sister once; I don't have it in me to do it again.

The silence in the car thickens. After a full minute, Tracee turns away as if she can't stand to look at me anymore. "You better go and get dressed for school."

"Aren't you going to ask me what happened?"

"Are you going to tell me the truth?"

I shut down. I hadn't planned on telling the whole truth, just parts of it. The Douglases couldn't handle the real truth. Not them, nestled in their green lawn suburban fantasy. Dinner at six, in bed by nine, and church every Sunday. What did they know about trying not to get punked or jumped in school by so many different gangs no one can possibly keep count? What did they know about falling for a guy who everyone keeps telling you you can't have? Or what it feels like to constantly battle my sister's wishes, but still rely on her and her status for protection?

"We'll talk about it tonight," Tracee says, turning and then climbing out of the car. She doesn't even wait for me to follow her into the house. In fact, it seems like she wants to get away from me as fast as she can.

An hour later, I'm dropped off at school. Things quickly go from bad to worse. With word of last night's battle between the GDs and Vice Lords, everyone is reppin' their shit hard. From the front door to my locker, I pass five fights where niggas are body slamming each other against every goddamn thing. Those who aren't fighting are just hollering and egging the shit on like it is all just a big-ass game.

I have never skipped school, but I'm seriously considering it. At least until everything calms down again. I search through the crowd, looking for my girl Essence. I don't know if she got locked up last night or if she just high-tailed it out of that muthafucka after the shit went down. Since she already has a rap sheet a mile long, she most likely just got the fuck on.

Some trick shoves her way through the crowd and shoulder bumps me so hard I hit the floor. "What the fuck?" I scramble back to my feet before niggas seize the opportunity to stomp on my ass.

"Hey, bitch," Qiana spits. "'Member me?"

Before I have a chance to respond, Qiana comes at me like a raging bull and slams me against a row of lockers. In the next second, she swipes her small loop earring out of her ear and a fist slams against the right side of my jaw. "I told your ass to stay the fuck away from Profit."

A fury I have never experienced before explodes out of me, and I just start swinging. Once I get started, I can't stop. I rage against the fucked-up street politics that keep trying to lock me up in a steel cage. My fists fly and connect against Qiana's short chin. Then I surprise the cheering crowd by spitting out a short razor I keep tucked in my cheek and use with lightning precision.

Just because I ain't in a gang don't mean that I don't come correct. Qiana is learning that shit quick, fast, and in a hurry. She tries to get the fuck out of the way of my blade when it comes slicing toward her face. She fails and cries out when her right cheek splits open.

"Ahh. Got damn!" A nigga laughs and points from the sidelines. "Cut that bitch again!"

The crowd cheers and kicks Qiana back into the circle when she attempts to flee with her hand holding her face together. Blood gushes through her fingers and drips onto the floor. Nobody gives a fuck, especially my ass. I'm ready to polish this bitch off once and for all.

"Come on, bitch," I taunt, waving her forward. "You've been talking shit for a minute. Let me show you how I get down!"

"Oooooh," the crowd choruses, and then waits to see what the fuck Qiana is gone do.

Qiana keeps one hand against the side of her face, but with the other withdraws a gray metal box cutter—old-school shit. "All right, bitch. You wanna do this?" she sneers with thick wads of spit popping out of her mouth. She slides back the lever, and a thin, rusty blade rises up. "Let's see if Profit wants you after I finish slicing yo ass up."

I cock my head and keep waving the girl forward. I can't wait to shut this bitch up once and for all. Maybe I'll finally start getting some respect of my own. It's way past time for a little bit of that. "C'mon, bitch. You think you're bad enough to do it, then bring on your nasty, tricked-out ass," I challenge.

Qiana inches around in a circle, but doesn't make any sudden moves. Clearly she is looking for her other girls to jump in and back her up. But of both us notice that there's just as many Queen Gs holding the line with their arms folded as there are Flowers.

This is my and Qiana's fight, and it's gonna stay that way.

I laugh. After all this time of talking shit, this bitch is too fuckin' scared to even make a move. "Whatcha waitin' for, huh? You want my man, right? Ain't that what this bullshit is all about? Profit doesn't want your diseased pussy that be funkin' up the goddamn hallways on the regular. Shit. Why don't you douche that mutha-fucka after you let niggas run a train on you? I can fuckin' smell you from here."

"Awwww sheeeiiit," niggas snap.

"Fuck you, bitch!" Qiana lunges, bringing the box cutter up high in the air.

I keep my moves short and quick, slicing open Qiana's other cheek like the muthafucka is made out of butter. Euphoria surges through me when Qiana drops the box cutter and more blood pours out the other side of her face.

"Whup that bitch. Stomp that bitch. Finish that bitch off," starts as a chant and then quickly sounds like a song. "Whup that bitch. Stomp that bitch. Finish that bitch off. Whoa!"

But the Flowers have seen about as much as they care to and surge forward to break the line. The Queen Gs do likewise and a full war breaks out.

"Break it up! Break it up!" Principal Davis shouts at the top of his lungs. Behind him a team of teachers pushes and shoves kids out of the way, but the crowd pushes back. One teacher screams when someone snatches her perfectly coiled bun and yanks her to the ground.

Principal Davis changes directions to help her. "Mrs. Fisher. Mrs. Fisher, are you all right?"

Somebody clocks me from behind, and I stumble to the floor where Qiana's blood smears across my jeans and T-shirt. I panic because the bitch is liable to have any goddamn thing. My attacker keeps at me, but since she is behind me, I can't see who it is.

"Get off her, bitch!" Essence's squeaky baby voice slices through the chaos.

I have never been so happy and relieved to hear from my girl. The feeling is amplified when Essence knocks my attacker off of me. With all the pushing and shoving that's going on, it's amazing that I can even get back on my feet without being stomped to death.

POP! POP! POP!

"Shit!" I duck. I should've known that it was just a matter of time for shit to pop off.

Everyone screams and takes off running.

POP! POP! POP!

"Come with me!" Essence shouts, grabbing me by the hand and jerking me toward one of the school's side doors.

"Wait, E!" I struggle to keep up with my girl. "What happened last night? Do you know where Profit is?"

"We're dodging bullets and you're asking me about some nigga?" E asks, incredulous. Outside, she pulls me to the side. "Yo, you're my girl and everything, but he's got your nose blown wide open, and, news flash, we in the middle of a muthafuckin' gang war, and you're two steps from getting us both killed. And now the whole school knows you that nigga's bitch. It's amazing that the Queen Gs even had your back."

"What? Nobody helped me fight that bitch Qiana."

"Yeah. You keep telling yourself that." She rolls her eyes and grabs my arm again. "C'mon."

"Look, I understand if you're still mad about last night, but I gotta find out what's going on with Profit. If he's been arrested or . . ." I finally see where Essence is leading me. I stop and jerk my hand free. "What the hell is she doing here?"

Essence turns. "She wants to talk to you."

I shake my head. "I don't have shit to say to her."

"Stop being hardheaded," Essence says. "You don't really have a choice. Either come with me or she'll just get someone else to drag you kicking and screaming." She folds her arms. "And you know she will."

Drawing a deep breath, I glare at E. "You're supposed to be on *my* side."

"I am—even when it doesn't look like it."

While kids still scramble out of the building, I force myself to swallow my pride and walk toward the burgundy Crown Victoria where LeShelle sits, drumming her fingers and glaring at me.

18

LeShelle

POP! POP! POP!

"**W**ill you hurry the fuck up?" I snap. I'm already pissed that I even had to come up to this bitch in the first place, and now Ta'Shara is acting like she has all the time in the world to get her ass in the car. I'm already agitated because I haven't slept in almost forty-eight hours. My mind's cluttered with questions. After I got separated from Python at the autoshop, I never heard from him. I know that he text-messaged McGriff that he was all right, but he hasn't contacted me. That shit is bugging me the fuck out, but right now, I'm in ass-covering mode, and I need to know what the hell is going on with Ta'Shara and that nigga who capped a few GDs last night. I ain't down for a blowback about shit I don't know about.

I want and need to believe that Ta'Shara was just at the wrong place at the wrong time and that she and that nigga have nothing to do with the war between the

Gangster Disciples and the Vice Lords. Sure, a few Queen Gs who attend Morris High School dropped dime that the two have been creeping around for a hot minute, but none of those bitches made it clear to me that that nigga was Fat Ace's little brother. What the fuck? His family? That's some violation shit that could get me caught up. My so-called sister couldn't have taken a bigger knife and twisted it in my back. How the fuck is Python going to react when—not if—he finds out? Because my nigga eventually finds out about everything. *Every muthafuckin' thing.* Hell, this kind of stuff could have niggas looking at me sideways and questioning my loyalty to the Folks Nation. I don't need or appreciate this bullshit in the slightest.

I glance around the busy street and expect the police to show up at any second. Of course, a shooting at Morris High School hardly shocks or constitutes an emergency nowadays.

Ta'Shara jerks open the passenger door and plops down while Essence climbs into the backseat. "You wanted to see me, Your Highness?"

"Don't you dare try to fuckin' clown me! Not today. I ain't in the fuckin' mood." I jam my foot on the accelerator and peel away from the curb like a bat out of hell. "Start talking," I demand.

Ta'Shara clamps her jaw tight and folds her arms under her breasts. "What do you want to talk about, the weather?"

Seeing red, I smack this smug bitch so hard her head rocks to the side and hits the window with a *THUMP!*

"Owww. What the fuck?" She places a hand against the side of her head.

"You think I'm fuckin' playing with your ass? You think this shit is a game?" I yell. "Trust that if you were any other muthafucka right now, I would put a goddamn bullet in the center of your fuckin' forehead. Please believe." I jerk the wheel and cut off some little old lady who's rolling at least ten miles an hour below the speed limit. "Shit. Why the fuck they let these old muthafuckas drive? I swear to God."

Still rubbing her head, Ta'Shara glares at me.

"I don't give a fuck if you're mad right now. You better scratch your ass and get glad."

Ta'Shara just pushes her bottom lip out even farther.

"I'm fuckin' waiting," I say, dead serious. "TALK."

Ta'Shara expels a long breath, but when she starts taking too much time, my hand comes back up. She ducks her head and puts her hands up to try and block the next blow. "All right. All right. Stop. Damn."

I return my hand to the steering wheel. "How long have you been fuckin' around with Fat Ace's *brother?*"

"Almost seven months," Ta'Shara mumbles.

"WHAT?"

Silence.

I pull my gaze from the road and stare at my sister. "Please, Lord, say this bitch ain't just said what I think she said."

Silence.

"Oh. So fuck me. Is that it?" I snap. "Fuck my muthafuckin' position or my muthafuckin' life when niggas find my sister is balls deep with Vice Lords. Is that it?"

Again this bitch is giving me the silent treatment.

"Oh, you ain't got shit to say about that, huh, ho?" I shake my head as my hands tighten on the steering wheel. "I swear to God, Ta'Shara. You don't appreciate shit. I should've had my bitches bust you in this game long time ago—make you earn the protection you've been taking for granted."

"I've never asked you to do shit for me."

"You didn't have to, did you?" I pound a hand against

my chest. "It's my fuckin' *job*. It has *always* been my job to take care of your ignorant ass—even though it's very clear to me now that you don't fuckin' appreciate the shit."

"Yeah. Whatever. You need any help carrying that cross, LeShelle?"

Angry, I whip the car into a Walgreen's parking lot and then slam on the brakes. Ta'Shara pitches forward and slams into the dashboard, while Essence damn near flips over the front seats. "END IT!"

Our gazes crash.

"Profit is not—"

"Don't say that nigga's name to me." I whack her on the head. "I *said,* end it!"

"Owww. Stop it. It's not funny," Ta'Shara barks back.

"Does it look like I'm laughing, bitch? This shit can blow back on *my* ass—not that you really give a fuck. You got your perfect little parents, living the high life in your bougie neighborhood and forgetting where the fuck you came from. *I'm* your fuckin' people. *I'm* your fuckin' flesh and blood, and it's my ass that makes sure that mutha- fuckas leave you alone while you fill your head with bullshit ideas like being a muthafuckin' doctor. I've al- ways had your back despite you giving me the back of your hand a couple of years ago."

"That is not how that went down and you know it."

"End it," I growl again, tired of the bullshit. "You se- riously think that Python . . ." I glance back at Essence. "Get out!"

Essence blinks.

"GET THE FUCK OUT! Don't you see I'm having a fuckin' private conversation with my sister?"

Knowing better than to argue, Essence jumps out of the car.

I wait until the door slams closed before continuing

my argument with Ta'Shara. "Python is not going to like hearing that my own sister is fuckin' a Vice Lord," I hiss. "My muthafuckin' neck is on the line. You got that?"

"Oh, I'm supposed to live my life according to the gospel of Python?" Ta'Shara challenges, squaring around in her seat and looking entirely too grown. "I'm not a gangsta bitch, okay? That's your bullshit. I'm not going to live my life according to a bunch of street rules that I never agreed to. And by the way, neither will Profit. He's not in the game."

"Oh, so my eyes were just deceiving me when I saw him kill three members of Python's crew? MY CREW. That shit alone means death."

"Memory serves me that y'all were the crazy mutha-fuckas who showed up shooting up a goddamn hospital in the middle of the night—like that's the muthafuckin' thing to do."

"You goddamn right. Fat Ace started this bullshit. I took a fuckin' bullet because of that grimy muthafucka." I jerk up the sleeve of my blue T-shirt and show my sister my bandaged arm. "So hell yeah, I went to that fuckin' hospital to return the fuckin' favor. Instead, I get there and my sister plants a knife in my back—*again!*"

"That's not—"

"END IT!" I yell. "I ain't asking—I'm telling you. End the shit or I'll end it for you. And trust me, you won't like it if I have to do it." I stare my sister down. Blood or not, I'll take this bitch out to maintain my spot. She needs to believe that shit. "Now get the fuck out of my car."

Ta'Shara glances around. "But we're—"

"I *said* get the fuck out. You can think about what I said while you walk your ass home."

19
Melanie

"Think, Officer Johnson. Are you sure you can't remember anything else?" Lieutenant Maddow of Internal Affairs presses. He leans forward in his chair with his brows knitted together and his dark, troubled eyes begging me for any golden nugget that would help solve the murder of my partner, Officer O'Malley.

I lower and shake my head. "I'm sorry. Everything happened so fast. O'Malley took off running down the alley, and I got pinned down behind the patrol car. I took fire for at least a good minute before some punk hopped in behind the wheel and took off. By the time I rushed down the alley to see if I could assist my partner . . ." I let the sentence hang and opt to stare down at my interwoven hands and twirling thumbs.

"I think that's enough," my father, Captain Johnson, says, stepping forward and placing a supportive hand on my back. "She's been at this for hours. She's answered all our questions. I must insist that we end this now. Let her go home and get some rest."

Maddow looks as if he wants to refuse the request, but then finally glances at his watch. "All right." He draws a deep breath. "I'm going to recommend you take a seven-day leave of absence."

"I'm being punished?" I ask, looking from Maddow to my father.

"Not punished," Maddow clarifies. "Just think of it as a mini vacation. I would like the opportunity to talk with you further, say maybe tomorrow, after you get some rest. Plus, I'd recommend that you speak with Dr. Woods—"

"The police psychiatrist?"

My father squeezes my shoulder. "You might think you're fine now, but these sort of traumatic episodes have a way of sneaking up on you."

I suck in a deep breath but clamp down the protest that's seconds from falling from my lips.

"Trust me," my father continues. "I've seen officers too afraid to ask for help. They usually end up eating a bullet. I don't want to see my own little girl going down that same road."

I cut my father a look that wills him to shut the fuck up. The last thing I want is for him to start treating me like I'm some fragile china doll. I've worked too hard for my colleagues' respect, and I'm not about to let him just sweep all that away.

My father seems to have read my mind. He lowers his hand from my shoulders and steps back.

"Really, Lieutenant Maddow, I'm fine," I say.

"You probably are." Maddow smiles. "But I'm going to have to insist."

I stand, not quite sure how to feel about being forced

to take some time off. Right now I've been up for nearly thirty hours, and I can use some sleep. It wasn't too hard to stage O'Malley's murder, being that one of his victims lay right behind him. The scene just looks like the perpetrator had squeezed off a shot before he died. I couldn't have dreamed up a better opportunity to get rid of that loudmouthed, racist muthafucka. As far as I'm concerned, I did the department—and mankind—a huge favor.

By the time our backup had arrived at the crime scene, Python had removed the blue flags from his fallen soldiers, promised that he would catch up with me later, and then took off into the night. There was nothing wrong in letting Python think that I'd dusted off O'Malley for him—because I would've had he asked. In fact, there is very little that I wouldn't do for him.

For twelve hours, I told my version of what had happened behind Goodson's Auto Shop. I'm certain the extensive questioning isn't because they doubt my account of what transpired, but because the department takes extra precaution to dot i's and cross t's whenever a cop is killed in the line of duty. In this case, the department had lost *two* cops in one night, and I had been on the scene for both of them. Add to that the horrendous shooting at the Med and now half the squad responding to a shooting over at Morris High School, it is no wonder the department is anticipating a public backlash about the growing violence in the city.

"I guess that's that," I say, eyeing my superiors and hesitating before walking out of the office. "You know how and where to reach me if you have any more questions."

"I'll walk you out to your car," my father says, placing his large captain's hat onto his head and then opening the office door. "After you."

I draw a deep breath and then march out of the office. As I thread my way through the precinct, a few officers who were on desk duty or processing perps toss a few sympathetic and supportive glances my way. I give most of them a slight nod but for the most part keep it moving—especially since my father is pulling up the rear.

Outside, I open the door to my red Ford Explorer and climb inside.

"Now, are you sure you're all right?" my father asks, trying to catch my darting gaze.

"Yes, Dad." I hedge a bit. "Or at least I will be," I add so I can look more shaken up about O'Malley's death.

Silently, he shuts the door and then leans against it as if he's waiting for something.

I try to ignore his penetrating stare by hurrying up and starting the car, but when he doesn't back away from the door, I have no choice but to meet his inquisitive stare. It's a mistake, because he immediately starts trying to read me like he used to when I was a kid.

"What aren't you telling us?" he asks bluntly.

My heart drops. "What are you talking about?"

He leans in close, as if he's afraid someone might overhear us. "Is someone threatening you? Do you feel safe to go home?"

I blink, not sure what to make of the question or even how to respond.

"I know you, baby girl. I know when you're not telling me everything," he says. "You say the word and I'll wrangle up a couple of officers to stake out your place and—"

"That's not necessary." I shake my head. "I'm good," I insist, and finally pull my gaze away.

However, my father keeps staring at me with his weight pressed against the door.

"I gotta go, Dad," I say, needing to end this standoff

before I do something stupid like start confessing all my sins. "I really need to hit the sack."

He nods but is slow to step away from the car. "I have a press conference to get to. Your mother and I will keep Christopher as long as you need us to. You get your rest. I'll swing by and check on you tomorrow."

Great. "Thanks. I appreciate that."

He pats the car door and finally backs away.

I waste no time shifting the vehicle into reverse and backing out of the parking space. Even as I pull off, I can still feel my father's heavy gaze following me until I disappear out of the precinct's parking lot. It's another ten minutes before my heart stops trying to pound its way out of my chest and I can release my death grip on the steering wheel.

My history with Python is long and secretive. We attended Morris High School together, at least until Python dropped out in his junior year. It wasn't love at first sight or anything. In fact, Python teased and picked on me mercilessly because of who my father was—and the fact that he was always in the paper for busting a lot of his homeboys on the block.

I rebelled at being viewed as a square, so I set out to prove that I was as down as the next chick. I drank, smoked, and partied harder than any of my friends. At home, I stole, lied, and just flat out made my teenage years a living hell for my parents, all for the sake of changing my image.

Much later, when I ran into Python at a block party that I'd snuck out to in my parents' car, he had no choice but to look at me differently. In just the one year since he had left school, I had filled out with enough tits and ass to make every nigga I walked past take notice. . . .

* * *

*Music was bumping all up and down Shotgun Row. I
never hung out that deep in Gangster Disciple territory,
because shit was known to pop off on the regular down
there. The minute I'd walked through Momma Peaches's
door, I caught a few people looking at me sideways, but
I kept it moving with my homegirl Shariffa.*

*In the middle of the living room, I spotted Momma
Peaches grinding all up on some young nigga like the
fucking rent was due in the morning. Niggas was clowning him, but he was letting the older woman have her
fun.*

*"Damn, girl. How you get all that ass in those
jeans?"*

*I glanced over my shoulder to see Python's best
friend, KyJuan, checking me out and licking his lips. I
rolled my eyes and laughed in his face.*

*"What the fuck so funny?" he asked with his chest all
swelled up.*

*"You," I say matter-of-factly. "Running the same
tired-ass line on every chick you come across."*

"Girl, I—"

"Please." I threw up my hand like a stop sign.

*KyJuan twisted up his face and raked me with a nasty
look. "Damn, girl. You rude as fuck. A nigga was just
tryna holler at you. I—"*

*"Hey, man. Fall back." Python's deep baritone floated
into the conversation. "I got this."*

*"Man, if you can thaw this frosty bitch out, you're a
good one." KyJuan tossed his hands up and then quickly
turned his attention to the next girl with a fat ass. "Yo,
shawty, what your name is?"*

*I whip my head back around. One look into Python's
hard, menacing face and my stomach started fluttering
like a muthafucka. A lot of bitches were afraid of Python.
They thought he was a bit hard on the eyes, and his love*

for snakes freaked them out, but not me. Everything about him turned me on, and I had a sneaking suspicion that he knew it.

"*Now what the fuck is supercop's little girl doin' hanging out in the hood after dark?*" *he asked, inching so close to me that I was sure he could hear my heart beating.*

After anticipating this moment for what seemed like forever, I was horrified when I couldn't actually bring myself to say anything now that I was standing in front of my secret crush.

He smiled and then took his time, looking me over. "You sure have filled out in all the right places since the last time I saw you." He reached out and boldly gripped my thick ass. "Must be eatin' a lot of red beans and rice, girl."

There were a couple of things I should've done at that moment: slapped his hand away or cussed him the fuck out. Instead, I stood there and blushed like the naïve schoolgirl I was.

Cocky, Python squeezed my shit a little tighter and then pulled me along his hard body so that I could feel his cock press against the bottom of my pussy. "You feel me, lil ma?"

I swallowed and bobbed my head.

"*Good, because I'm definitely feeling you.*"

At that moment, nothing and no one else existed in that house. Python was every good girl's fantasy: dangerous, mysterious, and powerful. For the rest of the night, I trailed behind him, sitting on his lap, laughing at his jokes, and, much later, following him to his room.

"*What's the matter, Ma?*" *he asked when I was taking too long to remove my clothes. His shit was off in damn near two seconds after he'd closed the door.*

"*I don't know . . . I . . . I . . .*"

He cocked his head. "Don't fuckin' tell me that you've just been teasing my ass all night," he said, his voice hard as shit.

"No, um . . ."

His eyes narrowed. "Have you ever fucked a nigga before?"

"I . . . um . . ." I was torn between telling the truth and lying my ass off. I'd worked too hard to change my image just so I could fuck it up now.

"Shit." Python shook his head as he glanced around.

My hopes plummeted.

"What the fuck are you doing up here, lil girl?" He shook his head. "Do you have any idea how the fuck I get down?"

"I . . . I can learn."

"I ain't runnin' no school up in this bitch."

My eyes glossed with tears.

He sighed and moved toward me, his fat dick drawing my attention. I wasn't completely innocent; I'd given a couple of niggas head before, but that wasn't like real sex. I licked my lips. "C-can I touch it?" I didn't wait for an answer, because I was still scared that he was just seconds away from telling me to get the hell out of there. The moment I wrapped my hand around his dick, I felt a delicious thrill shoot through my body. "I know how to suck it."

Python eyed me curiously. My breath thinned in my lungs. I was excited and scared at the same time. But so far he hadn't kicked my virgin ass out—that was a good sign.

"So what's up, Ma? You down here hanging with the niggas 'cause you tryna piss your peoples off? You think your ass can handle a hood nigga like me?"

I nervously licked my lips. "I came here 'cause I wanted to be with you," I answered honestly.

"Why?"

"'Cause I've had a crush on you since the ninth grade."

"Get the fuck out of here."

My face fell and I quickly turned toward the door.

Laughing, Python grabbed me by the arm. "That's a muthafuckin' expression, Ms. Virgin," he said. "Shit, girl. Chill." He licked his fat lips and looked me over again as he stroked his own meat. "For real—ain't nobody busted up in you before?"

I shook my head.

One side of his mouth curled upward. "And you came all the way down to this muthafucka so I could be the first?"

I nodded.

The other side of his mouth curled. "Shit. I don't think I've ever had no virgin pussy." He stepped forward and slid his hand between my legs to grab hold of the seat of my jeans. "I might have to check the calendar to see if it's my fuckin' birthday."

I smiled with relief.

"Take that shit off," he ordered, and then moved over to his cluttered bed to watch me.

I never moved so fast in my life. My midriff T-shirt flew over my head, followed by my one and only Victoria's Secret push-up bra. Python stroked his dick and watched the rushed striptease with hungry eyes. When I was finished, he took his time studying my young body.

"Anybody ever eat you out before?"

The question completely embarrassed me.

"Never mind, you ain't even gotta answer that." He chuckled. "Come over here. I want you to sit on my face." With one sweep of his arm, he knocked a lot of shit off the bed and onto the floor.

This was it. I took a deep breath and waltzed over to

the bed. But then something wiggling caught my attention and I jumped. "What's that?" My eyes landed on an aquarium next to the bed.

"Those are my babies, Beauty and Beast. They're ball pythons," he said, and then reached for my hand. "I'll let you play with them later. Right now, I wanna taste some of this fresh pussy." He fingered the soft curls between my legs. "Now climb on up here."

I looked down at him lying on the bed and started getting nervous again.

"Matter of fact, since you know how to give head, just turn around and we can do a sixty-nine."

Good thing Shariffa and I had snuck and watched a few of her father's pornos so that I knew what the fuck he was talking about. I climbed up onto the bed like I was mounting a Clydesdale—he was just that massive. But in no time, I had my pussy hovering above his face. When I picked up his heavy dick, I was scared I was going to choke on the muthafucka. The head was the fattest I'd ever seen.

"You gonna play with it or suck it?" Python asked.

I forced myself to stop thinking and just started feeling. It helped when he parted my young pussy lips and plunged his tongue so deep it may as well have been like a second dick.

"Ooooh."

"I thought you might like that shit."

His tongue plunged back in and completely unglued my world. Wanting to return the favor, I deep-throated his big dick. Before I knew it, I was lost in a new world. I rocked on his tongue while gagging and slobbering on his dick at the same time. I lost count of how many times I came, but I stayed on my job until he blasted off and coated my throat with his sour candy. After that, he pulled me off and then rolled me underneath him. He

*surprised me when he started kissing so that we could
share each other's taste. His sour with my sweet.*

*My toes curled and his dick got hard again in no time.
The next time he spread my legs open, I knew that I was
just seconds from becoming a woman. I pulled back to
ask, "You got a condom?"*

*He frowned. "Nah. I gotta feel what I'm getting into,
Ma. And this some new shit, too. I'm taking it raw."*

I stared at him.

*"Don't worry, baby. I'm clean." He kissed me for re-
assurance. "I wouldn't fuck you up like that—especially
since you letting a nigga be the first." The head of his
cock pressed against my pussy.*

"I don't want to get pregnant," I say meekly.

*"Why not? You said you love me. If you love me, then
you can carry my seed."*

I didn't know about that shit.

*"What? Don't you think I'd take care of you and my
seed?" He inched in a little farther. "You might as well
have my baby, because once I get in this pussy, the shit
is mine. You won't be giving my shit to nobody else."
Python locked gazes with me. "You hear me? If I ever
hear word fuckin' one about you smashing some other
nigga, then it ain't going to be nothing nice. You feel
me?"*

*I couldn't help but smile. Being Python's woman was
all I'd ever dreamed about for the last three years. "I
feel you."*

*"Good." He reached down and spread my legs so
wide I thought his ass was tryna make a wish. "Here we go."*

*Before I could suck in a breath, Python surged for-
ward with one powerful thrust. My eyes bulged as I
gasped in shock. I knew it was supposed to hurt, but not
like this. Punching at his chest, I tried to get him to stop.
I'd changed my mind. I didn't want to do this anymore.*

*He ignored me and kept a steady, deep stroke going.
"Shhhh," he whispered against my ear. "Relax, baby
girl. It's going to feel good in just a second. I promise."
He kissed my temple and kept stroking.*

*Tears leaked from my eyes. I didn't believe him, but I
welcomed the small kisses he planted down the column
of my neck and across my collarbone. Slowly but surely,
the pain between my legs eased and pleasure like I've
never known bloomed like a flower. Next, I was grabbing
and squeezing his thick ass cheeks while he sent my
mind to the fuckin' moon. It felt better than good—it felt
like heaven. My first time couldn't have been more perfect . . . and nine months later, I delivered a healthy
nine-pound baby.*

So did two other chicks.

My single-family ranch home sits in the middle of a
thirty-year-old subdivision in the Walnut Grove section
of Memphis. I inherited the place from my maternal
grandmother around the same time I'd completed the
police academy. It's also nestled right between Gangster
Disciple and the Vice Lords territory—a helluva place
for a police officer to live, as my father keeps reminding
me. But I've always liked living on the edge—just like
I've always been attracted to dangerous men.

After parking my car in the garage, I enter the house
through the side door and throw my keys onto the
kitchen table. I'm exhausted. No doubt a shower and a
twelve-hour coma would do my body good. First, I stop
off at the refrigerator and grab a cold beer.

A sound catches my ear.

My hand automatically goes to my holstered weapon
as I set my beer down and start a slow creep through the
house. Lord knows it wouldn't be the first time some

dumb punk has tried to burglarize my place. As I move through the house, I'm certain the noise is coming from my bedroom. Quietly, I place my hand on the doorknob and push open the door.

No one is in the bedroom—but there's definitely someone in the adjoining bathroom. I smile as I return my gun to my holster. Walking over to the bed, I remove my belt and kick off my shoes. When I reach the bathroom door, there he is: my afternoon delight. I chuckle under my breath and fold my arms as I take my time drinking in Python's muscled frame through the shower's glass door. There isn't an inch on him that I haven't committed to memory, and there isn't a position he can bend or twist me into that I haven't enjoyed over the years.

"Are you just going to stand there all day, or are you going to get your ass in here and wash a nigga's back?"

"What are you doing here?"

"What does it look like? I'm taking a shower."

I roll my eyes. "You know what I mean. What if my man came home with me?"

"What fuckin' man is this?" Python stops washing his large chest to stare me down. "I know you ain't giving my pussy to nobody else."

"Are you fuckin' serious?" I ask incredulously. "I hardly fuckin' see your ass anymore. You're too damn busy with your head up those silly Queen Gs' twats to give me the muthafuckin' time of day."

Python opens the glass door and pulls me inside. "Why the fuck are you giving me a hard time, girl?"

I squeal. "My uniform!"

"Like I give a fuck about this pig uniform." Python rips open my shirt. "Who the fuck you giving my pussy to?" He tosses the drenched shirt over the top of the glass door and then attacks the button on my pants. "You better tell me that you're fuckin' joking, 'cause I ain't had any of this good shit in a hot minute." He pulls me closer and smothers my full lips with a passionate kiss. I really get wet sucking on his sexy forked tongue and remembering what that muthafucka feels like drumming on my pussy.

Every fiber of my being tells me to fight this shit, but when it comes to Python, for some reason I just can't do it. He's always had a way of making my body feel things it shouldn't. The nigga has a string of women, and yet he always expects my ass to just sit on the sidelines, waiting with my legs crossed until whenever he feels like rolling through to hit me off.

In truth, I wasn't playing. I have my own sideline situation going on, but what Python doesn't know isn't going to hurt him. Niggas always think they're the only ones who know how to creep. Silly rabbits, tricks are for kids.

Right now, I'm just going with the flow, too thrilled that his ass has finally decided to drop in after a long absence. In our ever-changing relationship, the older we get, the harder it is to hold on. As much as I still loved his ass, it fucked with me on the daily that his dick was like a GPS—always on the creep for new pussy. Nowadays, niggas can't spell *faithful* let alone try to be faithful to no one chick. So at the end of the day, I'm no different than all these other baby mommas. I just carry a muthafuckin' badge.

My son, Christopher, now has so many brothers and sisters that I've lost count. When I found out about the other two women when I was pregnant, I broke up with Python for three years, in which time I graduated from school and then joined the police academy.

Some time after that, I'd pulled Python over for a routine stop, but instead of handing him a ticket, I turned up my ass and let him hit it from behind on the side of the road. My three-year celibacy streak was over with a snap, and then we pretty much been together off and on ever since.

We slosh around in the shower until Python manages to get all my clothes off; then he leans me up against the white tile and bounces me on that juicy dick. His shit is so good I get religious and start talking in tongues.

Python fists my hair and slams into me so hard that the wall of my pussy starts caving in. "You been giving other niggas my pussy?"

"No. N-never," I lie, and rotate my hips so that he's hitting my G-spot from the front *and* the back.

"This shit is always going to be mine." He reaches around and fingers my clit just how I like it. "You hear me, baby?"

"Yes, baby." I squeeze my nipples and then prepare to blast off. A couple more deep strokes and that's just what the fuck happens. I call the Father, the Son, and the Holy Ghost while my orgasms just keep coming. We go from the shower to the bed and then onto the floor. Python always knows how to fine-tune my body just right. I hate it because he's no good for me. Never has been, never will be. But neither my head nor my pussy wants to hear that shit.

When we're both sated and lying in each other's arms, Python lazily peppers the top of my head with kisses. "About last night," he starts. "Thanks for coming through for your nigga. I love you for that shit, yo."

I tilt my chin up. "Why don't you get out of the street game?"

"Why don't you quit being a cop?"

And here we are, back to the same old stalemate.

"I would've married you, you know," he tosses out there.

I roll my eyes. "Sure you would've."

"I still might one day," he adds, rolling me over and sinking his fingers in between the silky folds of my pussy. "In this crazy world, anything can happen." He plops one of my hard nipples into his mouth and starts sucking.

I know that he's just gassing me up, but my heart falls for his bullshit each and every time. Just like it's doing right now.

20
Yolanda

December . . .

For three months, I've been sliding down poles, contorting my body in every way imaginable and booty clapping my way into the hearts and minds of every nigga who walks through the door of the Pink Monkey. But Baby was right—bitches aren't stacking no eight hundred dollars a night. On the weekends I might make half that much, but that is a serious might. The only way some of those cheap bastards can make it rain up in here is by tossing they Laundromat quarters onto the stage, but that's Memphis niggas for you. They always want a whole lot of something for nothing. A couple of times, a few niggas who remember me from back in the day have tossed mini-packets of Lemonheads onto the stage, but I just ignore their ignorant asses because they still the ones up in here begging for some damn pussy.

Now, *Baby* knows how to make it storm. There's no

shame to her game when she rolls through the club with a fat-ass knot, smoking her la and sippin' on rum and Coke. Once the other dancers peep out how much Baby tosses on the stage, they focus their attention on her. Niggas are pissed every time they see her step through the door, but they sure as fuck don't say shit to her crazy ass. My girl is like my own personal cheerleading squad. At home, Baby helps me create and coordinate my routines. Now I look like I was born doing this shit.

But at least I'm having fun—more than I anticipated. I'm loving the attention I'm getting from men. Nothing gets me off more than watching how these niggas' dicks bust out of their pants like the Incredible Hulk whenever I'm grinding on they laps. As usual, bitches are hating on me, but I'm starting to listen to Baby.

"Bitches hate. That's what the fuck they do," Baby told me over and over again.

The more I look around, the more I find that shit to be true. However, I still want to move up in the Queen Gs. If bitches are going to hate, then hate me while I'm on top. You feel me?

At the Pink Monkey there are always chief enforcers, assistant overseers, and governors who drift through. The girls are expected to service them, pay or no pay, in the VIP room with no questions asked. That shit isn't right because niggas be trying to raw dog it and rip the lining out of a bitch's pussy.

I complained to Baby, but her answer was just a simple "Quit." I should've known better. Baby didn't care too much for a bunch of whining and complaining. "Don't talk about it. Be about it."

So I stopped talking about it, until Desire raced back into the dressing room.

"Yo-Yo, move your ass! You're wanted in the VIP room."

"Fuck that shit. My shift is over," I say, grabbing my bag.

Desire shuffles over to her vanity table. "It ain't a request. Python sent for you."

I freeze and cut eyes over at this bitch. She ain't fooling nobody. I know she can't stand my ass. "You shittin' me?"

"Bitch, I ain't got no time to be playing games with you. Python ordered you back there, and you can be a dumb bitch and not go if you wanna, but then I suggest you don't bring your ass back here thinking you still got a job."

Now that I know she's for real, I grab my favorite gold metallic thong and two gold pasties with hanging tassels, slick my body down with some baby oil, and then shove my feet into a pair of matching six-inch heels.

"You're really going back there?" Baby asks, watching me check myself out in the mirror.

"Of course I am. You know when I lock one of these big hustlers down, I'ma be able to upgrade and have a father figure for my babies when they come home."

"*If* they come home."

"C'mon, now, Baby. Don't be like that. You know what the game plan is."

Baby frowns. "Your momma dropped you on your head when you were a child. You know that, right?"

I roll my eyes. "Ha-ha. It's going to happen, and when it does, I'm going to dance around and sing 'I told you so!' "

"Whatever, bitch." Baby strokes her imaginary dick.

Satisfied that I'm ready, I flash Baby a smile. "Wish me luck."

"No," Baby says in a flat voice. "I'll do no such thing."

I shrug off Baby's disapproval and hurry out to the VIP room. But Python isn't the only one waiting for me. It was him, a nigga named Tyga, and McGriff. I didn't have to be Einstein to know that I'm the entertainment for an important meeting. For a second, I'm power struck, wondering who I should dance for first when the decision is made for me.

"Damn, girl," McGriff says, turning his attention from Python. "Don't just stand there. Get over here and give me a sample of that mean head game niggas been bragging about." He unzips his fly and surprises me with a dick that has to be the same size as a school ruler.

Fat too.

No wonder his girl, Kookie, be walking bowlegged.

Three sets of eyes shift to me, waiting to see what I'm gone do. It's the audition of a lifetime. I put on my biggest smile and wind my hips. I move closer to the table and then kneel down and suck his shit into my mouth like my middle name is Hoover.

"Fuck!" McGriff says, sliding his hand down my blond braids. "They weren't lying about your ass." He cocks his head and watches as my full lips suck and slobber all over his peanut butter–colored dick.

Tyga reaches down into his pants and pulls out his dick. What he lacks in length he makes up for in width. His shit is so fat it looks like a mini tree trunk while he strokes himself during my performance. "So whatcha thinking, Python?" Tyga asks, returning to business. "You think that grimy nigga Fat Ace is dead or what?"

Python shrugs and reaches for his beer. "Fuck if I know. Ain't nobody seen his ass since we put a couple of bullets in him that night at the hospital."

"Nah. That nigga ain't dead," McGriff chimes in, thrusting his hips and hitting my tonsils' bull's-eye. "We would've heard something by now. I'm—Whoa!" He leans his head back as I take his dick all the way to the balls, hold still, and squeeze my throat muscles. "Goddamn, bitch. Shit!"

I gag and choke while tears pour down my face, but I hold firm.

"FUUUUCK!" McGriff blasts off and my throat releases its grip so that I can gulp down his salty babies with a smile. "Whoo!" He looks over at Python. "You better hold on to this one. Bitch, where you learn to suck dick like that?"

I shrug. "My stepdaddy."

The niggas' faces twist, but then McGriff laughs. "Well, fuck. He did a great job."

"Will you focus, nigga?" Python says, irritated. "I don't like all this hide-and-seek bullshit with Fat Ace. The muthafucka appears and disappears like a ghost. That shit ain't sitting right with me."

"C'mon over here," Tyga says, reaching for me and jamming my head down onto his cock. "Don't worry about that big nigga, Python. We'll find him again."

"What about this brother, Profit?" Python asks. "Y'all still watching his ass?"

"Got him covered like Allstate," McGriff says, leaning forward to pull on my thong and take a peek at my ass while I'm bobbing on Tyga's cock. "But for real I think that nigga Profit is a square. The soldiers we got on him say that the muthafucka ain't in the game. He just goes to school and creeps around with his girlfriend."

"I don't give a fuck if he's in the game or not. He's collateral."

"So what you sayin'?" McGriff slides a finger into my pussy. "You want us to wet this dude up?"

Python sips on his beer and watches as McGriff slips another finger into my dripping pussy. He looks like he's in a trance before he finally answers, "I don't know. Let me think on it a little while. Who's his girl-friend?"

"Some chick out in midtown. We know the address. I can get you a name if you want it."

"See that you do." He catches the waitress's eye and signals for another beer.

Tyga starts sweating and squirming in his chair. "Sheeiiit."

"She gettin' it, ain't she?" McGriff laughs and gets up. "Stand up, baby."

I stand but remain stooped over with my mouth locked around Tyga's cock. I'm determined to suck this muthafucka's white taffy out before I give McGriff any more attention.

"I hope this pussy is as good as that fuckin' mouth of yours," McGriff says, spreading my ass cheeks and hawking a wad of spit at the back of my pussy for extra lube. Next, he straps on a magnum condom. I'm relieved he's not going to raw dog it. Before he enters me from behind, he leans down and places a kiss on my perfectly round ass. "Python, you sure you don't want to hit none of this?"

"Nah, nigga. Handle your bidness."

"Whateva, man. Pussy is pussy." McGriff holds on to my waist and slowly slides the head of his cock in between the walls of my creaming pussy. "Aww. Fuck yeah. You gotta keep this bitch around, Python."

"No doubt," Tyga cosigns.

"Glad you're enjoying her." Python smirks and accepts his second beer when the waitress returns. "What about that other shit? You checked out that nigga from up north? Is his shit legit?"

"Ooh." Tyga's eyes roll for a brief second before he answers the question. "Yeah. That nigga, Dmitry, is cool.

I've talked to a coupla niggas in Brooklyn who fuck with him. Nigga always comes through."

Python's eyes flash with irritation. He probably doesn't like Tyga tossing around names in front of mixed company. "So you're vouching for this nigga?"

"P-put my name on it. Fuck, this bitch is gonna make me fall in love." Tyga grabs hold of my head and holds me down to gag and slobber all over his shit as he blasts a couple of ounces down my throat. My mouth finally springs off Tyga's dick when McGriff sinks his long cock inside me from the back. I can feel the muthafucka all the way up in my chest.

"I know that you're loving this shit," McGriff brags, rotating his hips and beating up my walls.

I glance back over my shoulder. "Give me all you got." I slam my ass down harder on his shaft.

Python's brows lift with renewed interest. *Ah. He's an ass man.* I got his fuckin' number now. Python has seen his boy with other women in the VIP before, but none of them could take in more than just half his nigga's size. Now my big booty ass is backing all the way to the balls. I know they are all impressed.

A medieval grin covers McGriff's face as he takes my sassiness as a challenge. In the next second, he slings his dick so hard that I'm sure he's splitting me in half, but I continue to moan and throw my ass back like a cock addict. When I'm close to passing out, Tyga gets back into the mix. They toss me around like a rag doll. At one point, I have my leg locked around McGriff's waist while he digs out my pussy and Tyga's thick cock rams my tight asshole.

"Goddamn, you can take it all, can't you, you nasty bitch?" McGriff growls while he and Tyga bounce me up and down. "Your stepdaddy teach you this shit, too?"

At the table, Python watches the show while lazily rubbing his meat. I'm giving his boys just as much as I'm getting. I just want him to know that my little show is all for him. At every chance I can get, I lock gazes with him while one or both of his boys are beating my shit up. I'd welcome a full-out train if it meant I can get in good with Python. When he takes a woman, he brands her as his and then declares her off limits. Seeing how I get down, he has to be thinking I have potential.

Tyga roars and whips his cock out.

Python's black gaze zeroes in on the thick cum dripping out of my beautiful, golden ass. Yeah, it's just a matter of time before I'm doing a private show just for him, and he crowns *me* as the leader of the Queen Gs.

21
Ta'Shara

The police had been sweating Profit for months. But after a while, they had to fall back to their regularly scheduled program. He still had a court date for the illegal firearm, but he and his people seem to think that he'll be able to beat that charge. He had contradicted my story to the police by taking full responsibility for the weapon. The witness in the hospital lobby stuck to his story that Profit was actually a hero that night and saved his life, so that's a good thing in his favor. The main solid Profit is doing is not ratting to the cops where he got the gun. The muthafucka is clearly hot, since the serial number is filed off, but the ballistic reports couldn't place it at that shooting in Orange Mound.

Essence been sweating bullets and blowing up my phone every chance she gets. I understand. The last thing E wants to explain to the Gangster Disciples and the Queen Gs is how and why Fat Ace's little brother got hold her shit and mowed down members of their own set. I keep telling her to be cool, but the bitch is like a little Chihuahua and wrecking my nerves.

Profit will never do her dirty, and on that she's just going to have to trust me.

Meanwhile, the streets are still hot, and Fat Ace is still a wanted man with the Gangster Disciples. Niggas are now speculating that Fat Ace has nine lives, since he survived the five slugs he took at the hospital. The Vice Lords are resourceful if nothing else. Fat Ace's right-hand chick, Lucifer, pulled some real gangsta shit and saved Ace's life.

What makes me nervous is that Profit sounds more and more like he wants to finally clique up with the Vice Lords. Shit. I think he's done it already and is just looking for the best way to let me in on the program. It ain't like I don't understand. There's no such thing as a free agent in the street game. Everybody needs someone to watch they back. And when you have family as powerful as Fat Ace, it doesn't take a rocket scientist to figure out what's coming.

I just want him to lie to me just a little longer.

Profit glances up at me. "I love you."

My head springs up from the library book propped open on the table in front of me, and I stop playing footsie with him under the table. "Shhh." I glance around and giggle. "Someone might hear you."

"Like I give a fuck." His sexy lips stretch across his face as he leans forward and braids our hands together. For the last two months, I've been grounded. The Douglases have only allowed me to go to school, track, and the public library. Embarrassingly enough, Tracee drives me there and picks me up, ensuring that I'm exactly where I'm supposed to be. I ain't going to lie. The trust bond between me and the Douglases has seriously been severed, and I'm afraid that it will never be repaired. But I'm going to try, minding my p's and q's, like Profit likes to say—except that I do sneak him into my room and make love to him late at night. I can't help it. I love him. And I will always love him. I've never been more sure about anything in my entire life.

"Besides," Profit continues with our conversation. "The fact that you got me up in this muthafucka with all these bullshit books should tell everyone just how pussy-whipped I am."

"Pussy-whipped?" I arch a brow at him. "Most niggas wouldn't admit that shit." I laugh.

"No other nigga has what I have." He rubs his leg against mine. "And they never will." Profit levels me with a look that says he means business.

"You just keep on loving me the way you do and you'll never have anything to worry about," I sass.

He rocks his chin upward. "C'mere, you."

Self-conscious, I glance around the busy library, even though it's highly unlikely anyone we know is roaming around—that's why it's such an idyllic place to meet. At school, the tension between the various gangs has gotten worse, to the point the school board has voted to have security guards with metal-detector wands stationed at the doors.

Nobody snitched about the bloody fight between me and Qiana. I was spared having to see that nosy bitch again, because she never returned to school. Still, the hood vine buzzed. Nobody knew how to take or handle me and Profit officially coming out as a couple, so everybody fell back and watched from the sidelines.

"I'm waiting," Profit says.

Hands still locked together, I stand from my chair, lean over the table, and plant a fat kiss against his soft lips. We moan at the same time.

"Mmm. You taste like strawberry Bubble Yum," Profit says, pulling me back a bit but sucking on my bottom lip. "My favorite." Suddenly he releases my hands, hooks his arm around my waist, and pulls me across the table.

I squeal, causing everyone in the library to turn with their fingers pressed against their lips, shushing us.

Profit shoots them his middle finger while I giggle until he successfully pulls me into his lap and I almost piss in my pants. "Your shoulder!"

"My shoulder is fine. Just stiff," he says. "Now, you said you had something that you wanted to ask me," he says, snuggling my neck. "What is it?"

My heart flutters as I take a deep breath. "Well . . ."

"Well, what?" He lifts his head. "Are you blushing?"

"No."

Profit laughs. "Yes, you are." He smacks me on the ass. "What is it? Spit it out."

I twirl a lock of hair around my finger as if I'm shy all of a sudden. "Well, you know that the, um, prom is coming up?"

Profit's brows shoot up. "The prom?" He rolls his eyes. "Sheeiit."

"Yeah. I know it's silly but . . ." I draw a deep breath. "Well, you know . . ." I shrug and avoid his twinkling eyes.

"You're right. It *is* silly." He laughs.

I stop twirling my hair and drop my head in disappointment.

"*But*," he continues. "if my baby really wants to go, then . . . I guess I can turn this hustler into a G—for one night."

I perk up. "Really? You mean it?"

"Look at you." He grins. "You really want to do this?"

"It would be nice to get all dressed up," I say. "I'll be off punishment by then."

"What happened about not wanting everyone to know about us?"

"C'mon. Everybody already knows so . . . why not?"

Profit eyes me curiously. "Look. I'm cool with it . . . but what about your sister?"

My smile fades and my back stiffens. By no means have I forgotten my last talk, or rather lecture, with my older sister. How could I? I'm still pissed about it. "It's time I remind my sister that she doesn't run my life. I do what I want to do." I wrap my arms around Profit's neck. "And I date who I want to date."

And I mean that shit. I've had enough of LeShelle's bullshit. It's my life, and I'll live and love the way I see fit.

Profit's sexy smile widens. "I think you made that shit clear when you sliced Qiana's ass up," he jokes. "I'm beginning to think that underneath that honor-roll, good-girl persona beats the heart of a real gangsta bitch."

I take that as a compliment. "You think so?" I kiss the tip of his nose.

"Absolutely. Now we just need to come up with a street name for you and you'll be good to go. Something like, um, Lady Blade or Killa Blade—because ain't nobody going to forget that crazy shit you did to Qiana's face anytime soon."

"Shit. You're the muthafucka who taught me that shit."

"A teacher is as good as his student." He pimps his collar.

"Whatever, nigga." I roll my eyes and attempt to climb out of his lap.

"Wait. Wait." He keeps me locked in place. "So we're really gonna do this?" he checks. "I'm going to get a penguin suit and you're going to get all girlied up?"

"That's the plan." I almost can't believe I'm saying this shit myself.

"Limo? Corsage? Officially meeting your foster parents instead of listening to them from underneath your bed?"

"Yep."

Profit coughs and clears his throat. "And, uh, what about what normally happens afterward?" His lips kick upward.

Grinning, I remove my arms from around his neck and fold them beneath my breasts. "What? We're already—"

"Not in a fancy hotel," he cuts me off. "Not that I'm knocking your twin-size bed—it's kinky and all—but a tall brotha like myself could use a little more room."

"So you propose . . . ?"

"The Peabody Hotel." He shrugs. "Might as well do it up right."

I pretend to think about his proposition for a hot second. "All right. Deal."

Profit nods. "Guess that means our asses is heading to the prom. Just wait until niggas hear about this."

22
Momma Peaches

"**Y**our old ass should be ashamed of yourself," Josie yells as she storms into my house without knocking. "Where he at?" Her head whips around. "Arzell!"

I sit a platter of flapjacks down on the table and then settle my hands on my hips. "Will you stop all that hollering up in here? What's your problem?"

Josie swishes her wide hips over to the table. Time has not been all that kind to her face and body. Her once Pam Grier–like brick-house figure now looks like a brick wall, complete with elephant legs and doughy feet spilling out of orthopedic shoes. Her once-idolized long hair has lost the war against chemical perms and harsh dyes to the point her edges are as bald as a baby's bottom while the rest is a thin, gray, natural mess.

"My problem," Josie says, getting all up in my face,

"is my coming home from visiting my daughter out in California and hearing that you got your old-ass pussy all up on my grandson. What the fuck is wrong with you? You ain't supposed to do no shit like that."

I cut my eyes. "Girl, please. That nigga may be young, but he's good and grown. And I ain't heard no complaints, especially when he's tongue-boxing my clit. That's for damn sure." I laugh, shake my ass, and then return to the kitchen to get some syrup.

"This is a muthafuckin' joke to you, ain't it?" Josie follows me, huffing and wheezing the whole way. "That some foul shit, Peaches. You used to change that boy's diapers!"

"Chile, stop. Don't be tryna turn this into something it ain't. Like I said, the boy is grown and he can leave any damn time he gets ready. Until then, I'm going to ride your grandson's dick, because it keeps my back straight and my arthritis at bay."

On cue, Arzell shuffles up, naked, from the back of the house with a wide, goofy smile on his face and his fat sausage dick swinging in the air. "Hmmm. Something smells good," he declares, clapping his hands together. When he rounds the corner to the kitchen, he stops dead in his tracks. "Grandma, what are doing here?"

Josie gasps and clutches a hand over her heart. "Lawd, have mercy!"

I snicker. "Now you see why I fucks with him, don't you?"

"Go! Put! Some! Clothes! On!" Josie stomps her foot.

"Yes, ma'am." Stunned and embarrassed, Arzell turns and rushes out of the kitchen.

"Breakfast will be ready when you come out," I add, and cock my head to the side as I watch his firm ass muscles flex as he hurries out. "Sweet Jesus. You got some good genes running in your family. You hungry, girl?" I grab the syrup and butter and waltz back out to the table.

"I'm not playing with you, Peaches." Josie marches behind me again. "You've crossed a line. This shit ain't cool."

I set everything on the table and then retrieve my cigar box, where I keep the rolled weed that Baby Thug had hooked me up with. The shit is off the fuckin' chain. "For real, Josie? You're working my nerves. As many of my niggas you done fucked back in the day, you might as well charge Junior back there to the game."

"W-what?"

"Don't act all fuckin' tongue-tied now and spare me the shocked bullshit." I light my fat blunt and take a hard tug before blowing the smoke directly in Josie's face. "Now, if I made you think my ass was stupid all those years when you were creeping behind me and fucking all my leftovers, then my bad. But for real, most of that shit never bothered me. There are too many bitches going to war over these niggas, who are just going to dick us over anyway."

Josie blinks at me. "But he's my *grandson*."

"All that's important is that he ain't *my* grandson." I take a second toke and then pass the blunt over.

"Why can't you fuck somebody your own age? Shit. You got Rufus milling outside your door like a lost cat. Why don't you fuck him?"

"You fuck him. Why ride a colt when I can rock a stallion? Here." I thrust the blunt at her again.

Josie glances down as if she's thinking about refusing my peace offering. "You know I done stopped smokin' that shit."

"Girl, I ain't offering it again, and you know you need this shit to help you with your glaucoma or whatever else you got going on. Stop being so high and mighty just because you hollering in somebody's church nowadays."

Josie hesitates another second and then snatches the blunt from my hand and sucks on the muthafucka so long that I'm convinced she's trying to inhale the whole thing in one toke. I think about telling her that the shit is laced with some secret, potent shit, but I decide against it. Considering how old girl rolled up in my place trying to throw her weight around, she's getting just what's coming to her.

"Damn," Josie croaks, passing the blunt back and holding the smoke in her lungs. "What the fuck?"

"Some good shit, huh?"

Josie wobbles on her feet. "Fuck. I need to sit down."

I hide my smile but direct old girl back over to the table. "I'll grab you a plate." I disappear into the kitchen, and when I return, I get a good chuckle out of seeing Josie's round head lull around her shoulders like a bottle top.

"What the hell is in that shit?"

"Don't know. Baby Thug didn't tell me," I say. "All I know is that the shit is good." I reach over to the platter of flapjacks and fork a few onto her plate.

Josie shakes her head.

"What?" I ask.

"You'll never change." She grabs a couple flapjacks herself. "You always eat this shit after sex." Josie giggles and then catches herself. "That shit ain't funny."

"Then why the fuck are you laughing?" I know my girl is fucked up. I am, too. Despite all this bullshit, she's still one of my best friends.

"For the record, I wasn't *always* running up after your leftovers." Josie shrugs. "It just happened the one time."

"Yeah. But it was with my husband . . ."

* * *

Black Gangster Disciple Isaac Goodson was a mean muthafucka by way of Chicago. The minute he rolled into Memphis, supercop Melvin Johnson had him well within his sights and tried to take his ass down on the regular. But Isaac kept his shit tight and was always two steps ahead. The migration of national gangs was changing the game fast. Crack may have been destroying families and lives, but it was also fattening niggas' pockets like nothing anyone had ever seen in the projects. Isaac not only had mad connections that kept his niggas caked up, but the nigga also must have had an inside man in the military with the amount and types of guns he got his hands on.

When niggas saw how much weight Isaac was pushing and how he invested in the community, they all started looking up to him. Recruitment into the Black Disciples exploded. Everybody got educated into the Folks Nation quick, fast, and in a hurry. Isaac was all things to all his people. He kept niggas' pockets fat and stepped into the role as a father figure to a bunch of little niggas who never knew they daddies. And the women . . . sheeit. They lost they goddamn minds.

Isaac was thuggish fine: over six feet tall, bald headed with thick-ass muscles bulging on every part of his body and rumored to be rocking a Mandingo dick that put bitches to sleep. The minute I spotted his ass in his newly opened auto shop, my ass fell in love. Some real deep shit, too—like it was with Manny. Isaac talked big and did big things. He could outdrink a sailor and outsmoke a chimney, but he didn't personally fuck with the hard shit he was slinging to the weak and the trifling. He kept it hood with his mind on his money and his money on his mind twenty-four/seven.

Who the fuck wouldn't find that shit sexy as hell? And the feeling was mutual. When I waltzed through the door of that shop, he took one long look at me, smacked those fat, juicy lips of his together, and said, "I'm gonna marry you."

I was used to niggas talking shit, but for some reason I believed that muthafucka said what he meant and meant what he said. Isaac came at the right time, since I was stuck raising Terrell after Alice up and disappeared and Nana Maybelle had passed on. Terrell needed a father figure, and as far as I could tell, there was no better candidate than Isaac. Two days after we first laid eyes on each other, Isaac moved into my small place off Utah Avenue. A week later, we were married down at the courthouse. I had lost Nana's big crib due to back taxes, and I told myself that the move was just temporary until I stacked my money up—words to die by.

Terrell was used to niggas coming and going at my place, but he had never seen one of them move in and stay. He didn't like Isaac at first, didn't like having to share me all the time, and he didn't understand why he always had to do what this nigga was telling him to do.

Isaac was patient with the boy, always talking to him and trying to teach him shit. The biggest lesson came one day when four-year-old Terrell was out playing in the yard. All of a sudden, he was screaming his fool head off.

I was scared shitless and raced out of the house. Isaac, too, hustled from somewhere in the neighborhood when he heard the screams. However, when we found out what Terrell was screaming about, we were both pissed and relieved.

"Damn, lil man," Isaac said, approaching. "It ain't nothing but a snake."

Shocked, Terrell just stood there trembling as he

*watched the brown snake coil around a scrawny neigh-
borhood cat and begin choking the shit out of it.*

I moved forward to comfort my nephew, but Isaac
stopped me. He approached a trembling Terrell and
squatted down next to him.

"What you're seeing there, lil man, is a beautiful
thing. It's nature. All species feed off one another in
order to survive. Some are just more open and straight
to the point with their shit. A man should always respect
another's hustle." He draped an arm around Terrell's
tiny shoulders. "A real man learns to embrace and conquer his fears—whatever they may be. You understand?"

Terrell chanced a look over at Isaac and then slowly
nodded.

"Good." He stood up and removed his gun from his
waist. "What do you say we have a little something different for dinner tonight?" He smiled and then shot the
snake.

Terrell jumped.

Isaac patted him on the back. "Remember: all species
feed off one another—one way or another."

I smiled. I was convinced more than ever that I had
made the right decision marrying Isaac.

Six months later, I was still in love with Isaac's gangsta
ass, but the nigga definitely had a problem with keeping
his big dick in just one pussy. Every time I confronted
him on it, he would just respond with, "C'mon, Peach.
You know those bitches don't mean shit to me."

"So why do you keep fuckin' with them?"

"That's just it. I fucks with them." He'd wrap an arm
around my waist. "But I make looove to you, Momma."
Then he'd suck on my bottom lip, brush his big cock
against my pussy, and I would forgive and forget—until
the next time. Out of all the women my man fucked, the

one who hurt the most was Josie. True, she was going through a difficult time, she'd lost her husband in a fatal car accident, and she'd gotten hooked on crack shortly after. A lot of broke niggas who had been dying to fuck her since waaay back in the day now lined up to get they salads tossed or anything else they wanted for the low, low price of twenty dollars.

So why did Isaac want to dig Josie out when every muthafucka on the block was doing it? I could never get a straight answer on that shit, so I always suspected that Isaac's feelings were something deeper than just a casual fuck. The shit hurt, but I wasn't going to give up on my man over the shit—not yet anyway.

Around the same time I was fighting to keep my marriage together, I received a call from Alice. The girl had dodged a bullet after the botched robbery a few years back, because she convinced the police that she was just a customer who got caught up in the crosshairs. The police bought that shit because the security cameras in the place didn't work. Shortly after, with her crack addiction in full effect, Alice dropped Terrell off for me to babysit and never came back. Now she was calling and pleading for me and Terrell to come see her in the hospital.

The answer should have been a "hell no," but that old guilt landed hard on my shoulders again—or it never completely went away. The fact that my sister was fucked up in the head was my fault no matter how many times I tried to convince myself otherwise. So I loaded Terrell into the car and drove out to the hospital. It turned out that Alice's great emergency was that she had had another baby—a small wrinkly little thing who clearly had healthy lungs if nothing else.

"Heeey." Alice lifted a lazy smile when we walked into the room and then struggled to sit up. She looked like shit warmed over, and it was no surprise that Terrell

took to hiding behind my prosthetic leg. "Wow. He's so big now." Alice cheesed, cocking her head and trying to get a good look at her oldest son.

"Yeah. Children have the tendency to grow," I said sarcastically, and approached the small bed that my newest nephew wiggled and wailed from.

"Hey, Terrell. You want to come over here and say hello to Mommy?" Alice held open her painfully thin arms and pleaded silently with her watery brown eyes. She looked like she weighed about ninety pounds, and her matted hair clearly hadn't seen a brush, let alone some shampoo and water, in quite some time.

I glanced down and tried to push him forward. When he tried to push back, I bent down and whispered, "Remember what Isaac told you about fear?"

Terrell blinked and then glanced over at his mom.

"Go ahead. Go on." I gave him another gentle push, and he finally unrooted his legs and walked over to the hospital bed.

Alice lit up when she wrapped her arms around her son and rained kisses all over his upturned face. "Mommy has missed you sooo much." She squeezed him tight. "Have you been good for your aunt Maybelline? Huh? Have you been a good boy?"

I rolled my eyes at my sister's sudden maternal concern, but I wasn't in the mood to start a fight. "What's wrong with this little fella?" I asked. "He hasn't stopped crying since we walked into the room." I reached down and picked the runt up. "Awww. What's the matter?"

My new nephew just kicked and screamed as if someone were torturing him.

"Who knows what the hell is wrong with him," Alice said grumpily. "I don't think that he's shut up since the doctor smacked him on the ass."

I frowned at Alice. What the hell was with that tone? Alice went back to hugging and kissing on Terrell.

"Awww, lil man," *I said.* "It's gonna be all right." *I pressed a kiss against the boy's face and tried rocking him in my arms.* "Screaming and hollering is no way to spend a birthday," *I joked.* "Is your diaper wet?"

"No. And he ain't hungry either," *Alice groaned.* "He's been here six hours and he's already pissed at the world. Not that I blame him—I've been pissed about being here a long time myself." *She pressed another kiss against Terrell's head.* "You never cried like that when you were a baby," *she said.* "You were a good boy."

The hairs on the back of my neck stood up. My sister was getting at something.

"Can I hold him?" *Terrell asked, staring at his little brother.*

I smiled. "Of course you can, honey." *I walked over to the bed, still rocking the crying baby.* "Now, you have to be careful with him," *I warned.* "Hold out your arms."

Terrell turned from his mother and held open his arms to receive his baby brother.

"Okay. Here we go." *I gently transferred the baby into Terrell's outstretched arms.* "Careful." *I settled the baby in his arms and then watched something amazing happen: The baby stopped crying.*

Both Alice and I were stunned.

Terrell beamed a smile at his baby brother. "What's his name?"

"Mason," *Alice said, smiling.*

"Mason," *Terrell repeated, and then pressed a kiss against his brother's forehead. For our small dysfunctional family, it was the happiest we'd been in a long time.*

* * *

Arzell finally returns to the kitchen table fully dressed in black jeans and a fresh white T-shirt. "I hope y'all saved some food for me," he says, slapping and rubbing his hands together.

I snap out of my bittersweet memories and flash my young lover a bright smile. "You know I got you, boo." I wink and then cast my gaze over at Josie, whose disapproval has toned the fuck down with that good shit she is smoking.

"Let me get a hit of that, Grandma." Arzell reaches over and grabs the blunt from her hand.

"Now this is what I'm talking about." I wrap an arm around Josie and then Arzell and give them a big hug. "A family that smokes together stays together."

"Amen," Josie and Arzell testify. "Amen."

23

Yolanda

Things are really looking up for me. Not only is my money starting to stack, but also Python is showing up at more of my performances. He thinks he's being slick, but I've caught him peeping me out, so I make sure that I pop my ass just right and slither on the floor like one of his precious snakes to give him an idea of what I'm down for.

Baby Thug watches my shameless performance in the front row while tossing back one drink after another. Despite her disapproval of my working at the seedy club, Baby has yet to miss a single performance. After my private party in the VIP with McGriff and Tyga, she has to know I am on my way. My plan isn't looking so dumb now.

Baby isn't the only one in the set who has heard about me wildin' out in the VIP. Niggas from miles around have heard about how I handled two monstrous dicks at one time, and they are now all trying to get they dicks wet with me. They show up in droves, raining money like none of the other dancers have seen before. I am the sex freak of the moment, and I'm eating the shit up. See me, be me, bitches.

Now that Python is within my sights, I turn down the other offers for a private VIP show and just make bank off my new reputation by giving niggas a glimpse of my pretty pink monkey only when I'm working the pole. Hell, Baby is just as shook, watching me flash my pussy, as the other niggas strolling in from off the street. Her once-klutzy friend is now steadily building a fan base, and I am well on my way to making my dreams come true. If I can't get Python, maybe I'll cast my net on McGriff and snatch Kookie's man.

I crawl to McGriff's table with my thong buried deep into my round ass. I smile seductively as his gaze roams over my thick curves. McGriff is so turned on that he reaches down and squeezes his meat. I pop pussy in his face and watch this nigga go into a trance. Keeping my act going, I lick my lips and bury his head in between my breasts.

The club of niggas roar and applause. McGriff's sneaky ass latches his mouth over one of my fat nipples and sucks like a newborn trying to eat.

Jealousy kicks Baby hard in the gut. She clenches the glass in her hand so hard that the muthafucka shatters. Even then, she doesn't pull her gaze from the show I'm putting on.

McGriff reaches around and spreads my ass cheeks— wide. Niggas start getting out of their seats so they can get a better look at what my momma gave me.

"Oh my God. What happened?" the waitress asks Baby.

* * *

Until that moment, Baby didn't realize that she's still holding the broken glass and that she's bleeding all over the table. "Fuck!"

She leaps up and storms toward the bathroom in the back of the club. While she picks glass out of her palm at the sink, she tries not to let her imagination go wild about what is happening onstage, but the shit is hard. The best thing is just roll up out of there, but she can't get herself to do that either. Once she's sure she's gotten all the glass out of her hand, she runs cold water over it and wraps her blue bandana around the deep gash before heading back out into the club.

I see Baby just as my number is up, and I grab the last remaining dollars off the floor.

Baby stops at the bar. "Rum and Coke," she barks at the bartender.

Another waitress comes from the floor and puts in her orders.

"Hey, honey, what is that girl's name who was just on the stage?" a customer asks the waitress.

The waitress rolls her eyes. "Who? That blond bitch?" she asks, swiveling her neck. "Honey, you better stay away from that coochie. You might catch something your ass can't get rid of."

The old man at the bar laughs. "Sounds to me like somebody's been drinking the haterade."

"Hell, naw. I just know the silly bitch ain't nothing but a fuckin' retard from waaay back in the day. All her babies have different daddies, and up until a few months ago, every nigga on lockdown was digging her out for nose candy. Now she's up here rubbing that twat on anything that moves. Shit. We can't keep enough Clorox wipes in this bitch."

Baby's rage simmers but when it's clear that the

piece of shit waitress isn't about to shut the hell up, she quietly reaches over the counter and grabs a rum bottle. "SHUT THE FUCK UP!" Baby smashes the bottle against that slick-talking bitch's head and watches her ass hit the floor.

"WHOA! SHIT!" Niggas jump back, laughing.

"What, bitch?" Baby tosses up her hands and then stomps on the bitch. "You gonna act like your ass ain't got no damn kids? Huh?"

STOMP!

"You think you're so much better?"

STOMP!

"If I ever hear my girl's name come out your mouth again—"

STOMP!

"I will—"

STOMP!

"FUCK—"

STOMP!

"YOU—"

STOMP!

"UP!"

STOMP!

"Goddamn!" A man laughs, pointing at the whimpering waitress.

At long last, the club's two muscle-headed bouncers push and shove their way back to the bar. One grabs Baby around the waist, locking her arms at her side and then lifting her up like she weighs nothing.

"GET THE FUCK OFF OF ME!" Baby kicks and swings, trying to reach her gat, but the nigga who's manhandling her ain't playing that shit.

"I knew it was just a matter of time before your carpet-munching ass nut the fuck up," he growls.

"FUCK YOU, MUTHAFUCKA!"

The music keeps blaring and the chick on the stage isn't getting any love, because everyone's attention is focused on the drama Baby has stirred up. Some whoop and holler even though they don't know what the fuck is going on.

The moment the bouncer hip-bumps the exit door, Baby is airborne, and when she hits the concrete, she's sure the nigga's broke something because her leg hurts like a muthafucka. Still, she scrambles to get up, and when she does, the bouncers have two pistols aimed right at her head.

"I wouldn't even think about it, homey," Dwight, the meatier of the two ugly muthafuckas says. "You need to take your ass home and sleep that shit off."

Baby hesitates, at least long enough to allow reality and common sense to sink into her head. "A'ight, nigga. Whatever." She pinches the ridge between her eyes as if that will somehow stop the spinning that's going on in her head.

The bouncers lower their weapons. "Seriously, Baby, you need to consider yourself lucky, because I know for a fact Python was planning on firing that bitch at the end of her shift. If it wasn't for that, I would've been ordered to rock your ass to sleep out here. You don't take food out of a nigga's mouth. You feel me?"

"Yeah. Yeah." She pops a squat on the curb and hangs her head.

"Look, I'm gonna tell you like I tell all these other niggas—if you can't take watching your girl work these damn poles, then don't bring your ass 'round here."

"She's not my girl!" Baby shouts. "We're just . . . friends."

Dwight shakes his head. "Yeah, whatever." He and his boy turn back to go inside. "Y'all bitches carry on too much unnecessary drama." The door slams behind them.

Baby remains glued to the curb, shaking her head and fighting back tears. "We're just friends."

Backstage, I'm cheesing like a muthafucka while I stare at the six hundred dollars I've stacked for the night. The tides have turned, and I intend to ride this son of a bitch until the wheels fall off. The only thing I need to do now is save a little more and spend a lot less. With the money I've been pulling, I've been shopping at the white folks' mall out in German Town—not boosting like those bitches working for Momma Peaches, but buying the shit with cash money. I've traded in my synthetic braids for the real hair lace fronts like my idol Beyoncé. I've been upgrading my shit as fast as I was making it.

It's all good, because once I get my wardrobe tight, I'll work on getting my situation right. A new man, a new place, my own car, and then I'll file the papers to get my babies back. I put away my money and smile at my reflection. "I'm on the way up."

Desire storms back into our cramped dressing room and shoots me a hot look. "Girl, you need to get that baby dyke of yours under control."

I frown. "Who the fuck is you talking about?"

"Don't act stupid. You know exactly who the fuck I'm talking about: that diesel dyke who's been padding your pocket every night. She just busted up Aaliyah at the bar with a fuckin' rum bottle. Dwight and them just tossed her ass out of here."

"Baby?" I groan and reach for my jeans out of my duffel bag. "Fuck. What happened?"

"What? I look like Katie Couric to you? The bitch ruined my set, that's what happened." She holds up a small knot of dollars. "This shit ain't even enough to cover the gas it cost me to drive to this muthafucka tonight." Desire storms over to her bags in the corner. "I'm quitting this bitch. I got kids to feed and shit. I'm better off working at Popeye's."

I slam on a T-shirt, jam my feet into a pair of sneakers, and then race out the back exit, lugging my duffel bag. "Baby!" I glance around the parking lot as the back door slams behind me. Screeching tires catch my attention. I glance toward the main road just in time to see Baby's Impala jet out of the parking lot. "BABY!" I take off running and waving my hands. "BABY, COME BACK!"

I make it halfway across the parking lot and give up. Fuck this shit. My feet hurt. If Baby sees me clearly, she doesn't give a fuck. I stamp my foot and glance around. Baby was my ride home. It's two in the morning. Taking the city bus is definitely out of the question. Calling my mother will only result in me being cussed out, and taxis don't go down Shotgun Row. That leaves me with having to beg a ride from one of the other dancers. *Fucking great.*

I turn back toward the club while digging my cell phone out of my bag. Baby doesn't answer, and my call goes straight to voice mail. "What the hell, Baby? How could you just run out on me? Now how am I supposed to get home?" I huff out a long breath. "Call me back when you get this message." I disconnect the call and mutter another curse under my breath. The idea of Baby being upset doesn't sit well. It's one thing for us to talk shit every once in a while, but we have never truly been mad at each other before. I don't have other friends, so anxiety starts eating at me. What if I just lost my only friend? But what did I do wrong? Whatever it is, I want to fix it before it festers.

"What's wrong, Momma? You need a ride?"

I look up at a cluster of niggas spilling out of the club.

"Hey, that's that fine bitch who was grinding all up on McGriff," the shortest nigga of the group says, pointing. "The same one who got buck wild with that nigga and Tyga." He grabs his dick. "I *know* we can give you a ride to wherever the fuck you wanna go, shawty. Ain't that right?"

"Hell yeah!" The other four niggas cheese and lick their lips as their gazes rape my tight frame.

I shake my head and keep it moving. I don't know these niggas from the man on the moon, and I ain't so stupid that I'm going to get into a car with niggas I don't know.

"Hey, hey. Hold up, baby. I'm tryna holler at you."

I smile to myself but keep switching my hips as I walk away.

"Well, then, *fuck* you, bitch!"

"YEAH, FUCK YOU!" the niggas chorus as more niggas start coming out of the club, drunk as fuck and some singing off-key. A couple of brothers start walking up behind me—a little too close for comfort.

"Yo, baby. You looking for a date?"

"Get lost." I cut my gaze and bang on the back door.

"Now, why you got to be like that?" this sloppy, fat muthafucka who smells like corn chips says, stepping into my personal space. "A nigga is just tryna be nice to your fine ass." He reaches out and rubs a hand down my shoulder.

I pull back and bang on the door again.

"Now you're starting to piss me off." Corn Chip moves closer. "I'm like David Banner. You won't like me when I'm angry."

His sidekick snickers, sounding like a hyena. "True dat. True dat."

A siren blares and everybody turns to see an ambulance turning into the parking lot. "They must be coming for that waitress that one bitch clocked." Corn Chip chuckles to his partner. "That shit was out of control."

I pull and bang on the door again.

Corn Chip whips around, grabs my hand, and stands, tugging. "C'mon. Why don't you come and party with us?" He smiles and blows his funky breath down on me. "I guarantee you'll have a good time."

I try to pull my hand back, but his grip tightens.

"Damn, bitch. I ain't asking no more."

"Fuck naw. We ain't asking," his partner says.

The back door explodes open, and everybody jumps back when Python darkens the threshold. His black gaze swings around the small group. "What the fuck is going on back here?" His gaze sweeps my way. "Yo, these niggas friends of yours?"

I easily snatch my arm loose and rub my sore wrist. "Fuck naw."

"Whoa. Whoa, Python. Everythang is cool, man." Corn Chip and his buddies toss up their hands and look like they about ready to cry. "We were just hollering at your girl. No big deal."

Python glares at the men as if he can read straight through their bullshit. "You wanna talk to my girls, you go through me. Understand? Y'all niggas know how shit works around here."

"Yeah. Yeah. Our bad. We didn't mean no disrespect." Corn Chip starts backing away.

Python continues watching them until they turn and run off.

I sigh in relief and then coil Python a sly smile.

"Thanks. I don't know what I would've done if you hadn't opened the door."

Python nods, but he doesn't move from the door. He just takes his time, looking me over.

"My, um, ride seems to have left me stranded," I toss into the silence. "I guess I'll just have to hang around here a little longer."

Python finally shrugs his big shoulders. "Or I could give you a lift home."

My full lips bloom into a bright smile. I recognize an opportunity when I see it. "Thanks. I'd love a ride home."

24
Ta'Shara

"**Y**ou're going where?" Essence asks, staring and blinking at me like a deer caught in the headlights.

"I'm going to a party with Profit," I say, twirling around in front of my bedroom mirror. "And don't you dare rat me out to my parents. I told them we're going to the mall to shop for prom dresses."

Essence shakes her head and starts backing toward the door. "Nah. Nah. I don't want my name involved in none of this shit."

I glance up and see that she's serious. "E, don't punk out on me." I rush over and pull her back over to the bed. "I really, really need you."

"No. You need to get your head examined. Haven't you been in enough trouble as it is? I mean, damn, girl. Do you need a brick building to fall on your head?

You're going to a party where it's gonna be wall-to-wall Vice Lords *and* you asked that nigga to the prom?"

"Look, everybody knows we're together now. There's no reason for us to keep creeping. I'm Profit's woman. Now and forever. People need to start getting used to it."

"People meaning your sister?" Essence challenges.

"Especially my sister," I say. "It's past time for me to take a stand and live my life the way I want to live it. She made her choices, and now it's time that I make my own."

"Uh-huh. What happened to all those *other* dreams? You know, about becoming a doctor? You hardly come to school anymore, and when you do, you cut class. You got an F in biology this quarter. Damn. At least I got a D."

I don't want to hear none of this shit right now, and I can't believe that I have to beg my best friend to have my back right now. "Don't stress me, E. Tracee and Reggie have already done that."

She folds her arms and taps her foot like she my second mother or something. "And what did they say?"

"Are you for real?"

Essence just stares me down while her neck snakes like a cobra.

"I promised them that I'll get my grades up this quarter—and I will. Good Lord, it's like my first bad report card since I've been here. Cut me a break."

E is still shaking her head at me. "You're tripping, Ta'Shara. That nigga got you straight sprung, and you ain't thinking clearly no more. You used to know how this shit works. You used to know how many niggas have been dropped because of fucked-up street politics. It doesn't matter that you're not in the game. It doesn't matter that Profit's not in the game. You're both fuckin' pawns because of blood. GD versus VL. That shit don't mix."

"Pawns?"

"Yes, pawns, bitch. I know a thing or two about chess. And I know enough to know that you are in a fucked-up situation, *but* if you're as smart as your damn GPA used to suggest, then you'll cut this nigga loose until y'all can roll up out of this city."

I ain't trying to hear this shit. She's just making a mountain out of a molehill. "Look. I understand your concern and I appreciate it. I really do, girl. But I gotta start taking a stand for the things that I want—and I want to be Profit's girl. There's plenty of niggas whose families are in different gangs. This is no different."

"Different gangs?" E snatches her arm away from me. "You're thinking about joining the Vice Lords? You're going to become a Flower?"

"No. That's not what I'm saying."

"That's exactly what you just said." She jams her hands against her hips and stares me down like I'm something that just slithered out from under a rock. "You become a Flower, bitch, we enemies. Real talk."

"How can you say that? Profit has been cool with you from day one. Has he dropped dime about that gun? Has he told anyone that you were there at the hospital that night?"

Panic lights my girl's eyes. "And he better not either."

"He won't. Nobody is ever going to know. You got my word on that. I just need you to help me out right now. I'd do it for you."

Essence doesn't look convinced.

"I'm *not* joining the Vice Lords. I swear."

She still hesitates like I'm asking her to give me her damn kidney. "And we will *never* be enemies," I add. "Never."

At last, Essence draws a deep breath. "Girl, I sure hope that you know what you're doing."

I do, too.

Twenty minutes later, Essence pulls up outside the food court at Wolfchase Mall. No sooner do I step out of her beat-up Ford Escort than Profit pulls up in a sweeeet as fuck silver Range Rover with some crazy-ass rims that has every nigga in the parking lot checking out his ride.

"Hey, sexy. You want a ride?" Profit hits me with his perfect white smile and deep-pitted dimples while he turns down the bass bumping from his speakers. He's looking really fine with just a pair of black jeans, a fresh white T, and a single gold chain looped around his neck.

"Way not to draw attention to yourself," I criticize, reaching for the passenger door and hopping inside.

"What's the problem?" he asks as I settle into my seat. "I thought we were busting out of the closet? You haven't changed your mind, have you?"

Despite the knots looping in my stomach, I shake my head. "No." I lean over the armrest and kiss those juicy lips I love so much. Maybe Essence is right; this nigga really has my ass sprung like nobody's business. "I want the world to know that I'm your girl." The moment I say the words, I imagine LeShelle's head exploding and I just don't give a fuck. It's my life and she needs to fall the hell back.

We can hear the party long before we roll down Ruby Cove. Even though I spent the last couple of days preparing myself for this moment, my nerves are frayed and I'm chewing on my nails. What the hell was I thinking? What if some shit pops off and Profit can't protect me? My razor game is tight, but I can't fight off an army of Vice Lords and Flowers.

Profit takes one glance at me and starts laughing. "Chill, baby girl." He takes my hand and brushes a kiss against my knuckles. "It's gonna be all right. Ain't nobody going to trip. You're my guest. Everybody is gonna be cool."

"Fat Ace is going to be there?"

"Better be. He's the one who's throwing me the party."

"Throwing you . . . ?" I turn in my seat. I thought we were just going to a regular block party. "What's the occasion? Your birthday isn't until July twenty-third."

His smile broadens as he kisses my hand again. "Glad to see that you memorized it."

"And what's mine?"

"Ummm."

I snatch my hand way. "You better be playing."

"May fourth." He winks at me. "Now don't you feel stupid?"

"No—because it's May fifth." I reach over and mush him in the head. "Just like a nigga to not pay attention."

"You mean kind of like how my birthday is July twenty-*sixth*?"

Okay. Now I feel stupid. "I knew that. I was just testing you."

"Uh-huh."

I roll my eyes but then crack up at our ridiculous argument. I just played myself.

Old throwback cars line the curbs and driveways like Ruby Cove is just one huge car lot. Music blasts from all directions as every car and house crank up the bass. I try to take in the crowd, but there's so many niggas flagging and littering the yards that I just give up.

"Now there he go. Lil man and his lady," Fat Ace says, strutting slowly toward us from the yard in a Michael Jordan jersey and lily-white sneakers.

Just like last time, my heart damn near stops when I see Fat Ace's thick, muscled legs eat up the space between us. I still can't get over how massive and intimidating this man is. It's clear that he has mad respect, because every nigga's eye turns and head nods as he strolls by. I step closer to Profit and draw in a deep, steadying breath while the brothers exchange dabs.

"What's up, fam? I see you finally made it."

"Was there ever any doubt?" Profit cheeses and looks around the yard that's chock-full of Vice Lords. "We mobbin' deep today, huh?"

"All day, every day." Fat Ace takes off his shades, and his mismatched eyes shift in my direction. "What's up, lil lady? You can't speak?"

My face burns with embarrassment as I squeeze out a nervous "Hi."

Fat Ace laughs. "Don't be nervous. Chill. Make yourself at home, girl."

He plucks me from behind Profit and wraps a large arm around my shoulders. I feel like a puny no. 2 pencil getting ready to snap. "Drinks are in the house, and my nigga Bishop is burning it up on the barbeque. Trust me, he got mad skills."

I just nod along while the big man half walks and half drags me across the yard and introduces me to Lucifer, the pretty chick I saw the night of the hospital shooting.

"Trust me," Fat Ace brags. "Ain't no nigga's gangsta tighter than my girl right here. She saved my life that night at the hospital."

Lucifer nods her head toward me, but a smile doesn't crack her lips. She sort of reminds me of a taller Laila Ali: just as beautiful as she is tough. I'm introduced to a few more people in their crew as Profit's "lil lady" and can't help but blush every time. With everyone's eyes following Fat Ace, it also means everyone is looking at me, too. Then I see Qiana's ass glaring at me from across the way. I ain't seen her ass since I sliced her up at school, and no lie the bitch looks fucked up. The gashes on the sides of her face are black with these weird jagged stitches. It makes me wonder if she'd bothered going to the hospital or if she stitched the shit up herself. When she leans over and whispers to a couple of girls next to her, I get nervous again.

A few minutes later, I'm being handed a plate of some bomb-ass barbeque ribs, chicken, potato salad, and baked beans. "I can't eat all of this," I whisper to Profit. "I'll bust open."

He just laughs. "Wait until you taste it. You'll be back over here begging for more."

We find a pair of patio chairs in the backyard. Brothers constantly try to lure Profit into different card and domino games, but he refuses to leave my side. An hour later, I'm full, relaxed, and am getting only an occasional side eye when I pass up toking on the various joints that are being passed around.

Droopy, named so because his eyes are always so low that he looks like he's sleeping, tries to insist. "C'mon, girl. You better get yourself some of this here. This is some of that Super Skunk. Shit's smooth. It'll have your ass feeling like you're a muthafuckin' astronaut."

"No thanks." I smile and huddle closer to Profit.

"What, man. Your girl a square or some shit?"

"Nah, Droopy. Just go on with that." Profit brushes a kiss across my forehead and then passes me some mysterious punch in a red plastic cup. "You having a good time, baby?"

"Yeah. It's cool. Um, I gotta go to the bathroom."

"Bottom floor, down the hall. You need me to go with you?"

I want to say yes, but I don't want it to look like I need to be treated like a child. "Nah. I got it. I'll be right back." The minute I walk away from him, I feel like a dead woman walking. Every bitch in my line of vision is following my every step. For a couple of seconds, I think about holding my piss and just asking to leave, but then I think about what LeShelle would do in this situation, and I know her ass would just thrust up her chin and dare any one of these bitches to say shit to her. I stiffen my spine, copy my sister's swagger, and enter the house.

Nobody says shit to me. In the bathroom, after I empty my bladder and wash my hands, I take a few seconds to assess myself in the mirror. I look good with my MAC makeup still looking boss, my titties high, and my round ass filling out my jeans nicely. Real talk, I look better than the majority of the girls here. Smiling, I walk out the door and run straight into Qiana.

For a moment we're like two bitches in the Wild Wild West, staring each other down and waiting to draw our blades. I know this bitch is just itching to make a move by the slight twitch under her right eye.

"Is there a problem back here?" Lucifer barks.

When we don't answer, she turns down the hall and strolls toward us. "Don't make me repeat myself."

"Everything is cool." Qiana steps back but her eyes tell me that the shit isn't over—not by a long shot.

"Yeah?" Lucifer glances at me.

"Yeah," I confirm. "We were just catching up." I step around both Qiana and Lucifer and take my time switching my ass back out to my man. However, in the yard, everyone has formed a ring around Profit and some thick redbone nigga who is taking his shirt off. "What's going on?"

"Your boy is finally about to become a man, nah-whatImean?" Droopy pounds his chest and puffs out a cloud of smoke. "It's about fuckin' time if you ask me."

My heart drops. Is Profit about to get *jumped in* to the Vice Lords? I push my way through the crowd, determined to stop this, but I don't get more than a couple steps before Fat Ace effortlessly pulls me to his side. "This don't concern you, lil lady."

"Don't concern me? Everything about him concerns me." I try to push out of his arm, but of course it's useless.

"I hear what you're saying and it's cool that you're feeling my brother like this, but ain't nobody here twisting his arm. He knows he can't ride my coattails forever. A nigga on these streets need protection and a street family. And that some real shit. Profit could've got some real time over what happened at the hospital that night, and in the joint, blood carries you only so far. Niggas got to have they own connect—they own reputation. You feel me?"

I push and shove, but it's the sound of bone hitting bone that draws my attention back to the circle. Profit holds his own for a few swings, but it's soon clear that he's outmuscled by his opponent. Now, instead of trying to shove away from Fat Ace, I'm actually wincing and clinging to him.

The crowd whoops and hollers, and it looks like at any moment Profit is going to go down . . . but he doesn't. He takes punch after punch, but his legs refuse to fold. Tears stream down my face. How long does this have to go on? As more punches fly, there's a shift in the energy.

There's clear, growing respect for the punishment Profit can endure.

At long last, Fat Ace finally ends the fight. I race over to my baby and wrap him in my arms. "You're so stupid. I can't believe you did that. You're so stupid." The whole time I'm saying this, I'm raining kisses all over his face, grateful that his ass is still breathing after that vicious beating.

Profit chuckles while his eyes swell shut. His lips, too, are busted to hell and back. "All I want to know is, do you still love me?"

I laugh as I smother his face with more kisses. "Of course I love you. You stupid, stupid boy."

25
Melanie

"**F**uck Python." I disconnect the call on my cell phone and then throw the damn thing against my bedroom wall. I can never get that nigga on the phone when I need him. His visits have gone back to being too few and far between, which means that he's added another bitch to the dick Rolodex. Why the fuck do I keep doing this to myself?

Just remembering all that bullshit about him loving me and making me his wife has me feeling ashamed and stupid—again. I must have Boo-Boo the Fool stamped on my forehead. There's no other explanation. Terrell Carver is never going to change.

Things at the department have eased up a bit. No red flags have been raised over O'Malley's murder. But every once in a while, I catch my dad making a point to see me, but he never really has anything to say. It's odd and making me paranoid.

O'Malley received a hero's funeral, and I was assigned to desk duty until Internal Affairs was satisfied with my four visits to the department's shrink. Now that that stint is over, I'm back on patrol but currently without a partner.

"Mommy, am I still going to Grandma's house?"

Struggling to rein in my temper, I cut a hard look over to the door to see Python's mini-me staring wide-eyed back at me. It hurts to admit it, but I hate the fact that Christopher looks so much like his father. It's nothing but a constant reminder of the man who continues to fuck me over at every possible chance he gets. "Yeah. Hurry up and go get dressed," I snap.

Christopher lingers at the door. Undoubtedly he senses I'm angry about something, but he's too afraid to ask me about it because he doesn't want to get his head taken off. However, when he doesn't move, I explode anyway.

"I SAID GO GET DRESSED!"

Christopher races from the door.

Instantly I'm ashamed. "Fuck," I mumble under my breath. I don't chase after him to apologize, mainly because my temper needs a cooling-off period. Yet, it's hard to cool off when I still feel like a fool for falling for the same lies time after time.

Suddenly my stomach lurches. I slap a hand across my mouth and race to the adjoining bathroom. The moment I remove it, my breakfast splashes across, around, and then finally into the toilet. My face is hot while my stomach muscles clench as tight as a Charlie horse while it empties every little morsel it can find. Even after that, I dry heave until I'm begging God to end the torture.

When it is finally over, I pull myself up off the floor, stagger over to the sink, and splash cold water onto my face. *This can't be happening. This can't be happening.* I shut off the water and then pat my face dry before glancing at my reflection in the mirror.

"You dumb *bitch*." The tears come next, pouring from my eyes as if some invisible dam broke. I try to stop but then just give up and allow myself this one weak moment. Twenty minutes later, I end my pity party and clean up before rushing to finish getting dressed.

A few minutes after that, I go to check on Christopher, and I can't help but smile at seeing him all dressed up in his church clothes. Despite being just seven years old, Christopher is a meticulous dresser. His small black shoes shine, his suit is pressed, and his clip-on tie is straight.

"Now, aren't you handsome?" I ask, swiping away a tear.

Christopher smiles and turns away from the mirror, but the moment his small eyes sweep up to my face, he blinks. "Have you been crying, Mommy?"

I'm on the verge of lying when I feel one last tear slide down from my wet lashes. "Just a little bit."

My sensitive son rushes over and takes my hand. "What's wrong?"

Guilt washes over me. Just a while ago I was hating how much my son looks like his father, and now I realize that I don't deserve to have such a sweet and loving kid. "Nothing's wrong, baby. Mommy is all right." I lean down and press a kiss against one of his chubby cheeks.

Christopher looks as if he doesn't believe me.

"Are you about ready to go?" I ask, ready to change the subject.

He nods and then takes my hand.

I smile and rush us both out to the car. One glance at

the car's clock and I know that my mother is likely throwing a fit, because she's now going to be late for church—something she hates. My days of attending church ended the Sunday after I moved out of my parents' house for good. I never forgave the whole congregation for turning up their noses at me and my family when I got pregnant. Many of them had the teenage pregnancies, the drug addicts, and a host of other bullshit up in their own families, yet they sat up on their high horses and were just as giddy as flies in shit casting judgment on me. That is also part of the reason I never admitted to who Christopher's father was—it would have made things worse, especially with my father.

If only I knew then what I know now.

By the time I roll up into my parents' driveway, they are waiting outside and pacing next to the car. To spare myself a good tongue-lashing, I stay in the car. "Give me a kiss," I tell my son.

Christopher unbuckles his seat belt and leans over the armrest and kisses me.

"Be good," I warn, watching him turn and climb out of the SUV. I wave to him and then to my parents. True to form, my mother just rolls her eyes and then ushers Christopher into the car. A few minutes later, I pull up into the Pink Monkey. There are just a couple of cars in the parking lot. I didn't intend to come here, but what can I say? A part of me is still a glutton for punishment.

"Well, I'll be damned."

I turn toward a grinning McGriff. "Now, why aren't I surprised to see you here?" I ask, returning his smile.

"Because some things never change," he says. "I'm guessing you're looking for the big man?"

"Is he around?"

McGriff's lazy gaze drifts over my curvy figure. "Remind me why we never got together?"

I roll my eyes.

"Nah. Check it," he says, moving into my personal space. "Other than that pig's badge you be toting, you still got it going on."

"Uh-huh. Better not let your *boy* hear you talking to me like that."

"Please." McGriff laughs while his eyes roam freely over my tight curves. "That nigga got too many bitches as it is now. He needs to start spreading the love. Nah-whatImean?"

I clench my jaw and ball my hands at my side. "Where is he?"

McGriff's eyes light up. He knows he's struck a nerve with me. "In his office. I'm sure that he'll be happy to see you."

"Thank you."

"Don't mention it."

He steps aside and allows me to walk toward the back of the club. Sad to say, I know my way around.

Storming past McGriff, I take a deep breath. And as I approach Python's office, I'm still not sure whether I'm about to cuss Python out or just drop the news on him and keep it moving. However, the decision is taken out of my hands when I open the door and see Python ramming his dick into a woman on her knees and clutching at a belt that's wrapped tight around her neck.

"TAKE THIS DICK. TAKE THIS DICK, BITCH!"

The blond-haired black ho's eyes are rolling to the back of her head, and she's getting ready to pass out.

Python is so wrapped up in what he's doing, he either doesn't see me come in or he just doesn't give a rat's ass.

"AH, SHIT. I'm gonna come in this ass," he brags. "THIS MY ASS, BITCH. YOU HEAR ME? THIS MY ASS FROM NOW ON!"

The woman chokes and gurgles while one of Python's beloved corn snakes slides up between her full breasts.

Python roars and pulls out; his thick, gooey cum shoots out against the woman's round ass, back, and even in her hair. When he releases his tight hold on the belt, his plaything collapses, wheezing and gasping for air.

"What the fuck, McGriff? Are you taking notes?" Python pants and then turns toward the door. "Melanie . . ."

"Yeah. I'm taking a lot of notes, muthafucka!" I reach over and grab some heavy metal statue of some kind and hurl it straight at his head. The muthafucka ducks and the damn thing takes a chuck out of his desk. After that, I just turn and storm out.

"WAIT! MELANIE!"

I take off because at any minute I'm going to start crying again, and I can't have that shit. Not here. Not now.

"MELANIE!"

McGriff folds his arms as he watches me race by. "Make sure to come back and visit us again, *Officer.*"

I hop into my vehicle and tear out of the parking lot without a backward glance. Two blocks later, the dam breaks again. Tears flood my eyes and make it impossible for me to see straight. "Fuck that muthafucka." I slap my hand against the steering wheel. "FUCK HIM! FUCK HIM! FUCK HIM!"

Up ahead, I see a Walgreens and I suddenly know what I have to do. I whip into the convenience store and buy another prepaid cell phone. Back in the car, I dial and then punch in my code. After that, I wait.

Two minutes later, the phone rings.

"Hey, it's me. I need to see you." I sniff.

"Is there a problem?" the rough, gravelly voice asks on the other line.

"I need to see you."

There's a long pause and I find myself compelled to add, "Please?"

"All right. You know the spot, right?"

"Yeah." I nod. "Can I come over now?"

"Sure. I'll let the boys know my girl is rolling through."

"Thanks." I disconnect the call and start the car again. This time I drive in the opposite direction, toward Elvis Presley Boulevard. Ten minutes later, I pull into J. D. Lewis & Son Funeral Home. The parking lot is crowded with mourners for a late-morning service.

I remove my gun and place it in the glove compartment before climbing out of the vehicle. I keep my head down as I shoulder my way into the lobby and then work my way toward the back of the building.

"This must really be important."

I look up to see a familiar person dressed immaculately in a man's black suit, black tie, and polished shoes. The only odd thing about it is this person is clearly a woman.

"You clean up well," I say just for shits and giggles.

She cocks one corner of her lips while her onyx gaze remains flat. "Follow me." She turns and pushes through an exit door just as "His Eye Is on the Sparrow" cues up in the parlor.

I fall in line behind her and follow her through the funeral's prep room, past Sub-Zero freezers, out another door to the garage, and then finally to an adjoining office.

"Hold out your hands," she orders.

"What? You're going to pat me down?" I challenge.

"It's part of my job."

I start to argue but know that it won't do any good. "Fine." I hold out my arms.

She smiles and proceeds to give me a pat down——it

was a little too thorough. "Was it as good for you?" I ask when she's finished.

"Don't flatter yourself."

I shake my head and walk through the door.

"Mel, baby!" Fat Ace's deep baritone booms as one milky eye and one brown eye lands on me. He stands from a desk stacked high with bricks of cocaine and money. "Good to see you."

Fuck Python.

26

Yolanda

For the past half hour, I've been standing in front of my bathroom mirror, unable to pull my gaze from the bruises around my neck. They're nasty-looking: black, blue, red, and even yellow. I've stopped touching them, and I'm trying my best not to take any deep breaths. The rest of my body feels like it's going through trauma as well—my tits from Python's biting, my legs from being pulled in every direction, and my ass from being busted wide open. Python is a fuckin' beast . . . and all those damn snakes?

I shudder and then try to force that shit to the back of my mind. But it won't stay back there. It keeps flashing to that panic attack I had when Python first looped that leather belt around my neck and the dozen or so times when I thought I was seconds from dying. But I'd be lying to myself if I didn't acknowledge that there was *some* pleasure as well.

Still, is any of this shit worth it?

I lift my gaze to meet my stare in the mirror. Shit. I look like I've been run over by a Mack truck. Quickly, I rake my hands through my hair so it can lie flat, but just as quickly I give up. While I'm plotting and trying to make moves, clearly there's another bitch in the picture who hasn't been on my radar. But seeing how fast Python moved when she walked in on us means that heifer is somebody to Python. She wasn't no jump-off, that's for sure. But who is she—and does LeShelle even know about her?

My cell phone on the bathroom counter starts ringing, and I glance down to see Baby's picture and number pop up on the screen. This bitch got a lot of nerve calling after I ain't seen her ass since she left me stranded in the fuckin' parking lot. I should let the shit go to voice mail, but my curiosity gets the best of me and I snatch the shit up.

"Yeah?"

"What the hell kind of way is that to answer the phone?" Baby asks.

"It's my muthafuckin' phone, ain't it? I'll answer it how I want to answer it. Now what the fuck do you want?"

"Damn, girl. What's with you? You on the rag or something?"

"Oh, so you wanna play stupid. Is that it?"

There's a brief pause while I listen to Baby draw in a deep breath.

"Yeah. That's right. You were wrong and you know you were wrong. What the fuck were you doing wildin' out at my job, busting bottles over that bitch's head and shit and then leaving me to hoof it home?"

"Man, Yo-Yo, I was just . . . fuck it. I don't know. It just wasn't my fuckin' night, I guess. My bad."

"Your bad? That's it?"

"Shit. What else you want me to say? I'm fuckin' sorry. Damn."

She's putting bitches in hospitals and she's just sorry?

"Whatever." We hold the phone for a few seconds, neither of us saying shit.

"Well, all right. I was just calling to see how you were doing and everythang. I hadn't heard from you or nothing. I'm about to go out here and make this money."

"Thank you for finally acting like you give a damn. Better late than never, right? I'm fine and I'm gonna always be fine—especially now that me and Python have hooked up." I couldn't help but let her ass know that everything was going according to plan. Still, I don't know why I'm expecting her to congratulate me or something. That shit is not in Baby's character.

"What the fuck you expect?" Baby chuckles. "I ain't met a nigga yet who will turn down pussy, especially the ones always waving it in their faces."

"Fuck you, Baby."

"What?"

"Why can't you just be fuckin' happy for me? Shit. You know this was my plan from the giddy up."

Baby's laughter blasts my ear off. "I'm supposed to be happy that you've gone from hooker to ho? Is that what the fuck you're saying? Sheeeiiit."

"You know what, Baby? Fuck you and the pussy you came out of." I disconnect the call and toss the phone back onto the counter. I'm tired of haters hating. I swear to God.

Momma starts hammering down the door. "Yolanda, how long you gonna be in there?"

Now here she goes. "I'm getting ready to take a bath."
I turn toward the bathtub and turn on the hot water.

"DON'T BE IN THERE ALL DAY!" she shouts over
the running water, and then hits the door as a final excla-
mation point.

For real that bitch is on my nerve. I can't wait to roll
up out of here, collect my kids, and live ghetto fabulous
for the rest of my life. I bet everybody be kissing my ass
then. After sprinkling in some bath salts, I ease into the
hot water, hissing and wincing at the stinging pain in my
ass.

Is it worth it?

I can hear my momma stomping and bitching outside
the door. Her unappreciative ass ain't said shit since I've
been able to break her off a little of what I've been making at the Pink Monkey. In fact, the more I give her the
more she needs. Greedy bitch. And on top of that, I get
to hear about how I'm going to hell every time I turn
around. Shit. The only damn place I'm going to is the
muthafuckin' bank. Money moves every fucking thing
around Memphis. So the answer to my fuckin' question
is *HELL, YEAH.* I'm going to give it to Python just the
way he wants it and I'm going to smile, moan, and act
like I love the shit.

My cell phone on the counter starts ringing again. I
know that it's Baby, but she can just lick the crack of my
ass. Bruises heal, pride can be swallowed, and money
pays the bills. From now on, I'm just going to do me—all
the way to the fuckin' top.

27
Melanie

Fat Ace moves a bit slow and has a new scar jagging across his jaw. I haven't seen him since the night before the shoot-out at the Med. For the most part, he looks good; then again, I'm not all that surprised. I've come to suspect that the man has nine lives.

"Profit, I'm gonna have to call you back," he says, and disconnects his cell phone. "Well, don't just stand there, Mel. Come show your nigga some love." He smiles and opens his mountain-size arms.

I quickly rush into his embrace and relish how it feels being wrapped in a big warm blanket and how this big muthafucka always smells like fresh baby powder. "I've missed you. I've been soooo worried."

"Ah. Now that's what a nigga likes to hear." He leans down and sweeps his tongue into my mouth. I moan even though he doesn't taste as good as Python or even get my titties to tingle, mainly because Fat Ace has a habit of tasting like Hennessy and pistachios. Lord knows the nigga eats them by the pound. When we finally pull apart, I playfully swipe the residue of my coral lipstick from his lips and smile.

"I've been meaning to see you, but the streets are still on fire," Fat Ace says. "But you've definitely been on my mind."

"Now that's what a girl likes to hear." I keep my arms wrapped around his thick neck and try to work up the courage to do what I have to do. "How's your chest?"

"It's all good, Mel. You know you don't have to worry about your boy. Those paper gangsters can't find their own asshole while they shitting. You feel me?" He kisses the tip of my nose.

Behind me the door opens and Lucifer steps in.

"You know, Mel, I never thanked you for the heads-up when my brother was laid up in the hospital," Fat Ace says.

Now I start easing out of his arms while a different kind of tingle skips down my spine. "It's no thing. Once I realized who he was, of course I called."

Fat Ace nods while his broad lips start to lose their smile. "Yeah. I appreciate that shit, especially since it's possible that you're the one who put that bullet in him."

There's an accusation and a question in that statement. All I can do is draw a deep breath and hold my head up. "It's possible," I say honestly. "He was at the wrong place at the wrong time."

"There's definitely an argument for that," he says, turning away and folding his large frame back into his chair. "My only problem is figuring out how the Gangster Disciples knew that I was at that hospital."

The office roars with silence as my gaze shifts from him to the bitch standing behind me.

"I mean, I couldn't have been there more than . . . what?" He glances over to Lucifer.

"Fifteen minutes," Lucifer answers, glaring dead at me.

"Exactly what are you asking me?" I challenge, settling my hands on my hips and turning my stare back toward Fat Ace. "You think I told them? Are you suggesting that I set you up?"

Fat Ace's brows dip over his cataract eye. "I didn't say that . . . but it's an interesting question now that you've brought it up."

"Are you for real?" My eyes shift back over to Lucifer, whose hands are now inching toward her waist. "I don't fuckin' believe this shit. I didn't tell a soul that you were heading to that hospital. Why the fuck would I?"

Fat Ace shrugs. "You used to have a thing with Python."

My heart drops. "Who told you that?"

His gaze now looks as hard as the bitch standing behind me. "Niggas talk."

I have two seconds to defuse this shit or my baby is going to be an orphan. "That shit went down in high school. Ancient history."

"Then how come you never told me about you two?"

"For the same reason. It's ancient history." I make sure to hold his gaze and pray that his vision is just a little cloudy and he doesn't see that I'm lying my ass off.

"See there, Lucifer? I told you we didn't have nothing to worry about with Mel." His lips turn up into a smile again. "Now get over here and sit on Daddy's lap."

I don't waste any time popping a squat on one of his powerful thighs and pressing another kiss against his warm mouth. "Are we cool now, baby?"

"We're always cool, Mel." He laughs and pinches me on the ass.

Lucifer makes her exit and relief rushes through me like a tidal wave.

"It's all love. Heard about what happened to O'Malley. I'm sure you're all busted up over it." He eyes me as if waiting for some type of response. "You didn't happen to cap that racist muthafucka yourself, did you?"

"What kind of fuckin' question is that?"

"A serious one."

I turn away from his milky cataract because I don't think I can survive another round of his tight scrutiny. "Let's just say I haven't lost any sleep over his passing and leave it at that."

Fat Ace laughs and tosses up his hands. "A'ight. I'm gonna leave it alone. Less I know about how you legal gangstas do your dirt the better, right?"

The smallest smile flickers at my lips but then vanishes. If he can put two and two together, then how many people down at the station have been looking at me sideways?

"Uh-huh." Fat Ace snickers. "Like father like daughter."

"Not funny." I start to hop off his lap, but he easily holds me down.

"Aww, now. Did I hurt your little feelings? Don't worry. I'm not going to throw shade over his perfectly crafted supercop title. My lips are sealed." He leans in for another kiss and starts sliding his hand up under my shirt. "So to what do I owe the pleasure of this visit? Am I on one of your people's radar or have you finally come to your senses and want to come over to the dark side?"

"Very funny."

"I wasn't tryna be. This side of the fence pays better than that chump change the city tax dollars are paying y'all to dodge bullets. Believe that." He meets my gaze. "Ask your pops."

The tension thickens between us.

"Okay," he finally says. "You're not here for a pay

raise. So what's up?" He tilts up my chin so that my gaze
stops wandering around the room. "So what's so important that you had to rush over here in the middle of the
day?"

"I wanted to . . . share some news with you."

"I'm all ears," he says, nibbling on my ears.

"Well, you know the night before you, um, got shot?"

His smile kicks up a few notches. "Of course I remember. I plan on us doing a few of those positions
again as soon as these wounds heal all the way. I took
five plugs, you know." His hands slide down my back-
side so that he can give my ass a good squeeze.

"I'd like that," I say, easing closer. "But there's something I think you need to know."

"All right." He notes my serious expression and pulls
back a bit to fold his arms. "This looks serious. What is it?"

My smile wobbles. If I'm going to do this, I need to
just spit it out. Once I say the words, there's no going
back. "I'm pregnant." The tension only thickens while
the silence nearly deafens me. "Well?"

Slowly, Fat Ace's wide, rubber-band lips stretch from
ear to ear. "You're shitting me."

I shake my head while I try to evaluate if he really
thinks the news is good or not, but like Python, it's never
easy reading him. "I'm gonna have a baby!"

At long last, Fat Ace's face lights up like a Christmas
tree and his big meaty arms wrap around my waist like a
steel vise. "HELL YEAH!"

His voice nearly blows my eardrum out, and he starts
to swing me around the office like a rag doll. I really
hope I know what the fuck I'm doing.

28
Momma Peaches

Al Green is bumping on my old stereo. Not the new I-found-Jesus Al Green, but the old red-light-in-the-basement Al Green, who puts a smile on my face and has my hips rocking as I sweep off my front porch. "Oh, baby, love and happiness . . ."

"Aww. Sookie, sookie now."

I glance over my shoulder to see Rufus leaning against the front chain-link fence, grinning at me like I'm giving him a personal lap dance. "Now what the fuck do you want?"

"Right now, I'm just satisfied to watch you back that ass up. Now let me see you drop it like it's hot." Cheesing, he reaches into his pocket and pulls out dollar bills. "C'mon, girl. Make this money."

How can I *not* laugh at his stupid ass? "Get the fuck on with that."

"There you go. Here I am tryna help you out and this is how you act?" He returns the money to his front pocket. "A'ight. That young nigga must be breaking you off something lovely."

"In and out of bed," I brag, rolling my neck.

Rufus shakes his head. "That shit ain't right." He glances off toward a cluster of niggas mobbin' down Shotgun Row with clouds of smoke hanging over them.

"What ain't right about it? That a woman has the audacity to do what y'all niggas do all day every day? I seen you rolling up on some of these young girls out here, most of them too young to know better, and you got the nerve to throw shade on my game. Nigga, puh-leeze."

"Nah, nah. That was probably my niece you seen me with. I ain't out here like that."

This muthafucka damn near got my eyes rolling out the back of my head. Niggas and their double and triple standards.

"For real, Peaches. You know you're the only one who got my heart. It's time for you to stop breast-feeding these niggas in diapers and get in with the grown and sexy crowd." He claps his hands and strikes a Herculean pose so I can check out his guns . . . and they weren't too bad.

"Momma Peaches, you need to stop torturing that man," Chantal shouts from her front porch. "I ain't seen no nigga put in this much work for a woman in all my life."

"Shit. I ain't stuttin' this old nigga."

Rufus laughs. "I'm the same damn age you are."

"Whatever." At the sound of a souped-up motor, I glance up to see my nephew's Monte Carlo cruising down the block. A smile eases onto my face as niggas start pointing and waving their hellos. My heart warms every time I see Python. The weight he be moving and the amount of dirt he's buried in up to his neck, it's just a miracle he ain't locked down, let alone walking around breathing. However, when he pulls up to my curb in the middle of day, I know something must wrong.

My suspicions are confirmed when he rolls out of the car and I see his face. I know that face like I know my own. Clearly he's got a lot of shit on his mind that he can't work out on his own, and he needs his auntie.

Leave it to Chantal to point out the obvious. "Looks like you got company."

Rufus eases off the fence and tips his head so that my nephew can enter the gate. "S'up, Python?"

"Everythang is still everythang." Python looks Rufus over. "You still out here tryna holla at my aunt?"

"A real man never runs off the battlefield, nahwhat-Imean?"

Python snickers while he gives Rufus dabs. "Do you, nigga. Do you."

That shit just makes Rufus's lips stretch wider. "You see this, Peaches? This is like the Good Housekeeping seal of approval right here."

By the time Python is bouncing up my stairs, he's laughing his ass off. "How you doing, Momma?" He leans over and kisses me on the cheek.

"I was doing fine until you encouraged that fool with his nonsense. Now I'm never going to be able to get rid of his ass." Turning, I set the broom aside and slap my hands onto my hips.

"That nigga has been out here tryna holla at you since I was like fifteen. The only way you going to get rid of a nigga like that is to break him off."

"And let the church say 'amen and amen,'" Rufus shouts, waving his hands in the air.

Chantal and Python crack up.

"Boy, you can have these niggas out here thinking I won't bend your big ass over my knee if you wanna, but me and you know the real deal. Don't we?"

Python laughs and just heads on into the house.

"Yeah, that's what I thought." I follow behind him. "Now what's up? You hungry? I have some gumbo warming up on the stove from last night."

"You always trying to feed somebody," he says, plopping down at the table.

"That didn't sound like a no to me." Grabbing a bowl out of the cabinet, I quickly fill it up. "Besides, I like feeding folks."

"That explains why niggas are always running in and out your house." His eyes light up when I set the steaming bowl and a cold beer down in front of him. "Thanks, Momma."

"Uh-huh. You need to send LeShelle over here so I can teach her how to boil some water. Maybe that way you can keep your ass out of so many women's houses."

A pained look flashes in his eyes for a brief moment. "There you go. All up in my personal business."

"Oh, I'm sorry, but wasn't that you out on my porch telling me to break some nigga off some pussy?" I pop him on the back of the head.

That has him cracking up again. "A'ight. You got me on that shit." He shovels down a few mouthfuls of gumbo.

"Does she cook at all?"

"She cooks where it counts," he says, twitching his eyebrows.

"Clearly that ain't enough to keep your ass at home."

"Here we go." He sighs. "Check it. I love LeShelle. No chick come harder or is willing to go to the max for her man like my boo. In return, I take care of her and make sure she don't want for nothing. You feel me? But I'm a man, Momma P. We prey, hunt, and conquer pussy. That's just what the fuck we do. And Melanie just gotta understand that shit."

"Melanie?"

Python tosses down his spoon, props his elbows up on the table, and starts shaking his head. "Melanie rolled by the club this afternoon. She sort of caught me with, um, one the dancers."

I'm rolling the name around in my head. "You mean that cop's daughter you had a thing for back in the day? You are still messing with that girl?"

"She's raising one of my seeds," he says, shrugging.

"She and how many others?"

"Nah, nah. It's just . . ."

"Damn. You sprung on a cop's girl? Wait. Ain't she a cop, too?"

"If you start laughing, I'm gonna be out this bitch." He looks me dead in the eye. "For real."

Good thing he said that shit just before I really got going, because I find this shit absolutely hilarious. "Boy, I ain't gonna laugh at you."

Python takes a deep breath and holds my gaze for a while. Then he starts glancing around the house like we ain't the only two up in this son of a bitch. By the way he's acting, I'm expecting him to tell me he shot the president of the United States or something.

I reach out across the table and cover his hand with mine. "Terrell Jerome Carver, spit it out." *Before you give me a heart attack or something.*

"A'ight." He finally eases back in his chair. "Yeah. I still got a thing for her. You know, she was sort of my first love and shit. But circumstances and politics being what they are . . ." He shrugs his large shoulders and shakes his head. "Plus, her old man put so much heat on me back in the day. Word must've gotten to him about me and his daughter and that his grandson is my seed, because suddenly he was riding me and my niggas so hard we had to wave a white fuckin' flag. It was either that or let him drag our black asses down to the station each time we step outside. Don't you remember that shit?"

I nodded, remembering supercop Melvin Johnson and his men policing Shotgun Row so much it started looking like a fuckin' precinct down in this muthafucka.

"Was that what all that shit was about?"

"Fuck yeah. We couldn't move shit. Supplies dried up, customers took they asses to blocks the Vice Lords and the Crips were holding down. Shit. You know crackheads ain't got no loyalty. So I had to get that nigga off my neck some kind of way."

"So you had to stop seeing her?"

"Yeah. At least for a little while. Now I creep over there when I can—to see Christopher and shit. But for the most part I try to stay off that muthafucka's radar. You feel me?"

"Did you ever tell her?"

"Fuck naw. Melanie thinks his ass don't know shit. She would've just confronted his ass, and I would've been right back where I started—in the precinct Monday through Sunday, forced to stand in every fuckin' lineup for every fuckin' crime in the city. You know I got to be about this paper, staying on top of this game."

"And where does Yolanda fit in all this?"

"Yolanda?"

"Look. Normally I don't give a damn about which one of these fast girls you done run up on, but Yolanda— Yo-Yo? You know the kind of shit that girl has been through. And I ain't all that sure she's right in the head."

"Who said anything about my ass being with that girl?"

Leaning back in my chair, I give him the who-in-the-hell-you-think-you're-fooling look. "I was born at night, but it wasn't last night. Shit don't stay quiet in these streets."

"A'ight. Yeah, me and Yo-Yo hook up now and then. We both grown. But it ain't no thang. She know the deal, and she gonna play her position."

I don't know about that, but I'm the last one to be preaching. "So . . . Melanie walked in on you and Yolanda? That's what's behind the long face?"

"Nah . . . Yes. Fuck. I don't know. These damn bitches . . . I mean women." He glances at me and clears his throat. "Anyway, they just stressing me. It's gonna work out, though. I'm just gonna give Melanie a minute to calm down, and then I'll roll by and settle the shit."

"All right. But let me tell you—eventually women get tired of being sick and tired. You have my word on that. And when she does the little bit of hell you putting out, ain't shit on what a woman can do to you. Personally, the one I'd be watching if I was you is LeShelle. That girl ain't the fuckin' type to cross." I hold my nephew's gaze, hoping my message will sink in, but like all men, he's hardheaded and he's going to have to learn the hard way.

"The Chronic" starts blasting and Python scoops his cell phone out of his pocket. "Holla at me."

Since I'm not all that interested in his business, I get up from the table and fix my own bowl of gumbo and something to drink. When I return to the table, Python's face appears to be even more troubled and I have a sneaking suspicion it don't have shit to do with women. When he finally meets my gaze again, he's angrier than I've ever seen him.

"Problem?"

"Datwon," he spat.

"Your cousin?"

"Yeah. The muthafucka done turned fed."

29

Melanie

A few hours later, I return to my parents' place to pick up Christopher. Fat Ace had wanted me to go back to his crib for a private celebration, but I had to take a rain check. I'm trying to convince myself that I feel good about my decision in telling Fat Ace about the baby, but the truth of the matter is, there's a fifty-fifty chance that the baby is his. And unlike Python, Fat Ace doesn't have a whole bunch of babies sprinkled all over Memphis.

I met Fat Ace when I was slapping handcuffs on him at a BP gas station. I didn't quite appreciate having to chase his ass for seven blocks, but he seemed impressed that I could even catch him. I wasn't attracted to him or anything, but after he posted bail the next day, he didn't waste any time calling and hounding me for a date. At first I didn't pay any attention to his advances, but Fat Ace wasn't a man used to taking no for an answer. Three weeks later, I caved and then fucked him on the first night. He satisfied an itch during a time when Python was slithering from one bitch to another.

I shut off the engine to my SUV and took a moment to draw a deep breath. In my mind, I can still see Python fucking that girl, and I just barely stop a rush of tears from pouring down my face. "I'm not going to cry. I'm not going to cry."

Once I collect myself, I climb out of the car and head toward my parents' two-story brick home. Like every house on the street, the yard is emerald green and neatly manicured, as if everyone is in some silent competition to make the cover of *Better Homes and Gardens*.

I enter the house without knocking and holler, "Mom?"

"In the kitchen," she yells back.

My mother, Victoria, prides herself on being the perfect homemaker. Her home is her pristine castle, and cooking and gossiping about everybody in the church is her life. Unfortunately, today the smell of fried chicken and collard greens has my stomach churning.

"What's the matter with you?" my mother asks, looking up from stirring her homemade mac and cheese.

"Nothing," I lie, but I'm unable to stop my nose from trying to twist off my face.

She just gives me a look and opens the oven to slide in her crackling and corn bread. "Your father wanted me to tell you he wants to see you in his office upstairs when you got here."

I groan. The last thing I'm in the mood for is my father's long-winded stories about what's going on at the department. Unlike him, I like to leave the job at the job. "I really don't have time. I just want to pick up Christopher and get home."

"Aren't you staying for supper?" she asks, looking all butt-hurt. We go through this song and dance every Sunday. She just wants me to stay so when her gossiping sisters come over, she can brag about how much I've straightened up my life despite the child-out-of-wedlock episode I put her and Daddy through. Wait until she learns that I'm about to have my second one.

"Momma, I really don't have time."

"Make time," she tells me, washing her hands at the sink. "You need to start sitting down at the table with Christopher and not just always dropping him off somewhere. Besides, I told him that he can spend the night here."

"Well, I wish you would have told me that before I came. You could have saved me some time." I lean against the wall and fight down another wave of nausea. "Where's Chris?"

"He's in the backyard playing with his cousin Dewayne. And he'll still be out there while you go see what your daddy wants." She turns me around and propels me out of the kitchen. "Now go on."

There's no point in arguing, so I head on up to see what my father wants.

"And tell the captain that dinner will be ready in twenty minutes," my mother yells out.

"Yes, ma'am." *The captain.* I roll my eyes again. Beats the hell out of me why she always insists on calling Daddy by his job title. Growing up, it went from sergeant to lieutenant to now captain. It's weird but it's their little thing, so I let them have it.

I climb up the stairs in the foyer, grateful that my stomach is starting to settle as I get farther away from the wafting aromas. I walk past my parents' bedroom and head to my father's home office, which used to be my bedroom. Hoping that I can just cut this shit short, I knock one time and enter the room.

"Hey, Daddy. You wanted to see me?"

POP! POP! POP!

My eyes instantly fly to the thirty-two-inch television in the corner of the room and the black-and-white image of me running down the back of Goodson's Autoshop. Python has his hands up, and O'Malley has his gun aimed at the back of his head.

My father hits the PAUSE button on the remote and turns toward me. "Do you need for me to finish playing this?" he asks.

"No." I enter the room and quickly close the door behind me. Now, on top of my stomach sloshing around, a huge lump is clogging my throat. Never has his aging face looked more haggard and troubled than it does at this moment.

"Why, baby girl? Just tell me why?" His eyes plea with me.

"Who else has seen that tape?"

His eyes spring wide. "Nobody. What, you think I'm just going to hand something like this over? You think I want everyone down at that department—a department that I've devoted most of my life to—to know that my damn daughter is a fuckin' cop killer?"

"Who gave you the tape?"

"What the fuck does that matter?" he thunders, jumping to his feet. "I want to know what hell you were thinking!" He turns to the screen and points to Python. "And is that who I think it is?"

I suck in a deep breath and cross my arms. "That's Christopher's father."

My dad's hand falls away from the screen as he continues to stare at me. "What?"

"O'Malley wasn't going to arrest him. He was going to kill him."

"So you *killed* your partner?" he asks.

"I did what I had to do," I say honestly. "And I would do it again."

Still staring at me as if I'd just sprouted a second head, he plops down into his chair. "Oh, baby girl."

"I haven't been your baby girl in a very long time."

His big bushy brows dip together. "Excuse me?"

"And please spare me any sermon that you've been practicing for however long you've had that tape," I say, wanting to be spared the dramatics. "When it comes to doing our jobs, we've both done some shit that kind of colors the line of justice. Don't you think?"

"What are you talking about?"

"I'm talking about you and ole Smokestack. Word is, your affiliation with the Vice Lords runs pretty deep, Dad. Some would even say that they helped you build a career off the backs of the Gangster Disciples."

"Who told you that?" he asks, turning purple.

"Why? You want to waste your breath denying it?" While I watch him sputter, I push aside my guilt. I love my father, but he's no angel. "The Vice Lords have been greasing your palms and helping you with those career-making busts against the Gangster Disciples. You were always at the right place at the right time. You don't have to be a cop to know that not all gangsters are on the streets."

Shock chases the blood out of my father's face as he gives denial another shot. "I don't know who you've been talking to but—"

"Let's just say that Fat Ace and I are really good friends."

My father clamps his mouth shut. "He's been talking?"

"Tell you what, Daddy. Get rid of that tape and let's just forget we ever had this conversation. Agreed?"

He just stares at me, but I wait him out. I know his heart is breaking just as I know that our relationship will never be the same. At last, he hangs his head and glances away. "Agreed."

"Good. Momma says dinner is almost ready." I turn and walk out of the room, wiping away the tears that finally roll down my face.

Loyalty

30
LeShelle

March . . .

Sitting under the hair dryer at FabDivas hair salon, I'm reminded why I can't stand gossiping bitches. Lately, every time I walk into a room, a nail shop, or even a party, bitches stop talking and start whispering and pointing. It isn't that I don't know what they're jaw-jacking about. Clue one is Python's increasing absence from our bed, and clue two is that every time I turn around, there's Yolanda skinning and grinning in my face. I'm not stupid; I know the signs. Python has clearly been throwing dick her way for a couple of months, and now the retarded bitch is smelling herself.

As Python's wifey, I see the sudden shift in not just this crazy bitch but also in a couple of other Queen Gs' attitudes. There have been blatant signs of disrespect, and I'm not having that shit. It's now time to check these broads.

"If you got something to say, then just say it, bitch!" I

push up the hair dryer and glare at Yo-Yo over at the shampoo bowl.

Amusement dances in the bitch's eyes, but she keeps her mouth shut.

"Nah. Nah. Speak up," I say, not wanting to let shit go. "You obviously got something to say. I done watch you spit my name outcha mouth a couple times while I'm sitting right here in front of you. So speak the fuck up."

Another girl at the shampoo bowl chuckles and rolls her eyes like she done forgot who the fuck I am.

I know that heifer well. Octavia. She works down at the Pink Monkey, dancing under the silly name *Gucci*— like any nigga wanted a no-tittie stripper with pussy you could smell a mile away. How come bitches can't learn to douche their shit?

I turn my anger toward Octavia. "All right, Ms. Comedian. What the fuck is so funny?"

All eyes zoom back and forth between us. One of the stylists even turns down the radio so everyone can hear better. Now that we have an audience, Octavia's smirk fades. "I didn't say anything."

I twist my face as I stand up. "Didn't say anything?" My neck rolls like a cobra getting ready to strike. "Bitch, ain't shit wrong with my ears and my fucking eyes. Neither one of you bitches has stopped talking since you switched up in here." I shift my attention to Yolanda. "Especially your skank ass."

She glances around, probably to see if anybody has her back, but everybody suddenly got *real* interested in the old-as-hell magazines sitting in they laps.

"I'm talking to you, ho." My hand drums at my side, where everybody knows I keep my gat.

"Shelle, honey." Ms. Anna, the shop's owner, speaks up. "Calm down. I'm sure that child didn't mean any disrespect."

I stare Yolanda down. I know the smug bitch has something she's just dying to get off her chest, but she is just too scared to spit it out.

Ms. Anna tries again. "Chile, I really can't afford to have any trouble in here."

"It's all right, Ms. Anna. These bitches are just getting ready to apologize for ruining my morning." My eyes narrow on them. "Ain't that right?"

Octavia's jaw tightens as her gaze shoots daggers at me.

"You need some help getting that mouth to work?" The gun is in my hand before anyone has a chance to blink, and I make sure it is in her mouth like the dicks she likes to slobber on.

Fear finally leaps into Octavia's face as she starts stuttering. "I-I'm sorry," she muffles around the gun.

"And?" I prod, my trigger finger itching like a muthafucka.

Confused, Octavia glances around again.

"I'm waiting." I tap my foot.

Octavia swallows hard and tries talking around the gun again. "I'm sorry for ruining your morning."

I think about making the bitch lick the bottom of my shoes or something, but I'm already tired of her and want her out of my face. "Now, I think you were just leaving," I tell her, pulling the gun out of her mouth.

Octavia is so angry and humiliated that her face looks like a gigantic cranberry. Left with no choice, Octavia removes the smock from around her neck and stands her skinny ass up and walks out of the salon, wet hair and all.

The women in the salon crack the fuck up.

Bold as fuck, Yo-Yo kicks up another smile as she shakes her head.

My gaze zeroes back onto this bitch. My real enemy. My clit starts thumping and my trigger finger starts itching. I walk over to the empty chair next to Yo-Yo, sit down, and with one finger poke her on the arm. "I can touch you, bitch."

The bitch cuts her gaze away like I'm a bothersome child she doesn't have time to deal with.

"Yolanda," I say with my attitude barely in check. "Your ass needs to roll up out of here, too. For real, girl. I'm trying very hard not to waste your ass on Ms. Anna's floor."

Yo-Yo rocks her neck just as hard as I am. "I ain't gonna go no damn where. *Our* man broke me off some change to get my wig straight, and that's exactly what the fuck I'm doing."

Everyone gasps and then cracks the hell up. I'm stunned.

To prove that she means what she said, Yo-Yo crosses her legs and folds her arms.

"Bitch, what did you just say?"

Yo-Yo holds her own. "Girl, you heard me. I—"

I flip the gun in my hand and make a perfect golf swing with the butt of my Glock, crashing it against that smiling ho's face with a hard *CRACK!* Blood spews out of Yo-Yo's busted lip, and before the disrespecting heifer has the chance to clear her mind, I send the gun flying across the other side of her face.

Bitches scream and jump out of the way.

"WHO THE FUCK DO YOU THINK YOU'RE TALKING TO, BITCH?"

Whap!

"You think my man's dick is pumping you full of kryptonite? You think I won't kill your monkey ass up in here?"

Whap!

"CHILL OUT!"

Out of nowhere, I'm tackled from my right side. I

lose my balance and hit the floor with a thud. However, I still have a good grip on my weapon, but by the time I flip it to grab the butt, Baby Thug has her piece leveled at my head.

"I SAID, CHILL THE FUCK OUT!"

I can't believe my fuckin' eyes. "Have you lost your muthafuckin' mind?"

"Nah, but you have. Everybody up in here knows that this girl is pregnant."

Baby's words are like a swift punch to the gut. *"Pregnant?"*

"Yeah." Baby bobs her head. "Call me crazy, but I don't think Python will take it too lightly you tryna kill his seed."

Everyone in the salon starts whispering again, and the floor starts spinning beneath me. After a couple of deep breaths, I glare at Baby while Yo-Yo whimpers and bleeds by the shampoo bowl. "Get her the fuck out of my sight," I hiss.

Baby's chin goes up.

"NOW!"

Baby steps back and finally lowers her gun. "C'mon, Yo-Yo. Let's get out of here."

One of the girls working the shampoo bowl hands Yo-Yo a clean hair towel so she can take care of the blood gushing out of her mouth. Baby helps the girl up and escorts her to the front door, never once turning her back on me.

"By the way, Baby," I say, climbing back to my feet. "Watch your back. You just landed on my shit list, too."

Baby glares, pulls open the front door, and leads Yo-Yo's stupid ass out of the salon.

I dust myself off and walk back over to the dryer and sit down as if pistol-whipping a pregnant girl is something I do every weekend. "What y'all looking at?"

Everyone scrambles to look busy and the radio comes

back on. Despite looking calm, cool, and collected, my thoughts are in a state of chaos.

After my hair is done, I fake a couple of hours of happy shopping with my girls Pit Bull and Kookie. I'm shoveling Benjamins at a good clip at every register. But today retail therapy ain't doing shit for me. After I ditch my girls, I make a rare trip out to Goodson Construction near Winchester and march my ass up to the back door. I bang on it like it was Python's big-ass head. When no one opens the door, I try again and add a few kicks for good measure.

Killa Kyle busts open the door and then glances around to make sure I'm alone. "What the hell, girl?"

I shove my way past him. "Where's Python?"

Killa Kyle races behind me and grabs my wrist. "My man is a little busy at the moment, LeShelle. You're going to have to come back."

I snatch my arm out of his grip. "I don't think so. I have been laughed at and humiliated one too many fuckin' times. WHERE. IS. HE?"

"He's in a business meeting," he whispers. "Come back in about an hour."

"AHHHHHHH!"

I jump. "What in the hell?" I sidestep Killa Kyle and move farther into the warehouse.

"YOU BROUGHT A MUTHAFUCKIN' DEA AGENT INTO THIS MUTHAFUCKA?" Python kicks a body that's wrapped in plastic. "Y'ALL MUTHA-FUCKAS THOUGHT YOU WERE GONNA BRING ME DOWN?" He kicks the body again and then turns his attention to Tyga and Datwon, who are tied down in two metal chairs. Behind Python, a ring of Gangster Disciples have their forks up, looking as though they're just waiting for the word to start blasting.

"Python," Tyga sputters. "You gotta believe me. I didn't know this fool was a pig. I . . . I swear."

Python shakes his head and twists his lips. "Nah. Nah, man. I distinctly remember you vouching for this muthafucka Dmitry. Don't you remember? Your dick was tonsil-boxing my girl up in the VIP." He stopped in front of Tyga. "*You said* I could put your name on this deal. *You said* that you worked with the nigga before. Remember?"

Tyga's eyes look like they're trying to squeeze out of his head. He knows what time it is. He recognizes that crazy, manic look in Python's eyes just like the rest of the niggas in the room.

"Okay. All right." Tyga throws some bass in his voice so at least he won't sound too much like a bitch if his nigga snubs him out. "I know . . . I know I said that, but hear me out. Datwon came to me saying that the nigga was cool. He swore the nigga was legit. I was just tryna help the little nigga get back into your good graces, man. That's all it was. I didn't know your own cousin turned fed, man. I swear. I just felt sorry for the dude."

Python's narrowed gaze swings over to his cousin Datwon. He's sitting in the middle chair, trembling so bad he looks like a self-contained earthquake. "Were you tryna set me up, cuz?"

Datwon shakes his head. He looks too paralyzed to actually speak.

"Correct me if I'm wrong," Python says, scratching his temple with the barrel of his Glock, "but didn't I tell you this wasn't the business for you?"

Datwon swallows, his extra-large Adam's apple bobbing up and down.

"Help me understand this," Python continues. "You

steal, you lie, and now here you are tryna send me, your own cuz, to the federal pen. Did you really think you were gonna get away with this shit?"

"I . . . I—"

Python stops pacing and leans close to his cousin. "I'm sorry. What was that?"

Datwon licks his lips. "I'm s-sorry."

"Oooooh. You're sorry." Python bobs his head and then turns toward his blue-flagged army. "Niggas, y'all hear that? This nigga says that he's sorry." He tosses up his hands. "Well, fuck. I guess that settles everything. You're sorry." Then, quick as lightning, Python squares off and punches Datwon dead in the throat.

The loud smack sounds more like a crunch. When Python pulls back, there's this weird wheezing, as if air is trying to find an alternative way in and out Datwon's body, but isn't having too much success.

"Bring Damien on out here," Python instructs.

My brows jump at the order. Damien is Python's favorite pet . . . and his most dangerous. The twenty-six-foot python reticulatus has always given me the heebie-jeebies, and thank God Python keeps the menacing-looking monster in a big aquarium here at the ware-house office. It takes about fifteen niggas to carry the aquarium out to the middle of the warehouse.

"OH, FUCK!" Tyga starts bouncing in his chair. "OH, FUCK! NIGGA, NAH!"

Datwon looks like he's shitting a cement block in his pants.

Python just smiles. "Y'all know how I do. I like a little entertainment with my dirt."

"NAH, NAH! Y'ALL JUST SHOOT MY ASS!" Tyga shakes his head while still trying to sound all hard, but in truth a little bitchassness is creeping in strong. "Man, I can't go out like this."

"You lost that vote when you lied to me, nigga." Python turns to some more soldiers. "Y'all get this pig out of here. Chop that nigga up and make me a nice cement block to remember him by."

Niggas jump to it, grabbing the body wrapped in bloody plastic and running toward the back door. Killa Kyle and I move out of the way.

"Y'all niggas got any last words?" Python asks, looking over into the aquarium and making cooing noises at his beloved snake.

"D-don't do this," Datwon chokes, still trying to breathe through his collapsed windpipe. "I swear you'll never see me again. I-I'll leave town. I-I'll do whatever you want me to."

Python shakes his head. "Daddy brought you something good to eat today," he says in a loving voice. "Just consider it an early birthday gift." He chuckles.

"FUCK NAW! FUCK NAW!" Tyga starts jumping like he's going to hop all the way out of the warehouse tied to that chair.

Python laughs. "All right, man. Chill the fuck out." He snaps his fingers and points to a few boxes. The brothers rush over and pull out thick sheets of plastic. "Seeing as how you've been a true soldier for me up until this unfortunate incident, I'm going to do you a solid and let you go out like a soldier."

Tyga glances back as his brothers cut the ropes from his chair and then force him to stand on the plastic. Amazingly, Tyga looks a little calmer about the situation. He faces Python, lifts his chin and chest, and throws up his pitchfork signs. "ALL IS ONE!"

Raising his Glock, Python and the rest of the set shout back, "UNTIL THE WORLD BLOWS!"

Python squeezes off two rounds into the center of Tyga's forehead, sweeping him off his feet. The thick plastic does very little to soften the sound of Tyga's body hitting the concrete floor.

"Oh shit. Oh shit," Datwon moans, tears splashing down his face.

"You know, I'm actually going to miss that nigga," Python says remorsefully, and then turns to face his cousin. "You know, Aunt Peaches was right. It just takes one bad apple to spoil a whole bunch. I should've gotten rid of your ass a while ago."

Datwon keeps shaking his head. "P-please."

"All right. Pick this nigga up."

The crew rush Datwon, untying him and pulling him from the chair.

"LET ME GO! PYTHON, PLEASE DON'T DO THIS!"

"Nigga, stop all that hollering." Python grabs the chair Tyga was sitting in and pops a squat to enjoy the show.

"C'mon, Python. We're family, man!"

"Somebody tape that muthafucka's mouth."

Killa Kyle reaches over me and grabs a roll of duct tape. "I got it!" He rushes over eagerly.

Python finally sees me and smiles. "Yo, baby. C'mon over here."

He waves me over. I hesitate only because of Damien uncoiling in the aquarium behind him. I can deal with most of Python's pets, but that muthafucka scares me.

"Don't worry. Damien is going to stay where he is." He laughs.

I force my legs to move, stopping only briefly to hop over Tyga's body. "What's going on, baby?" I ask, even though I heard enough to figure out all the missing pieces.

Python brushes a kiss against my right temple. "I'm

just tying up some loose ends." He smiles. "I like what you did to your hair." He touches my soft wavy curls and then returns his attention back to the business at hand.

"PYTHON, NO! PLEASE!" Datwon screams.

Killa Kyle slaps a wide strip of tape across Datwon's mouth while the other guys tie his legs and hands together.

Python sits back down and pulls me into his lap. "This should be a good show."

I feel Python's dick harden as he watches the unfolding drama. The top of the aquarium is removed, and Damien's head lifts as if he senses the possibility of freedom. Next, two men grab Datwon's feet and two grab his arms and lift him like a stuffed pig ready for slow roasting.

"Hmumpt mummmph," Datwon muffles through his taped mouth.

"Drop his ass in there," Python says.

The brothers lower Datwon halfway, release him, and then scramble to put the top back on the aquarium before standing back to watch the show.

Damien wastes no time uncoiling from the corner and slithering over Datwon's squirming body. In less than a minute, he wraps his muscular body around Datwon and starts to squeeze.

I sit transfixed. I'm both horrified and fascinated at the same time. Watching Damien work, I can see his muscles move like a wave beneath his scaly skin.

Python locks gazes with his cousin as he screams behind his duct tape. Datwon kicks and bucks while his dark complexion turns a rich burgundy, then cranberry, and finally an ugly eggplant. A few seconds later, his body goes still.

The entire warehouse falls silent. A lot of the brothers just shake and hang their heads.

"All species feed off one another in order to survive," Python whispers.

I glance over at him, curious.

"This is what happens when muthafuckas try to cross me," he says as if reading my mind. "Family or no." He smiles and glances back at me. "Remember that. You don't let nobody punk you out."

Our eyes lock.

"Now what brings you down here?"

Suddenly it doesn't seem to be the best time to bother him about my issues with him fuckin' Yolanda's retarded ass. There's no telling what he'll say or do right now. "Nothing. I . . . just wanted to see you. You've been so busy lately."

He nods. "I'm always about my paper. You know that." His black gaze rakes over me while his hard-on still presses against the curve of my ass. "I've been meaning to ask you: How's your sister doing?"

The question is like a steel fist to my gut. "F-fine. Why do you ask?"

He shrugs, but his gaze never loses its intensity. "Just curious." He reaches up and brushes my hair back from my shoulders. "You got to be careful with these young kids today. Sometimes they fall in with the wrong crowd, you know?"

My heart races. "Not Ta'Shara. She's a good girl."

Python nods, licking his lips as he brushes a finger across my breasts. "Well, you can never be too sure. Good girls turn bad all the time." He pinches my nipple. "You should know that."

Oh, God. He knows.

31

Yolanda

I take another look at my busted mouth in the bathroom mirror. "Aaaargh! I can't fuckin' stand that bitch!" I throw the curling iron, and it hits a weak spot in the glass. The damn thing explodes as if I just unloaded an AK-47 into it. I gasp and jump back.

Baby Thug leans against the door frame, crossing her arms and shaking her head. "What the fuck did you think was going to happen? LeShelle ain't no punk. Did you think she was just going to let you play her in front of the other Queen Gs?"

"I ain't no punk either. And she ain't gonna be the head bitch for long." I storm out of the bathroom and brush past Baby.

"And just *how* do you know that?" Baby asks snidely. "Just because you're about to have that ugly nigga's kid?"

"Baby!"

"What?"

"Watch your mouth. That's our leader you're talking about."

"So? His ass is still ugly as fuck. He knows it, his momma knows it, and any damn body else who takes one look at him knows it," Baby says, marching behind me toward the bedroom. "And just because you're going to drop his seed don't mean that he's getting ready to kick LeShelle to the curb and make you wifey. Open your eyes. You're just his fuckin' jump-off—and you ain't the only one. That nigga got bitches all over the goddamn city, and all of them know how to fall back and give LeShelle her proper respect."

I whirl around. "Well, thanks a lot, *buddy*. With friends like you, I sure as hell don't need any enemies."

"If you didn't have a friend like me, then that bitch would've pistol-whipped you into the middle of next week." Baby shakes her head. "You're in over your head, and you don't even know it. Now you got me on that bitch's radar, and frankly I don't fuckin' appreciate it."

My eyes mist. "So . . . what? You want to run out on me again? Is that it?" I shrug my shoulders and sweep my arm toward the door. "Go! See if I give a fuck. I don't need you. I've been doing fine all by myself." It would've been more convincing if my busted bottom lip hadn't started quivering.

Baby cocks her head and stares at me.

"Y-you knew I've been trying to land someone high up in the set—and now I got the head muthafucka in charge and you wanna throw salt in my game like all those other haters?" I sniff. "You're just like the other bitches just wanting to throw shade."

"You also used to want to get your kids back, but I don't hear you talking about that shit anymore. Instead, you're about to pop out another lil crumb-snatcher you can't afford to feed."

"Python is breaking me off," I say, giving Baby my back as I go sit on the bed. "He's gonna take care of me. Watch and see." *Sniff.* "He's already spending more time with me than LeShelle, and he's been talking about getting me an apartment." I reach up and remove the silk scarf from my neck and toss it aside.

"WHAT. THE. FUCK?" Baby launches across the room and roughly inspects my bruised neck. "WHAT THE HELL HAPPENED TO YOU?"

I pull away. "Nothing. It's no big deal."

"No big deal?" Baby stares at me as if I've lost my mind. "Is that nigga beating on you?"

"No. Don't be ridiculous!" I roll her eyes. "It's nothing like that."

"Don't fuckin' lie to me." Baby's voice tightens with anger. "If that grimy muthafucka is hurting, he ain't got to worry about Fat Ace's ass no more, because I'll rock-a-bye that nasty-looking muthafucka *myself.*"

I stand from the bed and fold my arms. "He's not hurting me. We just like to play it rough when we're fuckin', that's all."

"Rough?" Baby reaches for my neck again, but I dodge her touch. "Damn, Yo-Yo. You letting that nigga choke you out? What the fuck?"

I shrug again. "It's no big deal. He really gets into it. I mean, he fuckin' comes like nobody I've ever seen." I laugh but it sounds like a misfired weapon, so I turn away again.

Baby just stands there not really knowing what to say.

"You watch. Python's gonna leave that bitch and make me wifey. Then all those bitches will have to bow down to my ass. The one they used to call retard and Lemonhead. I'm going to be the head bitch in charge."

Sniff. "You watch and see." Tears bum-rush my eyes and splash down my face. "These bitches are going to respect me."

I don't hear Baby move up behind me, but I melt when my best friend wraps her arms around me and pulls me close. The next thing I know, I'm sobbing and blubbering against Baby's collarbone. It's more than just my face and mouth that's busted; it feels as if something much deeper is going on. I put up a good front, but there's shit about Python and all those creepy-ass snakes and his violent sex practices that scares the hell out of me.

"Shhhh. Don't cry. Everything is going to be all right," Baby assures me awkwardly.

I know my girl isn't normally the comforting type, but at the moment I'll take what I can get. I've missed my friend, more than I want to admit. Who knows what could've happened if Baby Thug hadn't shown up when she did.

"It's all right," Baby whispers. "You know I'll always have your back."

I hear the truth behind her words, and then I feel Baby's soft but persistent lips press against my bruised ones. I don't immediately react. Then when my body starts to tingle, my thoughts slow and I find myself kissing her back. It's like a click inside my head, and for this one moment in time, everything feels *right*.

The way Baby caresses my body makes me feel both loved and desirable. I've never felt this way with any man. Ever. Now curious, I allow Baby to unbutton my shirt and unsnap my bra. My reward is Baby's strong but slender fingers spreading over my full breasts and squeezing their softness.

We ease down onto the bed. I stare at Baby like I'm truly seeing her for the first time. Even then I'm not sure what I'm seeing or feeling, for that matter. Baby is a petite woman with pretty brown eyes and long curly lashes, and her thick hair is cornrowed in neat, straight lines. Her subtle masculinity comes from her firm body, muscled arms, and thuggish attitude, which right now is turning me on.

Baby keeps her gaze level as she lowers her head and then sucks one of my erect nipples into her mouth. I gasp and moan when her tongue dances around my breasts. Encouraged by my reaction, Baby reaches down and peels my jeans and panties off my hips.

"Oh my God, Baby. I don't—"

"Shhhh. Just relax and enjoy, sweetheart," Baby urges, and then turns her attention to the other exposed breast. "Let me show you how I feel about you. Let me love you." She goes back to sucking and squeezing my breasts.

I run my hand along Baby's braided hair. I try to hold on to her, but the absence of a broad chest and thick waist slowly starts to pull me out of the fantasy that she's trying to create for me. I feel her slender fingers skim up my open thighs and then brush against my neatly groomed pussy. I quiver, deliciously so, while conflicting emotions flood my senses and a new wave of tears leak from my eyes.

This is wrong. This is wrong . . . but it feels so good.

Baby slips her index finger in between the lips of my swollen pussy and then swishes it around my slippery clit. Slowly, she inches down my body, planting small kisses as she goes.

This isn't right.

Baby pulls open my pussy and curls her long tongue beneath the base of my clit.

"No. No. Stop." I sit up. "I can't do this."

"What?" Baby looks up, confused.

I roll away and snatch my panties up off the floor.

"I'm sorry. B-but I can't. It's not that . . . that I don't have feelings for you. I do. But I can't love you the way you want me to."

"Let me get this straight," Baby says, her voice hardening. "You can fuck somebody else's *man,* but you can't fuck me? You can let that grimy freak choke you out, but you can't lay with a bitch who cares for you—who fights for you? Is that what you're saying?"

"Don't say it like that." I hang my head.

"How the fuck should I say it?" Baby hops off the bed. "I ain't good enough for you? Just fuckin' say it! You can't be happy unless someone is using and abusing you? Is that how you get off?"

"Stop it! Just stop it!" I toss up my hands. "It's not like that. I'm just . . . I'm—"

"You're just what, bitch?"

"I'M NOT FUCKIN' GAY!" I storm away from her, pressing my forehead against the palm of my hand. "No matter how much you wish I was or whatever, I just don't get down like that."

"Bitch, I just had my hand in your *wet* pussy! Don't tell me you weren't feeling me. You're just stuck on stupid. You always have been. Whether it's sucking nigga's dicks for Lemonheads or thinking a nigga like Python is gonna upgrade some chicken head just because he put a baby on you. If that was the muthafuckin' case, how come none of those other baby daddies didn't wife you? *Think.*" She taps her temple. "Only a retarded muthafucka would keep doin' the same thing over and over again and expect different results."

"Is that why you keep running behind me sniffing my ass?" I explode. "*Your* retarded ass thinks that I'm just going to magically turn into a muthafuckin' dyke so we can fuck with fake dicks and slurp down pussy juice?"

Baby cocks back a fist, but then catches herself before she sends the muthafucka flying.

"Whatcha wanna do? Hit me?" I glare. "Guess that don't make you no different from the rest of them niggas after all. Does it?" To my surprise, Baby's eyes gloss with restrained tears. *Never,* in all the years that I've known Baby, have I *ever* seen the girl cry. That shit just didn't happen. Baby is too strong, hardheaded, and rough around the edges to let anyone catch her slipping. "Baby, I—"

"Squash it." Baby relaxes her fist and holds up her hands. "I'm ghost." She turns for the door. "You're on your own." She storms out. "Peace."

I try to process what just happened. It feels like someone has just carved out my heart. What did I just do? "Baby!" I chase after her. "Please don't leave. I'm sorry." I race down the hall in just a pair of yellow panties. I hear the front door bang shut, and I speed up out the door. "Baby, come back! Baby!"

Baby Thug has already hopped into her blue Impala and is peeling away from the front curb.

"BABY!" I pay no mind to the lil niggas milling about, even as they laugh and point at my damn near naked ass. "BABY, COME BACK!"

In a rare and surprising move, my momma rushes out of the house and grabs my arm. "Girl, what the hell is wrong with you?" She drags me back toward the house. "Get your stupid ass in the house!"

"BABY!" I sob. "DON'T GO!"

32
Momma Peaches

"BABY, COME BACK!"

My head pops up from my pillow. "What in the world?"

Arzell's thick lips spring off my fat clit as he pulls the covers back from over his head. "Forget about all that noise. Just lay back and relax." He grins devilishly and then slides his hands beneath my ass so he can lift and plow back into his afternoon dessert.

"Oooh, sheeiiit." I rotate my hips, smashing my pussy against his open mouth so that Arzell's tongue gets in there good and deep. "Clean all that juice up, nigga. Ahhhh." My boo hits my magic spot and honey gushes out of my body. I quiver and shake and then quiver some more.

Arzell eats it up like a starving nigga from a third world country, smacking and slurping the whole way. I thrash around so much that I know I must look like I'm having an epileptic fit. Even then, Arzell climbs up my body, hikes up my one and a half legs, and enters me with such deft precision that I come on his first stroke.

My mind spins. This young nigga is going to be the end of me, but if a bitch has to go, then there's no better way than coming to death. An hour later, we're covered in sweat and smoking one of Baby's special blunts.

Arzell passes the blunt over and then reaches in between my legs and gives my sopping pussy a good squeeze. "How you feeling, Ma?"

"You know you handled your business, Daddy." I smile dreamily and blow a stream of smoke up toward the ceiling.

A wide smile stretches across Arzell's face as he drinks me in with his adoring eyes. "You know . . . I've been thinking."

"Was that what that smell was?" I laugh and cuddle closer. There are just no words to describe how it feels for a woman my age to have a young, beautiful, and virile body lying next to her.

"Ha-ha." He props himself up higher on the pillows. "Be serious for a minute, Ma."

I catch the serious look in the young brother's eyes and am instantly worried. I know that look. I've seen it on countless lovers before him. "No. No. No."

Arzell frowns. "No what? You don't even know what I'm about to say."

"Actually, I do." I pry myself away from the comfortable nook beneath his arm. "Do me a favor and let's not talk. Let's just float on this high for a while."

"But—"

"Tomorrow," I say. "I promise."

Disappointment washes over Arzell's handsome face. Clearly he doesn't want to wait and lose his nerve, and unfortunately, that's exactly what I'm hoping will happen. I try to take another toke off the addictive blunt but notice that the flame has died out. "Hand me that lighter off the nightstand," I instruct Arzell, since he's the closest.

Arzell grabs the red Bic and tries to flick it on. "It's empty." He sits up.

"There's another one inside the drawer."

He opens the drawer and rummages around. "Hey. Who's this?" He picks up a frame. "Humph. She's pretty. Is she related to you?"

I roll my eyes. "I asked you to grab a lighter, not to get all up in my business." I reach over and grab the damn lighter myself.

Arzell steals another peek at the picture, but clearly he knows better than to ask me about it again. Instead of putting the frame back in the drawer, he sits it on top of the nightstand and climbs out of bed.

"Where are you going?" I ask, suspicious that he's getting away from me because I have somehow hurt his delicate feelings.

"I'm hitting the shower," he says with a serious attitude.

"Whatever," I mumble under my breath, and flick on the lighter and inhale another much-needed hit. "These damn kids today." I toss the lighter over at the nightstand and hit the picture frame. Glancing over, I sigh at the sight of my smiling sister. I don't remember exactly when that picture was taken, but I certainly remember the last time I saw Alice. . . .

I worried about Alice's sudden interest in motherhood, mainly because she had dumped responsibility of her firstborn into my lap. Now her desire to be ghetto baby momma of the year stemmed solely from her wanting to prove that if I could do something, then so could she. That shit was questionable—especially since every time I did a roll-by of her Section 8 apartment in LeMoyne Gardens, the place was a total wreck and reeked of dirty diapers, spoiling food, and just outright BO.

Alice complained endlessly about not getting enough sleep or not having enough time to just take a decent bath, but whenever I offered to babysit, I would get accused of trying to steal custody of Mason. It was pointless to remind her that she was the one who had willy-nilly given up custody of Terrell and that it wasn't some sneaky, underhanded maneuver on my part. But facts didn't have a place in Alice's drug-induced perception.

Plus, Alice was being very secretive about Mason's father. Rumors circulated that it could've been anyone, since what my sister did to support her crack habit was the stuff of legends. Though my help wasn't wanted or welcomed, I still felt that it was my duty to check on my newest nephew.

"I say leave her alone," Isaac said as he shoved more bricks of cocaine into the deep freezer. "If the bitch doesn't want to be bothered, then don't bother her."

"I know, but I think that baby is sick. Every time I call, I can hear him screaming in the background. It ain't normal for no baby to holler like that all the damn time." I crammed my arm through the sleeve of my sweater. "I'm just going to run over real quick, and then I'll come back and start dinner."

Isaac gave up. "Fine. She's your sister. Just take Terrell with you because I gotta go handle some business over off Lamar." He grabbed his gat. "It shouldn't take too long, but I don't want lil man to get caught in the crosshairs."

"No problem. He's been driving me crazy about seeing his little brother again anyway. I just hope his momma will open the door and let us in." I kissed my husband on the cheek and headed out the door. "TERRELL!" I shouted, coming down my porch stairs. I spotted him across the street, playing with his best friend KyJuan. "Terrell, c'mon now. We gotta go!"

A door banged from off to my left, and I whipped my head around.

"I DONE TOLD YOU ABOUT TALKIN' BACK TO ME, GIRL!" Eddie, Betty's always drunk and deranged man of the moment, stumbled out of the house after a scrawny Yolanda.

"GET BACK HERE, YOU LIL BITCH!" Eddie waved a broken beer bottle. "I'LL TEACH YOU NOT TO TALK BACK!"

"What the fuck?" I raced over.

"MOMMY!" Yo-Yo screamed.

"Get away from that child," I demanded, not even thinking when I retrieved the switchblade from my thigh and swish, swish, swish.

"AWWW. FUCK!" Eddie hit the ground, grabbing the side of his face where his left ear used to be. "SHE CUT ME! THAT BITCH CUT ME!"

Suddenly Betty found it fit to come running out of the house, shrieking in outrage. "EDDIE! EDDIE!" She dropped to her knees beside him and was quickly covered in blood. "What the hell did you do?" She glared up at me accusingly. "YOU BITCH!"

I blinked at the stupid heifer and then went back to waving my switchblade. "Now you can get a little bit of this, too, if you want. I ain't about to be too many bitches out here."

Betty clamped her mouth shut and went about trying to help her man. *"C'mon, now, honey. Let me help you up."*

"GET THE FUCK AWAY FROM ME!" Eddie shoved her away and rolled himself off the ground. *"WHERE THE FUCK IS MY EAR?"*

Lil Yolanda started laughing.

I glanced over at the bony child and frowned. *"Chile, is you all right?"* That shit just made the girl laugh even harder. I stepped back. That girl wasn't all there.

Terrell ran up behind me, nosy to see what was going on. Hell, the whole block was pouring out of they houses to see what the hell was going on. Terrell looked at Yolanda like she was crazy. *"Mama Peaches, what's wrong with her?"* he asked.

"Don't worry about it, baby. C'mon." I returned the switchblade to my thigh garter and reached for Terrell's hand. But I jumped back when my hand brushed against something scaly. *"What the fuck?"*

Terrell beamed up at me as he held up a green grass snake. *"This is Python,"* he bragged. *"Me and KyJuan found him in his backyard. Can we keep him?"*

I rolled my eyes. My nephew had gone overboard ever since Isaac had told him to embrace his fears.

"Boy, I don't care. C'mon, let's go see your momma."

The ride out to LeMoyne Gardens was always interesting. Some hood nigga was cliquing up and starting to rise against the Black Gangster Disciples. Those lil ghetto hood rats were tagging damn near everything that stood still, and rolling through their territory was starting to be like going through inspection at the Mexican border.

Terrell glared at the cocky niggas but knew not to throw up the signs that repped Isaac's set. When we climbed the deep staircase up to Alice's apartment, Terrell wound and unwound Python around his wrist. "I'm gonna get me a gun and shoot all them niggas," he said under his breath.

"You ain't gonna do no such thing," I hissed, and tugged him along. I knocked on Alice's door. We waited for what seemed like forever before I banged again . . . and then again.

"Maybe she's not home," Terrell said, fidgeting.

"Maybe," I said, mainly because I didn't hear Mason screaming his little head off. I started to give up and walk away when something told me to try the door.

It was unlocked.

Curious and concerned, I pushed open the door and poked my head inside. "Hello? Alice?"

No answer.

I crept into the apartment. "ALICE. HEEEELLLLLOOO." I closed the door behind me and Terrell. A sound came from somewhere on the sofa in the living room. It took a moment, but I finally made out Alice lying facedown. "Alice?" I moved over to my sister and brushed back her hair. "Are you sick?"

"Hmmm?" Alice smacked her lips together and peered up at me. "Oh, hey, May." She tried to sit up. "Whatcha doin' here?"

I frowned. "Are you high?" I glanced over to the coffee table just as Terrell picked up his mother's glass pipe. "Give me that." I snatched the pipe from him.

Alice sighed and spoke drowsily. "Why didn't you call? I would've cleaned or . . . something." She swiped some clothes off the cushion next to her. "Sit down. Sit down."

I placed a hand under my nose. My sister smelled like

she hadn't taken a shower in weeks; in fact, the apart-
ment reeked of shitty diapers and spoiling food.
"Where's the baby?"

Alice stretched and scratched at her crotch. *"Hmmm?"*

The hairs on the back of my neck stood up at attention. *"Terrell, stay right here."* I took off running toward
the baby's room. It was just as cluttered and foul-
smelling at the rest of the house. More importantly,
Mason wasn't in his bed. I turned and raced toward
Alice's bedroom. It was just as messy, and my nephew
wasn't in there either. I searched the bathroom—
nothing.

Don't panic. Don't panic. I rushed back into the living room where my sister was preparing to light up her
pipe again. *"Alice, where's Mason?"*

"Oh, um, he's . . . he's back there sleep." Alice flicked
on the lighter.

"No. He's. Not. Where is he?"

"Shit. I don't know." She moved the flame over her
precious crack rocks, but before she could pull a good
toke, I slammed the whole thing out of her hands.
"STOP THAT SHIT AND LISTEN TO ME!"

"HEY!"

I grabbed my sister by the front of her sweatshirt and
jerked her up from the sofa. *"Mason is not here,"* I
hissed. *"Where the fuck is he?"*

Alice tried to pull herself free. *"Let . . . go."*

In response, I smacked the shit out of her. *"FOCUS,
GODDAMN IT!"*

"Oww. Stop," Alice whined, still trying to pull herself
free. *"What the fuck do you want?"*

Oh. My. God! *"Alice, I need for you to think
reeeeaaallly hard. When was the last time you saw
Mason?"*

My sister seemed confused by the question. *"Mason?"*

I glanced over at my nephew. "Terrell, get me the phone. I'm calling the police."

Alice's eyes grew wide. "Whoa. Whoa, why you gonna call the po-po on me?" She finally snatched herself loose and scrambled to gather her crack rocks. "You can't bring those pigs up in here. Are you crazy?"

I looked at my sister, but I hardly recognized the wild-eyed crazy woman who was shoving drugs into her pocket. "Alice, where did you get the drugs?"

"None of your damn business!" She swiped at her running nose. "You think I'm gonna tell you so your snitching ass can tell the po-po? Get the fuck out of here with that shit."

"Here you go, Momma Peaches." Terrell handed me the cordless phone and then stared at his mother, who'd retrieved her glass pipe and lighter from off the floor.

Angry and fighting back tears, I did something that I never thought I would ever do: I called the police. An hour later, still no one could get an answer out of Alice as to what happened to her baby, even though now she was coming down out of her high and panic was starting to settle in.

"He was here—I swear he was here," Alice repeated, glancing around. "I just . . . got a little taste, you know. Just to calm my nerves," she stressed to the officer who was snapping handcuffs around her wrists. "You don't understand. He wouldn't stop crying, and I just needed something to make me relax."

"Who did you buy the drugs from, ma'am?" another cop asked with his notepad out. "Do you remember what he looked like?"

Alice looked at the man like he'd just grown two heads. "Sheeeiit." She shook her head. She was faced with a hard dilemma: snitching or finding her baby. The *choice was clear in my eyes. But Alice wasn't seeing it the same way.*

"Tell them who was here," I pleaded. "We need to find Mason before . . ."

Alice licked her lips and scratched at her matted hair. "I . . . I just . . . don't . . . remember."

"What the fuck do you mean you don't remember?" I lost it and charged toward my sister. "YOU STUPID BITCH! HOW COULD YOU?" Four officers jumped into the mix and struggled to pull me away from her. "YOU FUCKIN' SOLD THAT BABY FOR A MUTHAFUCKIN' HIT?"

Alice started crying. "I . . . I don't . . . know. I can't . . . I wouldn't." She looked around for a sympathetic face, but didn't find one—not even from her son. "Terrell, I didn't. You gotta believe me. I would never . . ."

Terrell, holding his baby brother's stuffed teddy bear in one hand and his pet grass snake in the other, turned his back on his mother.

"Terrell, baby. Please. Listen to your momma."

"All right. Get her out of here." The one cop closed his notepad and shook his head.

"No, wait!" Alice screamed. "Terrell, baby!"

I gathered myself and shook the cops off of me. "Terrell, sweetheart. Come here."

Terrell waltzed over to me with his head down.

"You, bitch," Alice seethed as the police tried to drag her out of the apartment. "You're tryna turn my children against me. You got my baby. I know you do!" She glanced at the police tugging her. "She has my baby. Arrest her! I know she has my baby!"

I shook my head while tears streamed down my face. If anything happened to that poor child, I would never forgive my sister.

Never.

* * *

Arzell jerks open the bathroom door, and clouds of steam coil out along with him. He might have a body out of this world, with his hard, chiseled abs, slim waist, and muscled arms, but more and more I'm starting to feel our age difference creep in between us. "You feel better?" I ask, stubbing out what was left of my blunt.

He shrugs and removes the thick towel from around his waist so that his ten inches can just swing in the air. "I'm good."

I watch him wearily as he walks over to my side of the bed and sits next to me.

"You know . . . I hate it when you just shut me down," he says with a seriousness he hasn't shown before. He reaches for my hand. "I've been tryna get something off my chest for a minute."

Oh, Jesus. I struggle not to roll my eyes.

"Just hear me out," he says as if sensing my frustration. "Now, I . . . I love you. I know that might . . . I don't know, scare you or—"

"Arzell—"

"Let me finish," he insists. "For me this isn't just, you know, some sex thing. I wanna marry you, girl."

I bust out laughing.

Arzell's face twists as he lowers my hand. "What's so damn funny?"

I shake my head and wipe away a few tears of amusement. "Honey, I can't marry you."

Stunned and hurt, Arzell asks, "Why the hell not?"

"Because I'm already married."

33

LeShelle

I ain't forgot about that punk-ass shit Baby Thug pulled at FabDivas. Not for a muthafuckin' minute. Sure, I can't touch that high-yellow, Ritalin-popping bitch Python got knocked up at the moment. Mainly because word got to Python how I tried to work her over, so he rolled her out of Shotgun Row and stashed her simple ass someplace he thinks I can't find her. That's all right. It's cool. I'm going to let him have that for now, but he can't hide that bitch forever, so I'm just going to bide my time.

But Baby's ass is grass, and I'm looking high and low to mow that bitch down. Shit. I can't have bitches under me looking at me sideways like I'm just going to let that bullshit roll. If I let that shit go, then it's just a matter of time before the next bitch thinks she can try me.

For weeks I had every Queen G with her eyes and

ears wide open. If that I-wish-I-had-a-dick bitch is locking down a street, a corner, or even a curb, I want to know about it. Just so happens I'm dreaming about what I'm going to do to this bitch while Python's forked tongue is slapping my pussy from behind like it owed his ass money or some shit when my phone starts buzzing on the nightstand.

I can't answer because I'm facedown with a leather mask over my face, a red ball shoved down my throat, and my pink sugar melting in my nigga's mouth, not in his hands. It's hard to control my breathing, especially with my hands jacked down in between my legs with cuffs and a chain link that Python pulls whenever he gets ready.

The spike in my collar is digging into my neck, and the pain is shooting an unbelievable dose of euphoria that's only second to the pleasure exploding in my fattening clit.

"Skeet that shit into my mouth, baby."

Python's heavy hand smacks hard across my ass. I gasp at the stinging pain while my knees tremble and struggle to support my weight.

"C'mon, baby. Skeet that pussy juice."

My eyes roll to the back of my head just as the bottom of my pussy drops and wave after wave of my thick honey gushes into his open mouth. Ooh. I love this fucking shit. I've been with this freaky muthafucka for so long that he's turned me into a straight freak, too.

Python noisily smacks his thick lips. "That's right. That's a good pussy. Ahh." He wipes stray juices off the side of my leg and then makes a hickie on my inner right thigh.

I'm dizzy as fuck by the time he releases me and unzips the back of my mask. I gulp down a healthy dose of oxygen and then smile lazily as my body still vibrates with orgasmic aftershocks.

Python laughs, his warm breath rolling against my thigh. "Fuck, baby. You ain't come like that in a minute." Python crawls back up my body.

"I ain't come in a while, period. You're too busy giving my dick to those other bitches." I push him off me after he unlocks the cuffs. Just because he's given me a good nut ain't no reason for me to just forget about that other shit.

He props up on his side, laughing.

"I ain't said shit that's funny."

"Nah. You're just cute when you get jealous." He reaches over and squeezes one of my titties.

"Yeah. I wonder what your face would look like if you found out I was fucking some other nigga."

"What?" All humor melts out of his hard face, and the playful energy evaporates like steam.

"Nothing." I roll over and reach for my phone, which is buzzing again. But Python snatches me back by my shoulder and pins me down to the bed. "You fuckin' some other nigga, bitch?"

"Get off me!" This nigga is straight tripping. Before I can take another breath, he backhands my ass so hard it feels like my jawbone has been slammed into my eye socket. "Awww. Fuck, nigga!" I start kicking him. "That shit hurts!"

"Answer me!" His face is turning a demonic purple right before my eyes. "Are you giving another nigga my pussy?"

"NO!" It hurts to yell, but I got to stop this nigga before he hits me again and then offers to play doctor and reset my shit. "Now get off me. Damn." I push at his chest again and unpin my shoulders from the bed. I'm annoyed and pretend that I ain't scared that he's about to snatch a knot in my ass at any second.

The tension finally evaporates when he moves off me and climbs out of bed. "Better not," he says, grabbing my buzzing phone.

"Nigga, give me my shit!" This is a complete violation.

Python easily smacks my hand away. "What the fuck do you want with Baby Thug?"

"Where's your phone at? Let me start reading your shit." I twist toward the nightstand on his side of the bed and dive for *his* iPhone. Just when I'm about to reach his shit, he locks an arm around my waist and easily pulls me back.

"Stop fuckin' playing and answer the muthafuckin' question." He's back to laughing at my ass and waving my phone in my face. I try to snatch it from him and end up playing a couple of seconds of keep-away before grabbing my shit.

"Well?" he asks, smiling. "You chasing after pussy now? I might find that shit kinda hot."

"Get on with that retarded shit." I'm not tryna be charmed by his ugly ass, but a smile finally kicks up at the corners of my lips. "Me and old girl got some shit we gotta settle up."

"Uh-huh." His lips keep twitching. "I heard she got the drop on you at that hair salon." He strolls toward the adjoining bathroom with his fat sausage-size dick swinging low between his legs.

"Yeah? How did you hear about that shit—from that dyke's girlfriend you been fuckin' down at the Pink Monkey?" I charge.

Python just laughs and keeps it moving toward the bathroom. "Get on with that bullshit."

"Don't play me crazy, Python!"

He stops at the door and glances back at me. "How about you just play your muthafuckin' position? You think you can just handle that shit? Damn, you're practically my muthafuckin' wife."

"Practically ain't the same as is, now is it, nigga?"

Python rushes across the room and jacks me up on the wall by my neck. "You got a fuckin' smart-ass mouth. Now, I done asked your ass nicely to stop sweating me." His black gaze sears into mine, but I don't flinch.

"I better not catch that bitch slippin'," I warn. "That's all I fuckin' know."

We glare at each other for a while, and finally Python starts smiling again and releases me. "Oh, you bad, huh?"

"Nigga, you need to start acting like you know." I push past him.

"Don't let me hear you're giving my shit to no dyke bitch either." He chuckles and returns to the bathroom.

I roll my eyes and mumble under my breath. "Two-faced muthafucka."

"I HEARD THAT SHIT!"

"Whatever." I read the text message from Toxic and can't help but smile. My top girls with the Queen Gs have finally found Baby at Babylon—a well-known strip club on the Crips's side of town. "I got you, bitch." I hop up and rush into the bathroom with Python. He doesn't say much when I join him in the shower and block his ass from getting most of the hot water. Fuck him.

While I slide on a lace thong, I watch him splash on some of that loud-ass Obsession he likes and ask, "Where *you* going?" Now I know this muthafucka is 'bout to lie, and he doesn't disappoint.

"I'm just going to roll out with McGriff and handle some business," he says with a straight face.

Nigga, puh-lease. As he continues to get dressed, I stare and wish I had the balls to get one of Momma Peaches's hard-ass iron skillets and wear out the back of that fat head of his until he fucking apologizes for insulting my intelligence. I turn toward the closet and grab the shortest black skirt I can find, a white see-through top, and my best black hooker boots. I feel his heavy gaze shift back on me, but I finish getting dressed as if I don't know that I look like I'm about to go sell some ass. Twenty minutes later, I'm rocking smoky eye makeup and fierce cat eyelashes and my real black and white chinchilla cape. I'm a bad bitch from head to toe and I know it.

Grabbing my gat, I kiss my man and jump behind the wheel of my Crown Victoria. I'll worry about where Python is heading a little later. Right now my clit is just thumping at the chance to dump a whole clip into Baby's peanut head. Before I'm off Shotgun Row, I pick up Kookie and Pit Bull, and they're just as hyphy as I am.

"I know you gonna cap this bitch." Pit Bull laughs, pulling down the visor on the passenger side and checking to make sure her nappy hair is blending with her silky straight weave. It isn't.

"Fuck that. I'm gonna Jack Bauer that ass for a hot minute before I fuck her with this damn gat."

"We got your back, girl," Pit Bull says, showing off her .38.

"I'll cosign that," Kookie chimes in. "Queen Gs for life, baby."

We all stack our gang signs as I turn on the radio and blast some ill street shit.

"After this shit, we're heading to the club, right?" Pit Bull asks. "I'm in the mood to shake my ass tonight."

"I know that's right." Kookie laughs. "Who knows

when I'm gonna be able to get out the house, away from them damn kids."

"You got it."

"Now who's this Toxic?" Pit Bull asks. "How come I ain't heard of this bitch?"

"She just this chick I knew back in the day. We were at group home at the same time. The girl is bad, but she plays on both sides of the fence."

"Oh. She's one of those," Kookie says, rolling her eyes. "I swear to God it seems like these damn dykes are multiplying like a muthafucka. I hope that shit ain't in the water."

We all have a good laugh on that shit. "Anyway, apparently a couple of months ago, Baby Thug cracked a bottle over Toxic's girlfriend's head at the Pink Monkey, so she's willing to help me on this shit."

"Karma is a fuckin' bitch," Kookie says.

My phone buzzes and I quickly turn down the radio and answer.

"Damn, girl. Where you at?" Toxic hisses. "I've been blowing up your phone for the last forty fuckin' minutes."

"We rolling. You still with that bitch?"

There's a brief pause, and then Toxic's voice drifts back over the line a little lower. "Yeah. She's at my place. You better hurry the fuck on before I earth this bitch myself."

"Slow your roll. That bitch is mine," I warn. "You just shake your ass, keep that bitch wet, and me and my girls are coming through."

"How long you gonna be?"

"Bitch, I'ma get there when I get there. Hold your shit down and I'll handle it. A'ight?"

Pause.

"A'ight?"

"All right. See you in a few."

Toxic disconnects the call, and I flip my phone back into my purse. "I swear I hate working with bitches."

Kookie and Pit Bull just laugh while I jam my foot down on the accelerator. Toxic's crib is inside a gated community, but I just creep behind the car in front of me and hope the iron gate don't try to close on me.

"How are we going to do this shit?" Kookie asks, reaching for her own .38 between her thighs.

"Just follow my lead," I say, shutting off the engine and grabbing my burner. "Pit Bull, you stay down here until we verify we got this bitch locked down. If she makes it through us and out this door, you blast that ass. You feel me?"

"You know this." She raises her fist and I give her a solid fist bump before jumping out of my ride. My clit is thumping again as I head toward the door. As expected, the shit is unlocked and me and Kookie slip into the house like two careered burglars. Immediately we hear music playing at the top of the stairs.

I look over at my girl and press a finger against my lips. I want this shit to go down as smooth as butter. We creep fast to the bedroom, and I use my gun to push the door open and peek inside.

I immediately see Toxic jiggling and rolling her booty. Baby looks like she is in a trance as she dips her head forward and uses her teeth to grab the thin thong running down the crack of Toxic's ass.

"You like that, baby?" Toxic asks, bending over and stretching a hand down in between her legs so she can spread her pussy lips.

Baby lets the string snap out of her mouth as she hisses in a long breath. "Hell, yeah. Your ass got a beautiful pussy."

I kick open the door. "It's gonna be the last clit your ass is gonna see, pussy-ass ho!" I squeeze the trigger.

Baby jumps and surprises me by lifting her 9 mm and firing off a shot.

I duck and Toxic suddenly slices a blade down the side of Baby's face and splits that muthafucka wide open.

"FUCKIN' BITCH!" Baby turns her chrome toward Toxic and fires at point-blank range.

Toxic screams just as I come back up and start dumping my clip into Baby's right side. I'm fucking having an orgasm watching this bitch propel sideways up against the headboard and drop her shit. Somehow I manage to stop myself from going ahead and doing this bitch in. What can I say? A bitch likes to play with her food every once in a while.

I smile, cock my head, and stroll into the room like I have all the muthafuckin' time in the world. Baby is glaring straight at me while tryna take small sips of air. "Damn, Baby. You don't look so good."

"She's doing better than this bitch," Kookie says, crouching over Toxic. "She's dead."

I roll my eyes. Silly bitch. Why the hell she bring a blade to a gun show? "Well, that's all right," I say. "Baby here will be joining her in a minute."

"F-fuck you, b-bitch," Baby spits out, blood splashing down her shirt. "You might as well just pull that muthafuckin' trigger 'cause I ain't lost shit in this world."

"Sure you have. You lost your mind fuckin' around with me. But I *might* do you a solid and square things up if you tell me where your lil Yo-Yo is hiding out."

Baby laughs and coughs up more blood. "Why don't you ask your nigga where she at?"

My good mood slips a notch. "See, bitches like you don't know a good thing when it's fuckin' staring you in the face," I tell her, strolling closer to the bed. "Frankly, up until you pulled that stunt at the salon, I ain't had a problem with your pink mafia ass. But after that shit, well, we had ourselves a situation. Didn't we?"

"Fuck you. I should've plugged your ass when I had the chance."

"Yeah. You should have." I slide my gun up her right leg and then stop when it reaches the V where she wishes her dick was. "When you get to hell, tell the devil I said hello." Without blinking, I dump the rest of my clip straight into her pussy.

34

Yolanda

I miss Baby like crazy. I figured that by now we would've buried the hatchet and moved the fuck on. But I ain't seen hide or tail of her since she stormed out of my momma's house. And it ain't because I haven't tried to find her; I've been bugging every corner boy and chicken head I've come across, trying to find the block she's holding down. Nobody knows shit, or if they do, then they ain't telling my ass.

I ain't got the nerve to ask Python. Niggas already been gossiping about Baby and me being lovers or some shit. It's a headache and I'm hoping Python is ignoring the shit when it drips into his ear. He done already made it clear that if he's fuckin' with me, then it means my pussy is closed for business for all other niggas—bitches included, I guess.

He has different rules for his own dick. When he ain't

in my bed, I know he's slinging his shit hard to LeShelle and probably that other chick who interrupted us in his office that one time. But that's all right. I ain't going to be the bottom bitch for long.

I ain't forgot about that slick clowning shit LeShelle did to me at FabDivas—not by a long shot. Just as soon as I drop Python's newest seed, I'll be set and I can get my babies; then me and that bitch will resolve our situation. Ole girl may have beat my ass once, but, believe me, that bitch ain't gonna catch me slippin' again.

My new place is the shit. A fly studio off Madison Avenue that's way better than that roach-infested Shotgun Row. No doubt Python must be feeling this pussy all the way down to his muthafuckin' toes if he coming out the pocket to stash me here. I just wish I could celebrate with my best friend, but . . .

I choke up, surprised by a sudden rush of sadness.

I pick up my phone and dial Baby's cell. Who knows, maybe this time she'll answer. The line rings and rings, but just when I'm about to disconnect the call, I hear the line pick up.

"Baby?" A strange laugh tumbles over the line. "Baby?"

"I found you, bitch," a woman says, and then disconnects the call.

"Who the fuck?" I pull the phone away from my ear and stare it. Was that who I thought it was? I hit REDIAL, but then my doorbell rings and I hang up with the promise to try Baby a little later. Right now, I need to take care of my man.

I check my figure in the mirror and think I still look good, even with my small baby bump. I wrap a sheer white robe around my shoulders and stroll to the front door. One glance through the peephole and I know it's showtime.

"Damn. What took you so long?" Python asks, pimp

walking across the threshold and slapping me hard on the ass. "You got another nigga up in here somewhere?"

I roll my eyes. "How come you always ask that shit when you ride through? You know I ain't got nobody else up in here." I shut the door behind him.

"Don't worry about why I always ask. You just make sure you got the right fuckin' answer." He strolls through, checking shit out like he doesn't believe my ass ain't creeping.

"You hungry, baby? I can fix you something to eat." I head to the kitchen. Every Southern bitch knows that you can throw pussy at a nigga all day long, but the true way to a man's heart is through his stomach.

"What you got?"

"I got some short ribs, collards and mac and cheese," I boast. I can hear that nigga practically run up behind me.

"For real?"

"Uh-huh." I grab a plate out of the cabinet and start fixing him something to eat. This nigga is all up behind me, opening pot lids and sniffing my shit.

"Fuck, Yo-Yo. I think niggas been givin' you a bum break. Your ass got skills." He smacks his lips.

"It's all for you, baby. Just remember that shit." I pop a healthy hunk of homemade (not from no damn box) mac and cheese on his plate. "Here you go, boo. You want a beer?"

"Hell yeah." He takes his food and heads off to the living room.

I go to the refrigerator, pop the top off a cold one, and then meet him over on the couch. "How is it?" I ask, knowing my shit is hitting the spot.

"This shit is good," he says with a stuffed mouth. "A nigga could get used to some shit like this."

I keep smiling while I lean against him. "That's what I'm here for—to spoil you."

His fat lips twist up into a smile. I'm starting to think there's a sexiness to his ugliness. That shit sounds crazy but it's true. I reach for the TV remote control and put it on ESPN so he can catch the latest basketball scores. Trust that I'm doing everything I can to make sure that when he comes here to our crib, he ain't stressing about nothing. I just smile and watch his big ole lips smack over his food. Twenty minutes later, there ain't shit on his plate but bones. My ego is a fucking monster, and I love the fact that he's now pushing up on my titties and testing the wetness of my pussy.

I giggle and tease. "You ready for dessert, baby?"

"A nigga like me can always eat." He rolls me onto my stomach and spreads my ass cheeks open. "Look at this nice, fat ass."

He bends forward and glides that wet, forked tongue down the crack of my ass. I ain't gonna lie—that shit feels good as hell.

"Get on your knees."

I hop up and toot my shit up high. Python's tongue does a Dumpster dive and squeegee cleans every inch of me. My pussy juice gushes down my thighs. I know what's next, and I try to prepare myself, but I don't think anyone can really prepare for this nigga's fat mushroom-shaped cock turning their asshole into a fuckin' crime scene. The shit hurts. The trick is not to let the mutha-fucka know it. Actually, most of the shit we do hurts like hell. The choking, the spanking, and the occasional bag suffocation ain't like no shit I've ever done, and truth be told I just put all the shit in Jesus's hands and pray that the sadistic muthafucka don't accidentally kill my ass.

"Ahh. Shit. Your shit is so fuckin' tight," he growls, grabbing a handful of my hair and yanking my head back. I gasp while stars dance before my eyes.

"You love this dick, don't you, bitch?"

"Y-yes!"

He's balls deep and slow grinding. "You'll do anything for this dick, won't you? Over here cooking and shit. Sssss. Fuck."

I block out the pain and slam my ass down so hard I'm trying to break that dick.

"Yeah, bitch! Do that shit! Sssss."

I got that dick on the run now.

"I'm gonna nut up in this fat bitch," he promises. "Yeah. Sssss."

We keep at it until I feel his hot cum shoot up my ass and then spray all over my back. Even then I keep wiggling and jiggling while he uses his dick to smear it all over my back.

"Get over here and suck this shit off," he orders.

I hop on that shit quick while he continues to playfully tug on my hair and make sure that I do a good job. "You like that, baby?"

"It's a'ight," he jokes.

"Just a'ight?" I sit up and push him on his chest. "You ain't gonna tell me you get it like this at home. I can't even imagine LeShelle's ass cooking."

"See. You're worried about the wrong muthafuckin' thing. You just keep things tight over here and everything will stay good."

"Uh-huh." I cross my arms. I don't like how he still takes up for that bitch. It means that she still got her claws in good with his ass. Most niggas can't wait to start bitching what they girl or wifey ain't doing at home. *She stopped sucking my dick. She won't fuck when she's on her period. The bitch only cooks shit that goes in the microwave.* On and on. But Python never says shit about what goes on with him and LeShelle. It makes me wonder why his ass is even messing with me if everything is cool at the crib. However, tonight I'm determined to get some answers.

"So how come you and LeShelle ain't had no babies?" I lean against his chest but continue to stroke his dick. "Y'all been together for a hot minute."

"Sssss. Ooh. That feels nice."

I roll my eyes. I know this nigga hears me. "Can she even have babies? Is her belly rotten or something?"

He yanks my head back. "What the fuck? Why the hell are you all in our business?"

"I . . . I'm was just curious," I croak, and then wait for him to release my head. He glares at me for a while and then pushes me away.

"I would've thought you learned your lesson trying to fuck with LeShelle. She almost stomped your ass into the ground a little while back, didn't she?"

"I ain't fuckin' with her. I was just asking you a question. That's all."

He laughs at me. "You trying to fuck with her. I ain't stupid. I know how y'all bitches work. Let me just give you a little bit of advice: stay the hell in your lane. You got some good ass, you can throw down in the kitchen, and that may or may not be my muthafuckin' seed you got growing in that belly, but this shit here"—he gestures between us—"this ain't got shit on what the fuck I got at home."

I'm fucking blinking at this muthafuka like I'm stuck on stupid. *What the fuck did he just say?*

He laughs. "What? I'm just keeping it real so there ain't no misunderstanding. You're a sideline ho and you're always gonna be a sideline ho. Period."

"What? How the fuck you gonna say some foul shit like that to me?"

"Yo. You knew I had a wifey when you started slobberin' up on this dick. So don't be sweating me and acting stupid. I upgraded your situation, and right now you should be thanking my ass."

"Thank you?"

"Bitch, I got you off that pole, and I'm paying the bills up in this muthafucka. You got a problem with that shit, you can pack up and I'll move the next bitch up here who knows how to appreciate shit and stay in her fuckin' lane. And staying in that lane means that you stop trying to floss in front of my girl, 'cause I ain't gonna be responsible if she turns your ass into a grease stain."

I'm blinking again.

"So stop asking me about shit that ain't got nothing to do with your ass. All you need to know about my girl is that she don't fuck around and she ain't scared of shit. Now consider your ass warned. Stay in your lane."

35

LeShelle

"I can't believe that you shot that bitch's cunt out!" Pit Bull howls as we cruise down Parkway, heading out to the Blue Daisy to shake our asses. "What the fuck made you think of some foul-ass shit like that?"

"Shit. It just seemed like the right thing to do." I laugh, checking my reflection in the mirror. My shit still look fly—not a hair out of place.

"I don't know." Pit Bull shakes her head. "I'd haunt a bitch down for the rest of her muthafuckin' life if she sent me to the spirit world without my pussy. Sheeeit. My pussy done got me through some tough muthafuckin' times."

"You're preaching now." Kookie holds her hands up and waves them around like she's in the middle of church.

"Sheeit. Like Jacki-O says, Pussy pays my bills."

I crack up. "Y'all bitches ain't shit."

"You ain't either, ho. Now why the fuck you take that bitch's phone?" Kookie asks. "If we were gonna be boosting, there was a whole lot of nice shit in that apartment."

"That bitch Yolanda called and her number showed up," I tell them. "It's like God is smiling down on me tonight."

"Damn. You gonna track the girl down like the fuckin' FBI?" Pit Bull shakes her head. "Girl, you really ain't nothing to fuck with."

Blue and white lights flash in my rearview, and my foot eases up off the accelerator. "Fuck!"

"Aww shit." Pit Bull tosses her hands up. "How the fuck?"

"Be cool. Be cool," I tell them, pulling over.

"What the fuck you pulling over for? You actin' like we ain't just capped a bitch."

"Will you calm the fuck down?"

"Man, I can't be getting locked up tonight. My momma ain't gonna bail my ass out no more, and I ain't got no more strikes to play with," Pit Bull whines.

"Shut the fuck up!" Shit. This big bitch is riding my nerves.

Kookie doesn't say shit. She just eases back in her seat with her hand on her gat, ready for anything and everything. Now, she's the type of bitch I like riding with.

"Hand me my purse," I tell Pit Bull, since she's in the passenger seat. I grab my driver's license and my insurance card while I watch a female officer creep up to the driver's side. "Good evening, Officer. What seems to be the problem?"

I swing my gaze over and a surge of recognition hits me. This is the bitch cop whose patrol car I jacked months ago.

"License and proof of insurance," the cop says, completely ignoring my question. She's looking at me like she may be remembering that night.

I hand over my information and then tap my manicured nails on the steering wheel.

"Do you know why I pulled you over?"

Didn't I just ask this bitch . . . ? "No, Officer."

"You were doing sixty in a forty-five," she says.

I sigh in relief. "Oh. I'm sorry about that. I guess I must've pulled my eyes off the speedometer." I meet the cop's unsmiling eyes and know my ass is just seconds away from getting a ticket.

"Hey, don't I know you?" Kookie asks from the backseat.

I swear I want to stab Kookie in the throat now.

The cop's gaze shifts to the back as she shines her flashlight in Kookie's face.

"Yeah. Yeah. You used to go to Morris High School. You're that supercop's daughter who used to date Python back in the day." Kookie laughs. "I thought I heard you became a cop, too."

What the fuck? My gaze sweeps this bitch again, 'cause this is the first I've heard about Python dating some cop. Why didn't I know this?

Pit Bull and Kookie throw up our gang signs, and the bitch's expression doesn't change.

"Wait right here."

The cop turns and walks back to her patrol car with my cards. I watch her the whole time, and I'm able to make out that the chick has a nice frame on her. "How long ago was this bitch with Python?" I ask.

"Sheeit. Looong long time ago," Kookie says. "Like I said, it was high school."

That shit should relax me, but it don't. "Why they break up?"

"Who the hell knows? She never really was down for the set. I think she was just fuckin' with Python to piss her big-shot daddy off."

"Hell, I think they even got a kid," Pit Bull adds.

Now my mood is fucked up. "That bitch is one of Python's baby mommas?"

"Sheeit. Those bitches are all around this city."

"Damn, Kookie!" Pit Bull snaps. "How you just gonna talk about our girl's man like that in front of her? Shit."

"What?" She shrugs with a half laugh. "I ain't saying shit everybody don't already know. The nigga gets around."

I'm fucking hot under the collar now, but the bitch ain't doing nothing but telling the gospel. Everywhere I turn, I'm running into these muthafuckin' grimy cockroaches. It's like I can't fuckin' breathe.

"I wouldn't worry about it," Pit Bull says. "That shit is like ancient history. So the bitch may have squeezed out one of his seeds. So fuckin' what? His ass is with you. You fuckin' breast-feeding his ass now. Long as he's still finding his ass back home, I say your ass is good."

But he's finding his ass home less and less, I think to myself.

The cop slides out from behind her wheel and takes her sweet-ass time making it back up to me. I know I need to play this shit cool, but I have so many emotions rolling through me right now; I feel like I'm just seconds from flipping the script.

"I need you to sign here and here," she says, pointing to the two X'd spots on the ticket.

"Shit. You wrote me up?" I ask, incredulous.

"You were going fifteen miles over the speed limit. Be thankful I'm not hauling your ass in."

I side eye her hard. "What? I can't get no share-a-nigga discount?"

My girls snicker.

"Ms. Murphy, I suggest you calm down," the officer says. "If you want to dispute the ticket, your court date is printed on the ticket. Now sign."

I'm twitching and my clit is thumping, but this bitch is holding my gaze like she fuckin' wishes I would start some shit. The car grows quiet as my girls wait to see how I want to play this shit. Finally, I take a deep breath, snatch the clipboard and pen, and sign and initial my name. I also take the time to read her name at the bottom of the ticket. "Here you go, Officer Melanie Johnson."

The cop cocks a half grin and rips the yellow copy of the ticket out and hands it over to me. "You take it easy now . . . and tell Terrell I said hi." She pats her stomach, and my eyes damn near bug the fuck out when I notice a small lump before she strolls off.

"Is that bitch . . . ?" I turn toward Pit Bull to ask whether she just saw what I did, but my girl's mouth is hanging wide open.

Kookie starts cracking up in the backseat. "See? What I tell you? Baby mommas everywhere."

36

Yolanda

May . . .

It's been six weeks and I still can't believe Baby is dead. When I first received the call, I was in bed and I thought that someone was playing on my phone until I realized that I was talking to Ms. Gracie, Baby's grandma.

"Vivian is dead," she'd said flatly. "I knew that these damn streets would get her sooner or later. Turned out that it was sooner than I thought." She hung up the phone.

I continued to lay there with my heart melting out my chest, my head ringing, and tears streaming down my face. *Vivian*. Hard to believe but I never knew Baby's real name. She'd always been Baby Thug or Baby since the day I met her. When did she die? How did she die? When was the funeral? Her grandma didn't tell me any of those things, and she sure as hell didn't wait for me to ask.

I figured she must have gotten my phone number from my mother. I guess it really didn't matter. I was sure I'd find out the information eventually. I did—and when I heard how she died and what was done to her, I was devastated. I couldn't stop looping that last fight with Baby in my head. I remember the angry lines in her face, the clenching of her jaw, and the unmistakable love in her eyes. Baby loved me—probably the only one whoever truly did.

I didn't get out of bed for three days. I never knew that I could cry so hard or for so long. I should've tracked Baby down. I should've tried harder to get her to accept my apology. I should have done so many things.

Today, I stroll through the doors of J. D. Lewis & Son Funeral Home in a black dress and large matching hat, trying to hold it all together. I don't know what I was expecting, but I am stunned at the extremely low turnout—six people. I know that Baby had some beef with her people before they turned her out in the street, but I figured they'd squash that shit at a time like this. The minute I walk through the doors of the property's small viewing room, everyone's eyes zoom toward me. I want to run up out of here, but my gaze sweeps toward Baby's open casket and my legs carry me forward, not backward.

Halfway down the aisle, tears flood my eyes and make it nearly impossible to see straight. Still, I keep moving as if Baby's body is one large magnet. Baby's voice booms in my head: *I ain't good enough for you? Just fuckin' say it!*

I step up to the casket and stare down at my best friend. She is beautiful, though she doesn't look anything like the Baby I knew. The mortician had pressed her thick hair straight, and her makeup is impeccably done, even though Baby's beauty regime had been cocoa butter and ChapStick. I have the strangest urge to scrub the shit off and then sit down with my big old jar of Blue Magic and wide-tooth comb and braid her hair the way she liked it.

"I bet she's one of them," a woman whispers behind me.

"Lawd. It truly is the end of days with all this foolishness. Men sleeping with men and women sleeping with women."

My ears perk up as I swipe at my tears and glance over my shoulder. However, when my gaze levels on Baby's grandmother, the woman just glares back at me. She reminds me so much of my own mother that my heart shatters into even more pieces.

I touch the swell of my belly and think about my other kids, the ones I'm supposed to be trying to get back, the ones I told myself I was selling my body for. *Only a retarded muthafucka would keep doin' the same thing over and over again and expect different results.* The words are still harsh, and I'm suddenly flooded with so much shame that I nearly drop on the spot. Forcing myself to stand, I can't help but ask myself, *What the fuck have I been doing with my life?*

I turn back toward the casket and can't resist reaching out to touch Baby's face one last time. Yet, when I touch her skin, I'm repelled by its cold waxiness. This isn't Baby. This is just an empty shell.

With grief now as deep as the ocean, I turn away from the casket. The small crowd has now been reduced to just four. Baby's grandmother's eyes are still trained on me. I start back down the aisle, thinking I'm ready to just go home. But I stop in front of Ms. Gracie.

"I'm sorry for your loss," I whisper.

She glances away from me and stares straight ahead.

"I loved your granddaughter," I add. "Maybe not the way she wanted me to . . . but I did love her. I just wanted you to know that." Her bottom lip trembles, but her eyes remain dry. After that, I bow my head and walk out. However, there's a surprise waiting for me in the foyer: LeShelle.

"Well, well, well. Look at what crawled out of the gutter." LeShelle, impeccably dressed in a bright red silk dress, strolls toward me with her lips hiked up. Behind her are Pit Bull and Kookie; their gazes are just as hard as their leader's. Glancing around, I see other mourners getting ready to attend a different service in one of the larger rooms. I really wouldn't put it past LeShelle to start some shit up in here.

"What? You ain't got nothing to say, bitch? Or are you waiting for your girlfriend to rise from the grave to save your ass again?"

She stares into my eyes and laughs. The memory of someone picking up Baby's phone the night she was murdered pops into my head. For the first time in my life, I'm speechless. It's not that I don't know that the Gangster Disciples and the Queen Gs are responsible for body-bagging a good number of niggas in Memphis, it's just . . . this was my best friend.

"Yeah, I thought so," LeShelle sneers, raking her gaze over me like I'm something she just scrubbed off the bottom of her shoe. "You ain't me. You ain't never gonna be me. And you're not always gonna be pregnant." Slowly, she walks closer to me and then whispers, "Ticktock."

37

Momma Peaches

Arzell moved out.

I should've known that he would've been a bit sensitive about a little thing like my ass being married. Hell, I thought his ass knew. Everybody knows that my man, Isaac, is in the fed serving a twenty-year bid for drug trafficking and shit. I can't visit or nothing 'cause of my own record. We talks sometimes, about once a week, depending on whether his ass is in the hole for some macho bullshit that always goes on in the joint. One thing for sure, my man writes some beautiful letters. Shit he can't ever seem to say in person, but that's all right.

As far as me messing around with other niggas, all I can say is turn around is fair play. All those years he creeped out on me have finally come back to bite him on the ass. I can't say that he's completely cool with the shit, but I let it be known that I don't have the kind of pussy that can just chill on ice for twenty-something goddamn years, and the last time I checked, neither can his dick. So in the end, we just don't ask who the other is fucking and leave it at that.

Everybody's fucking happy.

Well, not everybody. Arzell can't play in his lane, so I told him to get the fuck out. To make myself feel a little better, I been taking these long peach-scented bubble baths and spending plenty of time down at FabDivas, getting my hair and nails done. On my drive back, I glance over at a car at the light and nearly piss in my pants when I see my parole officer, Cedric Robinson.

Is this muthafucka on his way to my place? Shit. I glance around, trying to think of a shortcut back to my place. If I get caught out and about without my electronic monitoring, my ass is heading back to jail and I ain't having that shit.

The light turns green, and I bank a right, jamming my foot on the accelerator. Because I've been the driver in my fair share of getaway cars, I'm floating and hugging street corners like a beast. I almost clip a couple of corner boys, but they recognize my ride and keep their gats at their sides.

I fishtail onto Shotgun Row with my tires squealing and my heart leaping into my throat. *Go, go, go.* Now, I don't know what the hell I was thinking when I left the house using my other prosthetic. Well, okay. Maybe I didn't think the electronic tag went with my outfit, but that shit seems silly now that I may be arrested if I don't beat my PO back to my house.

My house comes into view and I slam on the brakes, causing a thick cloud of smoke to engulf my car. But I don't give a shit because I'm jumping out of the mutha-

fucka and racing toward my front door like a runaway
slave.

"Damn, Momma Peaches. Where the fire at?" Rufus
hollers out from down the way.

"It's coming up behind me." I wiggle my key into the
lock and then sprint inside. Two minutes later, there's a
knock on the front door and I'm just barely getting my
shit together. Then the knocking becomes a hammering.

"I'M COMING!" I press my skirt down and rush
back to the front door. This nigga is still out there banging like he's trying to knock the door off its hinges. "I
SAID I'M COMING!" I snatch open the front door and
force a smile on my face.

Cedric Robinson, with his fine redbone ass, turns his
head from the shenanigans going on in the streets to
smile at me and remove his shades. His green eyes remind me of Manny, and I'm transported back each and
every time I see him. "Mrs. Goodson. I hope I'm not
disturbing you this morning."

I'm chugging in deep breaths and praying my ass
don't pass the fuck out.

Mr. Robinson frowns. "You been running?"

I keep my smile in place. "Only to the door."

He nods as his full, sexy lips split into a smile. "Mind
if I come in?" he asks, even though he's already shoul-
dering his way past me.

"Sure. Make yourself at home." I wink. I have to
admit I like flirting with my parole officer. I'm sure all
his female parolees do the same thing. He's just that
goddamn fine.

He immediately starts looking around, like I'm one of
those dumb hustlers who keeps her shit out with a glowing neon sign that says *arrest me*. "How have you been
doing, Maybelline?"

"Fine. And I told you to call me Peaches." I close the door and then just watch this muthafucka perform his half-ass inspection. I ain't gonna lie. I'm picturing his ass naked and wondering if he takes pussy payment for parole fees. How can I not? There's so much about him that has my ass reminiscing. His walk. His talk.

"Where's your lil boyfriend at?" he asks, turning toward me. "He's usually up in here eating pancakes when I come by."

"Out. Probably playing on someone else's playground by now." I fold my arms and hope he picks up on the hint that I don't want to talk about Arzell's ass.

That gets a laugh out of him. "You do like them young, huh?"

I rake my eyes over him again and guesstimate him to be in his forties, maybe fifties. "I like them with strong backs and big dicks—not necessarily in that order."

His laugh deepens, and even that shit sounds familiar. "Well, I can see why the kiddies are attracted to you. You're a woman who definitely believes in keeping herself up."

"Big dicks do a body good."

He shakes his head. "You're a hot mess." He kneels before me and starts checking my electronic tag.

"Nah. What I am is turned the fuck on. So unless you want a mouthful of pussy right now, you might want to hurry up reading that tag and get off your knees." Now, I'm just fucking with this muthafucka, so I'm completely thrown off guard when he slides a finger under my skirt, all the way up to my wet panties.

"You mean this pussy right here?"

His green eyes light up, and that old feeling hits me again. "Who your people?" I ask. "Were you born in Memphis?"

"I'm on my knees squeezing your pussy and you wanna ask me where I'm from?"

"You just remind me of someone I used to know." I reach down and caress the side of his face. "Someone I knew a long time ago."

Cedric turns his head and kisses the palm of my hand. "I was born and raised here. My momma was Eugenia Robinson. She passed away about ten years back."

"And your dad?"

"Never knew him. He passed away before I was born. The way everybody tells it, Papa was a rolling stone. He was a musician—a saxophone player who used to play with the usual suspects down on Beale back in the day."

No shit, it feels like my heart just fell out of my chest. "Manny?"

"Emmanuel Brooks." He cocks his head. "Did you know him?"

"I don't believe this shit. Hell yeah I knew him." I bust out with a big ole smile while I stare into Cedric's eyes again. He didn't get everything from his daddy, but the resemblance is there. I feel myself tearing up and force myself to back away.

"Sorry. I didn't mean to upset you." Cedric climbs to his feet, and for the first time since I've been assigned to him, an awkward silence hangs between us. "Um, I guess I got everything I need. Maybe I should go."

"No. That's not necessary. You just threw me for a loop. That's all." I suck in a deep breath. Manny's son. Here in my house. "In fact," I say, collecting myself and taking his hand, "I think maybe we should try to get to know each other better."

38

Ta'Shara

Prom night.

It seems like I've been waiting for this night for forever—especially since I've been grounded for most of the damn school year. It doesn't matter that Profit and I still get in our little dirt: school, secret meetings at the public library, and his constant sneaking into my bedroom in the middle of the night. What choice did we have? We are in love. What surprises me is that Tracee and Reggie act like they don't understand shit. They made it clear that they want me to concentrate only on doing my studies and getting into college.

No boys.

No thugs.

No gangsters.

Since the shooting at the hospital, things ain't been

right between us, and shit at school is even worse. The Queen Gs have clearly removed my veil of protection, and the Flowers have lowered a new, tenuous one—despite my slicing up Qiana. But word came down from Fat Ace himself, and that immediately shut down all beefs and past grievances.

The streets are still blazing more than ever with the Vice Lords making up ground like a muthafucka. Everybody is popping and everyone is dropping on both sides of the aisle, to the point that sideline niggas doubt the shit is ever going to end—especially me and Profit.

The school board is taking more drastic security measures, to the point that it seems easier getting in and out of Fort Knox than Morris High School. For a hot minute, it was rumored that they were going to scrap prom night altogether, but then the students raised so much hell that they had to backtrack.

I'm relieved. It's the one night I can break out of my suburban cage and participate in something that resembles me having a life. Now, the school green-lighting the prom and my foster parents giving me permission to go are two different things. The first time I brought the subject up, Reggie went from looking like David Banner to the Incredible Hulk in like two seconds. He wasn't having it. *No way, no how,* is what he shouted for like forever. In the end, it was Tracee who ran interference and seriously campaigned for me to go.

It didn't look like the shit was working until Tracee cut his stubborn ass off and made him sleep on the couch in the living room. That surprised me. You'd think she was the one who was going to miss out on the prom.

Three days later, Reggie stood in my door, looking a hot mess. "All right, if I'm going to agree to this, there's going to be a few rules."

Excited, I jumped up from my desk, raced over, and threw my arms around Reggie. "Thank you. Thank you. Thank you."

"Wait. Wait." He threw up his arms. "You haven't heard the rules yet."

"I don't care. I'm going! TRACEE!" I released him and took off running down the hall. "HE SAID I CAN GO!"

"Wait, Ta'Shara."

"What's this?" Tracee stepped out of her bedroom, only for me to nearly knock her down.

"I can go! I can go! I can go!"

Tracee's excited squeals matched my own as we became a tangle of jumping arms and elbows. "Oh, baby. I'm so happy for you."

Reggie was left sputtering in the hallway. It wasn't until we had returned with three different dresses to model for him that he finally set down a few ground rules. "This young man *will* pick you up here and introduce himself."

"You just want to interrogate him," I charge.

"Exactly," Reggie said, no shame to his game at all. "*Also,* he will return you back to this house by midnight. Not twelve-ten or twelve-o-one. *Midnight.*"

"But—"

"No *buts.* Take it or leave it."

I look to Tracee, hoping for an interception, but Tracee slides underneath her husband's arm, signifying their unity. Still, I try to negotiate a two a.m. curfew, but that shit wouldn't fly at all. It is midnight or nothing at all.

Now it's the big night. I settle on a sparkly, sky-blue, one-shoulder number that hugs my toned curves like a second layer of skin. When I model the dress for my foster parents, Tracee breaks out the camera while Reggie looks like he's just seconds from having a heart attack.

"I do not like this," Reggie mumbles, shaking his head and rubbing his chest. "I just got a bad feeling about all this."

Tracee laughs. "Will you calm down? I don't remember you complaining so much when you took me to our junior prom."

"I'm not going to even dignify that statement with a response."

Ding-dong!

"He's here!" Tracee and I squeal excitedly, and start jumping up and down.

Reggie rolls his eyes.

"Go answer the door," Tracee says, shooing her husband out of my bedroom. "And don't scare the boy away," she warns. "Be nice."

"Uh-huh." He strolls off, shaking his head. This whole thing is giving him indigestion, but by the time he gets to the front door, he has his game face on and is ready to put Profit in the hot seat. He jerks open the door and is temporarily thrown off guard when he sees that Profit is taller than him by a good four inches. Not only that, but he has also cleaned up well. In a tux, Profit looks grown—at least, too old for high school.

"Good evening, Mr. Douglas," Profit greets, jetting out a hand and holding a corsage.

Reggie looks at the hand but doesn't accept it. Instead, he glances down at his watch. "You're a few minutes early."

"Yes, sir." He smiles. "I figured you'd probably want to spend a few minutes grilling me before Ta'Shara and I head out."

"Smart man." Reggie steps back from the door and

allows Profit to enter. "C'mon in. Let's get this grilling started."

Profit crosses the threshold, determined to play it cool. After all, it's the first time he's entered the house by the front door. "What a nice home you have here, Mr. Douglas."

"Thank you," Reggie says tersely. "Take a seat."

Drawing a deep breath, Profit does as he's told and continues to smile.

Reggie remains standing. "So you're the young man Ta'Shara stole my car to race to the hospital in the middle of the night to see?"

Profit clears his throat. "Um, yes. I'm sorry about that, sir."

"Sorry?" Reggie crosses his arms. "Are you saying that you *told* her to steal the car?"

"Oh, no, sir. I would never encourage Ta'Shara to do something like that."

"Uh-huh." He holds Profit's dark gaze. "How did you come to get shot in the first place?"

"You don't have to have a reason when you live in Memphis."

Reggie cocks his head at the smart-aleck response.

Profit tries again. "I was just at the wrong place at the wrong time. Police shot me but then had to drop the charges when they realized they fucked—I mean, when they realized they made a mistake."

Reggie stares him down. "*Profit*. That can't be what your momma named you. What's your government name?"

"Raymond. Raymond Lewis."

"Raymond." Reggie bobs his head. "Nice, normal name."

"Thank you, sir."

"So what is it that your parents do, *Raymond?*"

For the first time, Profit appears to be a little lost for words.

"You do have parents, don't you?"

"Um, yes, sir." Profit sits the corsage down on the coffee table and clasps his hands together. "My mother lives in Atlanta. She, um, works at a doctor's office, and my dad, well, he and my brother own a funeral parlor."

Reggie's brows hike up at that, but before he can question Profit further, I make my grand entrance.

Profit jumps to his feet, his pearly white smile stretching from ear to ear. "Wow," he says, drinking me in. "You look beautiful."

I blush. "Thank you." It's odd. I feel like some fairy-tale princess getting ready to go to a ball. It's even stranger to see my man decked out in black tux and looking *GQ* fine.

A light flashes and nearly blinds me. "Okay, I think we have enough pictures," I joke, trying to get my vision back.

"No. No. We need some with you and your date." Tracee waves Profit over while she leans over and whispers, "He's cute."

Still smiling, Profit picks up the corsage and fumbles with the plastic casing as he walks over to me. My knees weaken when a whiff of Sean John's Unforgivable tickles my nose. *Oh, yeah. He's definitely going to get some tonight.*

Tracee snaps pictures while Profit awkwardly pins my corsage to the left side of my dress, right over my heart. Our eyes lock for a moment, which, of course, Tracee catches on camera.

"Are you ready to go?" he asks.

"Absolutely." I loop my arm through his and barely restrain myself from kissing Profit in front of my foster parents. "We better go," I whisper.

Profit nods and then turns toward Tracee and Reggie. "It was a pleasure to meet you, Mr. and Mrs. Douglas."

"It was nice to meet you, too," Tracee gushes, following us to the door.

"Make sure you have her back here by midnight," Reggie stresses. "I wouldn't want you to have to take another trip to the hospital."

Tracee and I gasp while Profit takes the threat in stride with a laugh. "Yes, sir. You can count on me."

Reggie gives him a look that lets him know just how much he trusts him.

Once we're out of the house and walking toward the stretch limousine, Profit wraps an arm around my curvy waist and pulls me close. "The things I do for you, girl."

"Just wait until you see the things I'm going to do *to* you later on."

"As long as you do it before midnight, you'll have yourself a happy man."

39

LeShelle

"**W**here the fuck is this nigga?" I disconnect the call after I'm transferred to Python's voice mail. "I'm getting tired of this muthafucka's bullshit." I toss the cell phone away from me onto the black leather couch. Lately, I don't know whether to be worried whether he's got clipped, jailed, or is still out fuckin' around on me. Yolanda, Melanie, Random Pussy—and he's fuckin' them all raw dawg and planting seeds. Meanwhile, I'm supposed to be the HBIC, and I ain't gave this nigga not one baby.

I take Beauty out of her tank and then go sit outside to try getting my mind right. Niggas are milling about, drinking, smoking, and talking shit. In a lot of ways, Shotgun Row is stuck in a time warp: old houses, old potholes, and a lot of overgrown grass. I'm both proud and sad to call this my home and my hood. In the distance, there's the unmistakable sound of police sirens and even a couple of gunshots.

Right now, I can't help but focus on my own problems. It's clear that my position in the Queen Gs is threatened. As I watch Beauty slither all around my arm and then up around my neck, I realize a bitch can't make a nigga be true. I used to know that, but when my ass caught feelings, shit blew up in my face. It's just this blatant disrespect that I can't handle. He used to be better about this shit, and I can't help but feel that all that I've worked for is about to go up in flames.

Fuck.

Python's ass doesn't even bother creeping no more; he just straight up lets it be known when he's rolling over to that trick's new crib and practically dares me to say shit about it. Everything is happening so fast it has my head spinning. Tears burn the backs of my eyes, but no way no how am I gonna let those muthafuckas roll. I vowed to never do that crying shit no more, and I'm nothing if not a woman of my word.

Up the block, I see Kookie come out of her house. I pray that she doesn't see, but sure enough she spots me and heads on down to interrupt my peace and quiet.

"Hey, girl," she says, switching her way inside my gate. "What you know good? What you doin' out here alone on a Friday night?"

She automatically hands over the woolie she's smoking, and I don't waste a second pulling on that muthafucka. "Nothing, girl. Just chillin' and relaxin'."

Kookie hikes up a brow and stares me down. "Waiting on your man?"

"Girl, don't start that shit with me tonight."

"All I want to know is how you gonna let some *retarded* bitch just steal your nigga, especially some bitch everybody in the set has dug out at least once."

"Including *your man*," I remind her, and then take another hit. "I heard about McGiff and Tyga smashing her in the VIP."

"But she ain't having *my* man's seed. That shit is on Python."

"We don't know that."

"*Yes, we do.* Python claiming that bastard all day every day. If you ask me, the muthafucka walking around like he found gold up her ass or something. The niggas ain't saying shit, but bitches are tripping."

"Python loves *me*. He's gonna marry *me*," I seethe. "I've worked too hard to get in this spot. I've done fought, robbed, and toe-tagged my share of niggas to maintain, and I ain't about to go out like no sucka on this. No fuckin' way." I shake my head. I'm not going to go back to having nothing. I nibble on my bottom lip while the wheels slowly turn in my head.

Kookie laughs. "Marry you? These niggas don't be putting a ring on nothing no more. When was the last bitch in the set you heard got married? You, of all people, should know better than that. You're either a chicken head, a jump-off, or a wifey. That's it. These niggas nowadays only see preachers and judges when they serving a bid."

"Get the fuck on. You don't know what the fuck you're talking about."

"All right. A hard head makes a soft ass." Kookie takes another toke.

My mind goes back to that night when Python told me that if I just kept playing my cards right, he was going to wife me. Hell, that night seems so long ago now. "Where did I go wrong?" I whisper.

"You ain't gave the nigga no babies," Kookie says. Her words are like a knife twisting in my empty belly. "Y'all been together how long? Every bitch he's ever

been with has dropped him off a couple of seeds. Those
nappy-headed bastards are sprouting like weeds in
Memphis. Please believe."

"Yeah and those baby mommas ain't holding it down
with him neither," I snap. "*I'm* wifey."

"True. Those other bitches cheated on him. Niggas
don't forgive that shit for nothing—especially Python.
Once he marks his territory, niggas know it's a death
sentence to touch what's his. That's the main reason he
yanked your ass out of the Pink Monkey and now Yo-
Yo's stupid ass. There's a method to that nigga's mad-
ness. Of course, I think he moved Yo-Yo to protect her
ass from you."

"Smart man. That bitch ain't gonna be pregnant forever." I continue to sit and think and then think and
drink. The problem is that I don't have that many muthafuckin' options. I don't have any bargaining chips.
Threatening to leave Python could result in him just
holding the door while I walk out and Yo-Yo smiling
when she walks in with my shit. I need Yo-Yo's trick ass
out of the picture. Period.

"Tsk-tsk. Don't be so hard on yourself. Shit. Let's
keep it real. Ain't no bitch come no harder than you.
Shit. When you let that nigga dig that bullet out of your
arm, a lot of bitches seriously respected your gangsta
ass on that shit. It wouldn't have been my ass. I need
someone with a degree cutting on me." Kookie shakes
her head. "I can't see too many bitches wanting to follow ole Lemonhead's ass nowhere, Python's main bitch
or not. He can ride that short yellow bus by his damn
self."

"You're just saying that shit to cheer me up." My lips
twitch up into a smile as I pry Beauty from around my
neck and let her curl around my arm again.

"Y'all and them fuckin' snakes." Kookie eases back. "But, nah. For real, girl. Yo-Yo ain't never gonna be nobody." Kookie's eyes lower while she gets good and fucked up. "Hell, I think her ass swings both ways. You saw how tore up she was at Baby Thug's funeral. McGriff says Python told him that she didn't get out of bed for like a week or some shit."

I nod. "Yeah. I heard about that."

"Fuck. Outside in her damn drawers, screaming and hollering 'Baby, wait!' " Kookie yells, sounding just like Yolanda. "Ain't that some shit?" Kookie shakes her head. "Now don't get me wrong. Baby could eat the shit out of some pussy, but, damn, that soap-opera shit is ridiculous."

I cock my head at my girl. "Now, how do you know about . . . ?"

Kookie tosses up her hands. "Don't ask me no questions and I won't tell you no lies." She laughs. "What you need to do is calm down on this shit. Python is going to realize that you're the real gangsta bitch he needs to ride with. Trust." Kookie laces a new blunt and takes her time rolling the shit up. "This shit right here is gonna hook you the fuck up."

"Nah. I'm cool." I jump to my feet and stomp my way to the bedroom, where I return Beauty to her tank. Kookie and I maneuver around piles of clothes, weight bars, and God knows what else littering the cramped room's floor. "I'm heading out to Da Club. Fuck this shit. Python wanna spend all his time on the creep, then I'm going out and shaking my ass, too."

"Careful now. You don't wanna cause these niggas to catch cases just because you can't keep your man at home."

My gaze cuts back to my girl.

"What? I love you, girl, but I'm just spitting the truth and you know it. Don't get mad—get even with the bitch."

"Trust, if it wasn't for that fuckin' baby she's carrying, the po-po would've found her body floating in the Mississippi a long time ago. Python will have my head on a platter if I hurt his kid." I yank out a black dress from the back of my closet. "It's time for me to remind Python what the fuck he's missing at home."

Kookie shakes her head. "Please, that nigga is stressing you on purpose. No way he done caught feelings for that Ritalin-popping bitch. He's just fuckin' with you."

My attention is piqued. "What do you mean?"

Kookie flicks her lighter until she catches a flame to blaze the end of her blunt. She tokes on it a few times and then passes the shit over to me. "Now, you know I ain't supposed to be repeating no shit that me and McGriff talk about in bed but . . ."

"But what?" I exhale a long stream of smoke. "Don't be holding out on me, bitch. If you know something, then spit the shit out."

Kookie retrieves the blunt and takes another puff. "All right, but you didn't get the shit from me."

"C'mon with it."

"My boo says that Python looking at you suspect because of your sister."

And there it was: the pink elephant that I have been trying my best to ignore. "Look, my sister ain't got shit to do with me. We're two separate bitches."

"Maybe . . . maybe not."

"What the fuck is that supposed to mean?"

"It means, as the head bitch of the Queen Gs, you, at the very least, need to be able to control your peoples— especially your blood. Look what the fuck Python had to do with his own. He let the nigga walk away once with a public warning; the second time he fed that muthafucka to his damn snake."

"Damien," I whisper, and then shudder. It will be a cold day in hell before I forget that fucked-up shit, especially when niggas broke out their camera phones and snapped pictures like they were at Sea World or something.

"Check it," Kookie goes on. "Fat Ace's brother is creeping with your sister. That makes it look like Fat Ace is making up ground on the Gangster Disciples and stealing niggas out of Python's backyard."

I open my mouth only to be cut off.

"Whether it's true or not isn't the point. On these streets, appearances mean everything. Some of our little niggas at Morris High say your sister and Profit are always snuggled up all kissy face, and a few times that nigga has been seen sneaking into her damn bedroom down on midtown."

"What?"

"Girl, don't act like you didn't know. Python has been scoping the situation out for a while."

"Goddamn it, Ta'Shara." The room spins while I try to take all this in. Why in the fuck am I the last to know about any of this shit? "McGriff told you all this?"

"Some of it. I pick up whisperings around the way, too."

"Why didn't you tell me this shit sooner? You're supposed to be my girl."

"Chile, I try to stay out of domestic shit. That's the fastest way niggas can get fucked up. Don't believe me? Ask Tyga's shot-up ass." Kookie sucks some more on her fat blunt. "Look, I wouldn't be surprised if Ta'Shara's ass is a full-fledged Flower by now. That nigga got her nose sprung all the way open. Shit. Word is they even going to the prom."

It's so much information that I have to sit the fuck down. "I told that bitch . . ." I suck in an angry breath and try to count to ten, but with each number I tick off, I only get angrier.

The front door of the house bangs open, letting me know that Python has finally found his way home. I roll my eyes, hoping he isn't just coming home to start no shit. Kookie hops up from the edge of the bed and makes a point to brush away any ashes that may have fallen onto the sheets.

"What the fuck y'all doing in here?" His narrowed gaze sweeps over us like he's just caught a couple of home invaders.

"Last I checked, I still lived in this muthafucka," I bark.

"You know what? I'ma catch up with you later, girl," Kookie says.

"Hold up." I reach out and remove the blunt from Kookie's mouth. "I think I'ma need this shit."

Not sticking around to argue, Kookie gets the fuck on, squeezing around Python at the bedroom door, since he makes it clear that his ass isn't about to move on his own. But once she's gone, his lips kick up into a smile. "What the hell is wrong with her scary ass?"

"Fuck her. Why didn't you come to me if you doubted how down I was for the set?"

Python's face twists. "Don't come at me with no gossiping bullshit." He moves into the room, tugging his white T over his head.

"So you don't have a problem with me?"

"Why would I have a problem?"

"Oh, so we're playing mind games now?" I charge, and roll my eyes. "I thought we were above that petty bullshit?"

Python's face hardens while his upper lip twitches.

I study every inch of his ripped and tattooed body while he gets undressed. It's funny that once upon a time, I'd looked to this man as just a means to an end, and he still is in a way, but he definitely means more to me now—more than I want to really admit.

"What, you want me to fall all out and beg you to leave these bitches alone? Is that it? At the very least that retarded bitch, Yolanda."

"She's not retarded."

I quickly jump in his face. "What, you're going to defend her to me, nigga? Is that what the fuck you're about to do?"

"Go on now." He pushes me away. "She's carrying my seed."

I toss up my hands. "Her and how many other bitches? Who the fuck is Melanie?"

Python's face changes up, and I swear to God my heart drops. This bitch means something to him.

"See. You worried about the wrong muthafuckin' thing," he says with so much bass I swear the floor is rumbling. "Melanie is Melanie. She's somebody who ain't got shit to do with you."

I don't believe what the fuck I'm hearing.

Python's gaze snags on the dress in my hand just as he reaches for a fresh pair of black jeans. "Going somewhere?"

"Don't fuckin' change the subject," I snap.

Slowly, Python's brows rise higher while the muscles in his chest make his tat python twitch. "Your fuckin' tone gettin' out of line."

"So this is how you wanna play this shit? I'm tryna talk to you and you gone play stupid?"

Python stops undressing to stare me down. "Who the fuck do you think you're talking to?"

"Somebody I thought was my man. Turns out you're

just the community ho, slapping me with a big ole FUCK YOU sign on the back of my head." I move up close to him and wave a finger in his face. "I've never disrespected you. NEVER. And this is how you roll? This is how you gonna treat me? Well, let me tell *you* something, nigga. You ain't never gonna find another bitch like me. You better believe that shit. So while you got that fat bitch riding your shit, better check yourself. When the shit gets tough, who the fuck riding with you? Who'll straight blast next to you? Huh? Any of them bitches you knocked up? Ever?"

Python's face softens.

I shake my head. "You got me twisted." I head toward the door, but Python snatches me by the wrist.

"Where you going?"

"Out. Just like you are," I say, thrusting up my chin and now daring his ass to say some stupid shit.

Python shakes his head. "Nah. Nah. I don't think that's a good idea."

"I'm a grown-ass woman. I don't need permission."

His jaw twitches as his grip tightens. "I don't think you're in the right mind to go partying tonight. You might do some shit you'll regret."

"Trust me, I ain't gonna do nothing you won't do."

Python roughly jerks me up, and out of reflex, my hand rears back and delivers a stinging slap across his face. It's like hitting stone. He doesn't flinch nor does he let on that he even felt the blow. To add insult to injury, he laughs.

To my horror, tears start stinging my eyes. *Don't you dare cry in front of this muthafucka. Don't fuckin' do it.*

Python's smile spreads wider. "You're gonna fuck around and make a nigga think you're in love with him."

"It's always about you, ain't it?" I jerk and try to pull

myself free, but Python isn't having any of that. "Well, go ego trip with your new trick down the way or that pregnant pig. I'm over it."

"Pregnant?"

"Please, save the stupid act. It's played out. I saw that bitch for myself."

He tries looking confused for a moment, and I just start wildin' out: kicking, punching. I swear on everything I own that if I had my gun on me, I'd turn this muthafucka into a crime scene. One of us has got to go.

Python releases my arm, but only so he can wrap his arm around my waist and lock me in place. "What? What you wanna do? You wanna leave?" He cocks his head and studies me while I continue to struggle for freedom. It feels as if his arm is trying to slice me in half. "Nah. You don't wanna leave. You wanna go from wifey to wife."

That shit gets my attention, and I finally stop kicking and our eyes lock. "You wanna show me how down you are? You really want my last name?"

I pull in deep breaths while nodding at the same time.

"Your sister," he finally says, evenly. "Handle that shit." He releases me. "Do that, and I'll give you my last name. Word is bond."

A corner of my lips curl when I see that he's serious. "Done deal."

40

Melanie

It's a fucking miracle I have a Friday night off—and what better way to spend that shit than to have your man stroke, suck, and lick the stress out of you all night long?

"Damn, baby, you got some good pussy," Fat Ace moans against my thighs.

"Eat it up, baby," I pant, rotating my hips as his thick lips smack against my throbbing clit. No lie, the nigga eats pussy like it's a bucket of KFC. I struggle to keep the noise down, because Christopher is a light sleeper. But tonight, Momma needs this nut in a bad way. The job has been stressing me out, my bills are all over the place, and Python is turning into a bugaboo, blowing my phone up so much that I keep that shit on vibrate. When the nigga had me, he acted like he didn't have time for me. Now that I've finally tossed his gangsta ass back to those gun-toting chicken heads he loves so much, he's blowing my cell up every time I turn around.

Fuck him.

I've wasted too much time on that nigga and those sweet lies he's been whispering in my ear since he first busted my cherry. It's time to move on with a man who knows how to appreciate what he's got. A thug nigga who always makes time for me and mine.

"Ahhhh. Ahhh." I start crawling up the bed, feeling my nut rise all the way up from my toes. Ace is really working my pink baby like a full-time job, and I swear if I had any money, I'd leave this big nigga a tip. "Ahhh. Ahhh." I can't breathe. I swear I can't. With each inch I take, Ace follows. The two fingers he has stirring my honey quickly turns into three and then four. Pretty soon, he's going to be fisting my shit and I'm going to shoot off like a fuckin' rocket.

I like shit that rough. Two seconds later, Ace doesn't disappoint. His fist pumps so sweetly that my pussy turns into a water hydrant, and his face is right there to get hosed down. My mind spins while he climbs up from in between my legs. I continue to gush, watching this huge mammoth of a man hover above me, anticipating his fat cock like a crackhead getting ready for her next hit.

Python's dick game is crazy, but a bitch can't sleep on what Fat Ace is working with either. The minute his thick, smooth cock enters me, my sugar walls melt. I wrap my arms around his tree trunk of a neck and my legs around his waist and hold on for the muthafuckin' ride.

"Tear it up, baby." I suck his right earlobe into my mouth and scrape my teeth along the tender flesh. As expected, I can feel an extra inch stretch my inner walls, and tears of ecstasy slide from the corners of my eyes.

"Like this?" Fat Ace growls.

His hips drill me oh so lovely. "Fuck, yeah." I try to catch my breath, but it's only second to getting this next nut. An hour later, we're still going at it. My head is hanging over the edge of the bed while Ace saws his big meat in and out my mouth like it's a second pussy. His mouth is busy bathing and sucking on my polished toes. There's always something new with this nigga, and I got to admit, I kind of like being surprised.

Finally, Ace tenses up. "Oh, shit. Open wide, baby. Here it comes."

I greedily stretch my mouth open and gulp down his gooey candy with relish. There's so much of it, I'm in hog heaven.

Ace tosses my words back at me. "Eat it up, baby." He rubs his dick around my face, smearing his semen into my skin.

It's all good. Nothing like protein to keep a woman's face glowing. He goes to the bathroom and brings a wet towel to wipe off my face and then lies down so we can spoon.

When I steal a few minutes in the shower, my mind goes back to Python's trifling ass. What the hell is wrong with me? My pussy is still aching from some-good ass dick and I'm still thinking about his ass.

Maybe it's true. A woman never gets over her first love. No. I'm just a glutton for punishment. That's what's up. I close my eyes and shake my head, and the tears that flow blend with the hot water that pelts down from the showerhead. Despite my tears, I'm still determined to keep Python in my rearview.

A cold breeze causes an army of goose bumps to

pimple my skin, and I turn my head to see Fat Ace easing his hunky, muscular frame into the shower with me.

"Figured you could use some company," he says,
grinning.

I force on a smile. If I keep faking this shit, then
maybe I'll start believing I'm happy. "I could always use
some help reaching my back." This is just an invitation
for us to add soap to our fucking frenzy.

I can appreciate a brother who can put in this much
work. After rinsing off, this big nigga carries me back to
the bed.

"Damn shame," he mumbles, running his hands over
my erect nipples.

"What?"

"You know what, *Officer Johnson*." He chuckles.

I roll my eyes. "Don't you start that shit." My irritation only seems to amuse him until I start to pull away.

"Whoa. Whoa. Hold up." He pulls me back. "No
need to get mad. I ain't tryna fuck up our flow. Po-po or
not, I'm going to be tapping that ass again in a few minutes."

"Is that right?" I smile and wiggle my rump at him.

"Damn, nigga. You must've had your Wheaties today."

"Nah. You got something extra in that pink monster
that has this thug strung out, baby. That's what's up." His
hands move from my breasts to the slushy mess between
my legs, and he slips his finger inside. "You'd done fuck
up and got a nigga wanting to come around more often."
He brushes his lips along the column of my neck. "You
know, some time when lil man is up, can you introduce us?"

My warm fuzzies disappear. I've never introduced
any sideline nigga to my son. Sure, I'll creep when he's
passed out, but this other shit—what Fat Ace is talking
about—can only lead to problems and complications.

"Ahhh. It's like that." Fat Ace chuckles and shakes his head. "That must mean that his daddy is still in the picture."

His fingers slip out of my pussy, and I grab his wrist before he can pull his arm from around my waist. "I didn't say all of that."

"You didn't have to, Ma," he says so smooth that I can't really tell if he's angry. "It is what it is. But, damn, if you're gonna be raising my seed now, then I should know what the hell else is going on in this muthafuckin' crip."

I flip over in his arms and try to get a good look at his harsh features while we continue this awkward pillow talk. Big and ugly but his body is killing it. "It's complicated."

"Does he still come around here?"

"No."

He doesn't immediately react to that. In fact, he stares me down like a human lie detector. "When was the last time he came around?"

"Why the fuck does that matter? It's over. He's not welcome here anymore." I know I'm getting heated, but I can't help it. I invited this brother over here tonight so I can get Python *off* my mind.

"Forget it. If you ain't gonna shoot straight with me." He shrugs his massive shoulders. "We can just squash this shit and I can just roll up out of here. It ain't that serious."

"It ain't serious, but a few minutes ago you were asking to meet my son?"

"*I* was serious. *You* are the one over here running game and thinking your ass is slick."

"What?"

"I call it like I see it." He sits up. "You wanted some dick and you got some dick. End of story."

"It's not like that."

"No? Then who's lil man's daddy?"

My heart drops. "What damn difference—"

"You bitches are all the same." He keeps shaking his big bowling ball–sized head.

"Time the fuck out!" I hop up on my knees in the bed so I can at least be eye level with his ass. "Ain't no man gonna sit up in *my* muthafuckin' bed and start calling me a whole bunch of bitches. NIGGA, IS YOU CRAZY?"

Fat Ace turns his head away from me, and I can see the muscles in his jaw twitching. "Get out my face with that." His baritone dips lower than usual. It's a sign that I'm skating on the edge of this Vice Lord whaling on me, but right now I really can't say I give a fuck.

"You know what? You need to go." I attempt to shove him off the bed, but of course he doesn't budge an inch. "Get to stepping." I plop back down and start kicking him.

"BITCH, I DONE TOLD YOU!"

Fat Ace grabs one of my legs, and I send the heel of my free foot sailing against the bottom of his chin. But the shit doesn't phase his ass, and it feels like I just broke my foot.

"What, you feel better now, *bitch?*"

He snatches my other leg and then yanks them both apart so hard I feel like a wishbone that he's snapped in half. "Get off of me, muthafucka!" I start swinging, slapping his face. "I ain't your bitch!"

He just laughs in my face as he hovers above me, his heavy cock threatening to slide into my open pussy.

"You ain't my bitch, baby?" he asks, releasing my

legs and now trying to grab hold of my hands. "You sure look like my bitch to me."

"Fuck you!"

"Funny. That's exactly what I had in mind." He chuckles. "But not until you tell me that you're my bitch."

This nigga must be crazy. I ain't saying shit.

"Oh, you gonna be stubborn, huh?" He pins both my hands with one of his above my head and then shoves his free hand in between our bodies, where he starts playing with my clit again. "Ah, yeah. Your ass is wet as hell and you up here talking shit. This pussy knows you're my bitch. Don't it?"

Suddenly, my ass ain't struggling too hard, and I'm biting down on my bottom lip to stop myself from moaning. But the shit doesn't work.

"Uh-huh. Look at you." He removes his hand and then starts teasing me with the head of his cock. "You want some more of this dick, don't you?"

Don't say shit. "Yessss."

"How bad do you want it?"

He squeezes a little bit of the tip inside and then pulls it back out. My moan turns into a whine of disappointment.

"If you want this dick, you know what you gotta say." He squeezes in and pulls out.

I whine some more.

"Say it." *Squeeze. Pull.*

Don't say it.

Squeeze. Pull. "Say it. Say you're my bitch." *Squeeze. Pull.*

"I'm . . . I'm . . . oooh. Stop playing, baby."

He chuckles. "I'll stop playing when you tell me you wanna be my bitch." *Squeeze. Pull.*

I suck in a breath because I'm feenin' bad. "I'm your bitch, baby. I'm your bitch. Now give me that sweet dick, Daddy." I try to push down on his shit because I'm tired of his ass teasing me.

"You want it? Here you go, *bitch!*" With one powerful thrust, he slams into my pussy and damn near clogs my throat. But the minute this nigga starts grinding, my ass is as lost as a muthafucka inside my head. Damn. Why in the fuck have I been wasting all that time with Python's stupid ass when I could've been getting sprung off this nigga? "Say you're my *nasty* bitch," he orders, pounding my shit with no remorse.

"I'M YOUR NASTY BITCH! I'M YOUR NAS-NASTY BITCH!"

"I'm gonna keep filling this pussy up with babies. This is my shit, and I better not see no other nigga coming around this muthafucka." He sucks in a long breath between his teeth, but his hips never stop. "You hear me, bitch? You tell Chris's daddy he better not come around this bitch no more."

"Y-yesss." He feels so good, my damn kidneys are having a fuckin' orgasm.

"Whose pussy is this, baby?"

"Y-yours."

"What's my name, baby?"

"Mmm . . . ooh!"

"What's my name, bitch?"

"MAAASSSOONN."

"What?"

"MASON!"

Suddenly there's a loud *BANG!* I look up to see the door kicked in and Python aiming his gun at Fat Ace.

"WHAT THE FUCK?!"

I'm stunned and can't move.

"WHAT THE FUCK?" Fat Ace jerks out of my pussy and makes a dive toward the nightstand for his piece.

"YOU'RE A DEAD MUTHAFUCKA!" *POW!* Python's gun sounds like a cannon.

I blink out of my trance and dive in the opposite direction just as Fat Ace starts returning fire. Right now I'm wishing that I didn't keep my own weapon locked in a safety box at the top of the closet, because judging by the look on Python's face, me and Fat Ace aren't walking out of this muthafucka alive.

41

Ta'Shara

I'm floating on cloud nine.

So far my prom has been everything that I'd hoped it would be. Well, almost. We weren't crowned king and queen. That honor went to the snooty captain of the football team, George Fletcher, and of course the school's head cheerleader, Sharon Jones. When those two squares took the stage, haters booed and hissed until the brother led her into the first slow jam of the evening.

Still, the whole evening played out like some magical fairy tale in which all the girls were certified divas and the boys, if you squinted and cocked your head to the side, could pass for gentlemen. It wasn't long before someone spiked the punch with some Cîroc and doled out some la in the bathrooms and out in the parking lot.

The school security knows the deal and elects to pick their battles. They pop up every once in a while to put out small fires and then pretend they don't smell the various different clouds of drugs. Success depends on getting through the night without a body being white-chalked.

Getting high isn't normally my thing, but tonight I was in full what-the-hell mode. "Oh, man. I'm fucked up." I giggle every other minute.

"I can see that." Profit laughs and pulls a deep toke before leading me out onto the dance floor. If his buzz has kicked in, he damn sure isn't showing it.

Essence and her date, Drey Faniel, avoid me and Profit like the plague. I don't blame her. As a Queen G, she can't appear to be sanctioning what Profit and I are doing.

"I don't know, Profit. Maybe we should sit this one out," I say and giggle again. "I'm not quite sure I can feel my muthafuckin' toes." I look down to at least verify that they were still attached to my legs.

"I got you, Ma." Profit chuckles and circles his arms around my waist. "Don't you worry about that." We rock steady to an emotional slow joint while our glassy eyes lock onto each other. "You having a good time, baby?"

My smile stretches so wide it feels as if it is bumping against each of my earlobes. "You know I am." His growing hard-on presses against me. "How about you?"

"It's all good." He peppers my face with a few kisses. "I'm just biding my time until we head out to the Peabody."

"I should've known that your mind is just on fuckin'."

"Yep." He bobs his head. "I ain't gonna lie."

I blush.

Profit whispers against my ear, "And when I get you to that hotel tonight, I'm going to take my time eating every inch of you."

A delicious shiver shoots through me as my own anticipation mounts. The game plan is to head out no later than nine-thirty so that we can have at least two hours alone in our luxury suite. I plan to get as loud and to buck as wild as I want without the fear of waking up my parents.

"I can't stand her ass."

I catch the loud diss but just don't give a fuck about what the haters say about me and Profit anymore. Queen Gs, Flowers, Cripettes—you name it, they are all trying to stare a hole in the backs of our heads. Truth be told, I'm getting used to the shit. All that matters is the man in my arms; however, Profit cares.

"Let it go, honey," I say, smiling to placate him. "This is our night."

"You know I love to see you smile like this, baby girl."

"Now, you know, I'm not your baby," I say.

Profit's brows jump. "Oh? Since when?"

I reach up and caress the side of his face. "Since I became your *woman*."

"My woman. Hmmm. I like the sound of that." He leans forward and kisses me so gently and tenderly that tears come from nowhere and start leaking from the corners of my eyes. Our bodies stop rocking, and Profit cups my small face with his large hands as if he's holding something fragile and precious.

Love doesn't encapsulate what I'm feeling. The four letters are too short and sound too casual to describe what is shaking me to my very foundation. Profit is as much a part of me as my own arm, head, or heart. Our kiss lasts through the rest of the song and into the next. When the small sips of oxygen I manage to steal are no longer enough, our lips finally pull apart.

"What do you say we roll up out of here?" His thumb traces the bottom of my lips while his eyes hold the perfect combination of adoration and lust.

"I say"—I press my body closer and loop my arm

around the back of his neck—"hell yeah." I smother his lips with another kiss before Profit laughs and immediately escorts me toward the exit.

A few heads turn and I blush like I have a neon sign on the back of my ass that reads I'M LEAVING TO GO FUCK NOW.

"You all right?" Profit asks as we step out into the dark parking lot.

Boldly, I reach back and grab his ass. "Never better."

"Aaah. All right. It's like that, huh?" Profit cups my fat-onion ass and gives it a squeeze. "Think your *man* can get in where he fits in tonight?" he asks, leaning over to make a playful nip at my ear.

"That's the plan."

Different groups of kids are chilling out back, smoking, drinking, and basically talking a bunch of shit as we thread our way through.

Khaled, a nigga who has always looked too old to be hanging out at a high school, looks up and gives his crotch a good scratch. "Awww. Sukie, sukie now. I know that shit going to get busted open tonight."

"What the fuck you say?" Profit flips on the nigga and starts charging.

I try to tug him back, but it looks as if he's finally had enough with all the cheap remarks tonight.

"Oh, shit. My bad, Profit." Khaled's hands shoot up, flashing the VL sign. "I didn't know that was you and your lady, man. I ain't never seen you in a monkey suit before. Sorry."

"Profit, baby," I beg. "Let it go. That nigga ain't worth it."

The crowd's interest piques at the prospect of a fight.

"It's all you, man. All day, every day," Khaled says, keeping his hands high in the air. "I ain't mean no disrespect. For real."

Profit glares, his face tense, his muscles tight. After a few more seconds, he backs away and pulls me into his arms. But off to the side, a few brothers stand tall with their gats out.

"Profit, man. You want us to blast this fool?" It's clear that Cash Money is just looking for an excuse to get something started.

"Now wait a minute," the nigga says, eyes bugging. "I done apologized. There ain't no need to take this shit to the next level."

I roll my eyes. Our wonderful night is on the verge of turning into one that will end with yelling, shooting, and handcuffs. "Baby," I pout, rolling my hand up the center of his back. "Squash this shit. You got more important things to take care of tonight." I plant a kiss against his hard cheek. "C'mon. Let's go."

A long, strained silence passes. The Vice Lords are cocked and ready for the go-ahead.

At last, Profit sucks in a breath, shakes his head, and returns his arm around my waist. "Nah, man. Let the crab go. We're supposed to all be chilling and having a good time. Ain't that right?"

Fat drops of perspiration roll down Khaled's square forehead. "Yeah, man. That's what I was saying." His awkward laugh shakes like he's having some kind of internal earthquake.

Cash Money looks disappointed but pockets his piece and then reaches for the joint that is in the middle of rotation.

I return to the nook under Profit's arm and march by his side as we make our way across the parking lot. When we reach the limo, Profit taps on the hood. The driver jumps, tosses his cell phone to the side, and scrambles to get out of the vehicle.

"Sorry. I didn't see y'all," the older man apologizes, and then scrambles to open the back door.

"Don't mention it, man. If you can get us down to the Peabody in ten minutes, there's an extra hundred dollars in it for you." Profit winks.

"I'll have you there in eight." He cheeses.

The moment I climb into the back, Profit is on me like white on rice, raining kisses on my face, neck, and collarbone. And when his strong hands start to make their way down my body, I can barely do more than moan my pleasure.

"You like that, baby?" Profit chuckles.

"W-what's not to like?" I pant, feeling my body come alive.

"Funny. I was just thinking the same thing." He licks the lining of my bottom lip. "Damn. You always taste so good."

Profit's hands shift directions and start traveling up, this time underneath my dress. Faintly, we're aware of the limousine's engine revving and the glass divider rolling up, but the only thing that holds our attention is how we're feeling.

The driver turns on the radio, filling the back of the limo with seductive old-school jams and getting me and my boo in the mood. I twirl my hand around his low-cropped hair and then run them down his smooth face while I nibble on his plump lips, drinking in the moment.

"Did you have a nice time tonight, baby?" Profit asks as he plants a string of soft kisses down my long neck.

"You know I did." I sigh and luxuriate at the feel of his warm breath caressing my skin. My senses are super sensitive, and my brain is still buzzing from that Cîroc and weed that were passed around at the prom. "Thanks for taking me tonight, baby."

Profit pulls back and stares me dead in the eye. "You know I'd do anything for you, baby."

This nigga loves me. As I stare at him, I can't get over that shit. We talk all the time, but it's not about the conversation. We laugh all the time, but it's not about the fun. We fuck all the time, but it's not about the sex. It's all that shit and then some.

"What?" he asks, taking in my goofy smile.

"Have I told you lately how much I love you?"

Profit's eyes light up as his smile becomes as goofy as mine. "Yes, but your man never gets tired of hearing it." He leans forward and kisses me until I'm so damn dizzy that I don't even notice my panties sliding off my hips and my dress hiking up higher and higher.

"Awww, baby. Look at you." Profit sucks in a deep breath and then peels open my pussy lips to see my hard candy. "You're beautiful, baby. Every fuckin' inch of you."

I slide my hands around his back, pull him in close, and proceed to grind against his hardening erection.

"Hey, now. This shit is rented," Profit jokes. "I don't think they'll like me returning things with pussy juice all over the front of it."

"If you're so worried, then clean me up."

Our gazes lock. "You know, that might not be such a bad idea." Profit slips his large fingers into my pussy and starts stirring things around. My moans blend with the music.

"Damn, girl. You're wet as fuck." With his free hand, he starts rolling down my one shoulder strap until he's looking at my creamy cleavage above my blue bra. "You coordinated your ass off with this outfit, didn't you, girl?"

"You bragging or complaining?" I reach behind my back and unsnap my bra.

He stares at my full breasts, hypnotized. "Now this is what I'm talking about." He flicks his tongue against my nipples until they have their own nice, shiny glaze. "We got to start coming to more of these damn proms."

"I was thinking the same damn thing." I unzip his pants and pull out my second best friend. We're both on the same page as far as getting in a good quickie before we reach the Peabody hotel. Lord knows it isn't our first time together, but something about this evening makes everything feel brand-new.

Profit shifts his body so that he hovers over me. "We only got a few minutes—spread your legs for me, Ma."

I reach down and pull my pussy wider just when the limousine veers sharply to the left and then screeches to a stop.

Profit pitches forward and slams headfirst into the back door.

"What the . . . Honey, are you okay?" I jump up, just as the other back door jerks open and a small army of niggas hops into the cab. "Who the fuck are you?"

POP! POP! POP!

I jump and then jerk my gaze toward the tinted windows, where I see our limo driver drop dead against the concrete. I panic. "What the fuck is going on?"

Profit struggles to get up but is slammed back down when this long-dreadlock-wearing muthafucka starts pistol-whipping him across the back of his head.

"STOP! GET OFF OF HIM!" I grab a fistful of the nigga's hair and snatch it back so hard I pull a couple of locks clean from their roots. I want to slice this nigga, but I don't have a blade tucked inside my cheeks. I'd stitched that baby on the inside of my bra, and that son of a bitch is on the limousine's floor.

"GET THIS BITCH OFF ME!" Dreadlocks shouts.

I turn my head toward the niggas he's yelling at,

only to have a fist crash against my jaw. My world explodes with pain, and my mouth fills with blood.

The back door slams closed, and the limo's tires squeal again as it takes off.

"Shit. That bitch gotta helluva grip on her," Dreadlocks says, shoving away and clutching the side of his head. "But I'm gonna let that shit go if that pussy is even half as sweet as it smells up in this muthafucka. He jams a hand in between my legs.

I clamp my knees closed. "Get away from me," I hiss through what feels like a broken jaw. "What the fuck do you want?" My gaze shifts to Profit, who's passed out on the floorboard. A steady stream of blood flows down the side of his head, and it's hard to tell whether he's even breathing.

"It's time."

My head whips to the small frame that was the last one to enter the back of the cab. "LeShelle?"

Calm and entirely too cool, my sister reaches up and pulls back her black hoodie. "Hey, sis." Her lips curl, but her smile never reaches her narrowed gaze. "Long time, no see. I hope you don't mind if me and a few of my closest niggas crash your lil prom night." LeShelle knocks on the glass divider. When it slides down, I recognize Kookie, but not the other two bitches, who are surely Queen Gs.

"What do you want?" I ask.

Dreadlocks laughs. "Shit. I came for some muthafuckin' pussy." He reaches out and tweaks one of my nipples. "And to welcome you to your new family."

I slap his hand away, only to be backhanded. Blood spews across the cab while my mind reels. It that moment, real fear creeps up the back of my neck. LeShelle and I have been through some foul shit in the past, but never in a million years did I think my sister would just sit back and watch some grown-ass nigga beat me down. Hot tears splash down my face as I glare over at my sister.

LeShelle looks down at Profit. "So this is the lil nigga who got your ass sprung." She cocks her head. "Muthafucka is definitely better-looking than his brother."

"Like Python is something to write home about." I tug my dress to cover my breasts. "You gonna fuck with something that looks like it crawled out of the muthafuckin' toilet and then you're going to come over here and lecture my ass?"

"Now there's that smart-ass mouth I love so much," LeShelle says.

Profit moans and stirs on the floor.

Dreadlocks delivers another blow to Profit's head before I have a chance to react.

"STOP IT. LEAVE HIM ALONE!"

"Tsk-tsk-tsk." LeShelle shakes her head. "If I were you, I'd be more concerned about myself instead of that dead muthafucka lying over there."

My heart drops. "W-what do you mean?"

"I told you to end it—or I would," LeShelle says evenly.

"You c-can't."

"Oh, yes the fuck I can." She laughs. "And I most certainly will." She holds up her Glock. "And I'm going to have fun doing it."

"Shelle—"

"Ah, ah, ah." LeShelle waves her finger in my face. "What did I say?" The limousine stops. "Worry about your damn self," LeShelle reminds me.

I don't have time to grasp her meaning before the back doors are jerked open and Profit falls out. I gasp and try to reach for him, but then Dreadlocks damn near wrenches my arm out of its socket when he jerks me out in the opposite direction. "LET ME GO!" I squirm and kick so much that the front of my dress slides down again, exposing my breasts for everyone to see.

"Feisty bitch." Dreadlocks chuckles and then blows his stank breath across my face. "I'm gonna have fun breaking your ass in. Just wait and see. I'll make you forget about that pretty lil nigga over there. I'm gonna make that pussy scream my name all fuckin' night long."

A rush of acidic bile burns the back of my throat as my wide eyes search around for LeShelle. It's dark and it appears as if we're out in the middle of nowhere. Though it looks bad, a small part of me is clinging to a sliver of hope that LeShelle won't allow any harm to come to me. She's just doing all this to scare me.

Dreadlocks drags me along as if I weigh nothing, all the while painting a very vivid picture of just what he wants to do with me once he gets me behind this abandoned brick building we're heading toward.

This is not happening. It's not happening.

Then I see those muthafuckas pick up Profit and drag him along. I can't help but think of the worst as his head lolls around his shoulders and blood pours down his head.

"Leshelle, please," I sob. "I'm sorry. I'll break up with him. I swear."

"Fuck that crying shit," LeShelle barks. "Time to put on your big-girl panties and handle this shit like a woman. You wanted to be grown and do grown things. Well, this is what happens when grown muthafuckas don't listen."

"Shelle—"

"Real talk? This shit is long overdue." LeShelle steps back into my view; her face is a cold mask of indifference. I've seen a lot of sides to LeShelle, but I have never seen this heartless bitch before. "You've never appreciated a muthafuckin' thing I've ever done for you. The protection I've always provided. All you've ever done is take and take. Well, tonight, baby girl, it's time to pay the fuckin' piper. I'm going to give you a little taste of my world: bullets and pain, baby."

"W-what do you mean?"

"It means that I can't have your narrow ass blowing up my shit because of a fuckin' nigga who don't mean shit. In this world, you don't get shit for nothing. I'm a Queen G and after tonight . . . so are you."

Our gazes lock and I know that my fate has been sealed. I'm going to be sexed into the Gangster Disciples. The gang way of branding bitches as their own.

"Wake that nigga up!" LeShelle orders.

Kookie unscrews the top off a bottle of water and then splashes it all over Profit's face. When that doesn't work immediately, she starts slapping him around.

"Fuuuck," he moans. "W-what?"

"Wake up, lover boy." Kookie chuckles. "You don't want to miss your special prom night, now, do you?"

I sob and continue to beg. "Leave him alone. I . . . I swear, I'll do whatever you want, LeShelle. Please."

"Oh, you going to do that shit anyway." LeShelle laughs. "Time-out with all that bullshit you've been getting away with. Starting *tonight*." She glances up at Dreadlocks. "Do you, nigga."

"Fuck yeah." He turns toward me and releases a barrage of punches. I'm shocked at first, but then it starts to feel like I'm being repeatedly rammed by a Mack truck, and there is absolutely nothing I can do about it.

"WHAT THE FUCK?"

Profit? I'm not sure if it's truly him or just voices in my head. I'm surrounded by so much pain that death seems like a logical escape.

"GET THE FUCK OFF OF HER! YOU GRIMY MUTHAFUCKA, COME PICK ON A NIGGA YOUR OWN SIZE!"

"Don't worry, nigga, we got something for you." Dreadlocks laughs. "But right now, I'm gonna brand this bitch as GD property so you slob niggas know to keep your muthafuckin' hands off." The punching stops and with one swipe, my dress is ripped off my body as I lie bleeding on a dirt road.

"Ta'Shara, baby. I'm sorry." There's a scuffle and the sound of more bone being pounded.

LeShelle squats next to me and snatches my head up. "I know you don't understand this shit right now, but one day you will . . . and you're going to thank me for it."

"Ta'Shara," Profit croaks. "Forgive me, baby."

I pry my eyes open, but they feel like they are already swollen shut. I push through the pain to open my mouth, gurgle some blood, and then spit out a tooth. "I h-hate you," I hiss.

LeShelle shakes her head like she actually feels sorry for me. "I guess that's the difference between us. I'm doing this because I *love* you." She shares a sad smile and then presses a kiss against my bloody lips. "It'll all be over soon," she promises, and then stands up.

Dreadlocks snatches my legs open and then shoves himself into my dry pussy, ripping me inside out.

The shock of it all allows me to escape into the dark recesses of my mind. *LeShelle said it will all be over soon. Just hold on.* I lie still, even though in my mind I'm curled into a fetal position.

Stroke after stroke, tears fall down my face.

"AHHHHH!" Dreadlocks blasts off. His cum feels like liquid fire burning my skin. "Now that's some good-ass pussy. I'm gonna have to get me some more of that shit later on."

"C'mon, nigga. It's my turn," shouts a muthafucka who's holding Profit down.

"Damn, nigga. Slow your roll. I'm coming."

Dreadlocks is replaced with another nigga who has an afro that looks as if he's dusted a whole house with it. His dick is much smaller than Dreadlocks'. I'm grateful that I can't feel him while he's huffing and puffing over me.

"Damn, nigga. You done stretched this shit all out," Afro complains.

LeShelle said that it will all be over soon.

"You feel this, baby? Huh? You feel me?"

LeShelle said that it will all be over soon.

Afro is quickly replaced by another and then another. I block it all out: the dicks, the sour breaths, the biting, and even Profit screaming in the background.

LeShelle said that it will all be over soon.

Finally the last nigga produces a switchblade and carves *GD* on the side of my ass cheek. Broken jaw be damned, I scream loud enough to wake the dead.

A beaten Profit is still fighting to get to me, but it's all useless.

"All right. Stop all that hollering," LeShelle says, as if she's bored with the whole thing. "It's over with. You're officially a Queen G, bitch. You fuckin' belong to me." She smiles, but it still doesn't reach her eyes. "But I gotta tell you," she says, shaking her head. "I'm not all that convinced that you've learned your lesson about fuckin' around with the Vice Lords. I mean, what's to stop you from showing me your ass again when we let you go?"

"Nothing," Kookie answers for me.

"Exactly." LeShelle taps her steel against the side of her head. "Logic says that there's only one way to settle this shit." She turns toward Profit. The two niggas holding Profit release him and jump out the way.

"YOU BITCH!" Profit charges toward LeShelle.

"That's *queen* bitch to you, muthafucka." LeShelle aims, smiles, and unloads her entire clip into Profit.

My eyes widen as I scream in horror, "NOOOOOOO-OOOOO!"

Acknowledgments

There are so many people to thank in this evolution that is De'nesha Diamond. First and foremost is our heavenly father, who's blessed me long before I had the common sense to realize it. To Granny, my baby Alice, who continue to inspire me though it's from up above now. My sister Channon "Chocolate Drop" Kennedy—you're still the best. My other sister, Charla Byrd, the funniest woman I know. My beautiful niece, Courtney—I love you. Kathy and Charles Alba—salt of the earth.

To K'wan, thanks for being my literary Godfather. Tu-Shonda Whitaker for keeping me laughing and sane. Brenda Jackson for being a good friend and inspiration. Marc Gerald for taking me under your wing. To Selena James for having the patience of Job.

And, of course, the Byrdwatcher family and The Diamond Girls book club—you lift me up. And to anyone I forgot, blame it on the alcohol. LOL.

Best of Love,
De'nesha

From *A Good Excuse To Be Bad*

1

If I weren't so screwed up, I would've sold my soul a long time ago for a handsome man who made me feel pretty or who could at least treat me to a millionaire's martini. Instead, I lingered over a watered-down sparkling apple and felt sorry about what I was about to do to the blue-eyed bartender standing in front of me. Although I shouldn't; after all, I am a bail recovery agent. It's my job to get my skip, no matter the cost. Yet, I had been wondering lately, what was this job costing me?

For the past six weeks, Dustin, the owner of Night Candy and my Judas for this case, had tended the main bar on Wednesday nights. His usual bartender was out on maternity leave. According to Big Tiger, she would return tomorrow, so I had to make my move tonight.

Yet, I wished Big Tiger would have told me how cute and how nice Dustin was. I might have changed my tactic or worn a disguise, so that I could flirt with him again for a different, more pleasant outcome. See, good guys don't like to be strong-armed. It's not sexy, even if it is for a good reason. Such is life . . .

Dustin poured me another mocktail. Although I detested the drink's bittersweet taste and smell, I smiled and thanked him anyway. It was time to spark a different, darker conversation. The fact that his eyes twinkled brighter than the fake lights dangling above his station made it a little hard for me to end the good time I was having with him.

"If you need anything, let me know." He stared at me for a while, then left to assist another person sitting at the far end of the bar.

I blushed before he walked away.

Get it together. I shook it off and reminded myself that I was on a deadline. I wanted his help, not his hotness and definitely not another free, fizzled, sugar water. It was time to do what I was paid to do.

When he returned to my station to wipe my area again, I caught his hand.

He looked down at my hand on his, glanced at my full glass, and grinned. "Obviously you don't need another refill."

I giggled. "No, I don't, but I do need something from you."

"I was hoping you would say that." He smiled and took my hand, then held it closer to his chest. "Because I've wanted to know more about you ever since you walked into my club."

"Great." I couldn't help but giggle back. "Does that mean I can ask you a personal question?"

He nodded. "Ask me anything, sweetie."

I leaned forward and whispered in his ear. "Do you have a problem with me taking someone out of here?"

"Of course not. You can take me out. My patrons don't mind, long as the tap stays open." He chuckled.

"No, Blue Eyes. I'm not talking about you. I'm talking about dragging someone out of your club. Very lady-like, of course, but I wanted to get your approval before I did it."

He stepped back, looked around, then returned to me. "I don't think I understood you, sweetie. You want to do what in my club?"

"Take someone out."

He contorted his grin into a weird jacked-up W. "And what does that mean?"

"It means that you have someone in the club that I want, and I'll shut this club down if I don't get whom I came for. I don't want to cause a scene, so I'm asking for your cooperation."

He scoffed. "Is this some kind of joke?"

"No, it's a shakedown, Dustin Gregory Taylor, and surprisingly, you're the one who sent me. So I need you to play along with me right now. Okay? Sorry for the inconvenience."

"Sorry?" He stumbled back and let go of my hand. "Who are you? How do you know my name?"

"You're causing a scene, Dustin, and that's not good for business. Why don't you come back over here and I'll tell you . . . quietly."

He looked around the bar. The club was jumping so hard only a few people around us noticed his confused facial expression and his almost backstroke into the glass beer mug tower that stood behind him. He ran his hand through his hair, then walked back to me.

He murmured, "Who told you about me?"

"We have a mutual friend." I pulled out my cell phone, scrolled to a saved picture, and showed it to him. "I'm sure you know the man in this mug shot. It's your cousin Cade. Correct?"

His brow wrinkled; then he sighed. "What has he done now?"

"What he always does, Dusty, robs banks and skips bail. But do you want to know the worst thing he's done?"

Dustin just looked at me. He didn't respond.

"Well, I'll tell you anyway. He convinced your mom to put a second mortgage on the family house, in order to pay his bail the last time he got caught. Guess what? He got caught three months ago and then he missed his court date, which means—"

Dustin yanked the towel off this shoulder. "Say what?"

"Your mom's home is in jeopardy if I don't find him tonight. My boss Big Tiger Jones of BT Trusted Bail Bonds is ready to turn your childhood home into his Smyrna office, if you know what I mean."

"Son of a . . ." He turned around in a full 360. His towel twirled with him. "This isn't fair."

I nodded. "Life can be that way sometimes."

"I had no clue he had gotten back into trouble. He didn't say anything to me, and my mom . . . No wonder she hasn't been sleeping well lately." He rung the towel in his hands, then snapped it against the bar. "I don't believe this."

"Believe me, I understand how frustrating it is to watch your family make horrible mistakes and you or someone you love pay the price for their burden." I thought about my sister Ava. "Dustin, I have to take Cade downtown tonight. We both know that he's here in Night Candy right now and has been sleeping in your back office since his ex-girlfriend Lola kicked him out of her house. So tell me how you want this to go down, nice or easy?"

"Neither." He folded his arms over his chest. "You can't do this, not here. It'll ruin me."

I sighed. "I know, ergo this conversation."

Last year after a stream of violence and crime, the Atlanta Mayor's Office and the Atlanta Police Department
issued a new ordinance against crime. Any businesses
that appeared to facilitate criminal activity would be
shut down. Night Candy already had two strikes against
it: for a burglary gone bad that ended in the brutal murder of Atlanta socialite and real-estate heiress Selena
Turner, and then there was that cat brawl between two
NFL ballers' wives that was televised on a nationally
syndicated reality TV show. The club definitely didn't
need a showdown between a habitual bank robber and
me. I'd tear this place up and anyone who stood between
me and Big Tiger's money. I'm that bad, if I need to be.

"Maybe it won't." I touched his hand with hopes that I
could calm him down. The last thing I needed was Cade
to notice Dusty's agitation. "But you must do as I say."

Dustin leaned toward me. His starry eyes now looked
like the eye of a hurricane. I shuddered. Man, he was hot.

"Listen to me," he said. "It's not you I'm concerned
about. Cade has made it clear to everyone that he'll
never go back to jail. He will fight. Lady, he'll burn my
club down with all of us inside before he goes back in."

I patted his shoulders. "I believe you, and that's why
Big Tiger sent me. See? Look at me."

"I've been looking at you all night."

"Exactly. This froufrou that I have on is a disguise."

"Didn't look like a disguise to me."

"That's my point, Dustin. I can sweet talk Cade out
the back where Big Tiger's waiting for him in the alley.
No one will suspect a thing, not even the plainclothes
APD dudes hanging around near the champagne fountain."

He looked past me toward the fountain, then lowered
his head. "I didn't see them there."

"That's because your attention was on me, just like

Cade's will be once he sees me." I grinned. "All I need you to do is to introduce me to him. I'll take it from there."

"Makes sense, but there's a problem." He ruffled his hair again. "Cade's in the cabanas upstairs, but I can't leave the bar. I'll let Ed, the VIP security guard, know you're coming. He'll parade you around for me. What's your name?"

"Angel."

"Angel, that name fits you." He looked at me and then over me. His eyes danced a little; then he frowned. "You're very pretty and too sweet looking to be so hard. Are you really a bounty hunter?"

I slid off the stool, smoothed down my hair and the coral silk chiffon mini cocktail dress my little sister Whitney picked out for me, then turned in the direction of the upstairs cabanas. "Watch and find out."

Night Candy sat in the heart of downtown Atlanta—underneath it, to be more exact—on Kenny's Alley, the nightclub district inside Underground Atlanta. Real-estate moguls, music executives, and Atlanta local celebrities frequented the club whenever they were in town. They also hosted popular mainstay events there. The upscale spot had become so über trendy that unless you were on the VIP list, getting inside was harder than finding a deadbeat dad owing child support. But getting admitted was worth the effort.

On the inside, Night Candy was its name: dark, indulgent, and smooth. Chocolate and plum colors dripped all over the lounge. Velvet and leather wrapped around the bar like cordial cherries. It even smelled like a fresh-opened Russell Stover's box. Dustin looked and smelled even better. I wished we'd met under different circumstances.

The club had three levels with VIP at the top and the best live music I'd heard in a long time: vintage soul, reminiscent of Motown girl groups with a dose of hip-hop and go-go sprinkled on top. My hips sashayed up the stairs to the music until I stopped.

I checked my watch and huffed. In three hours the judge could revoke Cade's bail. There was no time for errors. Cade had to go down now.

I texted Big Tiger. He had assured me he would be outside waiting for us. Trouble was, Big Tiger's promises had 50/50 odds. I promised myself to hire a male tagalong next time, preferably one as big as this Ed guy standing in front of me.

Whoa. I reached the stairs he guarded. Ed was a massive, bronzed bald-headed giant. He had brawn and swagger. My little sister Whitney would eat him up. Dustin must have given him the green light, because by the time I reached the top of the staircase, he was smiling and holding out his hand to help me inside the VIP lounge.

As he gave me a personal tour of what I called a Godiva version of a party room, I spotted Cade and exhaled. The Taylor men definitely had great genes. I didn't have to take a second look at his Fulton County Corrections Office booking photo to know it was him. He was drop-dead handsome—bald and dark, a bad combination for me. I'm a recovering bad-boy-holic. I hoped he wouldn't give me too much trouble, but the thought of a good crawl with this guy was enough to send me to church first thing Sunday morning.

I melted into a milk chocolate lounge chair across from his cabana and waited for his jaw to drop at the sight of me. And boy, did it. He was talking to a barely clad and quite lanky teenybopper when he saw me through the sheer curtain covering the cabana. I grinned and slid my dress up too high for a woman my age to ever do without feeling like some dumb tramp. I wished I could say I was embarrassed acting that way, but I couldn't. I liked having a good excuse to be bad sometimes.

The sad thing about all of this was that the young woman holding on to Cade didn't notice him licking his lips at me. After five minutes of his gross act, she stood up and walked toward me. My chest froze. Maybe she had seen him and was now coming over to warn me to back off or to claw my eyes out.

Yeah, right, like I would let that happen. Homegirl better think twice about dealing with me. But I didn't want to hurt her. I didn't get all shiny and done up to scrap with some girl over a fugitive. Besides, I promised Dustin I wouldn't show out up in here. So I gripped the chair as she approached and relaxed when she breezed past. I watched her enter the ladies' room, then patted my cheeks with my palms. I was getting too old for this crap.

As soon as the child left his side, Cade slinked his way over to where I sat. I looked below at the bar where Dustin watched me. I waved my fingers at him until he dropped the martini he was making. *Man, he was cute.*

While I daydreamed of a date with Dustin, Cade stood over me. "So you know my cousin?"

I turned toward him. "Is that your way of introducing yourself to me, or are you jealous?"

He smiled and reached for my hand. "My apologies." He kissed my hand. "I'm Cadence Taylor, but everyone calls me Cade. Don't tell my cousin, but I think you're stunning."

"No, I'm not." I giggled. "I'm Angel."

"I can see that." He sat beside me. "Like a guardian angel . . . no, a cherub."

"More like an archangel."

He clapped and laughed. "Not you. You don't look

like the fighting type. You have sweetness written all over you. You're definitely Dusty's type."

Oh, great. Now you tell me. I moved closer toward him. "And you have 'Bad Boy' written all over you."

He grinned. "You don't have to be afraid of me. I'm a good guy when I need to be."

I smiled back. "Can you promise to be good, if I ask you for a favor?"

He nodded. "Anything for you, Angel."

"I'm tired. I'm ready to go home. Can you escort me to my car? I was supposed to wait for Dustin, but I don't have the stamina for this club life."

"Of course, you don't, because you're a good girl." He stood up and reached for my hand. "Surprisingly, I'm not a clubber either. How about you leave your car and I take you for a quiet night drive through the city, then over to the Cupcakery for some dessert. By the time we get back, Dusty will be closing up this place."

"I don't know. I don't think Dustin would like that so much. Sounds too much like a date."

"Yeah, I guess so." He scratched his head like his cousin, another Taylor trait.

"Besides, your girlfriend would be upset if you left her here."

"What girlfriend?"

I pointed toward the ladies' room. "Her."

"Oh, her. We're not together."

I came closer and whispered in his ear. "Neither are Dustin and me."

He smiled and his eyes outshined the VIP lounge.

"Why don't you escort me to my car and follow me home instead, just to make sure I get there safe?"

He placed his hand at the small of my back. "I can do that."

Because Cade almost carried me out of Night Candy,

I couldn't text Big Tiger to let him know that I was coming outside. All I could do was hope he was where he said he would be.

We stepped outside. No Big Tiger. I hit the hands-free Talk button on my phone earpiece and voice-activated Big Tiger's phone number to dial. I got nothing. My heart began to race. Where was he?

"Is something wrong?" Cade asked. His hands were all over me.

I removed his hands, but said nothing. I had no words.

Sometimes bail bondsmen needed women locators to lure a defendant out of their hiding spot. I didn't mind doing it. Honestly, I needed the money, but we had a deal. I brought them out; he rode them in. So why was I out here alone? Well, not entirely alone . . . with Octopus Cade.

Cade watched me. "Are you having second thoughts?"

"I have a confession to make." I scrambled for something to say while fiddling for my handcuffs. They were trapped somewhere under the chiffon.

"So do I." He pulled me toward him. "I can't keep my hands off you."

I wanted to cuff him, but I couldn't, because he had wrapped his hands around my waist.

"Not here, not like this." I removed his hold on me again, but held on to one of his hands.

He smiled until he felt—I assumed—my cold handcuffs clank against his wrists. "What the—"

"You've violated your bail agreement, Mr. Taylor," I said. Still no Big Tiger in sight. "So you'll have to come with me."

He chuckled as he dangled my handcuffs—the ones I thought had locked him to me—over his head for me to see. A piece of my dress had wedged between the clamp. They were broken. My heart hit the floor.

"Unless these handcuffs are chaining me to your bed, I'm not going anywhere with you, sweetie."

Then, quicker than I anticipated, he head-butted me. I saw stars and fell to the ground. A pain so bad crossed my forehead, it reminded me of labor pains. I couldn't scream. I had to breathe through it to ease the pain.

The head-butting must have stung Cade, too, because he stumbled before he could get his footing. I caught one of his legs and clutched it. I closed my eyes and groaned as he dragged me down the alley. Through the excruciating bumps and scrapes I received holding on to Cade, past the onlookers who didn't care to help this poor damsel in distress, I asked myself, "Why wouldn't I let go?"

My forehead and my skinned knees throbbed now. I'm pretty sure Whitney's dress looked like wet trash. To make matters worse, I was angry with myself for putting myself in this position. I couldn't afford to be so cavalier anymore. I knew that before I took this stupid assignment. I knew it while I sat at the bar. I knew it the day I became a mother, but I did it anyway. What's wrong with me? I couldn't leave my daughter alone without a parent. Now I had to hurt this fool to get back to my baby in one piece.

Cade stopped and cursed. My heart beat so fast and loud, I prayed it would calm down so I could prepare for his next move.

"Angel, sweetie, I think we need to have a little talk."

He pulled me up by my hair, my store-bought hair. I wore a combed-in hairpiece because I didn't have time to go to a hair salon and I didn't want to damage my hair. However, Cade's tugging made the plastic teeth dig deeper into my scalp. I screamed to keep from fainting.

"Shut up!" He slapped me. "You stupid—"

Before he could say another word, I grounded my feet

then threw a round kick so high and hard with my left leg that I heard his jaw crack against my stilettos. He hit the ground, unconscious. While he was knocked out, I turned him over and handcuffed him again, but from the back this time and with the chiffon visibly gone.

I dialed Big Tiger. "Where are you?"

"Where did I tell you I was gon' be?" Big Tiger's voice seemed crystal clear. "Right here."

Someone tapped my shoulder. I jumped.

"It's a good thing I showed up when I did. You could have killed the man. I'da lost my money and then I would have had to take care of your raggedy bond." Big Tiger laughed, then helped me hoist Cade up. "Why didn't you wait instead of messing up your sister's dress? How many dresses have you slaughtered now?"

I looked at him and growled. "Say that again. I dare you."

"And your face, Angel Soft." He squinted. "I think we'd better call 911 after we put homeboy in my truck."

I walked toward Big Tiger with the intent to give him a right hook across his jaw. When I lunged, I think I fainted. I don't know what happened next and I almost didn't care until the EMS worker asked me whom I should call to let them know I was being taken to the emergency room.

"Call my sisters. Tell them where I am and make sure Ava comes to get me."

Then I faded back to black and it felt good. In my dreams, Dustin was on his knees proposing to me with some chocolates and a pink diamond.

His voice was so clear. "Angel, will you . . . be healed in the name of God."

God?

From *Someone Bad and Something Blue*

Just as I was about to cuff Misty Wetherington for ditching DUI court for the fifth time so she could hit the slots at Harrah's casino with her book club buddies, my phone buzzed. I looked down. It was my calendar app, reminding me that I had to be at Bella's school in ninety minutes.

"Crap, I forgot." I sighed.

My daughter, Bella, had asked me if I could join her at Sugar Hill Elementary School today for Doughnuts for Dads. It was a PTA event to celebrate fathers, more like a back-door way to get men into the classroom without them feeling awkward. However, Bella's best friend Lacy's mom came to the last one and, according to my friends at the Sugar Hill Church Ladies' Brunch, no one seemed to mind.

And . . . today was Bella's seventh birthday. I had to be there.

However, I was a little under an hour's drive from the school. If I could punch it without getting a speeding ticket, I would make it in time. The only problem was I didn't know what to do with Misty.

With the exhaustively long lines at the City of Atlanta's traffic court, who knew how long it would take to process her? I wondered as I looked down at her bleached, moppy hair.

She was still on the parking lot ground, face to the gritty, piss-stained pavement while I straddled her back. My handcuffs dangled in my hands.

"Misty, you have been caught on a particularly good day for you. . . ."

I placed the cuffs on the ground near her face so she could see them. I waited until she turned her head in the cuff's direction before I continued.

"Look. It's my daughter's birthday and I need to be with her. We both know that what I'll make for hauling your butt to jail is about the cost of two tickets to the Atlanta Aquarium, the Coke Museum, and one night's stay in the Georgian Terrace. So here's my proposition. Today, I let you go. I'll have Big Tiger finesse the city into giving you another FTA hearing, but on one condition: You fork over the money you were about to spend at the casino. I can surprise my girl with a kid-cation in Atlanta. What do you say?"

"And if I don't?" She grunted.

"How confident are you that the City of Atlanta will grant you a new FTA hearing after five no-shows without some help from Big Tiger? How confident are you that some other bail recovery agent isn't lurking behind any of these cars out here, waiting for the chance to take

you from me? And uh . . . where are your gambling buddies when you need them?"

Her gaze searched the parking lot. "Did they leave?"

"Darling, they are the ones who turned you in. Now
those are friends to keep. I can be your friend, too. Just
say the magic words."

She sighed. "The money's in my front pocket."

"Bingo." I hopped off her and flipped her over.

She reluctantly pulled the money out. I stretched out
my palm until she placed the money into my hand.
Misty was carrying five hundred dollars.

I placed the money in my back pocket and smiled.
"Happy Birthday to Bella."